A Fractu

by Geoffrey Sleight

Acknowledgement

With grateful thanks to my good friend Vanessa Chadwick for her time and invaluable help in preparing the book.

It is during our darkest moments that we must focus to see the light. Aristotle

CHAPTER 1

FLAPPING in a light summer breeze, bright bunting lined the balconies of Hardwick House. The colourful triangles worked hard to obscure the depressing dullness of the three-storey block of flats they now embraced. It was largely a losing battle.

Today the sombre, brown brick building had been tarted up and the usual scattering of litter and pools of urine on the grey, cold stone floor in the entrance lobby had been cleared away. But the obscene graffiti on the walls had proved harder to hide, a vivid and badly etched diagram of male genitalia in white paint being the most stubborn.

Hardwick House had never flickered so brightly with colour since the nightly illuminations of the wartime Blitz. A time when the heart of this community was bombed and blasted in the hell fires of Hitler's aerial attacks.

Even now, eight years since peace had come, the reign of death and terror still left its destructive mark, with vast tracts of brick and rubble scarring the neighbourhood like crude burial mounds where once familiar streets and faces were wiped away in the blinking of an eye.

The playground beneath in the shadow of Hardwick House echoed with children laughing, shouting and crying excitedly as they tore into the treats of drinks, jellies, ices, cakes and biscuits spread on rickety trestle tables. This was a rare street party feast to celebrate the coming of Her Majesty Elizabeth ll to the throne.

A fat balding man in evening dress wandered round the tables playing an accordion, smiling and sweating excessively as he pumped out a medley of happy-time tunes, slipping deftly from one jolly song to another.

But no-one paid him much attention as adults joined their children to gorge in the oasis of plenty, frequently waving little Union Jack flags in joyful displays of devotion to the newly crowned monarch.

Beside the playground ran Hope Street, a narrow cobblestone road separated from the playground by a low brick wall with a dark green metal railing running along its length.

Across the road from Hardwick House loomed the tall, abandoned Potters and Clarke pharmaceuticals factory, glowering gloomily over the festivity.

The lonely building stared through buckled, rusty metal grilles that had failed to protect its windows from volleys of stone missiles launched by children in mindless fun.

At the far end of Hope Street stood the Flute and Whistle pub. For many of the regulars in this dark and dingy refuge the only hope for a better life lived in dreams of alcohol.

Ricki Cellini was not a regular, the West End clubs were more his style, but today he had come to visit his mother at the Hardwick House festivities. Since alcohol was not available at the children's party he'd decided on a quick drink in the Flute and Whistle.

He parked his sleek, blue Ford Zephyr across the road and now stood outside the pub slicking back his black, Brylcreemed hair with a comb to make sure the crest of the quiff was neatly in place. His smart, light blue Italian suit contrasted sharply with the shabby den he was about to enter. The dark yellow brickwork along the front stood pitted with arcs of urine stains. The brown paintwork had virtually peeled away from the window frames leaving mostly rotting bare wood, and the smell of stale beer and cigarette smoke wafted out of the half-open frosted windows.

Ricki faltered as he approached the entrance door. As a minder at one of the seedier night clubs in west London, his expectations of class and presentation though not high, exceeded what lay before him. But he was here and would press on.

Stepping over the dry patches of sick which had hardened on the pavement outside, he pushed open the door and stepped onto the filthy lino floor. It was covered with dog ends and a myriad of dirty pock marks that lent themselves to a form of random design.

In one corner a tramp sat at a small table littered with crisp bags and crumbs from a half eaten sausage roll. Through a growth of knotted beard that obscured most of his face, he drew on a badly hand-rolled cigarette and then sipped at his free pint of Coronation brown ale. In between these actions he mouthed insults and curses to himself and the world in general.

Today was special for him. Normally he swigged meths under the railway arch just down the road by Lyle Street. But in an act of uncharacteristic generosity brought on by the general air of national pride, the landlord on this occasion had not barred his entry and indeed had given him the ale which he now slurped.

At another table nearby two evil-eyed, scruffy men, nurtured beer jugs in their hands, whispering secretly to each other over the froth as if planning their next robbery.

Ricki walked to the bar and narrowly avoided placing his hands in the puddles of spilled alcohol trailing across its surface. Beside him a shapeless, beer gutted man in a grubby, sweat stained check-shirt leaned on the bar. He was chatting to the local coal man whose face, hands and threadbare clothes from tilted cloth cap to gaping hobnail boots, were ingrained with coal dust.

The daily grind of heaving one hundredweight sacks of coal on to his back had deformed him into a partial hunchback and he looked middle aged before his time. But his eyes shone like beacons from his dusty face, sharp and mean as a ferret, briefly diverting his gaze towards the new arrival, swiftly sizing-up this unfamiliar spiv.

Ricki noticed a group of four other men sitting round a table playing cards beneath a poster of the new monarch which had been hastily tacked to the murky green wall, and served to cover a large area of crumbling plaster. Apart from that, no-one could have guessed that a new Elizabethan era had just begun.

Bunting and flags would have been excessive at the Flute and Whistle. It was the high altar to alcoholic worship and nothing was more important than that cause. For happiness and celebration booze-ups, everyone went to the Lord Raglan pub down the road.

One of the four men sitting beneath the new queen rose grudgingly from the card table, taking his time as he shuffled through a small opening leading behind the bar. This landlord was not one to stand on ceremony for his customers. He looked as though he had just crawled fully clothed out of bed and was badly in need of shaving and grooming.

"Yeah?" he snarled, approaching Ricki.

"A vodka and tonic," Ricki ordered, reaching into his pocket for some money.

The landlord picked up a glass and rammed it under the optic. The shapeless, beer gutted man talking to the coal man turned for a moment to stare at Ricki.

"What's that funny smell that's just come into the pub, Jack?" he called to the landlord. Jack grinned and reached for the tonic bottle on the counter behind the bar. The coal man was the only darkened complexion that he normally served on the premises.

"It's coronation day," Jack justified his usual break from tradition. "We have to welcome our overseas friends Ron." The tonic bottle hissed as he lifted the cap with an opener.

Ron heaved his beer gut round to face Ricki.

"Have your drink and fuck off," he threatened. "We don't like your sort round here. Sod off back to Africa."

"I come from Corsica," Ricki informed him, shrugging off the insults and taking a swig at his drink.

"You're all the bloody same to me," Ron retorted with authority.

5

"Hold on a minute," the coal man chipped in, "I know who you are." He directed his words at Ricki. "You're that Chilli bloke ain't you? Lives at number 16 down the road."

"Cellini not Chilli," Ricki corrected him. "Ricki Cellini."

"Yeah, that's right. I've delivered coal to your mum. You've done time ain't you? Nicked something didn't you?"

Ricki looked down, momentarily embarrassed. "That's behind me now, I've got a proper job," he excused his past.

"Oh yeah, what's that?" the coal man probed.

"I work in the West End, for a club."

"What one of them strippers clubs in Soho," Ron interrupted sneeringly. "You're a bloody pimp ain't you? I suppose that's how you get your money for all them fancy clothes."

"I've come back to see my mother and family for the coronation. I don't live round here anymore," Ricki attempted to steer the talk on to a civil path, but Ron preferred to be hostile.

"A fucking good job too. Why don't you take your bleetin' mum and family back up west with you, or better still, piss-off back to where you come from."

Ricki felt a surge of anger. He had a vile temper which hadn't been good for holding down jobs in the past, but he'd learned to bite his lip better as he grew older. He finished his drink and prepared to depart.

Ron the shapeless had not finished. His hatred of all things foreign ran deep.

"Number 16. Ain't that the one where that mad ol' slag lives. You know that dago woman who runs a shagging shop."

6

Fury ignited in the pit of Ricki's stomach and burned like fire to his brain. He wasn't even aware that he had reached into his jacket pocket and drawn out a flick-knife, the button pressed and a deathly click as the vicious blade sprang open for action.

Ron stared in horror, slipping off the bar stool and backing away. All eyes were now upon them save for the tramp who ceaselessly continued to mumble to himself.

"Take that back," Ricki demanded, "my mother is not a slag or a prostitute."

Ron could not lose face in his domain, especially to a foreigner. He summed up false bravado, aided by the several scotches he'd already downed.

"Just fuck off out of here, you scum." He faltered as he spoke, now less certain of himself and starting to back further away. But it was all too late. Ricki sensed the fear in his quarry and with uncontrollable rage sprang forward sinking the blade into Ron's ample gut.

Blood spurted, soaking Ricki's hand and jacket. For a second he'd felt immense joy and relief as his anger flowed along the blade into his victim. Then suddenly the terrible thing he had done dawned. He could be hanged for killing.

Ron groaned and reached clumsily for the bar to support himself, knocking over a stool. But his strength ebbed and he slumped to the floor.

Ricki held the bloody blade, daring anyone to seize him. He had to escape. He had to lie low. He couldn't see his family now. He would break his mother's heart. Why in God's name did he walk into this hell? His friend Charlie Sullivan at the night club would hide him 'til it all blew over. Charlie was always getting away with murder, literally.

Ricki backed away towards the door. The men beneath Her Majesty's poster were now standing, poised ready to fight or flee. Even the tramp had stopped mumbling, though to him the events were no more real than moving images on a cinema screen.

A pool of blood began to cover the dirty lino beside Ron's lumpy frame. His shirt soaked red.

"For Christ's sake we've got to call an ambulance," the coal man pleaded piteously. "He's dying."

Ricki felt no emotion for his fallen foe. He was more interested in getting safely out of the pub. In the commotion he hadn't noticed that the two evil-eyed conspirators, who'd been sitting near the tramp when he'd entered the pub, were no longer present.

While Ricki had driven in the blade, they'd slipped deftly into a small alcove beside the door. Their stock-in-trade of housebreaking had skilled them with cat-like softness of movement.

Now, as Ricki backed away towards the door, one of them stepped out behind him and swung a beer bottle into the side of his head. He jerked as the glass shattered and the liquid cascaded over him, tottering for a moment before collapsing on the dirty floor. With seasoned precision, Ricki's attacker and companion disappeared out the door.

******

8

THE revellers at the playground party had now satisfied their stomachs, the stocks of food and sweets practically all consumed. A group of children were dancing in a circle round the accordion player.

Another child, Tony Selby, remained at the trestle table studying a silver-plated coronation spoon. The aldermen of Stepney Borough Council had decided in their generosity to commission these commemorative items of cutlery and donate them at street parties to the underprivileged slum children of London's east end, in an act of devotion to the Crown. Tony was wondering what the initials ER II meant, stamped on the handle.

"You look after that," his mother Irene told him, more by way of command than request. She wore a floral print dress which she'd made at home on her sewing machine, specially for the occasion. Her wavy auburn hair had been carefully crafted by an uncomfortable night in net and rollers. The woman was a rose in appearance, but her thorns would severely gouge anyone who dared cross her.

It wasn't that she thought her son would be careless with his new acquisition, but more her fear that some thieving hand in the crowd would have it away. At the age of ten, Tony did not understand the value of his possession in the same way as his mother. One day it might be worth something she thought. Irene always kept trinkets in case they might be valuable one day.

Tony held out the spoon to his mum. It would be better if she looked after it than have her constantly nagging him. After all it was only a boring thing used to stir tea.

He brushed back his hair. It was always flopping onto his forehead. He'd inherited the hair colour as well as high cheekbones from his mother. Now after making the most of the treats on offer, his best and only white shirt and beige shorts were streaked with squash stains.

The street party arrived at its formal point as a dignitary from the local council wearing his gold chain of office mounted a makeshift podium erected in the playground for the occasion. Rapping the lectern in front of him with a small hammer he called for silence. The laughter and music gradually ceased.

In the opening seconds of this tribute speech to the new royal era, Tony's mind began to wander. He'd seen a really good Dinky toy car in the shops when he was out with his mother yesterday. It even had built-in suspension.

He turned to focus on the empty pharmaceuticals factory across the road and wondered if he could steer a stone through one of the protective grilles at a rare remaining pane of glass. Then he stared at the flat that was his home on the first floor of Hardwick House. From the playground he could just see his bedroom window over the top of the balcony.

Tony wondered if he could leap from the balcony and land without breaking his ankles. He noticed one of the kids further down the table pulling a face at him. He pulled a face back and was clouted round the ear by his mother.

After what seemed an age, the official droning came to an end and the accordion player began playing God Save The Queen, the adults joining in to sing the national anthem.

At first Tony thought he was imagining bells ringing in the background, but they grew urgently louder. Faces turned towards the source of the sound, distracted from singing. The council dignitary urged the accordion man to play on, but it was impossible. Car tyres screeched to a halt at the far end of the playground outside the Flute and Whistle. Now the singing had stopped and only the accordion player battled on for a few more bars.

A wave of people began to flock towards the pub. An ambulance drove into view racing down Hope Street towards the police bells. A small group of uniformed officers ordered the crowd to move back as a buzz of questions began to sweep through the onlookers. Tenants started lining the rows of balconies hoping to get a better view of what was happening.

"Someone's been stabbed in the pub," a voice cried out. A groan of concern rippled through the gathering mass.

"It's one of the Cellini brothers," another voice shouted.

"Not my son, no please God, not my son," a woman in the crowd screamed.

She was heavily built and used her large frame to barge through to the front, but was pushed back by a growing group of policemen, now being reinforced by another team of officers bursting out of the prison van and brandishing truncheons. When a stabbing happened in this area, they turned out in force.

Moments later two ambulancemen emerged from the pub carrying a stretcher. A blanket had been placed hastily over the knife victim. They lifted him into the ambulance.

Mrs Cellini cried out, "oh my Ricki, let me go to my Ricki!"

The police linked arms to stop her going any further. In her distress she couldn't see that the body on the stretcher was twice the volume of her son.

Moments later Ricki Cellini was escorted out of the pub by two officers, arms handcuffed behind his back. He walked unsteadily, blood streaming down his face.

Mrs Cellini was in turmoil. Her feelings of relief and dismay welled into a state of panic and confusion. "Ricki, Ricki, what have they done to you?" she clawed at the cordon, attempting to break through again but without success.

The crowd murmured at the sight of Cellini being led from the pub, Maria's world collapsed in ruins. Why were they taking her son away? She was truly thankful he was alive, my God, yes, but how would her family live if he went to prison again? She sobbed bitterly. Why were they cursed with such a miserable life?

Ricki turned his head towards the sound of his crying mother. "Don't worry mama....." he attempted to reassure her, but he felt a brutal fist impact in the small of his back, urging him to silence and into the prison van.

Maria Cellini buried her head in her hands as the heavy back doors were slammed shut and the vehicle sped away. Life had been an uphill struggle for the woman and nothing ever seemed to improve for long. She'd come to Britain from Corsica as a young bride in her late teens with her new husband Joseph. Her older brother, Santo, had emigrated to London some years before and he urged Maria to come and live over here.

They believed the opportunities to advance were so much better than back home. Joseph was granted a work permit and he and his bride came to live in Stepney. Joseph, however, had an unfortunate liking for alcohol. At first he got work as a bus conductor, but his habit made him unreliable and he was sacked. He then found some menial jobs fetching and carrying in the street markets, but there were too many tempting pubs on the corners. He began stealing to buy drink.

Being good Catholics, Joseph and Maria were blessed with children at frequent intervals. Ricki was her first, followed by son Silvio. Her husband Joseph was badly deteriorating by the time their daughter Angelina arrived and matters had totally degenerated by the time Johnny came along. Joseph was regularly lifted out of the gutter by the police or a passing good Samaritan.

Eventually he choked to death on his own vomit in a pile of rotting vegetables and cardboard boxes which the street traders had left for the dustmen to collect. It was a freezing December night and he'd crawled among the rubbish to get some warmth.

By now, Maria had taken to selling herself along the Whitechapel Road, just to get enough money to feed her family. Local jobs in the factories just didn't pay enough. Her sister Rosemary minded the kids while she set about her night work. There was nothing sophisticated, a cheap shag in a doorway or in a back room at one of the more amenable pubs. Maria was never quite sure who was the father of her fifth child, Dominique.

They were bad years and she feared for the future of her son Ricki, who was brought before the juvenile courts on several occasions charged with stealing wallets and handbags in Club Row, Petticoat Lane and the labyrinth of other street markets that straddled the area. Finally in his mid teens, he'd progressed to holding-up shopkeepers at gunpoint, by which time the courts decided to send him down.

When he came out Ricki seemed to have changed. He got jobs working in the London night clubs. Maria wasn't sure what he did and she didn't really want to know, but he began earning good money and he sent on £10 to her every week. It was enough to pay the rent and buy food and clothes for the younger children.

By now, her frumpy looks didn't attract the punters anymore and she was relieved of the burden of work that had only made her feel shame. She took a cleaning job, and with the money from Ricki, life had become a little better. Until the harrowing event that had just taken place. Even now she could hardly believe it was true.

******

TONY Selby lay in bed pondering the events of the day. The lamp-post light in Hope Street shone over the playground below, and penetrated the flimsy light green curtains of his bedroom, dimly illuminating the flaking ceiling.

Part of the window was obscured by the silhouette of his dad's tropical fish tank near the foot of the bed. The door to the room was slightly ajar and light shone onto the side of his wardrobe which just fitted the short space alongside the doorway.

He could hear muffled shouts and thuds through the wall adjoining the Cellini household next door. Maria Cellini was taking her frustration with life out on her kids. They were shouting back and it sounded like furniture, glass and crockery were being used as missiles in the bitter dispute. Her wails and sobbing penetrated his bedroom.

On the other side through the door opening Tony could hear his mother and father arguing. He was used to it. They were always arguing.

"How do you expect me to get all the shopping when you only give me two pounds, ten shillings a week?" his mother Irene demanded. "I have to bloody well go out and work in a sweatshop pressing clothes all day to help keep this place going."

She was sewing a button on a shirt, sitting forward on a shoddy wing chair, its dark yellow fabric and springs worn beyond endurance. It was one of a pair, positioned to face the television, which Irene's mother had bestowed on the newlyweds to help them set up home. She in turn had acquired them from a tinker 15 years earlier who'd redeemed them from a rubbish tip.

"You're just a nasty vindictive cow," her husband Gerry fought back. "All you ever want to do is live in this dump. I want to get on."

"I don't want to live in this bloody dump. You're the only one holding us back with all you're bleedin' airs and graces." Irene knew how to wound him.

Gerry's face turned red with anger, highlighting the black of his wavy hair and neatly trimmed moustache. He shook with fury. It was all he could do to stop himself striking his wife.

Not so long ago he'd been held in respect, joining the Royal Air Force at the outbreak of war as an ordinary aircraftman, and working his way up to become a sergeant.

Flying over Hitler's Germany in a Lancaster bomber, he was the bomb aimer and wireless operator. Weaving through the explosions of flak lighting the night sky at 20,000 feet, any deadly one of them could send him and the crew plummeting to earth in fiery cremation.

In one raid the bomb operating gear got stuck and Gerry climbed down into the bowels of the aircraft to literally kick one of the bombs free. It was risky because one slip would have sent him down with the ten ton payload. He was commended for his bravery.

He met Irene in the Prospect of Whitby pub at Wapping during a short spell of leave in 1944. They must have experienced love, because Tony was conceived in those brief days they spent together. Perhaps the emotion was brought on by the turbulent times and the high possibility of a short life, but they hadn't experienced much love together since. With the war ending the following year and Tony on the way, a hasty register office marriage was organised.

Irene's war days were spent in the woman's Auxiliary Training Service, posted to various locations around the country. It gave her the chance to see life after a claustrophobic, ill-educated girlhood in Stepney where the furthest she'd ever been afield were the hop fields of Kent on working holidays picking hops. But her prospect of any further new horizons came to an abrupt end with the arrival of son Tony.

Gerry's eyes had been opened by the war and the RAF. The closed environment of his Wapping home fell away and with it his otherwise destiny of joining his father in a lifetime job on the railways. He'd met people with new and different ideas and he'd decided he wanted to become a lawyer. That meant a lot of study.

"Why don't you get a job on the docks? You can get good money," Irene urged him.

"Because I don't want to spend the rest of my days living in this slum," Gerry exploded.

"Well you're not gonna get far as a solicitor's clerk. They pay peanuts," Irene derided him.

"Yes, but I'll get a lot more money if I can pass my solicitor's exams," Gerry tried to drive home the point, frustrated that his wife didn't understand the longer term better prospects for the family.

"It's bloody impossible trying to study for them with you nagging me all the time and that bloody noise from upstairs and the Cellini's next door. They're all bloody criminals that family. They ought to be locked up." His frustration spilled out.

"My brother works on the docks. He gets good money," Irene wanted better prospects now.

"I don't want to be a bloody docker and spend the rest of my life in a council house in Stepney." Gerry picked up his pipe from the table and started knocking the spent tobacco into an ashtray. His pipe was his comfort and support in these times.

"You've got big ideas you have. What d'ye want to go mixing with all them nobs for? They're not interested in you." Irene's denigration of her husband's aspiring status in life rankled with him.

In the RAF he'd mixed with well educated men from wealthy families. On many occasions their lives had depended on his radio skills while they were under heavy fire. They'd treated him as an equal. The world was changing. Working class people now had new opportunities. But the point was lost on Irene. Her mind remained steeped in the old order. It gave her security.

Gerry looked around the cramped living room. The small, black and white television in the corner staring from its cabinet. The cast iron cooking range set in an alcove and now only lit to heat the flat in winter.

Two apples in a fruit bowl and a women's magazine lay on the table in the middle of the room. In the corner by the window, which overlooked another bleak council estate, stood a glass fronted cabinet stacked with plates and dishes.

"I should have stayed in the RAF," Gerry reflected sorrowfully. He struck a match and held it to the bowl of his pipe, sucking vigorously. A thick cloud of smoke began to waft across the room. It calmed him a little.

"I could have made it to officer level if I'd stayed in," he continued to voice his regrets.

"Oh you'd have loved that, wouldn't you, hobnobbing it with all the sirs and generals," Irene continued her derision.

"You stupid cow, they don't have generals in the RAF," Gerry rejoiced at his intellectual superiority.

"I expect you'd like to be one though," Irene laughed, knowing he truly would.

She finished sewing the button, snipped the thread with the scissors and put the dress over the back of the dining table chair. She rose and took a few paces to switch on the television.

"I don't want the TV on," Gerry barked.

"Well I do," Irene sized up to him. "Anyway it'll take five minutes to warm up, so you've still got a bit of time for all your big talk." Gerry puffed furiously on his pipe, great jets of smoke shot out across the room. He couldn't get any peace here. This was their multi-purpose family room, dining room, lounge, sitting room all squeezed into a meagre space. There was nowhere else to go in this flat. Only the two squashed bedrooms, the kitchen vying for space with a cast iron bath and the lavatory designed for use by a contortionist.

Gerry had been standing beside the range. Now he stepped forward and stooped to turn off the television. Irene grabbed his arm.

"No you fucking don't," she warned him. He wrenched his arm from her grasp and with it swung her a sharp wack in the face. She flinched in pain, then recovering quickly turned on him, punching and scratching at his face. She hit his pipe and it flew from his mouth smashing onto the table, the tobacco spilling out over the cloth. He tried to grab hold of her arms, but she broke through gouging four fingernail tears in his left cheek. Enraged, Gerry began punching back. She crouched to protect herself and he rained blows to her side and back.

"Get off me you fucking bastard, get off," she screamed. Gerry backed away, heaving for breath.

"I hate you you cow, I fucking well hate you," His eyes filled with tears, remorse at what he'd done and anger were all mixing up inside.

Irene stood up, she hadn't finished baiting him yet. "They won't make you a fucking general if you go around hitting women," she snarled, daring him to attack her again. Gerry touched his cheek. It was sore. He looked at the traces of blood on his fingertips.

"You bitch," he growled.

"Explain that to them at work," Irene goaded triumphantly.

Gerry was shaking, but he resisted the urge to strike again. He caught sight of his pipe and snatched it from the table, storming from the room. A few minutes later the front door slammed shut.

Irene knew he'd soon be consoling himself with a pint or two in The Feathers, one of the few pubs in the area that had a fitted carpet and signs on the walls asking customers not to stub their cigarettes on the floor. The television hummed and a picture of Jimmy Jewel and Ben Warriss larking and joking came fuzzily into view. She'd have a couple hours to herself now. But it might come to blows later, when he came back from the pub, all those emotions and frustrations fired with alcohol.

Tony heard the row from the bedroom. He was upset at his mum and dad fighting but it wasn't unusual. For him it was the natural course of life. He did know some friends whose mums and dads sometimes kissed and hugged each other. But they were a bit strange. He couldn't imagine his mother and father doing anything like that.

He began to feel drowsy as the TV comedians' jokes wafted through the gap of his bedroom door. In the flat above a record player burst into life, and a loose flake of paint from the ceiling fluttered on to Tony's forehead as the couple above broke into a thudding dance routine. He brushed the flake away, turned on his side and fell asleep.

******

"COME on hurry up, you'll make me late," Tony's mum called to him. He'd not long woken and was getting dressed in his hated, grey school uniform. The rough material of the shorts always made his thighs feel itchy.

Irene was spreading margarine onto a slice of bread in the narrow L-shaped kitchen. Bracketed into the wall, above the worktop where she was preparing her spam sandwich lunch, rested a black electric meter. It made strange ticking noises which occasionally kept beat with the 'Music While You Work' programme coming from the radio in the living room. The medley of happy tunes seemed to emphasize the bleakness of Monday morning.

21

To the right of Irene a bulbous, creamy white gas geyser with a silver spout overhanging the cast iron bath, throbbed and roared unnervingly, straining to heat a volume of water deep inside.

"Don't forget to wash your face and brush your teeth properly," Irene ordered Tony. He pulled on his grey jumper and stepped across the passageway into the kitchen. Squeezing past his mother, he approached the porcelain sink wedged in a small gap at the foot of the bath.

Ignoring the carbolic bar of soap on the draining board alongside, he began to splash his face half-heartedly, shuddering to the touch of the chilly liquid running from the solitary cold water tap.

"Do it properly," his mother ordered again. "Here, I've just boiled some water." Irene came across with the kettle, placed the plug in the sink and poured in the steaming water. She then ran the cold water tap, testing the temperature of the shallow pool with her finger. Reluctantly Tony lathered the evil smelling soap and sparingly applied it to his face.

"And clean your teeth," Irene barked at him. She sliced her sandwich in two and popped it into a brown paper bag. After glancing round to make sure Tony was carrying out his ablutions to order, she left the kitchen and took the few short paces down the passage to the living room.

From a rose patterned china bowl resting on a small, dark brown cabinet in one corner, she selected a shilling and some pennies to cover her bus fare to work in nearby Poplar.

Gerry entered the room from their adjoining bedroom, dressed in his vest and pants. He looked round for the morning paper.

"Have you boiled me an egg?" he demanded of Irene.

She said nothing, dropping her bus fare into her purse.

"Did you hear me?" Gerry pressed.

"No I bloody well haven't boiled you an egg," Irene retaliated with a sharp blast of vitriol. "I suppose you want fucking bread soldiers to dip in it too."

Gerry should have known better than to invoke Irene's ire, but as far as he was concerned a woman's place was to look after her husband first and foremost. That meant making him breakfast. Despite a decade of marriage, he still could not come round to the idea that Irene did not see herself in the traditional woman's role.

"I've got to go out to work. Do yourself a bloody egg," she concluded.

"That's not a job, working in a sweatshop pressing clothes all day," Gerry used his anger to make Irene feel small. But she knew how to play that game.

"Well if you earned some proper money, I wouldn't have to work in a sweatshop," she goaded him. "If it wasn't for me working we wouldn't be able to afford the rent." The day had begun in its usual way. Gerry picked up his copy of The Daily Telegraph from the dining table.

"You'll always be a cheap eastender," he sneered at her. "At least I'm trying to better myself." He glanced at the front page and decided to head back for the peace of the bedroom to read the story before getting dressed.

"Oh yes, we all know you're Mr Wonderful," Irene jibed as he slammed the bedroom door. Then she saw Tony standing in the passage, staring at her. "Don't take any notice of him, he's just carrying on again. Go and get my ten Weights."

It was the morning ritual, Tony being sent to the local corner shop for Irene's pack of ten Weights cigarettes. He was clutching the one shilling and sixpence she'd left him in the kitchen for the purpose.

There was drizzle in the air as he closed the front door and made his way along the balcony past Ellie Pitchfork's flat beside the block's main stairway. Ellie Pitchfork lived a more or less reclusive life, rarely seen outside her front door. She was stooped with age and probably in her seventies, but she always ridiculously described herself as being "a little over forty".

Whenever she opened her front door, a foul stench of the unwashed drifted out on to the balcony. Tony hated the smell and always passed the door in fear that it might suddenly be opened. For some reason he couldn't fathom, she always wanted to speak to him when she saw him, but he always recoiled from her withered approach. He'd seen witches in books that looked a bit like her. Once she had offered him a sweet, but he ran away in terror, convinced that it was poisoned.

He passed her door without incident and ran down the stairs, carefully leaping over the pools of piss trailing down the steps. He climbed the low wall and railing bordering the playground, preferring to do this than use the entrance into Hope Street marked by two stubby brick columns.

At the turn of the L-shaped street was a small grassed area surrounded on three sides by flats. Tony saw a group of four slightly older boys kicking a football around on the grass, then realised one of them was his arch antagonist Brendan Healey. With short cropped hair, everything about him was taut and muscular. It seemed to be his mission in life to set on Tony everytime he saw him.

Usually Tony could outrun him and now he was already gearing himself up for flight. Sure to form, Brendan saw him and began to mouth insults. "I'm going to smash your head in," the sentiment usually began. Tony took off as Brendan and his mates began to pursue their quarry.

Tony knew that if he could make it to the corner shop in Turner Street, just a few hundred yards away he'd be safe inside. But he would have to use animal cunning to get back home without a good punching.

The shouts of his pursuers gave Tony the shot of adrenalin needed to sprint for all he was worth. They were close as he rounded into Turner Street and now it was just another fifty yards. Safety was in sight, but his toe caught in one of the uneven cracked pavements and next second he was aware of his left shoulder impacting painfully on the kerb and his body rolling uncontrollably into the dirty gutter.

His attackers were now almost upon him screaming with joy at the prospect of running their quarry to ground. But with lightning reactions that only deep fear injects, Tony was somehow on his feet again and ready to flee. Brendan caught hold of Tony's left arm, but Tony pulled away causing him to lose his balance and spin round. As he tried to keep upright his right arm swung out catching his attacker a sharp blow in the face.

Shocked for a second, the boy released his grip. His mates attempted to grab Tony, but he was off again swift as a fox, making it breathless to the corner shop and crashing through the door.

"Hey, hey, hey," he heard Rita shout out as he careered into her store. "You'll break my door. Be careful!" Tony only half heard her as he quickly slammed it shut. Brendan and his friends gathered and glowered outside. Rita realised they were chasing Tony and came to his aid. She opened the door and called out in her strong foreign accent, "go away or I'll have the police on you." For a moment Tony knew he was secure, but they would be waiting for him around the corner.

Rita was a grumpy old woman but kind hearted. Tony came to her shop for his mum's cigarettes every morning and a relationship of familiarity had built between them. It usually consisted of Rita pouring her heart out about the cold. She always felt cold.

Save for the hottest, humid summer days, Rita was buried in a heavy overcoat and thick layers of self-knitted woollies, huddled beside her paraffin heater in the middle of a jumble of goods ranging through cheap toys, sweets, cigarettes, packets of cereal and tinned food. There was a small counter but it was covered in cardboard boxes and loose products. She gave change from a leather pouch that looked something akin to a horse's oat bag.

No-one was quite sure where she came from, possibly somewhere in Eastern Europe about forty years ago. It was thought she'd had a husband at one time, though no-one was aware of ever having seen him.

Rita hobbled to the back of the shop and returned with a packet of Weights cigarettes. Then she went to a colourful display of glass sweet jars on a shelf behind the counter and selected one filled with liquorice sticks. "Here's your spanish," she said, fishing out one of the sticks and presenting it to the boy. Tony loved liquorice, or spanish as it was known in these parts. It was his reward for getting the ciggies. Tony handed Rita the shilling and she delved into the horse's pouch for a penny change.

"Now go on home and keep out of trouble," Rita advised him. Then she returned to her seat by the paraffin stove muttering to herself about the cold. Tony knew Brendan and his cohorts would be hiding around some corner. The glass pane in the door was largely obscured by faded and torn advertising stickers. Tony peered out between them to see if the coast was clear.

His aggressors were gone, but he could sense they were out there somewhere waiting for him. The bottom of the door scraped on the floor as this time he opened it carefully and cautiously looked around. A man walking his pitifully unkempt Scottie dog passed by. He was going in the direction Tony wanted. He thought that if he walked closely behind the man, Brendan would not attack him with a grown up present.

He tailed the man up to the corner that led into Hope Street. The man crossed the road and went straight on. He was no longer going in Tony's direction. Two other grown-ups passed by, but they weren't going his way. Tony pressed on, looking round fearfully and ready to run. He began to relax as he neared the grassed area and saw no-one there.

Brendan must have given up. Suddenly his arch enemy and mates sprung up from behind a low wall bordering the area. They leapt over it shouting and screaming in triumph. Tony was taken completely by surprise and by the time he realised what was happening they had surrounded him.

Brendan approached menacingly, fists raised. His clothes were spattered with mud from the game of football. Although he was only a year older than Tony, his long black trousers gave him the look of being several years ahead of his victim dressed in school shorts. Tony looked for a gap between the boys, calculating if he could bolt for it. Their semi-circle was too tight.

"Come on, fight me," Brendan invited.

"But it's five of you against me," Tony protested the odds. The group laughed.

"Alright then, stand back the rest of you," Brendan commanded his troops, "and I'll fight you myself."

It was the opportunity Tony needed. As the others stepped back he made his break for it like a wildebeest outmanoeuvring a deadly trap of lions.

They lunged at him but he slipped past their fingertips. He heard their shouts of abuse at being outwitted, but dared not look back as he raced away in case a glance over his shoulder would slow him down. Only as he neared the porch entrance to his home did he turn to see if he was being pursued. The coast was clear. They'd obviously decided to leave him alone for now.

A few huddled figures making their way to work, glanced at him as he stooped to gain his breath before climbing the dirty stairway to his front door.

"What have you been doing?" his mother demanded angrily. "You've been ages."

"Some boys chased me. They were trying to hit me," Tony complained.

"Well why didn't you hit them back?" Irene was unsympathetic.

"They were bigger than me," Tony protested.

"You hit them back, they'll soon leave you alone," Irene insisted. "Come on, give me my cigarettes, I'm going to be late for work and I've still got to get you to your nan's."

Tony's grandmother Joyce Ryder looked after him while her daughter Irene was at work during the day. Tony was very fond of her and she gave welcome relief to the brashness of his mother.

She had a ruddy complexion of broken veins and always smelled of cold cream, which she liberally plastered on her skin. Each morning she would walk Tony to school about half a mile away, before going on to buy daily provisions and have a ferret for a good bargain on the stalls at nearby Watney Street market.

She remembered the days when the area was a close knit community. She'd lived with her mum and dad and seven other brothers and sisters in a tiny, cramped two up, two down. It was in a row of dozens of similar terraced dwellings with tiny back yards. They were all crammed into one bedroom, sleeping alternately head to toe to fit into the bed and on the floor, arguing whose turn it was to enjoy the comfort of the mattress.

Then the authorities began to tear down the slums and in the 1930s Joyce, who by now was married, moved with her two sons and three daughters into the luxury of a block of flats, Conway House in Hope Street. Now her offspring had flown the nest, but daughter Irene had moved only a short distance away to Hardwick House at the other end of the street.

It took only a few minutes to walk the length of the playground to Conway House and Joyce was waiting for her grandson and daughter at the entrance to her block. Irene exchanged a hurried greeting with her mother, kissed Tony goodbye and soon disappeared to catch her bus to work.

Tony's nan adjusted the knot of the dark blue scarf she was wearing and made sure the buttons of her fawn raincoat were all done up against the light drizzle of the morning. She picked up her shopping bag and set off with Tony by her side.

As they walked the tarmac of the estate, the enclosure gave way to pavement and Tony began to play hopscotch on the alternating slabs.

"Behave yourself," his nan called out as he began to get ahead of her. "You'll fall over." He stopped and waited for her to catch up. Soon they turned into Cable Street busy with shopkeepers opening up for the day's business.

Checking there were no cars coming they crossed the road into Fairclough Street. On the corner was a bomb site, a large rectangle of brick and concrete rubble scattered with vicious shards of broken glass bottles, piles of rubbish and rusty skeletons of metal tubing which once had life as prams and bicycles.

Weeds now flourished through the countless cracks and crevices. Before the wartime blitz the setting had been a thriving community of small terraced houses. As they walked beside the tangled heaps, Tony's attention was drawn by a rotting carcass. He stopped to study it. Maggots were teaming over the last fragments of flesh and fur. It was a dead dog. Tony picked up a stick nearby and began to prod at the creamy coloured parasites eating their way round the half revealed skeleton of the unfortunate creature.

"Leave it alone," Joyce called back to him. Tony was fascinated by the sight and made a mental note to return to it after school, lobbing the stick as hard and as high as he could into the mass of dereliction.

Further down the street a rag and bone man in a dusty black overcoat was plying his trade. Sluggishly he pushed his barrow piled high with a jumble of old clothes along the road. His approach was signalled with frequent shouts of something that sounded like "any ol' rags". But the drawl of his cry made it difficult to tell.

Tony felt a sense of guilt as the sight of the hardened traveller reminded him of an unfortunate episode a month or two earlier, when he had taken a few dresses out of his mother's wardrobe without telling her and given them to a rag and bone man for the princely sum of sixpence.

Tony thought that if he bunched some other clothes into the wardrobe space, his mum wouldn't notice. But she did. And they were her favourite dresses. That was when Tony found out what the term 'boxing someone's ears' really meant. Irene had been absolutely furious. Tony would never repeat such folly in a hurry.

Fairclough Street school's grim and foreboding elevations soon came into view. Queen Victoria had not long been laid to rest when its construction began to darken the landscape. The high brick wall surrounding the structure for some length marked it as a place of punishment rather than education. Only a lack of bars at the tall windows peering loftily over the wall gave any hint that it was not a penal colony.

Tony waved goodbye to his nan and turned towards the school entrance. It was a narrow, arched opening with the legend BOYS inscribed sternly in a cold slab of concrete above. His left shoe felt loose and he stooped to re-tie the lace.

As he rose, he noticed a group of boys larking about on the other side of the road. One of them caught his eye and for a moment they stared at each other. Tony didn't know the boy and from the glowering expression in the stranger's face he wanted to keep it that way. Now the rest of the group stopped pushing, shoving and shouting at each other, taking an interest in their companion's gaze. They saw Tony and began to mouth abuse and threats at him.

"Who you fuckin' staring at?" they rounded. They weren't dressed in uniforms and Tony took comfort from the fact they didn't go to his school. He quickly turned away but sensed they were crossing the road and coming towards him.

Quickly he ran into the school grounds, normally a dominion that depressed him but which now offered security.

The tarmac playground was teeming with the energetic excitement of a couple of hundred or more boys and girls chasing, teasing, shouting, daring. Tony slipped into the comfort of the crowd and caught sight of some friends talking together on the far side of the walled enclosure. Sidestepping ball games and hopscotch contests he precariously made his way over to them.

"Hey Cisco," his friend Stephen greeted him in a hardly recognisable Mexican accent. "Hey Pancho," Tony replied, trying hard to sound like an American. They were imitating the heroes of their favourite TV cowboy series The Cisco Kid. It was an interest that united them in games and conversation and immediately they began pretending to shoot each other, ducking behind other boys and girls in the playground.

Stephen's eyes smiled through the thick lenses of cheap, flimsily framed spectacles. Without them the boy was almost blind. Tony thought they made Stephen look intelligent, and he'd once asked his mum if he could have spectacles hoping it might help him to do his schoolwork better. His mother had laughed and told him he'd have to work harder if he wanted to be clever. The suggestion didn't appeal.

"We're going to Clacton for our holidays this year," Dougie, another boy announced as Tony used him for cover, narrowly avoiding Stephen's hail of imaginary bullets. Tony had no idea of Clacton's location except that it was a seaside holiday place.

He'd stayed with his aunt and uncle just outside London near a town called Romford a year ago, where there were grass landscaped areas. He thought that was the countryside.

"We went to Clacton last year," Annie, a dark haired girl dressed in a pink gingham dress standing nearby retorted smugly.

"Well my dad's getting a car." The proudest boast came from John Atkins as he joined the group. He always had to go one better than anyone else. Owning a car in this area was a statement of great wealth.

"You're dad hasn't got enough money for a car," someone else derided. John Atkins stoutly defended his dad. The gathering descended into argument while Tony and Stephen slipped away to carry on their cowboy game elsewhere, using the multitude of children milling around the playground for new cover.

As they enacted their shoot-outs, Tony's attention was taken by a huddle of boys just inside the school entrance.

"Got you," Stephen shouted, blowing at the two fingers of his right hand that represented his smoking six-gun. Tony had dropped his defence. The game disappeared as he recognised the group by the entrance as the gang who had threatened him just outside the school. They appeared to be looking for someone.

"Do you know who those boys are?" their was disquiet in his voice.

Stephen squinted across the playground, but couldn't make them out. A fat lad nearby, who they'd used as a large make-believe rock to shield behind in their cowboy game knew the answer.

"That's Ronnie Sutton and his gang," he told them. It sounded more like a warning than a statement. "They got chucked out of Blundell Street school down the road for threatening a teacher with a knife. They say Ronnie Sutton's killed someone."

A sense of deep fear gripped Tony and he used the fat lad for cover again, this time shielding himself from what he knew to be a potential real threat of harm. Peering from behind the boy, Tony was relieved to see Ronnie Sutton and his gang of hangers-on leaving the playground.

A teacher ringing a handbell emerged from the entrance to the school at the top of a small flight of stairs. It signalled the start of lessons and the noisy commotion in the playground began to subside as the children funnelled onto the steps and into their classes.

Tony realised that he needed to have a pee and he quickly made his way against the flow towards an outside toilet block. The foul stench of the overflowing urinal gutter inside caused him to try and hold his breath as he relieved himself against the dirty, stained wall.

As he buttoned up his flies, he thought he heard a noise behind. For some reason he felt another twinge of fear and quickly turned his head. Ronnie Sutton and his boys now blocked the doorway of the toilet.

"Gotcha, you little scumbag," Sutton was delighted that his quarry was so entirely trapped. Tony was petrified and felt like he was going to pee himself, though there was none left to come. His mind was racing to think of a way to escape, but there were only high frosted windows above the urinal which couldn't be opened.

"I haven't done anything to you," Tony pleaded.

"You stared at me and I don't like people staring at me," Ronnie Sutton accused him. He had a prominent, bony forehead which he used frequently and skilfully to floor his victims. His eyes were deep set and glowed with a triumphant evil smile.

"But I wasn't staring, I just caught sight of you."

In his heart Tony felt it was hopeless to try and plead his way out.

The thug was several inches taller than his followers, who now stood beside and behind him edging their way towards Tony.

Sutton raised his fists. His forearms were sinewy and heavily tattooed. "Get hold of him Benny," he commanded. One of the boys at his side stepped out. He was stoutly built and had the look of brute dimness. His pleasure came as much from obeying his master as walloping people.

"You hold him Benny, while I piss on him," Sutton relished the prospect and began unbuttoning his flies. His followers began to laugh.

Benny grabbed hold of Tony, twisting his arms up behind his back. Tony winced with pain, struggling a little but mainly too fearful to move.

"Don't piss on me too," Benny jested. The four other boys in the gang had now fanned out on each side of

Sutton, anxious to get a ringside view of the sport. They laughed heartily at Benny's quip.

Sutton moved closer and pulled out his dick aiming it at his victim. Tony prepared for the worst. Suddenly to his amazement, Sutton came flying forward at breakneck speed, shooting past him and impacting head first on to the urinal wall with a loud crack. The boy groaned half-conscious, and slumped into the urinal gutter. His hands flailed around on the dirty floor.

The boys who'd been standing alongside Sutton were now being punched in their sides and heads by a figure delivering blows so quickly none of them had time to think about defending themselves. In seconds they were doubled-up in pain. The lad Benny, still holding Tony, released his grip looking about in bewilderment, stooping to help his floored leader.

In the next moment Tony's mind was able to focus on his rescuer, an older lad by several years he'd never seen before. He had short, dark hair and a hard face like a seasoned boxer who'd taken some knocks. Tony sensed that events were now on his side.

"Get off your arse and piss off Sutton," the stranger erupted. His fists were ready for further action, directing them at any potential challenger. Sutton's supporters hadn't the stomach to fight him and heads bowed they fled out of the block.

Sutton began to heave himself to his feet. Benny, who'd helped him, now turned to face the stranger.

"You fuckin'......." he launched a counter attack. He was taller and bigger and the impact from his fist would have caused a lot of damage. But his adversary was faster and sidestepped the offensive. Even as Benny was finishing the hammer delivery into thin air, the stranger shot forward again landing him a savage blow in the kidney.

Benny screamed in agony as the continuing swing of his futile punch threw him completely out of balance. He crashed into Sutton who went down for a second time, now with the full weight of Benny on top of him.

The huddled, defeated heap rolled around on the floor, gradually separating and staggering awkwardly to their feet

"Go on, get out. Pick on people your own size you coward Sutton," the stranger commanded.

Ronnie Sutton and his sidekick Benny brushed themselves down, their clothes spattered with wet urine stains. They moved cautiously around their adversary towards the door. At the exit when he felt sure enough he could make a speedy escape, Sutton turned scowling. "I'll get you for this Billy Walker. You won't be so big when I've knifed you."

"Bugger off Sutton," Billy turned raising his fists again. Benny raised two fingers in a half-hearted, defiant gesture. Billy moved towards them and they were off, running at first and then trying to retain some dignity by slowing to a walking swagger as they neared the exit from the playground.

"Are you alright?" Billy turned to Tony who was staring at him in disbelief and total admiration. He'd never been rescued by anyone like that before. He nodded that he was okay.

"Watch out for Sutton, he's a nasty piece of work," the youth warned.

"I've never seen him before," Tony was bewildered. "I didn't do anything to him."

"You don't need to do anything for him to pick on you," Billy turned to look at Sutton disappearing through the school exit in the distance. "He's a bully. But like all bullies he's a coward too. Come on, he's gone," Billy reassured him. "You'd better get to your class or you'll be in trouble." They re-entered the playground.

"Do you go to school here?" Tony asked.

"Me?" Billy seemed surprised. "No, I work in my dad's fish and chip shop in Cable Street. Just round the corner."

Tony knew the chippie. His mum and nan sometimes bought fish and chips there for a Friday night treat.

They now approached the flight of steps that led up into the school building.

"And where do you live?" Billy was getting ready to part company, stopping at the bottom of the steps.

"In Hope Street," Tony mounted the flight.

Billy nodded recognition and walked off as Tony pushed at the heavy wooden door to enter the school building.

Inside the gloomy entrance hall, a long corridor with doorways along its receding length lay before him and to the right a stairway led up to the landing where his classroom was situated. He raced up the stairs, now worried he'd be late for class.

"Stop running!" a teacher boomed from the hall below. Tony slowed his pace.

Reaching the landing, Tony's classroom was a few doors down on the right, along another characterless corridor with frequent patches of brown flaking paint and brightened only marginally by a few art class paintings taped to the walls.

As he pushed open the classroom door, he heard Mr Salmon explaining something about multiplication and chalking some figures on a blackboard at the front of the class. He turned to further explain the symbols he had written and saw Tony. The teacher stopped and gazed at the latecomer. His narrowing eyes pierced the thick lenses of his dark spectacles, the main feature of his face save for the menace of its stare.

"Why are you late?" Mr Salmon growled. The other thirty or so boys lining the room in neat rows at their desks turned eagerly towards this welcome distraction from arithmetic. It was always good when someone else was in trouble.

"I…I was hit by some boys….in the playground."

"Hit? Hit by who?" Mr Salmon was both curious and disbelieving, but certainly not sympathetic.

"I…I don't know." Tony moved slowly towards his desk at the back of the classroom with his head lowered, believing that if he didn't look at the teacher the affair would be forgotten. The next second he clutched at his head as a piece of chalk stung him on the left ear.

"Stand still!" Mr Salmon raged as he had launched the projectile. "Look at me."

Reluctantly Tony turned to look at him, covering his ear lobe in fear of another attack.

"You're lying aren't you," Mr Salmon accused.

"No, look my coat's torn here," Tony lifted the bottom of his jacket.

"You've been larking around and you're late. I shall be reporting you to the headmaster. Now sit down and get your class books out." Mr Salmon picked up another piece of chalk from his desk and turned to the blackboard again. Tony's classmates whispered insults and laughed as he passed through the rows of desks to his own, several sticking out their legs and attempting to trip him on the way.

"Shut up!" boomed Mr Salmon without bothering to turn from the blackboard.

Education was a mysterious practice to Tony. It seemed to serve no obvious purpose other than to be a constant reminder of his failings. He longed for ticks in his exercise books, but found it difficult to work out the method by which they should be achieved. The greatest problem was in trying to remember what the teacher had taught him. Or, indeed, trying to understand what the teacher was saying. The knowledge apparently poured out, but not evidently in.

He was quite good at reading, but the present subject of arithmetic was the greatest puzzle he had ever encountered. In this classroom he was not totally alone in that respect, although he did have the distinction of always coming bottom.

Mr Salmon's words of instruction drifted out on to an ethereal plain. A distant realm of multiplication, division, addition and subtraction existing in the nebulous far reaches of the ornate, plaster floret in the middle of the ceiling, with the electric light cable dangling from its centre. After a few minutes Tony shifted his stare to the arched window in the classroom, overlooking roofs and chimney pots of terraced houses in the adjacent street.

"Selby!"

Tony froze in terror.

"What are you doing boy?" Mr Salmon eyed him viciously. He was holding a blackboard duster, which he half raised in fury and then thought better of it, tossing the implement on to his desk.

Tony wasn't sure of having done anything which could incur such wrath. He stared at his inquisitor, bewildered.

"You're day dreaming boy. That's what you're doing." Mr Salmon loomed towards him.

"What have I just said?"

"That I was day dreaming sir."

Roars of laughter broke out.

Mr Salmon towered above him. He grabbed Tony's left ear, still sore from the chalk assault, and began to shake it.

"You haven't listened to a word I've said have you?" Tony' face screwed in pain as his superior visibly grinned at the suffering. After an extra hard tug, Mr Salmon released the grip, leaving Tony to nurse his sore, red ear.

"You haven't even opened your text book," the teacher accused, flipping the pages.

"Here, long division," he pointed to the matter in hand.

Tony looked at the page, which might just as well have been written in Chinese.

"I want you to find the answer to this problem," Mr Salmon indicated the section with stabbing thrusts at the page.

"Now if you've been listening, you'll know how to do it."

Tony hadn't and didn't, for which no doubt he would be rewarded with another assault later in the lesson.

Tony's encounter with education drifted on like this. Playground breaks were a welcome relief to the monotony of learning, and being told off or beaten were largely routine aspects of going to school. He could cope with that. The part he dreaded most of all though, was when now and again word filtered through to his father about his stunning lack of academic ability.

Gerry already had big plans for his son to ride high in society. For Tony's own sake, of course, although it would be nice to bask in the reflected glory of an industrial or academia supremo. Unfortunately, Tony presently did not manifest any signs of the raw material necessary to build such a fine career. Gerry raged whenever he read his son's school reports. Those were not good days.

The present day, however, rolled on and after what seemed a grinding age, the bell rang at the end of the last lesson and it was time to go home. Tony remembered his encounter that morning and was in a state of fear as he approached the school exit. Cautiously he peered round the opening into the street outside. Groups of schoolboys and girls made their way home singly or in groups, but he couldn't see the boys who had attacked him earlier.

He stepped out and started the homeward journey. In the next moment he was thrown forward as a strong blow impacted on his back.

Tony stumbled forward, petrified as he braced himself for a vicious assault. His earlier attackers must have been hiding ready to pounce.

"Daydreaming Selby!" boomed a young, high-pitched voice. Tony was confused. It didn't sound like his aggressors. Quickly he turned round. It was one of the boys in his class, laughing and goading him. Being the fool was infinitely preferable to an attack by a gang of bullies and Tony felt relieved rather than angry.

"Well you're no good at sums either," Tony retaliated.

"Better than you though," his tormentor sneered. They continued trading insults in this way walking down the street, then the conversation changed to which teacher they hated the most. They had found common ground and were laughing and joking as they parted company down the road.

Saturdays were good days for Tony because he didn't have to go to school. The day started as normal with his mother and father having a row. Something about Gerry needing a button sewn on to his shirt.

"I've got to get the shopping, it'll have to wait to later," Irene began, placing her bags on the floor in the living room and starting to put on her raincoat. Gerry considered that as her husband, his needs should take precedence over the business of buying their weekly fruit and veg at the market stalls in Watney Street. Anyway she was going out to enjoy herself. Women like shopping, he knew that only too well.

Their priorities clashed further and ended as Irene slammed the front door with a departing "sew the bloody button on yourself then".

Tony hardly noticed. He was constructing a building on the floor, carefully balancing one upright comic annual on top of another until the structure had reached a level even higher than the dining table top. Then with a toy car, he'd propel it hard into the bottom annual, causing the whole building to collapse, and all the imaginary people would rush out or be crushed. And fire engines and ambulances would all zoom to the scene, sirens blaring.

His father muttered curses under his breath, throwing the shirt in question on to a chair. He stepped over the derelict ruins of Tony's building and reached for his beloved pipe on the sideboard. Stabbing tobacco agitatedly into the bowl and sparking it into life with a match, he puffed furiously considering his slight.

"Can I go out to play, dad?" Tony looked up at him from the floor. Gerry was too absorbed to hear him.

"Please dad, can I go out to play?" his son urged.

Slowly the request sunk in as Gerry half focussed his attention on the boy.

"Downstairs in the playground, but not on the bomb sites," his father commanded. "You know you cut your foot on the broken glass the other week."

"No, I'm just going to play in the playground, honestly dad."

Gerry reached out and rubbed the top of his son's head as Tony rose from the floor. Here was Gerry's most treasured possession, but his love strained to manifest itself, bursting out in occasional moments of affection like this. Otherwise his mind was too troubled with the everyday of life.

"But clear up your comic annuals first," his father caught sight of the calamity beneath.

"They're not annuals dad, they're buildings," Tony corrected him.

"Your buildings then," Gerry smiled, and then returned to distant thoughts of vengeance in the episode of the un-sewn shirt button, thick billowing clouds of pipe smoke rising ominously over the room.

Tony left the house and made his way along the balcony to the stairs, running quickly past Ellie Pitchfork's door just in case the old crone should suddenly open it and pounce on him with the offer of a poisoned sweet. Stepping over the fresh tributaries of piss trickling down the stairs he made his way into the playground below.

He saw a group of children playing hopscotch, jumping nimbly into the squares chalked roughly on the tarmac surface and he approached them hoping to join in the fun. He knew them, but had never really developed a close friendship with any of them because his father thought they all came from scum families and were not to be fraternised. As a result they thought he was a bit snobby. Eddie Allen in the group greeted him.

"What d'ye want?"

Tony looked at the boy who was dressed in scrappy, short dark trousers covered in mud stains and a shirt that was once bright white in the custody of a previous owner. His long thin face complimented the grubbiness of his clothes and he seemed totally unaware that his nose was running.

"Can I play?" Tony pleaded.

"Go away," Eddie snarled.

"Oh let him play," a girl intervened, as she scooped up the stone at the end of her hop.

Tony knew Jean Nash a little. They'd played games before and he'd found himself strangely attracted to her. Her bright red, cotton dress stood out particularly vividly in contrast to the scruffy clothes of Eddie Allen, and she reminded him of an idyllic, smiling fair haired girl he'd once seen in a story book about a family living on a farm.

The other children in the group grudgingly agreed to let him play, even though it meant they'd all have to wait longer for a turn. The game had continued for about ten minutes when Tony became aware of an onlooker standing a short distance from the group.

"Hey Tony, what you playin' with all the babies for?" the onlooker called out with a derisory grin on his face. It was Johnny Cellini, brother of the now infamous Ricki Cellini involved in the Flute and Whistle pub stabbing a few months earlier.

In the setting of the post war days in these parts, Johnny's darker Mediterranean skin set him apart from most of the other children in the immediate locality. He was foreign and that meant he was separate and different to start with. Now his family link with the stabbing set him further apart. People also saw Johnny's matted black hair, sharp narrow nose and darting eyes as another reason not to trust him.

47

But Tony had a grudging respect, even a fear of him, because Johnny Cellini could look after himself. He was never beaten in any fights. In fact he'd beaten up Tony's arch-enemy Brendan once, and to have such a warrior on your side was fantastic. Not that Johnny had ever stepped in to defend Tony. His motives lay much more in self-interest, though whether he was born with a selfish streak or circumstances had led him to that pass was debatable, and at this stage far beyond Tony's mental capacity to even perceive such heady concepts.

Johnny Cellini had accused him of playing with babies. Tony was not a baby, so he would have to stop playing baby games in order to retain Cellini's respect. Anyway, they were both about the same age, and if Johnny acted like a grown up, surely Tony must too.

"I was bored so I'd thought I'd play this stupid game for a while," Tony defended his temporary plunge in status.

"You begged us to play," Eddie Allen was intent on stirring it.

"No I didn't!" Tony was embarrassed.

"Fuck off Eddie Allen, or I'll stab you," Johnny Cellini stepped forward. Tony's eye caught a glint of silver as Johnny withdrew a flick-knife from his trouser pocket, pressing it into action with a deadly click.

Eddie Allen's face froze with horror. Everyone was stunned into silence.

"Don't stab me," Eddie began to plead, "please!" Tears began to well in his eyes.

"Now clear off before I kill you," Johnny's countenance had now changed to fury. Eddie began to step backwards, then at a safer distance he turned and ran for his life, quickly disappearing from view round the corner of a building. The other children began to wander away.

Tony wasn't quite sure if he should run too. He was very afraid. His fear subsided somewhat as Johnny closed the knife and placed it back in his pocket.

"I'm gonna do a warehouse break-in, d'ye fancy coming along?" declared Johnny baldly, as if it were as natural as going for a Sunday afternoon stroll.

Tony felt it wasn't so much an invitation as an obligation if he wanted to retain his status, after all *that* certainly wasn't playing baby games. On the other hand, he knew it was wrong, and he could hear his father warning him never to play with Johnny Cellini. It was akin to saying don't play with the devil.

But peer pressure is strong and somehow Tony's strings were no longer in his possession. He was being operated by a far more powerful force.

"You're scared ain't you?" Johnny goaded with another of his derisory grins.

"No I'm not," Tony sounded less sure than the sentiment expressed by his words.

"Come on then," Cellini started to walk off. Tony began to follow.

"Where are we going?"

"To Fox's Wharf, near the river."

Tony had never heard of Fox's Wharf, though he knew there were dozens and dozens of warehouses lining the river near Wapping.

"What's happened to your brother?" Tony knew all about the stabbing, the gossip was rife just after it happened.

"He's being done for murder. The bloke died. It's all lies though, he was attacked, he only did it in self-defence," Johnny exonerated brother Ricki.

"My dad says he's been in trouble with the police before," Tony reported.

"Well your dad's an arsehole," Cellini stopped abruptly, rounding viciously on Tony, whose father had had words with Johnny on many occasions about his swearing and anti-social behaviour

"But I was only saying what I'd heard," Tony was fearful of that knife being produced again.

"Everyone who lives around here's fucking liars," Cellini began walking again. Tony decided this particular topic of conversation was over.

They picked their way through the dull blocks of flats, kicking empty milk bottles, old rags and discarded tin cans littering the tarmac enclosure linking the buildings. Then into the old streets of dark terraced houses, much of their continuity collapsed into tracts of bomb-site rubble, and on towards the River Thames at Wapping.

Now towering rows of sullen warehouses lining the cobbled streets beside the river's edge rose into view. A strong, distinct smell of mixed spices started to pervade the atmosphere, seeping from the innumerable bales of imported oriental herbs heaped inside the buildings.

The cargoes arrived here from sea ports, transferred on the final leg of their long ocean journey aboard wrinkled tugs, hauling endless flotillas of barges along the river.

Haulage lorries parked in the shadows of the storehouses stood stacked with the cargoes as teams of warehousemen lowered the bulging bales on to them, using hoists projecting from openings three, four and five stories up, shouting commands, warnings and profanities as each situation dictated.

The boys had to weave precariously around the lorries as chunky iron hooks and chains swung to and fro, now and then thrashing into the sides of the buildings and sometimes crashing on to the ground below.

A little further on they came to a narrow passageway cutting through to the riverside. The arm of a crane was visible at the far end, partly obscuring the staggered outline of wharves on the far side of the rippling divide.

The sounds of the river traffic echoed down the length of the passage's enclosing brick walls, disfigured with crumbling pointing and separated by cracked, uneven flagstones. Hooting, spluttering tugs, the shouts of dockers unloading goods from the barges, clanking machinery, an energetic ship's horn renting the air, and in the background the river softly slurping over muddy shingle.

Halfway down the passageway Johnny Cellini stopped, furtively looking up and down to make sure no-one else was nearby.

"What are we going to do?" Tony was becoming apprehensive about the mission. Naughtiness was within his remit, but breaking into somewhere and stealing, well, he knew that was very wrong.

"We're going to get in here," Johnny Cellini pointed to a thin metal grille protecting a window set low into the wall beside Tony. The novice thief hadn't even noticed it, mainly because it had never entered his head until now that anyone would want to gain access to a building by this route.

"But it's covered over," Tony protested. Johnny wasn't listening. A corner of the grille was not properly fixed to the wall. He eased his hands behind it and began to pull. His face turned red as he heaved and a rusty bolt fixing began to dislodge from the brickwork. A bit more heaving and it came away.

"Go and make sure nobody's coming," Cellini ordered Tony, "up there by the street."

Tony complied with the order, cautiously creeping to the corner. The warehousemen further down the road continued with their labours unaware of the felons.

A moment or so later, Tony heard a faint sound of breaking glass and looked towards his companion. Johnny's right foot was inside the grille, pumping at the window. Content he'd made a big enough hole he called for Tony to return.

The protective metal cover was now bent back far enough for two slim people to crawl through. The window was sufficiently smashed to allow similar passage, but small, sharp fragments remained on the edges of the frame. Johnny quickly pulled off his grubby white T-shirt, revealing the taut, sinewy muscles of his arms and chest.

He folded the garment and draped it over the fragments for protection.

Hands on the ground and feet first, Johnny backed into the opening. In a few moments he had disappeared inside.

"Come on." Cellini's voice echoed from within. Tony attempted to imitate his master's prowess, but his feet caught the grille. Making another attempt he suddenly felt his feet being grabbed and hauled inside. The protective T-shirt fell away as Tony's arms passed the shards remaining in the frame.

He felt searing pain in the palm of his right hand and cried out. In seconds he was inside the warehouse and lying on the concrete floor, a few feet below the level of the pavement outside. The pain was intense, he looked and blood was pouring from his hand. He began to panic, calling out, tears welling in his eyes.

"Shut up!" Cellini whispered with suppressed fury. He clamped Tony's mouth with his hand. "You'll be all right. Here…" he grabbed his T-shirt, now lying on the floor, and folding it lengthwise tied it around Tony's hand fastening it with a bulky knot. Tony was grateful but still very frightened.

"That's nothing," Johnny re-assured him. "I slashed my leg right down to my knees when I was breakin' in somewhere once," he drew a line with his finger across his trousers, indicating the wound beneath. "It happens. You gotta get used to it."

Tony was becoming rapidly convinced a life of crime was not for him. He wished he was back home playing hopscotch.

"Right," Cellini had been kneeling beside Tony, but now sprang to his feet. He surveyed the scene. Row upon row of canvas spice bales, were stacked throughout the storage bay, lit by a line of grilled windows along the riverside length of the building. The sweet smell was overpowering and he fought hard to resist sneezing.

He reached inside his pocket and pulled out his flick knife. He then proceeded to slash at the canvas bales, slicing gaping tears in the fabric from which brown, powdery spice poured out on to the ground. Tony was too engrossed with nursing his wound to notice at first what was happening. When he looked up, Johnny had carved up eight or more bales, the smell of spice was becoming overpowering.

"What are you doing?" Tony was bemused. "I thought we were going to steal something?"

"No, not this time. Next time," Johnny pursued his activity with fury.

"Why are you cutting them?" It was destructive without any purpose Tony thought.

"For revenge," Johnny's tone was bitter. "The manager of this wharf is gonna give evidence against my brother. He was in the pub when Ricki was forced into that stabbing."

Tony forgot the pain in his hand for a moment as he sensed a deeper evil than just vandalism or stealing.

He knew some families in the area worked for really bad men, people who were into murder, gangland killings and revenge attacks, or so he'd overheard the grown-ups saying when they thought he wasn't listening. Even in his own naivety something told him there was a deeply sinister thread to Cellini's actions.

"Come on that'll do for now," Johnny closed the knife and returned to Tony. He looked at the lad's hand and the blood stained T-shirt. "You can pay me back. That was a good shirt," he told Tony.

"I'll get my mum to wash it," Tony promised.

"Sod that, I don't want your mum knowing how you cut yourself. You better not tell her what I've done or I'll get you," Cellini waved the closed knife in Tony's face.

"No, no, I won't tell her," he insisted. He wouldn't dare anyway for fear of what *she'd* do to him.

"Besides, you're a criminal now," Johnny smiled. "If the police find out, you'll go to prison too."

The realisation of what he'd become deeply shocked Tony. It was true. He'd committed a crime, albeit in truth unwittingly. It was hardly the crime of the century, but the police could have him. Destroying other people's property. He knew that was an offence. He felt the hairs on the back of his neck rise. The throbbing increased in his wound.

"Come on, let's get go," Johnny made for the window. Tony feared he'd cut himself again on the way out. Cellini stooped to the side of their exit and grabbed an old brick which had become dislodged over time from the crumbling pointing.

Using it to knock away as quietly as possible the sharp fragments of glass in the lower frame of the window, he then lobbed the brick contemptuously at a spice bale.

"Come on," he leaned forward, craning his neck to see if anyone was in the passageway outside. The sounds of the riverside returned. Content that the coast was clear, Johnny heaved himself through the opening, the metal grille rattling as his right arm brushed it.

"Hurry up!" Cellini called back. Tony had placed his hands on the window frame to hoist himself out, but even through the T-shirt the pain from the cut made him wince.

"Quick, there's a copper," Cellini was frantic.

Panic gripped Tony. The police! In seconds he had launched himself into the open, falling awkwardly on to the pavement. But he felt no pain. He was on his feet in a flash starting to run when he felt Johnny's restraining hand on his shoulder.

"Only joking," Cellini laughed. "See, you can do anything when you think plod's after you. Had you out of there in no time, didn't it." He was extremely amused with this ruse.

Tony's joy at learning the police weren't after him was quickly supplanted by the pain in his hand returning with a vengeance and a growing ache in his right shoulder where it had sharply impacted on the pavement.

In his rush, the T-shirt had come untied and had fallen on the ground. He now gazed at a large gash in the palm of his hand, still trickling blood. A life of crime grew less appealing every moment. He picked up the shirt, now covered in dirt and bloodstains and pressed it on his hand to stem the flow.

"I haven't got a shirt now," Johnny protested. "Give me yours."

Tony was about the same size as his companion so there would be no problem in the fitting. But how would he explain to his mum why his shirt was missing, or even worse that he had given it to the hated Cellini?

Johnny could see the reluctance in Tony's face. "What's the matter? You gonna refuse to give me your shirt after I helped you," he seemed deeply pained.

Tony was puzzled. He couldn't work out how Johnny had been his benefactor. On the contrary he was the cause of the trouble he now found himself in. But events were moving on rapidly in Johnny's mind. "Tell you what, keep the shirt and you can nick another one for me in Watney Street. He was referring to the traders' marketplace. It seemed a reasonable compromise to Tony at that moment, though he was a total novice at street theft.

"Let's go home," Cellini strolled back up the passageway, peering cautiously into the main road where the warehousemen carried on their duties unaware of the vandalism that had taken place. With the air of someone taking an innocent stroll, Johnny stepped out into the highway, whistling.

Tony followed head lowered, lest the guilt in his eyes should give him away. They took yet another route through Wapping that was unfamiliar to Tony. He wished that he could recognise the street in which the grandparents on his father's side of the family lived nearby in the area. He could do with some comforting right now.

The smell of the spice had now faded and Tony began to see familiar houses and flats. Johnny had been recounting numerous episodes of his life in petty crime some of which Tony took in, but much of which didn't penetrate beyond his own thoughts of how he was going to explain the gash on his hand to his mum and dad. Somehow, they always seemed to know when he was telling lies. But he certainly couldn't tell them the truth on this occasion.

"Right, see ya," Johnny abruptly announced after finishing another tale from his extensive larceny memoirs. With that he walked off briskly and soon disappeared into a nearby housing estate. Not his own. Tony wondered if he was going to break into a flat.

Sore and thoroughly miserable from his exploits, his mind was frantically searching for an innocent explanation of his injury that would convince his parents. Deep in thought, he turned a corner and almost collided with Brendan. For a second both froze, in a crossfire of delight and misfortune. Tony's oppressor was flanked by his usual cronies. They broke into baiting howls and jeers.

After briefly allowing himself a gloating smile, Brendan leapt at Tony, grabbing his shirt-front. Quickly surrounded by his other opponents, this time there was absolutely no escape. Brendan's right fist struck Tony's face. The boy jerked back, but was held in place by the grip on his shirt.

"You're not fucking escaping this time, runt," Brendan's failure to snare Tony in their last encounter added impetus to the pleasure of this triumph. As Brendan drew back his fist to deliver another blow, his supporters joined in with frenzied kicks and punches at every available part of Tony's body.

"Oi!" A man's voice broke into the vicious attack. "I'll call the police!" Brendan and his followers laid in a few more blows and sped off down the street.

Tony staggered backwards and fell on to the pavement.

"Are you alright?" Through a daze he saw a wrinkled, unshaven face under a cloth cap peering down at him. "I'll call an ambulance."

No, Tony didn't want an ambulance. He wanted to be at home. His head was spinning, but somehow he managed to get up. His rescuer seemed very distant to him and his words didn't have any coherence. It was just a voice with tones of concern. Then fragmented scenes of wandering down streets and into his estate and along the familiar balcony. He didn't remember much about his parents either. Questions and more expressions of concern.

"Some boys beat me up," he mumbled. Then a huge sense of relief flowed through him as his mum tucked him up in bed.

CHAPTER 2

TONY was practicing whistling as he stared absentmindedly out the back window of his home at the street below. He was kneeling on a chair beneath the window with its back to the wall, resting his elbows on the sill and cupping his chin in hands.

A small group of boys were playing football in the road, moving to one side as a car occasionally interrupted their game. Tony had only just learned to whistle and now practiced it at every opportunity.

He tried to accompany the light orchestral tune coming from the radio in the corner of the room, but lack of skill in the art and unfamiliarity with the melody resulted in complete disharmony, the general sound punctuated by shrill bursts.

He felt considerably happier now the pain from his bruising was easing. As a result of Brendan's attack he'd been off school for the last few days, spending much of the time with his nan while his mum and dad were out at work. Staying away from school was always a bonus.

A figure walking down the far end of the street brought his unmusical repertoire to an abrupt halt. The background orchestral music carried freely on. Tony was now gazing intently as the figure grew closer. It was his avenging angel, Billy Walker. Quickly he slipped down from the chair and ran to the front door calling out "mum, I'm just going out for a while…"

He vaguely heard her telling him not to go too far from home, but his attention was elsewhere. Rushing down the stairs he tore round the block of flats running after Billy. He caught up with his hero fielding a stray shot from the football game Tony had been watching from the window.

Billy dribbled the ball before booting it back to the group of boys. As he turned to resume walking he caught sight of Tony approaching.

"Hello Billy, it's me," Tony blurted out eagerly.

Billy stared at him for a moment, searching to remember any previous encounter with the boy.

"You remember," Tony prompted, "those boys who attacked me in the school lavatory." Billy's eyes suddenly registered the occasion. "Oh yeah, that's right, you're…"

"Tony Selby."

"Tony, is it? I didn't know your name." Billy studied him for a moment. "It looks like they got you. The state of your face. Those bruises on your cheeks."

Tony looked down for a moment, as if slightly ashamed. "No, some other boys did that. My stomach's all bruised too." Tony touched his shirt to indicate the sore area.

"My God, don't you ever hit them back?" Billy began walking again and Tony followed by his side.

"I'm no good at fighting. I don't like it. I don't like hitting people." He spoke as if it was a shameful confession.

"Well I don't either, but that's the way it is. Sometimes you have to," Billy enlightened his subject. "I'm totally amazed that you've never learnt to look after yourself. Especially in a rough ol' area like this."

Tony remained silent, feeling as if somehow he'd failed his hero.

"We're gonna have to do something about it. Have you ever done any boxing?"

Tony looked towards Billy and shook his head. "Have you?"

"I box at the Junior League Club at the Town Hall."

Tony couldn't have been more impressed if Billy had just announced that he was the current middleweight boxing champion of the world. "You need to do some. But round here you also need to play dirty too. See in boxing you mustn't hit below the belt. But round here, it's the first place you should go for."

Tony wasn't quite sure what he meant.

Billy could see his puzzlement. "Come over here."

Tony followed him off the pavement onto a nearby bomb-site, stepping gingerly over heaps of rubble until they came to a small concrete clearing in the ruin.

"Put your hands up like this," Billy began to show Tony some basic defence and attack boxing tactics. For about ten minutes Billy simulated blows and showed the young boy how to counter them.

"Now punch me." Billy ordered.

"What really punch you?"

"Yes."

"I don't want to."

"Just do it." Tony obeyed, aiming a fairly limp punch at Billy's shoulder.

"Not there, my face. And hard."

Reluctantly Tony threw a hard punch. Instantly it was knocked away and Billy responded with an attack at Tony's undefended stomach. The bigger lad stopped short of a hard impact. Tony was surprised at the swiftness of the reprisal.

"You've got to keep your defence up as well," Billy insisted, "or you go down." He lowered his arms.

"Look, why don't you come over to my place in Cable Street after school, and I'll give you some boxing lessons. We can use the living room. I get a break while the shop's closed between shifts, and my mum and dad are usually in the back getting stuff ready for the night's frying."

Tony felt honoured by such an offer from someone he considered an expert at the sport.

"I have to go to my nan's after school while my mum and dad are out at work. But I'll ask them if it's okay," Tony replied eagerly.

"Alright. But in the meantime, for your own safety and defence, this is a very effective move. Put your hands up again as if you're gonna hit me." Tony obeyed. He was expecting a pretend punch to his body or face, but Billy swiftly raised his right leg and aimed his foot at Tony's balls. Thankfully the blow stopped short.

"In the meantime, use that one if anyone attacks you. It's not allowed in boxing, but around here it's very useful," Billy delivered words of wisdom instead of pain.

The boys picked their way back over the rubble to the street pavement again and parted.

Tony's parents agreed to let him see Billy after school, but only after his mum Irene insisted it would be okay. She knew Billy's parents, who were a well respected family in the area, and she often got a larger portion of fish and chips from Billy's dad, Albert, a well rounded, cheerful man always with a smile for his customers.

Gerry wasn't so keen for Tony to be associating with local boys. He had plans in hand to raise his son to a higher status above the commoners who lived in this run down area. But if this lad was teaching him to box, that could be a useful skill, so he relented.

After school next day Tony made his way to the fish and chip shop in a street lined with many stores and several pubs. Scatterings of squashed chips that had been crushed underfoot littered the pavement outside.

Billy had seen Tony through the shop's glass frontage and opened the door as he was about to knock.

The novice boxer followed his coach up a flight of steps to a small living room upstairs.

"We've got an hour before the shop opens," said Billy, moving a table and chairs in the middle of the room to one side, and revealing a hole in the brown linoleum floor covering beneath. Faded wallpaper displayed tropical birds that seemed gloomy from the ageing. A couple of ballerina figurines stood on a shelf looking sad.

Billy gave his pupil a pair of scuffed boxing gloves.

"I used these when I was younger. They should fit you though," he said, putting on the pair he now wore in boxing tournaments.

Tony's first lesson took in the basics of defence and attack as well as some footwork, and a few tips not in the Marquess of Queensberry rules of the game. Eye pokes, groin attacks, foot blows to break knee joints and a few other street fighting techniques.

Over the next few weeks, he started to become proficient at striking and defending blows, and ironically in this time none of his aggressors had been around to attack him. Until one evening when he was coming home from playing with friends at a neighbouring housing estate.

Terry Purvis and Dave Jepson stood in the entrance porch blocking the stairway to his landing. These were not boys, but young men in their twenties who took to wandering around the local area terrorising children. Their shirts and trousers were dirty and crumpled from sleeping rough under the railway arch they called home down the road.

Some said they were simple in the head, but Tony only saw them as big bullies, and he'd felt their blows before. They had a tactic of standing aside to let their victims pass, then leap on them.

Tony was quick at ducking and diving to avoid their punches, but some of the blows would get through before he could get up the stairs. On this occasion he felt more confident watching them as they stood in his path.

"Come on then," Tony raised his fists in the boxing stance Billy had shown him.

The wicked smile on Terry Purvis' face turned puzzled under his thick crop of straggly black hair. The eyes in his lighter haired companion lost the gleam of relishing an easy conquest. Then they perked up. The boy would be a pushover.

They moved away from the stairs rounding on Tony. As they grew near he delivered a hard punch to Purvis' face. The man staggered back in shock.

Angered, his friend shot a blow at Tony, but the boy raised his arm fending off the blow and stepping back. By now, Purvis had recovered from the shock of the punch and furiously lashed out at Tony. The boy ducked and walloped him in the stomach, causing him to recoil again. Now his companion was moving away. He didn't want to get hit. That wasn't the plan. They should have demolished the youngster by now.

Terry Purvis wanted to strike Tony again, but now looked warily at the boy. Jepson put a hand on his friend's shoulder, pulling him back.

"I'll fucking get you next time," Purvis yelled, pointing his finger threateningly. The two stepped away, shouting threats as they retreated, completely thrown by the defeat from a squit half their size.

Tony was amazed at what he'd done. Billy was right. Bullies don't want to get hurt. But his glow of triumph was ebbing away as the pain in his right fist grew. Delivering a hard punch to someone's face without boxing gloves had bruising consequences. The fist was red and swelling.

As he returned indoors his mother immediately noticed it, mostly because Tony had entered awkwardly sideways trying to hide his hand.

"What have you been doing?" Irene snapped,

"I was playing and fell over," he offered an explanation. His mother would think he was lying if he told her he'd just seen off two men. Fooling around with friends was acceptable.

"You're filthy dirty," she said, clipping him round the ear. "Get undressed while I run the bath."

Tony shuffled into the bedroom. There was no retaliation in his mother's domain.

******

OVER the next few afternoons Billy had to help his aunt Emma redecorate her living room. She lived alone a few miles away in Bethnal Green. This left Tony having to check in everyday after school with his nan.

It wasn't so hard because she was always generous with cakes, sweets and soft drinks she bought at the market, along with American imported Marvel comics. Tony was content to spend an hour or so reading the adventures of Batman, Superman and Captain America, and he'd developed a particular crush for Veronica in Archie.

One afternoon while he sat in an armchair enthralled by the amazing comic superheroes, his nan went to answer a knock on the door.

It was his uncle Frank. His favourite uncle. Of the three males and two other females on his mother's side of the family, uncle Frank came top followed by aunt Ellie. The fact that the man always gave Tony some money for sweets and Ellie always seemed to have a Mars bar to spoil him, did greatly influence the boy's judgement. But Frank was number one. He could do coin and card tricks too.

"Your nan spoiling you again with cakes and comics," Frank winked at Tony as he entered. In the small living room dominated largely by the square dining table in the middle, Frank's muscular frame, in a white, open neck shirt and dark blue trousers, looked gigantic.

His face was frighteningly threatening when serious, but cheeky and impish with a smile. Tony could only see a good side in him.

Look," Frank took a coin from his pocket. Tony stared, his uncle was going to perform a trick.

"The coin's in this hand," Frank held it between finger and thumb on his left hand. Then he reached with his right covering the coin to take it. With a gesture he waved his clenched right hand, 'abracadabra', then opened it. The coin should have been there. It wasn't. Tony was amazed.

"How did you do it?"

"Ah, magic," his uncle replied.

"I've made you a cup of tea," Joyce called to her son through the open kitchen door.

"Now behave yourself," Frank pointed at his nephew with a smile. "I'm gonna have a word with your nan."

He entered the narrow kitchen containing a gas cooker, sink and draining board on one side, with storage cabinet, larder, and small work space on the other. There was hardly space for two people to squeeze past each other.

Frank leaned back on the draining board as his mother took the whistling kettle off the gas hob.

"I'm thinking of jacking in labouring on the building sites," he announced.

"Why?" she seemed puzzled.

"It's good money. Cash in hand. No tax. But I'm sick and tired of lugging bricks, mixing cement, unloading deliveries. It's dead end work."

His mother was silent as she took a bottle of condensed milk from the larder and poured some into the cups on the work space, then lifted the teapot to pour the liquid through a tea strainer.

"Have you got something in mind?" she asked.

"I've been offered a job driving a van for the Parker brothers."

Joyce froze for a second.

"The Parker brothers?" she wasn't happy. The brothers had a reputation in the area for racketeering, extortion and violence. "I don't think you should work for them. They're serious business."

Frank smiled.

"There's a lot of nonsense talked about them. They supply lots of shops with goods, and they've got a nightclub," he assured her.

Joyce took a sip of tea. She frowned disapproval of her son's choice. She was well aware the Parker brothers had a hand in bank robberies and insiders in the dock warehouses stealing imported cigarettes and spirits along with clothes and spices. Those were the black market supplies to shops they provided as well as their own nightclub.

"Well, I'm going to take the job. It's really good money and it'll give me a chance to put some aside for a deposit on a house. Brenda and the kids deserve a better place than the shithole flat we've got in Limehouse," Frank had made up his mind.

Joyce knew his wife Brenda had been constantly on at him to get a job with more money so they could buy a house for them and their two young daughters. She couldn't blame him for wanting better.

"Well, you've got to do what you think is right," she advised. "But be careful. I don't want you spending twenty years inside."

Frank knew the brothers' reputation, though he was prepared to take the chance.

Tony had been engrossed in Lex Luthor getting his comeuppance from Superman, but his ears had pricked up on the kitchen conversation when his nan's voice seemed to take an unhappy tone. What was Frank saying to her? Parker brothers meant nothing to him, although the name had appeared to unsettle her.

Frank re-entered the living room. Unknown at that moment, his life changing decision would one day link him and his young nephew in deep, far reaching consequences.

"What you been up to?" he asked Tony. The boy lowered the comic on to his lap.

"I've been learning to box," Tony announced proudly.

"Have you?" Frank placed his teacup on the table. "Come on then, box me," he raised his fists.

Tony threw the comic to the floor and sprang up raising his fists. Towering above him, his uncle delivered pretend punches. Tony struck the man's stomach several times, which had no effect on penetrating the rock hard muscles, but he feigned pain and declared Tony the champ of the match.

"Now remember that coin I made disappear? Well it's here." Frank opened his right hand to reveal a shilling coin giving it to the boy.

Tony was thrilled. With the money he could buy loads of sweets.

"Don't go spending that all at once," said his nan, entering the room.

"No nan, I won't," Tony lied.

"Well, I'd better get on," Frank hurriedly finished his tea and Joyce accompanied him to the door.

The youngster no longer wanted to read the comic. Sweets beckoned.

"Can I go to the shop?" he asked when she returned.

"Go on. But don't be long. And don't spend all the money."

Tony headed for the newsagent a few streets away.

******

ON Saturday morning, Irene went out as usual to join her mother shopping for the week at the local market. For some time she'd been suggesting her husband should buy a car on hire purchase. It would make shopping easier and allow them to go on outings.

But Gerry's aspirations to progress as a lawyer overrode all. He bought expensive suits and shirts and as a solicitor's clerk his pay was low. A few daily beers after work also depleted the income. So there was no money left for buying a car.

On Saturdays he liked to relax. Listen to the radio, read a book and go out in the evening with Irene to a pub on the riverside, The Prospect of Whitby in Wapping, where they'd first met over ten years earlier. But now the desire between them had died. They often spent the evening there stony faced together for a while, before Gerry joined his friends at the bar to laugh and joke until closing time.

Meanwhile Tony would be left outside the pub with a packet of crisps and a lemonade, occasionally playing with other children whose parents were also drinking and enjoying themselves inside.

On this particular Saturday morning Tony was involved in a game of Knock Down Ginger with friends in the playground. It involved knocking on people's doors and running away to hide.

Their target today was a middle-aged woman known as Mad Anna living in the ground floor flat below Tony's. She occasionally woke the neighbourhood in the middle of the night screaming 'Help! Murder! Police!' Her terror was totally unfounded. No-one was being attacked or murdered.

Children were fascinated by her deluded mind and rambling mumblings whenever she made a rare appearance from her flat. And Tony with his friends had no understanding of the woman's desperate need for psychiatric help which never came. They'd played the game on her door a number of times before, and her yelling at no-one as she opened it fascinated and amused them as they peered hiding behind the low wall bordering the playground.

"Go on Tony, your turn to knock," a scruffy haired friend challenged him as they ducked below the wall to start their game.

Tony leapt over it and ran to the woman's door. He was about to knock when the door flew open. He stared in terrified surprise at her deeply lined face and bulging furious eyes.

"Bastard! Bastard!" she screamed, rushing out to attack him. Tony swiftly stepped aside, turned and ran leaping back over the wall. His friends were scattering in terror. The woman stood uttering more curses by the door, then returned inside slamming it shut.

Tony stood alone, stunned by the event not turning out as planned.

"What you doing?" he heard someone call. The voice sounded familiar. Rounding the street corner was Johnny Cellini.

"Nothing much," Tony replied, placing his hands in his pockets and trying to hide the scare of flight from a botched game plan.

"There's nothing going on round here," Johnny sneered.

Tony was envious of Cellini wearing long trousers making him look grown up, while he was confined to short ones advertising childhood. Johnny also wore a smart, open neck blue shirt in contrast to the grey or plain white he was condemned to wear. The approaching youngster could see Tony studying his clothes.

"You need to learn what grown-ups do. How they can make good money," Cellini began his enticement. He knew a naive boy when he saw one.

"Come with me and I'll show you how it's done."

Tony had run into trouble once before getting involved with Johnny. But there was a fascination about it. The attachment of trouble to him and his family seemed to possess a magical sparkle of excitement. Defying authority.

"I'm seeing a friend who's got a car. Come with me, we can go for a drive," Johnny invited him.

Not many people in the area owned cars. They were generally the better off. Tony had only ever been for a car ride once, in a black Morris Oxford owned by his dad's friend, and he'd loved it.

Tony hesitated. His dad had warned him off Johnny Cellini.

"You gonna come or not?" the lad grew impatient.

"Alright."

Tony followed down narrow cobblestoned passageways between houses and along streets that were gradually becoming unfamiliar to him. He began to feel uncertain. A few more streets and passages and they arrived at a row of brown brick terraced houses lining the road. Halfway down, Johnny stopped at a dark green door and rapped on the brass knocker.

A balding, unshaven man opened it wearing a white string vest and grey trousers. He stared aggressively at them.

"Yeah?"

"Is Duke in? It's Johnny Cellini. He's expecting me."

The man turned back inside and shouted.

"Barry. Someone here to see you."

Tony was confused. His friend had asked for Duke, not Barry.

The boy didn't know that Barry Welling had renamed himself Duke to his associates because he thought it sounded more upmarket than Barry. His dad standing at the door gave his son no such pretensions.

The man disappeared inside and a few moments later Duke emerged. He was older than the two boys. At seventeen fully grown to them.

For a second Tony was dazzled by the lurid blue suit he wore. It seemed to have a speckly shine. The purple shirt and white tie added to the bizarre image confronting him. He knew his own dad would instantly hate someone dressed in a showy way like that, the sort of thing foreigners might wear he'd say. Not that Duke was foreign. Born and bred in east London.

"Who's this?" Duke stared at Tony through suspicious eyes set in a thin face. He raised his hand sweeping back his black, oily hair to ensure it was neatly in place.

"He's a friend," Johnny explained. "I've brought him along for a ride."

Duke gave a knowing smile.

"Johnny says you've got a car," Tony gleamed.

"Yeah, that's right. It's parked a few streets away."

Tony was surprised he parked his car a few streets away, but had no reason to doubt it was true.

"Come on," Duke stepped from the doorway and the boys followed him. Again they weaved along several passageways and streets.

"What's happening to your brother Ricki?" Duke asked.

"He's inside waiting for his trial. Couple of months I think."

"Well I hope he gets off, but he'll probably get stitched up by the coppers," Duke sounded resigned to the injustice of being punished for committing crime.

Tony remembered the talk of Johnny's brother stabbing a man in the Flute and Whistle pub. For a moment he visualised his father warning him off the Cellinis. But a car ride wasn't a crime.

They turned another street corner and a little further reached a small cul-de-sac. Parked at the end was a light blue Ford Zephyr. The setting had a high wall on all three sides, obscuring any view from the back windows of houses surrounding it.

"This is the one," Duke whispered to Johnny so Tony couldn't hear. "Saw it the other day. I'll have it started in no time."

"This is my car," Duke turned to their newest recruit. "A friend borrowed it and left it here."

As they reached the vehicle Duke searched through his trouser pockets starting to look annoyed.

"Shit, I've left the keys at home. I'll have to break in."

He reached inside his jacket and produced a gun, then smashed the driver's window with the handle releasing the door from the inside.

Now even Tony's naive mind was beginning to figure that Duke didn't own the car. But the man had a gun. He might get shot if he tried to run away while his companion opened the bonnet to hot wire the engine. All traces of relaxed friendliness had disappeared.

The motor started and Duke leapt into the driving seat with Johnny joining his side.

"Now anything that happens next and you don't say a word or else I'll shoot you," Duke threatened Tony.

"You're in the big time money," Johnny crowed to him as their driver swiftly pulled away.

The car travelled along streets that were now entirely alien to their reluctant new gang member. It was turning out to be an exciting car ride in a way he'd never expected.

After a while Duke pulled up in a high street lined with shops.

"Okay, we're here," he declared opening the door. Johnny followed suit telling Tony to get out. They were parked outside a jewellers.

Duke turned to Tony.

"I want you to stand at the door and tell anyone who tries to come in that the shop's closed for five minutes."

Tony could see him reaching for the gun inside his jacket. Johnny followed his leader as he pushed open the shop door.

The boy's instinct was to flee. But the gun. If he escaped he feared Duke would track him down and shoot him. He stood at the door, knees trembling, hands shaking.

Several people walked past and he prayed no-one would try to enter the premises, fearing the lie of telling them it was closed would sound unconvincing. This was an armed robbery taking place. Even Tony's limited knowledge of the world extended to understanding that.

A few minutes later the shop door flew open as the pair emerged, Johnny carrying a bulging drawstring bag. They leapt into the car, ignoring Tony, and pulled swiftly away.

Seconds later the middle-aged owner emerged, his face puce with fury. Tony looked terrified as he approached him.

"Did you see…?"

The youngster didn't wait for the rest of the question. In panic he took off.

As he ran, he became aware the man was in pursuit. If he got caught he'd be blamed. The police would come and then his father would thrash him.

He weaved down passageways totally alien to him. The man was catching up. Across the road was a bomb site. He sprinted towards it. Agility could give him the advantage. He was used to leaping over rubble and weeds.

After a few minutes the ruse worked. The man was tripping and stumbling in pursuit and soon gave up the chase, as Tony left the dereliction and disappeared down a side street.

Now Tony was desperate to seek refuge at home, but completely lost. He kept looking back, wondering if the jewellery shop owner might suddenly re-appear. The police had probably been called by now. They could be after him too.

Reaching a busy main road, he saw a bus with Plaistow signed at the front. He'd heard of the place, but didn't know where it was from home. And with no money, he couldn't catch a bus anyway. For a couple of hours he wandered the streets, everywhere unfamiliar.

A woman in a dark red coat noticed Tony staring around lost.

"Are you looking for somewhere?" she asked.

Tony felt heartened by her kind, enquiring face.

"I was playing with my friends and I've lost my way home," he replied, avoiding the fact he'd just been innocently involved with armed robbery.

"Where do you live?"

Tony told her.

"You're a long way from home then. You'll best catch a bus!

His face fell.

"Have you any money," she asked.

Tony shook his head.

The woman reached inside her black handbag, opened a purse and took out sixpence handing it to him.

"Go to the end of this street, turn left and wait for the bus that comes with the Aldgate sign at the front."

Aldgate was familiar territory to him. He'd know his way home from there. Tony thanked the woman and made his way down the street. She watched as he left, not convinced the boy had told her the real reason why he'd strayed eight miles from home to here in Barking. But she couldn't leave a little boy lost.

Tony got off the bus, happy to see home surroundings again, though with a growing sense of being betrayed by his so-called friend Johnny Cellini. He began to realise his dad's warning about their neighbour was true.

His relief at reaching refuge was suddenly aborted as he approached the entrance porch to his flat. Terry Purvis and

Dave Jepson were sitting on the steps, waiting for young victims to approach. Right now Tony had suffered enough stress, but the sudden prospect of being attacked fired a rush of aggressive adrenalin.

"You want another fight?" he shouted at them.

Wicked smiles on their faces descended into doubt. They remembered the last encounter with him. Getting hurt was not part of the plan.

"Move!" Tony pointed at them. The pair looked at each other as if agreeing to discard their plan, then sheepishly got up and left the entrance, walking away across the playground mumbling curses.

Tony's victory helped to raise his otherwise flagging spirit brought on by the day's events.

"Where have you been?" his mother opened the door demanding.

"Playing with friends," he lied, slipping past her into the flat.

"No you haven't," Irene closed the door and followed her son.

"I have."

"Mrs Miller at number fifteen said she saw you going off with Johnny Cellini."

Tony hated some of the neighbours who were always spying and poking their noses into other people's business.

"I went out playing with him."

He was terrified word might have got back he'd been involved in a jewel shop raid, but his mother made no mention of a crime.

"Your father's told you not to have anything to do with the Cellini boy. He'll get you into trouble. And on that I agree with your dad."

Tony was already wishing he'd obeyed the advice.

"Get in the living room. Your dad wants to talk to you."

Now Tony was really worried. A talk from his dad was usually a telling off. He entered the room.

Gerry was standing at the window looking towards the blocks of flats across the road at the back. He took a few puffs of his pipe then turned to his son.

"It's alright. Relax. You're not in trouble," Gerry reassured him. "Sit down."

Tony pulled a chair from the dining table, entirely baffled by the summons, and sat facing his father.

"Do you like your school?" Gerry asked.

Tony hated it. The bullying and boring lessons. Teachers that shouted at him because he didn't understand things. But he said nothing to his dad. His sullen face spoke for him.

"How would you like to go to a good school?" Gerry asked.

The lad had no concept of a good school. Nothing to compare good or bad. Again he said nothing and just shuffled his feet.

Gerry could see his son felt awkward. He wasn't going to be given a choice anyway with the decision already made.

"At the start of the new school year in September, you'll be going to a new one. A private school where the teachers will be good. You'll learn lots of new things there."

81

Tony had no idea what his father meant, but the thought of no longer attending the present one seemed good news.

Gerry had plans to lift his son out of a dead end future, to which he'd be condemned from the poor education on offer where they lived. He'd discussed it with Irene. She was steeped in a deprived upbringing and poor education herself, and he struggled to make her see that it was possible for even the lowliest to rise in the world. But in spite of all her rough edges, she loved her son and Gerry had convinced her it was possible for the youngster to make the leap.

Next hurdle had been to convince her on the cost of a private school. They'd have to pare their own outgoings to pay the fees. Irene knew her husband would be unlikely to curb his own lifestyle, and that she would have to earn more on overtime to make up the deficit for her son.

"Alright Tony, that's all I wanted to tell you," Gerry took a few more puffs at his pipe.

The boy stood up and left. He could smell dinner cooking, so he went to his bedroom to play with some toy soldiers on the floor before his mum called him for the meal.

******

THE following morning Tony met up with some friends on a bomb site. Finding weed covered rubble that had openings into cellars was a favourite. The three boys and a two girls spread out, searching for a new discovery.

Once before Tony had found a cavity leading into a cellar. It was virtually pitch dark inside save for a narrow beam of sunlight streaming between the weeds. In there, he and his friends discovered an emaciated dead dog, that must have found its way in and got trapped, a tin bath, smashed crockery and a broken table.

But the prize discovery was a tobacco tin with St Bruno's Flake just discernible on the faded, scuffed container. Inside was a five pound note. They'd struck a treasure trove. A further search in the dirt and dust revealed no other treasures of value to them, so they climbed out again with the tin. It soon became the focus of an argument.

"Finders keepers, losers weepers," declared the boy Steve, who'd found it. Another boy punched him in the arm, which set off a general scrap as the boys rolled around on the rough pieces of concrete and bricks, while the two girls watched them laughing.

"Shut up!" Tony finally shouted getting up.

The cry brought them to their senses.

"Look, there's five of us. Let's go to the corner shop and spend a pound each," he calculated a fair solution. They'd all been happy with that.

Today though, their search proved fruitless. Instead they decided to have a stone fight, which girls were not allowed to play because they could get hurt. They just had to observe from the sidelines. The boys spread apart and began to lob pieces of broken brick and concrete at each other, the obvious objective to avoid getting hit.

After a few minutes, Tony got whacked on the shoulder, and then another boy George took a painful smack on the side of his head, which began to stream blood.

As he staggered out of the fray to wander back home clutching his injury, Tony and Steve decided to call a halt to the game. Agreeing with the two girls to meet for another bomb site search next weekend they all returned to their homes.

Tony's mother greeted him with a cuff round the head. The green pullover she'd knitted for him was covered in dirt and brick dust.

"And you're late for your lunch. Go and sit at the table," she ordered.

After eating, they settled together in the living room to listen to a comedy show on the radio, Life With The Lyons. It was a family tradition to listen to the radio together for an hour or so on Sunday afternoons. Tony enjoyed it the more because in that brief period his mother and father were not constantly at each other's throats.

Today though, the brief harmony was abruptly shattered. Shouts came from the balcony. Maria Cellini was screaming.

"Let him go! He's done nothing!"

Gerry and Irene rushed into their son's bedroom, with a window overlooking the commotion. Tony followed.

Three police officers were hauling a struggling Johnny Cellini. His mother behind them shouting.

"Why are you picking on him? He's done nothing!"

As they moved past the window and on towards the stairs, Tony's mother opened the front door and stepped outside, followed by husband and son.

Mrs Cellini's protests echoed from the stairwell. Across the road below a police car waited.

Still struggling with the handcuffed young Cellini, the officers bundled him into the back of the car, which swiftly took off blasting the air with its siren bell.

Mrs Cellini stood at the empty space by the roadside crying.

"They're taking all my sons," she buried her head in her hands.

After a few moments she made her way wearily back to the stairwell, watched by neighbours now lining the balconies to witness the event.

Tony and his parents went back inside their flat. Gerry and Irene didn't want Mrs Cellini to start wailing at them about the injustice done to her son. They were unaware of the sinking feeling growing in the pit of their own son's stomach. Tony sensed Johnny's abrupt removal had something to do with the raid on the jewellery shop. Would the police return to take him away? He was terrified to his soul.

What he didn't know was that the car Duke had stolen had been found abandoned and identified as the vehicle used in the robbery.

Not being the brightest of sparks, the fingerprints they left matched records already held by police for previous petty crimes. A third set of prints were identified by size to belonging to a child. But there was no record held for them.

Obviously Tony didn't know he was in the clear on fingerprints, but for now his greatest fear was that Johnny and Duke might tell on him.

It didn't help when his father launched into a lecture.

"You see. That's the Cellinis," he warned his son yet again. "They're all criminals."

Tony listened dutifully, but his father's words were distant as the terror of the police returning for him gripped his thoughts.

That night even the music penetrating his bedroom from the flat above seemed far away. It often comforted him as he slipped into sleep. This night, however, would be restless.

The following day after school he went for his boxing training at Billy's. So far the police hadn't come for him and he was starting to relax a little.

When he arrived at the fish and chip shop he was greeted with unwelcome news.

"My dad's sold the business," Billy announced as they put on their boxing gloves. "We're moving to Dagenham. He's buying a chippie there."

Tony had been to Dagenham some years ago, visiting an aunt who lived there. It was only ten miles away, but the place wasn't part of his everyday life and it might as well have been on the moon.

"Sorry, but I won't be able to give you any more coaching," Billy delivered Tony a blow more painful than a punch.

The youngster felt deeply sad. He was going to lose his friend.

"Are you going to work in the shop there too?" Tony asked.

"For a while. I want to join the police force. In a year I'll be old enough to start in the police cadets."

Tony was amazed at Billy's choice of career. The police were not popular in the world he knew. He'd often heard some grown-ups saying 'all coppers are bastards'.

"Why d'ye want to be a policeman?" Tony wondered, as they prepared to size up to each other with the gloves.

"Because I don't like scum. Low life stealing stuff that don't belong to them. Attacking people for nothing. Killing. One's like the rubbish trying to beat you up just because they think they can get away with it." Billy grew animated and nearly delivered a seriously hard punch at Tony, pulling back just in time.

The youngster grew troubled with the guilt of his unwilling connection to the jewel raid. His dark secret. He imagined the shame he'd feel if his friend was now a policeman coming to arrest him.

Billy began jabbing at him, and seeing a gap in the boy's defence moved in to strike a winning blow to his head. Tony swiftly fended off the attack.

"Good move!" his coach was genuinely impressed.

CHAPTER 3

A FEW weeks later school half-term arrived. Tony was at his nan's reading comics and stuffing generous quantities of cakes supplied by his doting grandmother.

Late morning uncle Frank called in. As well as cakes, the boy now anticipated some money coming his way.

"Why ain't you at school," Frank greeted him

"It's half-term."

"Half-term?" When I was a boy, I had to help dad on his milk rounds in any spare time I had. You kids today don't know how lucky you are," Frank winked at him.

Tony's grandfather Reg, sadly missed by his nan, Joyce, had become worn out lifting heavy crates on and off the horse drawn cart he drove to deliver milk in the neighbourhood from age fourteen. In the winter smogs and cold, he eventually developed bronchial pneumonia and died when he was fifty.

"What you need is a job," Frank told his nephew.

"Leave the boy alone," Joyce broke in. "He needs to learn things at school so he can get a good job, not scrape around for bosses and get hardly any money like us."

"Well I'm getting good money now with the Parker brothers," Frank boasted, reaching into his pocket and pulling out a wad of notes. He handed it to his mother.

She looked at it contemptuously for a moment. Joyce didn't approve of the Parker brothers' reputed criminal activities. But money was always welcome. Her state pension and part-time office cleaning job didn't bring in much. Conscience could be put to one side.

The adults went into the kitchen for a cup of tea, leaving Tony to his comic. He thought uncle Frank must be a millionaire judging by the bundle of notes he'd given to his nan. Maybe his uncle would be as generous to him before leaving.

A short time later Frank returned to the living room.

"Come out in the van with me. I'm making a delivery. You can find out what working life's like," he invited his nephew.

"He doesn't want to get mixed up in all that," Joyce rebuked her son. "His dad's gonna send him to one of those posh schools, where he'll learn to be clever."

Frank whispered into his mother's ear so Tony couldn't hear.

"His dad's a puffed up ponce. Got lots of airs and graces. Thinks he's better than our family."

Joyce didn't disagree with his sentiments about Gerry, but Tony was her grandson. She wanted him to have a better chance at life than her own. Virtually no education and a drunken father who left her mother to bring up six children alone, gradually driving the woman to insanity.

"He'll be alright," Frank assured her. "I'm just delivering to one of the Parker brothers' clubs in Soho. It's not far. Won't take long. It'll be good work experience for the boy."

Joyce looked doubtful, but trusted her son to look after him.

"I'll drop him back in a couple of hours."

Tony was game for going out with his favourite uncle. It sounded exciting, and highly likely he'd get some money at the end of it.

Climbing into Frank's black van parked in the street below he was filled with pride as they set off.

"If you do a good job, I'll give you some pay," Frank promised, confirming Tony's hope. Now he was an extra willing recruit.

As they entered London's west end, Tony became mesmerised by the streets teeming with people, bright lights in enormous stores and an atmosphere of liveliness entirely absent from the drab streets he knew back home. Yet they were not many miles apart.

Frank turned off Oxford Street and shortly entered a small service road, pulling up at the back of a nightclub. Tony followed his uncle as he descended the short flight of steps to a small enclosure containing a bin overflowing with rubbish and litter strewn on the ground. Taking out a set of keys he opened the rear door entrance to the club.

Neither of them were aware of three men sitting in a black Vauxhall Cresta parked a short distance away in the service road.

Returning to the van, Frank opened the back doors to reveal a stack of cardboard boxes. He pointed his nephew to one.

"You take that."

The boy could just about get his arms around the box, but it wasn't too heavy.

His uncle lifted another. There was a clink of glass. Tony wondered why his uncle wanted to take glasses into a place, completely unaware it was knocked off bottles of booze.

As they entered a dark storeroom, Tony noticed the top of his box was half open, He could see part of a name Player's Navy something. He'd seen them in shops. They were cigarette packets. Frank noticed his nephew's insight.

"You don't say a word about any of this, or else you won't get paid," he warned.

It was the first time his uncle had ever sounded serious to him and he became frightened.

"I'll never tell anybody," Tony promised, worried their friendship would be at risk.

"You're a good boy," Frank smiled. Tony was relieved his kindly uncle had returned.

After they completed carrying goods from the van, Frank led his young employee up another flight of steps into the main premises.

"This is the Scorpio Club, owned by the Parker brothers," Frank announced.

Tony had never seen anything like it. Tables and chairs spread across the broad room, a bar stretching the length of the back, and a small stage with a microphone stand at the front.

The stand caught Tony's attention.

"You have singers here," the boy had seen them on the small TV screen at home. To think they had real singers on stage here seemed amazing. Famous people.

Frank didn't enlighten him that most of the performers here were neither famous or glamorous. Mostly downbeat blue acts filling the gaps between striptease shows.

And at that moment Frank was not enlightened to the fact that the three men in the black Vauxhall Cresta had left the vehicle and were approaching the rear entrance to the club.

"You've been a good help and here's your pay," Frank took out his wallet and handed the boy a five pound note.

"Hello Frank. How you keeping ol' mate?" A man emerged from the back of the club wearing a light grey raincoat, a wry smile on his creased face.

Detective Sergeant, Doug Squires, was no ol' mate of Frank's, nor was he interested in his well being. Two broad shouldered men in blue suits followed the police officer into the room. One with a long scar on his right cheek, the other a vicious sneering face pummelled out of shape from endless fights.

"Not on official business then," Frank replied to the detective, who was now flanked each side by the two heavies. He recognised them as members of a rival gang.

"We don't do official business do we Frank? Your masters the Parker brothers have a special off-contract agreement with me, as you know," the detective referred to his cosy arrangement with them. They could get away with all sorts of criminal activities as long as he received generous payment in return.

Tony had no idea of what was going on, seeing only that his uncle looked uneasy in the presence of these men.

Your bosses have been refusing to increase my wages," detective Squires continued the conversation. "A very unwise move."

"That's nothing to do with me," Frank dismissed the problem. "And I've got no influence with them."

"Indeed you haven't," the officer turned to survey the club bar. "Nice set up. Would be a shame to spoil it."

"Now don't do anything hasty," Frank knew what was coming next.

"Just fuck off little man," Squires snarled. "Go on lads."

The heavies upturned a table and lifted a couple of chairs, then swiftly made for the side entrance to the bar. Frank leapt forward and landed a hard punch at the scarred face. He staggered, dropping the chair. His partner turned back. The bar optics and bottles would have to wait for a second as he redirected the chair at Frank.

Two legs smacked heavily into his back. Frank flew forward, colliding with a table. The heavy raised the chair to bring it down on his head. Frank ducked aside, avoiding the impact by a fraction, and delivered a powerful blow to the man's head sending him flying to the floor. The scarred face had now recovered and picked up another chair to attack Frank.

Tony hated these horrible men. He could box, but was no match for their enormous frames. So he'd slipped behind the bar and picked up a beer bottle from the shelf. Creeping back just as the nasty man raised the chair to hit his uncle, Tony sprang up behind and for all he was worth smashed it on his head. The bottle shattered spraying beer everywhere. The attacker wasn't felled, but swayed stunned for a moment. Just enough time for Frank to move in and deliver a knockout punch.

93

By now the other man still half dazed had picked himself up ready to launch another attack.

"Stop!" the detective sergeant shouted. Everyone froze.

He looked contemptuously at the two he'd brought along to teach the Parker brothers a lesson and force a pay rise. The club was meant to be in ruins. Save for some broken chairs and a beer bottle it was still intact. His henchmen, nursing their injuries, gathered sheepishly by his side.

"You fuckin' tossers," he sneered at them. "Christ knows why Mickey Rogers employs you two for security. A bloody kid can take you on."

Mickey Rogers was a rival gangleader. For a long time he'd been attempting to take over the Parker brothers' business, and DS Squires knew it.

Rogers paid the detective too for turning a blind eye to his activities. The gang leader was eager to expand and hoped Squires would help him drive the brothers out, by offering a much higher payback.

What Rogers didn't understand was Squires would help the ones who paid him most for protection from the law. Loyalty had no part in the game. If Frank's bosses could be forced to make a better deal, he'd go with that. The visit was all part of his plan to up the stakes.

"Get back in the car and wait for me," Squires ordered the shamed heavies. They sloped out.

Tony stood by Frank's side, hardly believing what had happened, but bristling with pride that he'd helped his uncle fight some very unpleasant bullies. He intensely disliked the man in the raincoat now facing them, but sensed he had strong power over his uncle.

94

"Tell your bosses I want double what they're paying me now, or I'll pull my protection. I'll have this place shut down for touting illegal booze, prostitutes and pornography, and I'll have this place and their other clubs trashed so they won't even have anything left to sell." DS Squires gave his terms.

"I'll tell them," Frank agreed. "They won't be happy. That's a big rise."

"I know they won't be fuckin' happy. But they'll be a lot unhappier if they don't." The detective pointed at the boy. "He's a bit handy. He'll go far one day. Good to see you're starting him off young. Keeps us in business. New blood, low life criminals."

Squires smiled smugly, turned and left.

Frank put his arm across Tony's shoulders.

"I'm sorry about this. I didn't know they'd be coming." He reached for his wallet again and handed Tony another five pound note. "This is a reward for being brave and helping me."

Tony gleamed. He now had ten pounds. He was rich. Visions of endless sweet supplies filled his thoughts.

Frank locked the back door of the club and they made their way to the van.

"I'm just going to see some people before I take you back to your nan," said Frank as he pulled away.

Neither spoke for a while as Frank made his way down busy Oxford Street, and back towards the greyer setting of Whitechapel in East London.

Tony broke the silence with something that had been puzzling. Something the detective have said.

"What are prostitutes and por… por… porno…" the boy couldn't remember the whole word.

"You don't want to know yet," his uncle replied.

******

FRANK parked the van in a street lined with semi-detached houses.

"Come with me, I'm just going to see some friends," he told his nephew. Tony followed and after a couple of raps on the knocker of a red door, a woman with long blonde hair opened it.

Tony was struck by her heavily rouged lips and thick, black eyeliner. She looked like a toy doll. Her chest bulged in a white lace top and her dark skirt seemed too tight around her waist.

"Frank!" she greeted him with a beaming smile. "And who's this?" The woman bent down and treated Tony to an even bigger smile that seemed to rise halfway up her face.

"He's my nephew, Tony."

"Oh, ain't he a cutie?" she chucked his chin. Tony grimaced at the annoying intrusion, moving his head aside.

"He's shy ain't he?"

"This is Lindy," Frank introduced the woman to his nephew. She was the wife of Dave Parker, one of the notorious brothers. Tony smiled weakly, not wishing to be rude because she appeared to be a friend of his uncle.

"Come in, come in," Lindy invited in her usual over excited manner.

Tony followed his uncle along the hall, decorated with palm trees wallpaper. The place seemed so high and wide compared to his own small home. Lindy opened a door and beckoned them inside.

The elegance to the boy was beyond belief. The large room contained a huge sofa and armchairs. His shoes sank into the plush, deep pile red carpet. The wallpaper teemed with bright flowers. Frank thought the place was a bit tacky and overdone, but would never voice his opinion in this hallowed dwelling.

Dave Parker's rise from poverty meant he needed to make a statement of wealth to all lesser mortals who visited his home. The man himself was sitting in an armchair reading a newspaper.

"It's Frank," Lindy announced, entering the room with the visitors.

"Frank." Dave closed the paper, dropping it to the floor. He stood up, revealing a towering muscular man in smart blue shirt and black trousers.

"What brings you here?" The brothers' minions didn't usually show up unannounced. Normally they were summoned. There must be something urgent. Dave caught sight of the boy standing beside Frank.

"Who's this?" he approached Tony, bending down to his head level. The man was smiling, but Tony sensed heartless aggression behind the shine of his eyes. The close cropped brown hair and sinewy face gave him the impression of a wild animal waiting to pounce. Frank introduced his nephew. Dave nodded then raised himself back to full height.

"So you've brought him here as our latest recruit?" The man's tone was jokey, but also carried a hint of sarcasm. Why a mere operative had brought along some snivelling kid was beyond him. Only his wife Lindy's presence and her ridiculous soft spot for children kept him from exploding into fury.

"He'll be a bloody good recruit one day," Frank countered, annoyed at the subtle contempt inferred on his nephew. "He helped me save the Scorpio Club being smashed to pieces, not more than an hour ago."

The news struck Dave Parker a hard blow. He stiffened. The threat of his lucrative investment being damaged was worse to him than being badly slashed in a knife fight.

"Explain," he demanded.

"The kid," Lindy interrupted, approaching Tony.

"Get the kid out," Dave waved them away.

"Your brother Lenny will be here in about ten minutes. Remember, he wanted to have a word about the new Aquarius Club opening," Lindy reminded her husband, taking Tony's hand.

"Alright, we'll wait a few minutes 'til he gets here. Sounds like he ought to be in on this one," Dave agreed. "But get the boy out of here. Take him to see Lucy. They can play some games upstairs."

Frank didn't like his nephew being taken away from him, but it was a temporary annoyance compared to the vengeance that would descend on him if he tried to overrule the brothers' commands. They weren't averse to cutting their enemies into segments and feeding them to pigs on a friend's farm. Dropping their bodies through manholes into

98

sewers, or blasting their brains out in remote parts of the countryside.

Lindy led Tony up to a dark blue carpeted stairway to a door on the landing.

"Lucy darling," she called, opening the door. "Here's a friend to see you." Tony followed the woman into the room.

Kneeling on a red carpet, a young girl in a light yellow dress held a miniature toy sofa in her hand.

"This is Tony. He's come to play with you for a while," Lindy introduced him.

Lucy was similar in age to her visitor. She turned her head to study him, long fair hair trailing over her back.

Tony forced a smile. She looked pretty he thought, but felt shy from this unexpected meeting with a girl completely unknown to him. And she looked cleaner and better clothed than the rough girls he and his male friends would sometimes allow to join in their games back home.

"Hello Tony," the girl said, turning back to open the hinged frontage of a doll's house and carefully placing the miniature sofa in the living room.

I'm leaving Tony here with you for a few minutes while your dad has a talk with Tony's uncle," Lindy explained to her daughter. She smiled at them both and left.

The girl continued moving pieces of furniture in the doll's house. Tony stood there feeling awkward. He looked around the room. He saw some comic annuals scattered untidily on a small desk. A Beano annual on the top. He liked the characters in The Beano.

Lucy's bed looked plump with a thick golden eiderdown. Until this moment, he'd never given a second thought about beds, but now the image of his own seemed flat by comparison, a faded patchwork cover bearing loose threads coiling limply across its surface. He wouldn't have wanted the wallpaper of fairy castles surrounding Lucy's bedroom, but it looked so fresh compared to the paper of leafy bamboo canes, browned almost beyond visibility in his own bedroom.

Silence prevailed for a while, as Tony felt increasingly awkward watching Lucy kneeling with her back to him positioning furniture in the house.

"I've got a toy fort at home with soldiers," Tony broke the silence. Lucy continued to ignore him for another minute then turned to face him, sitting on the carpet.

"Well I've got a pram with dolls in the other room," she boasted, staring intently at him. Tony was taken by her bright, shiny eyes. He felt his heart flutter a little. A strange new sensation.

"I don't have dolls, but I've got a teddy bear." Tony instantly regretted admitting he had a teddy. That was his secret, known only to his mum and dad. His friends would torment him for being a little baby if they knew. Now Lucy would laugh at him.

"Is he a nice teddy?" Lucy asked.

Tony half-heartedly nodded. He didn't want to pursue this line.

"Do you like comics?" Lucy could see she would get no further on the subject of teddy bears. Now Tony nodded enthusiastically. He glanced at the annuals on her desk. She saw his interest.

"D'ye want to see these?" Lucy stood up and walked over to them. Tony moved for the first time to join her.

"Come and sit on my bed and we'll read them." Lucy had carefully studied the boy with auburn hair, the worn stitching on his red and white zig-zag pattern pullover, and grey trousers thinning at the knees. It was the mark of poor kids from flats on rundown housing estates. Her father had told her he used to live like that when he was a boy. But she would always enjoy the finest.

Tony's clothing seemed not to matter to the girl. She thought he had a kind face with lovely long eyelashes. He sat beside her on that soft eiderdown as she opened the Beano comic annual.

Half an hour later when Lindy returned she heard laughter coming from the room. Opening the door she saw them sitting on the bed with annuals spread across it.

"You two having fun?" Lindy smiled. "Your uncle's ready to take you home Tony," she held out her hand to take his. Tony didn't want to be led by the hand, feeling she was treating him like a baby. But she was nice, so he got off the bed and took her grasp.

As they left he turned his head to smile at the girl. She smiled back. Lucy had smitten him.

Lindy took him back to the room downstairs where his uncle stood with Dave Parker, now joined by his brother. His face was softer than his brother's. He had longer, side-parted hair and looked more handsome in a smart, well-tailored grey suit. He could pass as an ordinary business

101

man in a city street. But there the difference between brothers ended. He too stood tall and broad and carried the same ruthless inner streak.

"I'm Lenny," the man stooped, reaching out to engulf Tony's hand in a congratulatory shake.

"Your uncle Frank and my brother tell me you've been a real hero."

Tony raised a smile, but with no idea what he meant.

"You helped your uncle beat off the bad men," Lenny resumed his towering height.

Tony saw helping his uncle as a loyal duty. This man obviously thought it was something special. Though he was pleased to be called a hero. Like Batman or Superman.

The adults resumed talking, rounding off their conversation.

"Okay, I'll settle the payoff business with Mr fucking important Detective Sergeant, Doug Squires," Dave snarled.

"Dave!" Lindy was still in the room. "Children present."

"Sorry," he mumbled.

They began moving towards the door.

"Thanks for saving the club. Good man." Lenny patted Frank on the back.

As Frank drove Tony back to his nan's, he asked the boy to solemnly promise not to say a word to anyone of what had happened, especially not to his nan or mum and dad. Tony solemnly made the promise, but at that moment his mind was captured by the wonderful time he'd spent with Lucy.

102

A FEW weeks later Tony was at home in his bedroom playing with toy cars on the carpet. His father entered smoking a pipe.

"Just want to have a word about the new school you'll be starting soon," Gerry sat on the bed. Tony settled beside his toys.

"It's a preparatory school called Spencer House at Sloane Square near central London."

Tony listened with no idea what was a preparatory school, but his dad must think it alright and he wanted to get back to his game with the cars.

"You'll meet some boys there who come from well-off families and the teachers will be much better than the ones you've got now."

The boy was silent for a moment, then came up with a vital question.

"Do I get the same holidays as now at the new school?"

Gerry frowned.

"You need to concentrate on learning, not worrying about holidays." He stood up and left the room, fearing that his son lacked scholarly attributes. Tony returned to the important business of playing with toy cars.

Next day, after school, he set off to meet some friends on a nearby bomb site. As he walked down the street towards the rubble he heard someone call his name from behind. The voice sounded familiar. He turned. It was Billy, who he hadn't seen for some time since his move to Dagenham.

"How you doing?" Billy asked as Tony walked back to greet his friend.

"I'm over this way to see my granddad," Billy announced. "But I thought I might catch you coming out of school."

"I miss our boxing," said Tony. Billy smiled.

"Me too, but that's the way it goes."

"D'ye like your new place?" asked Tony, hoping Billy would say no and that he was moving back.

"Yeah. Dad's business is going great guns. It's a nice shop with a flat over it. A palace compared to what we had."

They walked on chatting and arrived at the street corner. Billy stopped for a moment to tie a loose shoelace. Tony waited. Suddenly, just around the corner, he caught sight of his arch enemy Brendan approaching with two friends.

"Tony Selby!" the boy shouted, a grin rising on his face in anticipation of giving him a good beating again. The three began bearing down on him when Billy appeared from round the corner and reached Tony's side.

The three stopped in their tracks for a moment, sizing up the new arrival. Tony felt much more secure with Billy beside him. The three began approaching again only more cautiously. The one by Tony's side looked bigger and ready to pile into them.

"We're not after you," Brendan called, growing closer. "Just him." He pointed at Tony.

"Anyone who's after my friend is after me," Billy growled, raising his fists.

The two beside Brendan began to back away. They didn't want the prospect of being beaten up by someone who appeared capable of demolishing them.

"Right, there you are Tony. It's one to one. You and this geezer. Use your skills."

"He's the one who's always bullying me," said Tony.

"I know him. Always picks on smaller kids," Billy replied.

Brendan looked less certain now his allies had dropped back, but he couldn't afford to lose face in front of them. He leapt forward flinging wild blows. Nimbly moving back, Tony swiftly raised his fists in defensive guard, dancing about to avoid the punches. Suddenly he side-stepped, landing a hard right fist into the side of Brendan's jaw and a left into his stomach.

The boy yelped, tottering sideways and falling to the pavement. Tony stood, fists still ready for a second onslaught as the dazed Brendan slowly stood up.

"Alright, alright," he raised his hand defensively. "That's enough."

Tony couldn't believe that the boy who'd previously filled him with terror was readily conceding defeat. Brendan's allies were now walking away from the scene not wishing to risk conflict with both Billy and Tony.

"Look, I'm sorry," Brendan, wiped away a trickle of blood from his split lip. "Let's be friends," he held out his hand. Billy watched suspiciously at the gesture of friendship. It was an old trick to strike when your opponent's guard was down. But the gesture seemed genuine and Tony extended his right hand.

"My uncle runs the King's Head pub a few streets away. "come round and have a lemonade with me. Let's be friends from now on." Brendan raised a smile on his swelling lip. Tony felt surprised by the change in the boy's personality, but tended towards peace rather than conflict.

Billy had planned to see Tony for a short while before going on to his relative. Now he was worried Brendan might be enticing his protege into a trap. He invited himself along too, in order to keep a protective eye.

The pub looked grim. The metal nameplate above the doorway into the dark brick building, faded and pitted with rust leaving it barely readable. The sash window frames each side of the door bared and rotting, with the last traces of green paint curling as if to escape from the clutches of decay. Dried patches of sick stains adorned the pavement outside.

The door would be locked until official opening time at six o'clock, so Brendan led Tony and Billy down a narrow path to an unlocked door at the side. As they entered the stench of damp and rot struck their noses. The place was a shithole, but they followed the boy along a narrow hallway to a door leading into the bar.

The stink of stale beer rising from a filthy, stained carpet was the next evil odor to strike. Tony wanted to leave, but felt tied by the uneasy new bond of friendship offered by his former enemy.

Brendan beckoned them to sit on a wooden bench seat backed against the pub's front window. Dull, cloudy light struggled through the dirty lace curtains, browned like the dismal bar area with tar from tobacco smoke. Pools of beer beginning to dry from the lunchtime opening glistened on the table in front of them.

"Want something strong?" Brendan asked. He knew his alcoholic uncle would be upstairs sleeping off a heavy intake of whisky from the earlier session and wouldn't stir for a couple more hours.

"Just an orange juice," said Billy.

"Me too," Tony followed.

Don't you want a drop of gin in it?" Brendan encouraged.

"No." Billy was insistent.

Tony wavered. He didn't want Brendan to think he was an innocent who just followed Billy's lead. He could be Tony in his own right.

"Just a little drop," he said, causing Brendan's swollen lip to rise in a mischievous grin.

"You sure that's a good idea?" Billy cautioned.

"I've drunk alcohol before," Tony protested with a lie.

Brendan prepared the drinks behind the dirty bar, choosing gin and tonic for himself, then brought them to the table sitting on a seat opposite the pair.

"God Bless the Queen," Brendan raised his glass. Tony followed suit, taking a cautious sip. The taste of gin diluted in the orange juice was strange, but not unpalatable to him. In fact he quite liked it. Billy was keeping a watchful eye on him.

The two younger boys chatted about good places to play in the area and Tony learned that Brendan no longer went to school. He'd been thrown out of two. His mother had left home and his father was serving six years in prison for a series of burglaries. Now he lived with his uncle and helped out in the pub for a bit of money.

"Come on, let's 'ave another drink," he said, finishing his own.

Tony was starting to feel a buzz from the alcohol, everything growing a little fuzzy, distant, but it was a comforting feeling. He held out his glass despite sensing Billy's disapproval.

Behind the bar, Brendan shot another generous amount of gin into Tony's orange, an even wider grin breaking out on his face. He'd guessed the boy was an alcohol novice.

As Tony took more gulps, the pleasant, relaxed feeling began to transmute into a different sensation. His stomach was launching a rebellion. His head began to lose control, everything in the room starting to spin, no matter how hard he fought to control it.

"I feel sick!" he stood up, swaying clumsily.

He was hardly aware of Billy grasping his arm and leading him out into the street. The world echoed and spun recklessly. Fresh air swept across his face. His stomach churned, and in the next second he spewed on to the pavement, the mess joining dried patches laid earlier by men who'd grown older, but not wiser.

Billy guided him back towards his home, steering the boy's wandering legs. While he thought Tony had been stupid, it was probably a good lesson for him to suffer and learn from the experience. Back at the pub Brendan felt satisfied. He might have been beaten in the fight, but he got revenge another way.

Back at Tony's flat, Billy knocked on the door and left. As it opened, Tony staggered in. Irene looked alarmed.

"What's happened?" The boy was pale and groaning. She feared he'd been attacked.

Tony slurred something incomprehensible, wandering towards his bedroom and slumping on the bed. Irene grew suspicious. Her suspicions were confirmed when she smelled his breath.

"You bad boy!" she raged. "You've been drinking," her anger fell on deaf ears. Tony was out of it.

Irene reported their son's condition to Gerry when he came home from work.

"It's this bloody place. The boy's going downhill with the rubbish living round here. Got drunk with some yobs, no doubt." Gerry took off his overcoat while Irene went to make a cup of tea in the kitchen. They settled in the living room.

"I've been to the local council today and applied for a transfer out of the area," Gerry lit his pipe, resting on a scuffed leather armchair in the corner. "There's a new out of town development going up at a place called Roehampton, near Richmond Park with plenty of greenery. We need a fresh start."

Irene wasn't so sure. Moving away from the only world she knew would be a big step. Her mother. Her brothers and sisters. She'd never heard of Roehampton. In her mind it was a thousand miles away. In reality only ten. That triggered the start of another argument between them. However, Gerry's insistence that it would give their son a better chance in life, finally swayed her.

CHAPTER 4

GERRY accompanied Tony on the underground train from Aldgate East near their home to his new school. The journey took them from the deprived, poor region of the capital into the wealthy, upmarket climes of Sloane Square in the Royal Borough of Kensington and Chelsea.

As they entered the street at their destination, Tony was struck by the grand buildings all around. Apartments with balconies, the Royal Court Theatre, a large department store. Everywhere looked so much cleaner and fresher than the drab surroundings where he lived.

Cars busily circled the road surrounding the central square, office workers scurrying across in a rush not to be late.

Ahead of father and son a group of chatting schoolboys, about Tony's age, wore the same uniform of blue blazers, grey shirts and short trousers, heading in the direction of his new school. After a few turns, a long row of five-storey, red brick terraced house rose majestically above the street, crowned by Flemish-style pitched roofs. An array of white window frames peered over the setting.

Approaching a short flight of steps leading up to one of the dwellings, they followed the schoolboys through a black front door, bearing a silver plate engraved with the school's name, Spencer House.

The group of schoolboys began to disperse to their classrooms. With the poor schooling Tony had received up until now, he was unaware these boys were two years ahead of him in education.

Still accompanied by his father, the pair crossed the chequered floor tiles of the entrance hall and ascended a wide stairway to the half landing where the school office was set through a door to the side. Gerry knocked and they entered, to be greeted by a grey-haired man wearing a black master's gown. He introduced himself as Selwyn Turnberry, the head of the school.

Gerry had met him on a previous occasion, when discussing his son's entry into Spencer House, and matters of fees.

"So this is young Selby," the man shook Tony's hand, then turned to Gerry.

"Right Mr Selby, I'll show your son to his new classroom. He will have a lot of catching up to do, but I'm sure with good effort he'll make the grade."

Tony didn't understand what the man was talking about, being more fascinated by a large wart on the side of his neck and layers of wrinkles under his eyes, magnified by rimless spectacles.

"He'll start the first day or two out of the mainstream with Miss Ferguson's class for younger pupils, so he can get used to the place," the head continued, "then he'll join the boys in his own age group for serious education."

That's what Gerry wanted to hear. A proper education for his son. They parted, with Gerry reminding the boy he'd meet him later for the homeward journey.

Tony was gripped with loneliness, now in the presence of total strangers in an alien environment. The headmaster showed him to Miss Ferguson's class in the school basement. Drawings and paintings adorned the walls. Bench seats surrounded a large central table where Miss Ferguson helped the children with artwork and making things from paper and cardboard.

She was a young woman and very pretty in Tony's eyes. Kind and smiling. He felt out of place among kids below his own age, but loved the painting and drawing. If only life could have remained so sweet for him at the school.

His introduction to the 'serious business of education' among boys his own age began in Class 3b, where the sweet life began to turn sour.

Mr Spears, the English teacher, sat at his desk facing the rows of schoolboys at their desks.

"We have a newcomer," he announced, glaring at Tony who was seated towards the back of the classroom. A man in his mid-forties, Mr Spears fixed his gaze under a wavy crop of black hair. His sloping nose reminded Tony of a fearsome hawk with a vicious beak that he'd seen in a picture book.

"Stand up Selby so everyone can see you," the teacher commanded.

Sheepishly Tony obeyed, his cheeks growing red at being the object of attention among strangers.

"Can you read and write boy?" Mr Spears demanded.

Tony nodded.

"Speak up boy, I can't hear you."

"Yeah,"

"Yes sir! In this school you call teachers sir. And you do not speak in that common East London accent."

"Yes sir," Tony obeyed, forcing himself to try and speak poshly. He'd never thought his accent was out of place until now.

"Good. Then you'll know all about prepositions, because that's what we're going to do today."

Tony knew absolutely nothing about things called prepositions. Even from his poor education to date he'd learned to read and write reasonably well, but grammar was an unknown universe to him. The man might just as well be speaking a foreign language.

Mr Spears chalked a sentence on the blackboard.

"Come up here Selby and underline the preposition in there."

Tony shuffled to the front, all eyes fixed on him as the teacher handed over the chalk. The boy had no idea which to choose and selected a word randomly.

"That's a verb!" The teacher almost delighted in Tony's ignorance at selecting the wrong word. He knew the boy came from a slum area of London, and resented those who he deemed lesser people entering the hallowed portals of expensive education. Post-war aspirations among the lower class were becoming too liberal for him.

"You don't know what they are, do you?" Spears growled. Tony shook his head.

"Bend over."

Tony was puzzled. He hadn't noticed until now that a cane rested on the teacher's desk. Spears picked it up, gripping the end with relish.

"Bend over!" he shouted.

Tony obeyed and the man delivered a hefty whack with the cane on Tony's backside. The pain seared through him. He recoiled, gripping the cheeks.

"Keep bending over!"

Spears delivered another two hard strikes. Tears welled in Tony's eyes. He didn't want to be seen crying in front of the other boys, but he couldn't control the flow.

"Now that will help you remember everything I say."

The teacher replaced the cane on the desk, a visual display of his punishing authority.

"Get back to your seat."

The soreness made it difficult for Tony to sit comfortably again, and in fear of receiving the same dreadful beating, the class remained deadly silent unless required to speak.

"Who can underline the preposition?" Spears threw out the question.

"Clark," he pointed to the boy who'd raised his hand. Clark was the bright one. He walked to the blackboard and underlined the correct word. The teacher smiled at him.

If Tony thought the encounter was the only woe he would suffer at Spencer House, he was mistaken. After a few lessons with teachers of a kindlier nature, his next nemesis was Mr Fitchmore.

The balding, grey-haired man with eyes piercing through his gold rimmed spectacles, took great pride in his Master's Degree in Languages. He always wore his flowing university gown when taking lessons.

"God knows why the headmaster is allowing scum, riff-raff into the school," he'd remarked to his colleagues in the common room, when learning of Tony's acceptance at the place.

"I think the head must be a closet socialist," his friend Mr Spears had replied, sitting back in an armchair sipping a cup of tea beside Fitchmore.

Selwyn Turnberry, their boss, was a reforming type and had inherited these two teachers when he took on the top job six months earlier. But he was also a pragmatist and if people from a poor background were prepared to pay the school's high fees, he wouldn't create any barriers.

"Selby," Mr Fitchmore boomed as he entered the classroom that afternoon to take the lesson.

"Do you know any Latin?"

Once again someone might have been asking Tony the question in an alien language. He shook his head.

"Stand up boy!"

Tony obeyed.

"Have you ever learned Latin?"

Again he shook his head. Fitchmore tutted, now shaking his head in disgust.

"This boy," the teacher addressed the class, "comes from the slums of East London. He is ignorant and will never rise to anything worthwhile." He turned to Tony.

"Sit down Selby, and hopefully I might be able to drum something into your tiny brain."

Given that Tony hadn't the first basics of this Latin language he'd never heard of before, the entire lesson that followed was gobbledegook to him. When Fitchmore set homework for the class to do that evening, Tony might just as well have been given orders to fly to the moon.

His first bright spot arrived a few days later when he encountered Mr Wells, the sports master. A coach took the class to a sports field a few miles out into the suburbs. Tony took to the game immediately. He'd only ever played in the streets and the wide open space of a green field pitch was amazing.

"Well done!" cried Mr Wells, as Tony weaved skilfully past his opponents to score another of several goals.

The master's praise made Tony bristle with pride. At last he'd done something which had attracted praise instead of beatings.

The man cheering him on was fifty years old, with a slightly wrinkled face and bushy grey moustache. His profile was older than the traditional school sports master, but he remained almost as fit as his younger self, back in the days when he played in a top London football team.

A couple of days later the sports teacher was in the master's common room pouring a cup of tea from the urn on the refreshment table.

"That boy Selby has some terrific skills at football, he's a natural," he announced to his colleagues, seated and chatting during the lunch break. "I think he'll be a credit to the school team."

Spears and Fitchmore were in their usual armchair positions beside each other, grumbling about the falling standards in education these days.

"He won't be much credit to the academic achievements of the school," Fitchmore responded. Mr Wells approached him, cup of tea in hand.

"Life isn't just about heady scholars," he replied. "You've got a very narrow outlook on the world."

Spears and Fitchmore considered Wells to be a lesser person because he only took sport lessons. They glanced at him sourly.

"You're both just a couple of fucking twats," Mr Wells gave his considered opinion of them. They looked away dismissively. Tony would have loved hearing his advocate's reply to them. But the teachers' common room was sacred ground, in another galaxy to mere schoolboys.

In the same lunch break, the two hundred Spencer House pupils sat at rows of long tables in the school dining room, using spatulas to lift sections of cauliflower cheese on to their plates from large metal trays spaced along their length.

"You talk really funny," said one of Tony's class mates sitting next to him.

"Does everyone in east London talk like you in that strange accent?" another boy sitting close by asked.

Until now, Tony had found the boys in his class had accepted him as one of their own, despite lagging behind them in lessons. His beating by Mr Spears had formed an unspoken bond of initiation with them. They had all carried bruises from beatings by the man.

Now Tony suddenly felt apart from them. They spoke in what he considered posh accents, like all people from educated, well-off families as he'd been led to believe by those from his own so called lower class. To him the way they spoke made no difference if they were friendly.

Another boy nearby mimicked Tony's accent. "I dunno ow ya do that."

"That means, I don't know how you do that," another translated, taking pride in his powers of converting it into correct speech.

Unfortunately for the boy who had mimicked Tony, a teacher with searing eyes that looked like they could literally fire arrows was passing the table at that moment. A fellow idealist and friend of Fitchmore and Spears, he too feared the rising tide of lower class people.

"Harrison!"

The boy trembled under the teacher's gaze.

"How dare you pretend to speak in a common language like that. You are properly educated and not a child of the slums. Your parents would be ashamed of you. Go to the washroom and rinse your mouth with soapy water. Then go to my study." The boy knew it would be for a vicious caning.

Tony felt guilty even though the situation was not of his making.

"He was only playing sir," he leapt to the boy's defence.

The teacher glared poisonously at him. "Be quiet Selby! You are destined for the rubbish heap where you belong. If only a good wash could clean away the stink of your people."

The dining room had fallen silent as the drama unfolded. Fear that if any of them made a sound, a beating would follow.

******

SEVERAL weeks later, Tony met Brendan while nearing home. Gerry had stopped accompanying his son to and from school, considering the boy should stand on his own two feet in life as early as possible.

"Ain't seen you for ages," Brendan greeted him.

Tony was weighed down with doing lots of homework after school and at weekends. By the time he'd worked his way through essays and arithmetic, he was too tired to go out and play. Fear of being caned if he didn't complete the work drove him on.

"You feeling better now? You looked pissed out of your head when you left my uncle's pub the other week."

The memory of feeling ill after drinking the orange juice laced with gin was indelibly stamped on Tony's mind.

"It's alright. I'm okay." Tony dismissed it, feeling embarrassed that it had made him look a wimp.

"What's all the fancy fashion? And that bag over your shoulder?" Brendan studied Tony's school uniform and the satchel containing his evening's homework.

"My dad's sending me to a posh school. All the kids there are rich."

"What's he doing that for?" Brendan looked genuinely puzzled.

"He wants me to be clever. But I'm not," Tony replied gloomily.

"Clever at what?" Now Brendan was mystified.

"English, sums, Latin."

"What the fuck's Latin?"

"Some old language."

Brendan's screwed his faced in disgust.

"That's sounds fucking stupid. What the hell for? Won't do you much good around here."

Tony felt just the same. The wider horizon of education and the opportunities it could produce was way beyond his present understanding. The boys began walking down the road together.

"You can get good jobs in the docks, driving lorries, working in the street markets. And the clubs." Brendan listed the work opportunities on offer. "There's bloody good money to be made in the clubs if you join up with the right hard men. They can rake it in with booze, cigarettes, strip shows, protection services." The boy was well versed in the advantages of crime.

The mention of hard men put Tony in mind of his uncle Frank. He didn't fully understand what was going on, but the fight he helped his uncle with at that club, and the men Frank visited afterwards at Lindy's, made him think they were hard men. Gangsters even.

The thought led him to remembering Lucy, and for a moment his troubles seemed to melt away. He was in love with her. She was so beautiful and friendly. How he longed to see her again.

"Who are those two geezers?" Brendan's voice brought Tony back. They were approaching the railway arch near his home.

Tony immediately recognised them as Terry Purvis and Dave Jepson, the tormentors he'd encountered before. They were holding beer bottles, looking ready to give trouble. The pair approached, sneering.

"It's that fucking git who wanted to smash us up the other week," slurred Purvis, full of alcohol.

"Did you?" Brendan asked Tony.

"Yeah. They ran off."

"What's all those funny clothes he's wearing? Looks like some rich kid," Jepson offered his slurred opinion.

"Piss off!" Brendan shouted.

"See, now he's got a friend 'cause he's too frightened to go around on his own," Purvis laughed triumphantly.

Tony was preparing for an attack, raising his fists.

"Don't worry about those pussycat drunks," Brendan assured his friend.

"Who are you calling pussycats?" Purvis drew near, raising the beer bottle in his hand. Brendan stood his ground, defying the retreat his opponent had expected. The man's expression turned to fury. He swung the weapon violently at Brendan's face.

The boy tilted in a flash avoiding the impact and sprang back to snatch the bottle from Purvis' hand, swiftly smashing it on his attacker's head. The man collapsed in a heap.

Now Jepson lurched forward swinging his beer bottle at Brendan. Again the boy stepped aside evading the blow and grabbing the weapon from his off-guard opponent. Gripping the neck he smashed the bottle on the ground raising the jagged remains of glass and swiping it across Jepson's face as he turned to attack again.

Blood poured out in a streaked line across his cheeks and lips as the man staggered back screaming in pain and terror.

"That's a lot fucking quicker than boxing," Brendan boasted to Tony, throwing the remains of the bottle away.

Tony's jaw dropped in horror, realising he'd got off lightly in his fights with the boy. He was obviously capable of extreme violence. It was terrifying. And the sight of blood gushing from Jepson's face deeply shocked him. Tony's feelings had no time to sink in any further.

"Oi! You lot!" a voice echoed down the street.

"It's plod!" Brendan shouted "Quick!" He grabbed Tony's arm to pull him into a sprint. As they took off, Tony glanced back to see a police officer at the far end of the railway arch racing towards them. They darted down several side roads to evade capture.

After what seemed ages the boys stopped, gasping for breath and looking warily along the narrow footpath they'd taken lined by rows of houses on each side. The officer had lost them, outpaced by their frantic escape. Satisfied they weren't being followed, they walked to the end of the path coming out to a main road.

"I reckon you ought to wait a while before going home," Brendan advised. "The copper might recognise you in that poncy school uniform."

Tony saw they were beside the busy Whitechapel Road. A broad pavement lined the street with market traders shouting encouragement from their stalls to the teaming crowd of shoppers looking for a host of bargains.

"D'ye think you killed that bloke?" Tony was terrified that the police would hunt them down and stick them in prison, Even hang them maybe.

"No. I only scratched his face with the bottle. A few stitches and he'll be alright," Brendan was unconcerned by his vicious attack.

"Let's go to me uncle's pub and we can have another drink," he invited his accomplice in crime.

"I'm not drinking any of that gin," Tony pulled a face.

"Yeah. I bet you had a right fucking headache the next day," Brendan laughed. "He placed his arm round Tony's shoulder. "I'll just give you orange juice this time. Promise."

As they began walking to the pub, Tony became aware that he no longer had his satchel. He must have dropped it in the escape from the police officer. His homework, his textbooks lost. His mum and dad would kill him. And the school teachers.

"What's the matter?" Brendan saw the dismay in Tony's face.

"I've lost my school bag."

Brendan creased with laughter.

"Fuck your school bag. All that learning's a waste of time. Come and have a drink with me." He lead Tony on to the pub.

Brendan's uncle was there when they arrived, stacking beer bottles on shelves behind the bar. He stopped when they entered through the back door and took a swig from his whisky glass.

"What you doing in 'ere?" he eyed the boys suspiciously. The man had not long got up from his afternoon nap, wearing a dirty white vest and brown trousers that he changed out of every so often. Days of stubble growth covered his face and his dark, greasy hair splayed out longing for a wash and comb.

Tony took an instant dislike to him, his mean narrow eyes. He wished he hadn't come.

"Just come in for a drink uncle Ted," Brendan explained, not expecting his uncle to be out of bed yet.

"You're always stealing my drinks you bloody little sod. And who's this one with you in the posh blue jacket?" Uncle Ted's eyes pierced Tony.

"Just a friend."

"Just a bloody friend," Ted mumbled. "You can have a drink, then sod off." The man returned to stacking beer bottles.

"It's alright, he'll be pissed again soon. Won't even notice we're 'ere," Brendan confided to Tony.

The boy helped himself to a double gin from the optic and opened a bottle of orange juice for his new friend, pouring it into a glass this time without any alcohol additive. Then he picked up a pack of cards from behind the bar.

"Come on. I'll show you how to play poker," he led Tony to a table.

A couple of hours passed as he tried to teach his pupil the beginner skills of the card game, but Tony's mind kept straying to the shattered beer bottle slicing across Jepson's face, mingled with thinking up an excuse to explain how he'd lost his school satchel. He was now on his third orange juice. Sitting opposite him at the table, Brendan had downed several double gins, but seemed none the worse for wear.

125

Regulars began to fill the pub at early evening opening time, laughing, playing cards and swilling generous pints of beer.

"I'd better get home," said Tony, after losing yet another hand at the game he had great difficulty in understanding.

"Yeah. I expect the police dragnet will be over by now," Brendan joked.

Tony didn't see it as funny. He was terrified there would be a manhunt in progress for them."

"D'ye know your way back?"

Tony nodded.

"Alright. I'll see you around."

The boys stood up. Brendan placed his hand on Tony's shoulder.

"I like you. I like you because you had the guts to fight me. If I didn't like you, I'd have come back to sort you out."

Tony smiled. It was good to hear an affinity of friendship had grown between them since their first encounters. But Tony felt wary of his new companion. There was something unsettling about Brendan. As if beneath that easy going temperament there lurked an unstable volcano. His cold-blooded slashing of Jepson would remain a chilling memory.

"Thing is, you need to toughen up to keep living round here," Brendan offered his advice, removing his hand from Tony's shoulder. "Look after yourself."

Leaving the pub, the problem of explaining to his parents the loss of the school bag loomed imminently, coupled with the fear of a police officer in hiding ready to arrest him as he neared home. His fear of the law proved unfounded. In the fading light of the evening all was quiet near the railway arch and he reached the flat safely.

"Where have you been?" Why are you late?" his mother snapped at him. His father stood behind her puffing heavily on his pipe.

"I met a friend. We were playing I didn't realise the time." Tony's excuse sounded hollow.

"You're a bloody naughty sod," Irene clipped his head with a swift blow. "I was worried sick."

"Where's your school satchel?" Gerry removed the pipe from his mouth. Tony hesitated, puzzling which one of several excuses he'd been working on to use."I put it on the seat beside me on the train and forgot to pick it up when I got off."

Gerry and Irene doubted that was the real story, but had to consider it was a possibility.

"Get into your bedroom. No dinner for you, and I'll speak to you in the morning," Gerry ordered his son.

Tony was hungry, but it was a welcome respite from the anger he had expected. Though he knew he'd be in the doghouse for a day or so to come.

******

BACK at school, his floundering education continued. The loss of the satchel didn't help. New text books had to be provided, paid for by his parents, and he had to do extra work to make up for all the essays and arithmetic that disappeared with the bag.

127

The languages teacher, Fitchmore, didn't help in soothing Tony's misery.

"You're totally hopeless," the man declared in front of the Latin class, all eyes fixed on him while he struggled to translate a passage in a textbook.

Streaming out of the classroom with the other boys at the end of the lesson, one of them turned to him shouting 'you're totally useless' mimicking Fitchmore. He was a favourite of the teacher and carried with him the same lofty arrogance.

The jibe blew Tony's stress fuse. He lashed out giving the boy a hard punch in the face. He lurched backwards, raising his hand to the pain. Blood started to run from his lip. As he lowered his hand and seeing the blood started bawling.

"Selby!" A man's voice boomed. Fitchmore was leaving the classroom and witnessed the attack.

"You vicious little sod. Get to the headmaster's study now!"

Tony felt his knees begin to tremble. Now he really was in trouble.

Fitchmore went to the injured boy's assistance, taking out a handkerchief to dab his lips. The class had frozen witnessing the scene in amazement.

"Get to the headmaster's study!" Fitchmore ordered Tony again, as he too stood locked in terror. Reluctantly he obeyed. Being sent to the headmaster's study was the school's equivalent of receiving the wrath of God.

Fitchmore briefed the top man on the incident, before Tony was summoned inside.

128

Selwyn Turnberry sat behind a large desk, an open folder in front of him and several more stacked to the side waiting for his attention. Fitchmore stood glowering at Tony when he was called to enter.

Turnberry rose from his seat and approached him, his black master's gown adding to the looming sense of grim judgement about to descend.

"Attacking another boy is a very serious offence," he declared gravely.

Tony's bottom chin began to tremble. He could feel tears rising. The head saw his terror. Inwardly the man gained no satisfaction in reducing a child to such depths of fear. He wanted to nurture, unlike the man standing near him, who in his heart he despised as a bigot. Turnberry was a reformer, and held the strong belief that children with a lesser start in life should be given same the chance for better opportunities as those whose parents were wealthy.

However, attacking other boys could not go unpunished.

"Why did you punch your classmate?" he asked.

"Because he was making fun of me," Tony explained, doing his best to hold back the tears.

"He attacked because he's a nasty common boy," Fitchmore couldn't restrain his spite.

The head raised his hand for the man to remain silent.

Tony had committed an act that could lead to him being instantly expelled from the school. But Turnberry was of a mind to give him another chance. He knew Fitchmore would despise him for it, but he loathed the man and would gradually take steps to make him find another teaching job elsewhere.

"For the next month you will stay behind in class during lunch break periods and continue with your schoolwork," the headmaster declared his terms. "You will apologise to the boy you attacked, and I will tell your parents what has happened."

Tony considered the punishment harsh, since he believed he was the one who had been wronged. Losing his lunch break was hard enough, as well as having to say sorry to the boy who'd insulted him. But telling his mum and dad. That was the worst of all.

"Now go," the head ordered. "Any more trouble from you and you're finished at this school."

Fitchmore grunted and followed Tony out of the room without saying another word to his superior. He was angry. He'd fully expected to see the boy thrown out.

When Tony's parents received a letter from Turnberry a few days later about their son's behaviour, there was mixed reaction. While not praising what Tony had done, inwardly Irene was proud he'd given the boy a thump. It was the sort of justice she'd grown up with. An eye for an eye, a tooth for a tooth.

Gerry saw it differently. He gave his son a good thrashing.

"Sending you there is costing us a fortune. If you mess it up, I'll throw you out on the street," he raged.

His words were not intended as a genuine threat. But they struck terror in him.

CHAPTER 5

TONY managed to survive another three years at Spencer House by generally keeping his head down.

Fitchmore and Spears had resigned a couple of years earlier in disgust at the way the headmaster was reshaping the school. That helped Tony weather a few bad behaviour difficulties with more tolerant teachers taking a softer line. But his progress in education still trailed.

The lift-off into higher realms of ability and knowledge that Gerry had planned for his son was not materialising.

"I'm good at sport," he defended himself, when his father confronted him with yet another poor school report after summoning him into the living room at home.

"Yes, but playing football in the school team won't get you very far in life," Gerry grumbled.

"My friends think I could play for a big team when I grow up," the boy was desperate to show some worth.

"And your friends will all get well paid jobs while you'll remain at the bottom of the pile," Gerry warned him.

Tony had made some good friends at the school through his football skills. Andrew Marsh, one of his best, was not only clever, but gifted at sport too. His father was the managing director of a subsidiary American oil company, based in London.

Andrew did all he could to help Tony with his studies, sometimes even letting him crib off his homework. The boy had invited him to his birthday parties at his parents' spacious, grandly furnished Mayfair house.

When Tony had wanted to reciprocate the kindness, Gerry flatly refused.

"You're not bringing any friends back here so they can go home and tell their parents what a dump we live in." Gerry was climbing his way up the ladder at the legal firm where he worked. Still not great pay as a lowly minion, but the prospect of better things approached. He wasn't going to let anyone from work or his son's school see the rundown area he inhabited.

Tony continued to play with some friends at home, but Billy no longer visited the area and Brendan had been caught breaking into a shop, stealing money and cigarettes. He was now serving time in a young offenders institute.

On a Saturday afternoon Tony was reading comics and eating cakes at his nan's when uncle Frank called round. He hadn't seen his favourite relative for over a year.

"Do a magic trick for me," he urged, as Frank entered the living room greeting his nephew with a pat on the shoulder.

"I've come here for a cup of tea, not to be a flamin' conjuror," he smiled. Tony's face fell. Joyce went to the kitchen to put on the kettle.

"Are you smarter than us now, learning lots of things at your posh school?" Uncle Frank's voice was full of sarcasm.

"No. They all think I'm stupid," Tony replied glumly.

"You don't need to learn lots of stuff to make money," Frank gave his considered opinion. "All you need is this,"

132

he reached into his pocket and produced a gun, opening the barrel to show bullets inside.

Tony's jaw dropped. It was real. Not like the cheap plastic ones he and his friends played with. He'd only seen cowboys with real guns on the television. A real one looked terrifying. Cowboys killed people with them.

You don't kill people, do you?" Tony was shocked that his uncle might be a killer.

"Put that away! Fancy bringing that here!" Joyce reappeared from the kitchen. "You'll frighten the boy."

Frank instantly obeyed his mother, reassuring Tony with a lie.

"It's alright, it's only a toy. Just looks real."

The boy believed him completely. It was his uncle playing a joke.

Joyce returned to the kitchen and brought back a pot of tea and cups on a tray, placing them on the table.

"I reckon you need to learn more about life," Frank announced to his nephew as Joyce poured the tea.

"How do you fancy a Saturday job at one of the clubs where I work? Bit of pocket money?"

"Not sure if he's ready to work in one of those." Joyce wasn't keen on the idea.

"Well it won't be evening work. Just afternoons," Frank explained. "We get mostly drinkers in then. None of the night stuff. He could help with general jobs."

Tony's nan knew the 'night stuff' referred to the crude cabaret acts, and personal services offered to men. She didn't like to think of her grandson being involved with strip clubs and prostitution. Euphemisms suited her better. And anyway, if he wasn't present for that it would be fine.

"Would you like a Saturday job?" Frank asked.

Tony nodded enthusiastically. Working for his uncle would be fantastic.

"Not sure his dad will agree," Joyce seemed doubtful.

"He's a stuck up snob," Frank turned aside, whispering to his mother. "Irene can persuade him," he laid faith in his sister's power of persuasion.

Tony overheard the whisper. He felt inclined to agree with Frank's comment about his dad.

******

JOYCE was right. When Tony told him about the Saturday afternoon job offer, Gerry exploded.

"Not a chance!"

Irene was with them, sitting on the armchair stitching a sock. She stopped to join in.

"I've talked to my brother Frank about it. The boy will only be helping at the back of the club mostly, stacking crates and helping to take drinks and cigarettes to the bar for stocking." Irene didn't think it would hurt her son to do some labour for a bit of money.

Gerry was not a happy man.

"Tony, go to your bedroom."

The boy slunk away, fearful the plan would founder.

"It's a bloody strip joint, and your brother is a gangster," Gerry looked furious and began drawing heavily on his pipe to relieve stress.

"He's not a gangster," Irene protested. "He's got a good job and earns a lot more money than the high and mighty Gerry Selby." Now fury gripped her too.

"I'm trying to get him away from your shithole family. Bloody deadbeat no hopers. Your other brothers Jack, a lorry driver and Ted, a low life navvy. Frank...." he paused as the disgust rose in him "....a bloody gangster."

"Your family's no better. Your workshy sister, Lizzy. Your moaning, miserable mum always pretending she's got something wrong with her." Irene struck back. "I say the boy can do a Saturday job in the club. Frank's not gonna let him near you know what stuff. Work will be good experience for him."

The burning tobacco glowed red in the bowl of Gerry's pipe as he puffed even more heavily, pacing the room in agitated thought. Finally he came to a decision.

"He can do it for a couple of Saturdays. Then I'll decide if he can continue after that." Gerry left the room and came back a few minutes later wearing his overcoat.

"I'm going to the pub for a couple of pints." He left again, slamming the front door behind him.

Tony lay on his bed. He'd heard the sound of his parents arguing through the wall, but couldn't make out what they were saying. When his mother entered the bedroom a short time later to give him the news, the boy was ecstatic. He'd be working for his uncle.

Frank picked him up from his nan's flat the following Saturday at noon. He didn't collect Tony from his home, because he wanted to avoid a confrontation with the boy's father. The few times they'd met, Gerry's holier than thou

135

attitude had irritated him. Frank had been tempted to hit him, but that would cause family upset. So with much will power he'd resisted the urge.

"Where's your van?" Tony asked as he climbed into the front passenger seat of Frank's car, a shiny black Rover 12.

"I got rid of that a long time ago," Frank smiled. "There have been a few changes," he explained to his nephew, starting the engine.

"Now first I'm going to stop off at my house," he pulled away.

Twenty minutes later Frank drew up outside what looked to Tony like a small mansion in a tree lined avenue. The property sat among refined Victorian terraced houses with neatly trimmed hedges bordering the front gardens.

"I thought you lived in a flat at Limehouse?" Tony was puzzled. He'd been to his uncle's flat some years ago.

"Not any more." Frank led him down the pathway to the front door. As they entered, Tony was surprised to see Lindy coming into the hallway to greet them. She didn't look as heavily made up as the last time he remembered her, but the rouge on her lips was vivid.

"Hello Tony!" she gave a broad smile. "Oh, you are growing into a big boy ain't you?" She bent forward and kissed him on the forehead, which he immediately wiped away with the back of his hand.

Tony hadn't seen Frank's wife Brenda for years. He knew his uncle wasn't married to Lindy. She was married to one of the Parker brothers. And Frank had two daughters that he'd played games with sometimes at the flat where his uncle used to live. Something strange had happened.

"Come into the kitchen and I'll get you some lemonade," Lindy took Tony's hand while Frank left for another room.

It was an amazing kitchen, large with lots of cupboards and work surfaces. Even more amazing was that it had a fridge, which Lindy opened to take out a bottle of milk for the tea she'd just made. Tony had seen pictures of fridges, which kept food fresh and cold. His mum wanted one, but couldn't afford it. They were the height of luxury.

Frank entered the kitchen and could see the boy was impressed by the surroundings.

"Sit down and drink your lemonade," he beckoned his nephew to a chair at the table. Frank leaned back against a counter.

"Lindy's moved into my new home for a while. Her husband and brother are going to be away on business for a long time. So Lindy's staying here for a bit of company," the man explained.

It seemed a bit odd to Tony, but then Frank was his hero. To be trusted without question. In fact, what his uncle had told him was a pack of lies.

A year previously the Parker brothers had been put on trial as the masterminds of a bank robbery in which two of the teller staff were seriously injured leading one of them to suffer life-changing disability.

Frank vividly remembered the flight of the brothers from the police. It was the middle of the night when he was woken by loud banging on the door of his flat, the doorbell repeatedly ringing.

He opened it to see the brothers in a state of panic. They rushed past him into the living room.

137

"The law's after us," Lenny Parker announced breathlessly. Frank was baffled. He thought bribes usually kept the police at bay.

"We organised a big bank robbery. A huge amount of cash," the other brother Dave explained. "But one of our lads shot two of the bank tellers. The stupid buggers thought they could overpower our men."

"A couple of days later plod lifted three of ours and took them in for questioning," Lenny sat on a chair, lighting a cigarette to calm his nerves.

"It would have been alright," said Dave, "but Mickey Turner broke down and agreed to spill the beans on us in a trade-off for a lighter sentence."

"I told you he was a weak link, we should never have got him on board," Lenny criticised his brother.

Frank was stunned. He had no idea of the robbery even being planned.

"Can't you pay-off the law?" he asked.

"Too serious Frank. When innocent people get shot, the public get angry. The coppers in our pay won't risk looking the other way when the heat's on from their bosses and the newspapers." Lenny's face was pale with fear.

"Why didn't you tell me you were planning the job? I could have told you Mickey Turner was unreliable," Frank sounded disappointed.

Dave approached him, placing a hand on his shoulder.

"We didn't tell you because we wanted you as a back-up, no connection," he explained. "You've done well for us over the years as you know. That's why we put you in charge of the clubs."

Frank's readiness to sort out trouble as well as his usefulness in organising staff had impressed the brothers, and they valued his loyalty.

"We thought about the possibility of things going wrong, and now they bloody well have it's likely plod will pick us up for questioning."

Frank wondered what Dave was leading up to.

"You're clean. Nothing to do with this, so we want you to be caretaker of the business if we go down."

"We've got a good lawyer and we think there's a chance we could get off with a light sentence," brother Lenny stood up. "But right now we're off to a place in Southend that'll give us a bit of time to sort out our story before the law catches up with us. John Marriott, our accountant, will fill you in on all the bookkeeping stuff. We put our trust in you Frank."

The brothers prepared to leave.

"I want you to look after my wife Lindy and the kids. See that they want for nothing," Dave gave Frank his final orders. "The law will probably call on you. Don't tell them we've been here."

Frank had no intention of telling the police of their visit.

At that moment Frank's wife Brenda entered the room in her dressing gown.

"What's going on?"

"It's okay love. Nothing important," Frank reassured her.

The couple's two daughters appeared in their nightdresses following their mother into the room.

139

"Back to bed," Frank ordered them, waving the girls away. "Everything's alright. Go back to bed." They left the room.

The Parker brothers nodded a brief greeting to Brenda then quickly let themselves out of the flat.

"What the bloody hell are they doing here in the middle of the night?" Brenda demanded.

"Nothing to worry about. Just a bit of business," Frank attempted to calm her.

"In the middle of the night?"

"It's alright. Nothing to worry about," he repeated.

"Nothing to worry about? Ever since you started working for those two I hardly ever see you, and you carry loads of secrets," Brenda's frustrations came spilling out, her usual tolerance weakened at being woken so abruptly in the night.

"Yeah, and we've been a lot better off with money since I started working for them," Frank hit back.

"Look after Lindy, did I hear Dave say?" Brenda rounded on him. "You've been fucking her for ages, haven't you?"

Her words sliced through him like a knife. He thought his affair with Lindy was a complete secret. Somehow Brenda knew. He realised it would be useless to deny the fact.

"It's nothing. I don't love her," Frank offered a feeble defence.

"We are done. We are finished. I can't put up with this anymore, knowing you're happy to fuck other women and working for those bastard gangsters. You'll all end up inside one day leaving me and the girls destitute." Brenda stormed out of the room.

Frank did love his wife and daughters, but he loved the money more. And now there was the prospect of taking over the Parker brothers' operation. That was power. He was not going back to being an odd job van driver, or as a labourer on the building sites just to satisfy his wife's peace of mind.

In the event, the Parker brothers were picked up by the police and, despite the best efforts of their lawyers, were found guilty of masterminding the robbery. The sentence was twenty years behind bars. Frank had become top man.

The split with his wife and daughters had been painful, but he made sure they didn't suffer financially, and visited the girls often. He also fulfilled Dave Parker's wish looking after his wife Lindy, though in an intimate way the man hadn't envisaged, as well as providing for daughter Lucy. Frank's unexpected rise to the top brought him much greater income. Enough to buy a grand house where they now lived together.

The door opened while Tony was in the kitchen with Frank and Lindy. Lucy stood there in a pink frock, a red ribbon tied in a bow on her long fair hair. Tony's heart fluttered. She looked beautiful.

"You remember Tony, don't you?" Lindy asked her. The girl smiled.

"Come and say hello to him."

Tony got up from the kitchen table as she approached. It was a long time since he'd last seen her and she appeared so much more grown up now.

141

"Do you still like comics?" the girl asked. Tony nodded. He was feeling shy in her magnificent presence.

"Come up to my room. I've got more annuals," Lucy invited him. Eagerly he began to follow her.

"You can't do that now," Lindy interrupted. "Tony's going with his uncle Frank. He's going to help him at work."

Tony stopped, bitterly disappointed. He was besotted with the girl and wanted to spend more time with her.

"Come on Tony. Time to go." Frank began walking to the door. The boy followed, smiling at Lucy. He wanted to kiss her on the cheek, but resisted in fear of an adverse reaction from all present.

As Frank drove off in the car, Tony plucked up the courage to ask a question.

"Can I see Lucy again soon?" he felt his cheeks flush red with embarrassment as the words came out. He didn't want people to think he was in love with the girl. Grown-ups could tease about such things.

Frank grinned.

"Why, are you in love with her?"

Tony's face flushed redder. He wished he hadn't asked. Silence filled the air for a moment. Frank broke it.

"Well, if you work hard for me, it could be arranged."

The boy resolved to work very hard for him.

******

FRANK took his nephew to the same club in Soho where he'd been several years earlier, helping his uncle in a fight.

142

The small yard at the back looked cleaner, no scattered litter or overflowing dustbin. His uncle led a more professional operation with the passing of the Parker regime, but the lucrative seedy side of the business continued as normal.

Tony was put to work in the club basement, unpacking crates and boxes of beer, spirits and cigarette packs for supply to the bar.

A middle aged man called Ron, whose craggy face through over indulgence in alcohol had etched the appearance of a seventy year old, helped him with the unpacking. He wore a white shirt with rolled up sleeves that begged for a good wash. He was a friendly person, but had to stop every so often to take a swig from the whisky bottle perched on an upturned crate.

"I used to run this club for the Parker brothers," Ron boasted to Tony during a drink interval. "All changed now. They don't want me anymore."

Ron replaced the bottle on the crate and scratched his thinning grey hair as if for a moment he couldn't remember what he was meant to be doing.

Tony thought him a bit strange, though likeable enough.

As the two of them got back to work again, a man's head poked round the door leading up the stairs to the bar.

"I need a bottle of gin and whisky," he called to them. The man disappeared.

"It's Luke the barman," explained Ron. "Here, you take them up," he reached for the bottles on a shelf and handed them over.

Men sat drinking at the bar as Tony entered. He remembered the club room from his last visit, but everywhere now looked brighter. The place had been completely refurbished.

Handing the spirit bottles to Luke, he was about to return to the basement when a young woman with peroxide blonde hair, dressed in a dark satin top and short black skirt, entered from a door beside the bar. She began crossing the room towards another door on the far side when she caught sight of Tony.

"Oh you little cutie," the woman came over and stooped to kiss him. As she bent down her short skirt rose to reveal her knickers. Whoops and wolf whistles flew from the men at the bar. For the second time that day Tony's face flushed with embarrassment, suddenly having all attention focussed in his direction and being treated like a little boy.

He pulled away from the kiss.

"He's shy aren't you little one?" she reached out and patted him on the head.

"I'm not shy! Come and give me a kiss Annie," one of the men called from the bar.

"I don't kiss ugly sods like you," Annie retorted giving him a V sign. The other men burst into laughter. Tony wished the floor would swallow him.

"What's going on?" a voice boomed above the commotion. A beefy man in a dark suit entered the room. The club bouncer.

"I'm making a date with my new boyfriend," Annie replied, smiling at Tony.

"You shouldn't be out here right now," he snarled.

144

"Just going to the dressing room." The woman gave him a sarcastic curtsy and continued to the door on the far side. The men at the bar resumed their conversation and drinking. The bouncer's stare was enough to make them behave.

Tony returned to the basement totally humiliated. He'd felt like a big man working in his uncle's club. Now he'd been deposed as a small cog in a baffling adult world. Why wouldn't they stop treating him like a little boy?

The feeling of inferiority passed in the next few hours, and when his uncle returned from business visits to other clubs in the area, Tony's spirits rose again.

"Ron tells me you've been a really good worker," Frank greeted him. Ron's shift had ended for the day and he was now upstairs in the bar adding a few more whiskies to his liver.

Frank drove the boy back to his nan's, and just before Tony got out of the car his uncle handed him a ten pound note.

"Your wages."

Tony's eyes widened in sheer amazement. He'd never been given so much money in his life.

"You get good rewards for doing what you're told," Frank said. "I see a great future for you and me." The last remark baffled the boy. But it didn't matter. He was rich. Ten pounds!

When he arrived home his mother opened the door.

"Look how much uncle Frank paid me!" he showed the note with pride. Irene's eyes widened in amazement.

145

"Don't show it to your father," she looked concerned. Tony's moment of joy fell flat.

"Why?"

"Because I'm telling you, that's why. Now give it to me. It's a lot of money and you can have it bit by bit."

"But it's my money," Tony protested, reluctantly handing the money over.

Irene looked down the hallway to the closed living room door hoping her husband watching TV didn't come out to see them.

"Don't tell your dad," she ordered her son. Now the boy was totally confused. He thought his dad would be really pleased to see he'd earned so much money.

"Now go to your bedroom and get undressed. You're having a bath."

Bitterly disappointed with his mother's reaction to the triumph he'd earned, Tony sloped off to his bedroom.

Irene was thrilled with her son's fabulous earnings, but she couldn't let her husband know. The money was almost as much as Gerry's weekly wage. It would greatly rankle if he learned the boy had picked up nearly a week's money in one afternoon. The money would stoke another furious argument, likely leading Gerry to forbid him working for his uncle again.

Irene wished her husband would wise-up and get a job maybe connected to her brother's obviously lucrative enterprise, instead of spending years studying and taking exams on a small income to eventually become a solicitor. They needed money now, not when they had grey hair.

Tony kept to Irene's wish, telling his father that he was paid with free drinks of lemonade and packets of crisps. The subterfuge allowed him to continue working on Saturdays at the club for another month before two major changes took the family in an entirely new direction.

The first was Gerry announcing that his application for a council house transfer to a newly built flat in Roehampton had been approved, promising a new life away from the rundown setting where they lived, to a leafier place in the outer London suburb.

Irene was still unsure about moving ten miles away from the only area she'd ever known, relatives and friends. But as well as Tony's future, she was encouraged by the prospect of having a modern kitchen, bathroom and two larger bedrooms. The place also had the luxury of central heating. She was swayed without further argument.

The second major change focussed on Tony.

"I'm taking you out of your present school and sending you to a new one," Gerry told his son after calling him into the living room for a chat. Tony was not disappointed he'd be leaving Spencer House. He had a few friends there, but none of a particular attachment. They all lived in a higher strata of life far removed from his own.

However the next part of the change lined up for him left the boy uncertain.

"It's a boarding school in North Wales," said Gerry. Tony was puzzled, he had no idea what his father meant.

"It's a school where you stay away from home. You get holidays when you can come home, but you live there while you're away."

That didn't seem like a good idea to the youngster.

"Where's North Wales?" he asked. Gerry was surprised his son hadn't learned that in geography lessons.

"A country in Britain where Welsh people live."

"How far away?"

"Your school is in a place called Wynngryth. It's about two hundred miles away."

Tony's jaw dropped. That sounded like the outer universe.

"Why are you sending me away? Have I done something wrong?" Tears began rolling down the boy's cheeks.

"No son, I just think it will be better for you," Gerry placed his hand on Tony's shoulder attempting to comfort him. Tony shook it away and rushed off to his bedroom.

Gerry stood there. His own ambition to rise above the lowly class he'd been born into was driving him to instil the same ambition in his son. So far, it wasn't working out that way. He'd been called to the headmaster's office at Spencer House a month earlier. Selwyn Turnberry told him that Tony was not making good academic progress, and perhaps he would do better being sent to a boarding school that took him out of his home environment.

"Somewhere that the boy can learn to survive in his own right. Teach him to stand on his own two feet," Turnberry advised. "I think that would persuade him to take his education more seriously, free from street people outside school who, shall we say, in his present circumstances are not a good influence on him."

Gerry knew the head was referring to the bottom rung of society as he saw it, for whom the daybreak on a brighter

148

future for their lives would always be fractured from birth. Lack of good education condemning them to a lesser existence.

Gerry's first step to physically uproot from the area was being fulfilled. Now moving his son to a setting where distractions out of school would be minimised seemed the next best step.

Of course private education, especially at boarding schools, was expensive. But he could rely on Irene to work more overtime to help supplement the extra cost involved. He couldn't work overtime in his own job, since junior legals were expected to put in longer hours without extra pay. And he had other expenses.

"Money burns a bloody hole in your pocket!" Irene's cry at Gerry's spending habits on new suits and beer often haunted his mind.

After much researching he'd found a school with fees that looked affordable at a pinch. Sandalwood College at Wynngryth, North Wales.

The place would become an education for Tony, but not remotely in the way Gerry imagined.

CHAPTER 6

THE new family home turned out to be a maisonette at the top of a high rise block. Tony had never lived in a place with upstairs rooms. He loved his new bedroom on the second floor with space for a bedside table, a chest of drawers and a wardrobe. The room was enormous compared to where he'd lived.

Irene had never looked so happy, thrilled by her new kitchen with room for a twin-tub clothes washer and fridge, when she could afford them, as well as plenty of cupboards and shelves.

The views from each side of the place stretched high across houses and trees into the hazy horizon. At night the landscape was lit by homes and street lights illuminating the vast setting.

"It's just like fairyland," Irene would often remark at the sight. Day and night the new home was unimaginably different to the drab world they'd left behind.

In the evening Gerry contentedly filled the spacious living room with pipe smoke, sitting on the sofa watching television. Tony had never know such lengthy peace between his parents, hardly an argument passing their lips.

But his experience of harmony was short lived. Two weeks later he stood dressed in his new Sandalwood College uniform, a navy blue jacket and dark grey trousers, ready to board the train at London's Paddington station for the two hundred miles journey to Wynngryth.

His parents were there to see him off, and Irene's eyes filled with tears at the prospect of not seeing her son again for three months until the school holidays. Tony felt tearful too at the parting, but daren't show his emotions with all the other college boys present on the platform bidding farewell to their parents.

Gerry stood stiffly resolute in his smart charcoal suit, managing a goodbye tap on his son's shoulder. He strongly believed in the stiff upper lip to deal with feelings of emotion in public. Irene kissed Tony on the cheek and he boarded the train with the other boys.

His compartment was filled with newcomers, and for the early part of the journey hardly a word passed between them, absorbed in their own thoughts and already feeling homesick on the journey into the unknown.

After a while, one of them ventured to change the mood.

"Where do you live?" he asked the boy sitting next to him.

"Purley," he replied.

"I live near there at Sutton," another came in.

The ice was broken and conversation filled the air.

A couple of hours had passed when the compartment door was drawn open. An older boy dressed in the college uniform stared at the group from the corridor.

"All new boys, eh?" He grinned wickedly. "Missing your mums? They won't be able to kiss and cuddle their little darlings where you're going."

The patronising tone of the intruder annoyed Tony.

"Oh, we've got a big boy here, have we?"

The older boy, who Tony guessed was seventeen, stepped into the compartment and approached him. He reached into his jacket pocket and pulled out a knife. With a click the blade opened.

"You want to watch yourself sonny," he warned Tony, pointing the blade at his face. "Or you might not live to go very far." With his other hand he closed the blade.

"I'll be looking out for you," the youth sneered, then gazed contemptuously round at the newcomers before returning to the corridor.

The comradeship that had been building between the boys was silenced for some time, all fearful of what hell might be awaiting them in the loneliness of their new world.

Gerry thought he was sending his son to a college of young gentlemen. He was badly mistaken.

******

THE BOYS were taken by bus from the Wynngryth station to the college situated a mile away. As the vehicle travelled down the long entrance driveway, a huge greystone stately home came into view, topped by four mansard roof towers at each corner.

Once owned by a wealthy family, the property had been converted into a college when the last of the family line found the upkeep too costly and sold it.

The building seemed steeped in gloom under a heavy sky threatening rain. Tony wanted to leave for home, but it would be difficult travelling two hundred miles without any money to buy a train ticket. Similar thoughts ran through his new companions' minds, one of them starting to cry.

On arrival at the front entrance with a couple more coachloads of pupils, they were led into a large dining room, long tables and benches spread across its length to accommodate the three hundred boys at the college. Large trays containing shepherd's pie were placed on the tables to provide them all with an evening meal.

Tony scooped a portion with a spatula on to his plate. The general opinion was that it looked and tasted revolting.

In early evening, the thirty newcomers were summoned to the assembly hall, another huge room with dark wood panelling all around. A grey-haired man draped in his university gown stood on a podium staring curiously at the new intake through gold rimmed spectacles.

"I am Dr. Goldacre, the headmaster of Sandalwood College, and I wish to welcome you all," he began when they'd settled quietly.

"What a boring looking man," Tony said to the boy next to him.

"What did you say?" the headmaster's hearing was not as decrepit as Tony had imagined.

"Nothing sir," his face turned red.

The head continued staring at him for what seemed an eternity, then resumed.

"We hope everyone here will work hard and be happy. But we will not tolerate insolent or bad behaviour," the man concluded his talk, directing the closing remark at Tony.

As they broke up to be shown their dormitories, some of the boys thought Tony had been quite heroic.

"I wouldn't have dared say that," one patted him on the back.

"Lucky he didn't cane you," came another.

Their excited chatter was short lived as they followed a man leading them up a broad flight of stairs and filtering them to different dormitories.

In Tony's, green paint was peeling off the walls revealing crumbling plaster beneath. The metal frame beds numbering eight each side of the room were covered with thin blankets. Sheets worn threadbare peered over the top. Battered cabinets, for clothes and personal possessions, stood sadly in line beside each bed and the bare floorboards showed signs of woodworm.

Tony and his roommates undressed and put on their pyjamas, unpacked earlier by the college matron from their luggage trunks. Next it was ablutions in the adjoining washroom and then into bed.

That was the hard part. Literally. Tony's mattress was deeply worn and near wafer thin. Not a spring in its guts. Although it was early September, the night air of Wynngryth, set close to the Snowdonia mountains, grew chilly. Devoid of any heating, he shivered beneath the spartan bed covering.

Tony could hear one of the boys trying to stifle a cry of homesickness. Another started snoring. He lay awake for ages, the moon now free from a passing cloud shot a beam through the tall curtainless window beside his bed, highlighting the peeling paint on the opposite wall.

Thoughts of home drifted through his mind as he drifted into sleep and it didn't seem many moments had passed when he was woken by shouting.

"Come on, come on, wake up!" an older youth stood in the dormitory calling commands and loudly clapping his hands. Being new, the youngsters didn't know he was Stevens, a prefect, responsible for this wing of the college. They soon would, as his rousing morning calls became a regular feature. It was seven o'clock. The sun was rising above a distant mountain peak, streaming across fields and valleys, making the gloomy dormitory appear a little brighter.

After breakfast of cereal and scrambled egg, another prefect shepherded Tony with a group of other new boys into a classroom of grim desks, carved with countless initials of former pupils, and badly in need of replacement. The first lesson on the timetable was mathematics.

A few minutes later an elderly man appeared, his university gown flowing around his shoulders like an aged spectre. He jerked forward in small unsteady steps taking position behind the desk at the front of the classroom.

His bald head with a deep dent on one side were the only smooth features on his otherwise deeply wrinkled face. To the youngsters watching him he appeared to be knocking on the door of one hundred years, soon for it to open into the next life.

Swaying slightly he stared at the boys and in a feeble voice told them to sit down. They looked puzzled and remained standing. It took the teacher a few more moments to realise why he hadn't been obeyed. There were no chairs in the classroom.

"No chairs," he uttered as if it was a revelation to him.

He turned and slowly shuffled out. When he'd gone, the boys burst out laughing.

"He looks like an old Dracula," one of them joked. The boy was unaware yet that ol' Drac was his college nickname.

For some time the class waited in belief the man had left to organise a supply of chairs. They waited and waited for the full forty minutes of the lesson, but he never reappeared.

Over the next few days after chairs were eventually provided, the class had a succession of the oddest teachers they'd ever come across.

Hamilton Crosby had a nervous delivery of words as he attempted to educate the class in biology, often stopping mid-sentence before continuing. He frequently kept striking his forehead hard in twitchy attempts to brush back hair from his side parting which constantly flopped down.

Tony couldn't help giggling as the man continually struck his head.

"What are you laughing at?" Hamilton Crosby demanded.

"Nothing sir."

Yes you are. Come here!" The man began shaking with rage.

Tony made his way cautiously to the front.

"Bend over the desk!" Crosby's face had turned red with fury, his eyes manic. He tore off his shoe and started to thrash Tony, except the man was in such an uncontrollable frenzy most of the blows struck the desk. But those that hit home really stung.

The teacher's insane performance drove the rest of the class into stifled stitches of laughter almost making punishment worthwhile to see the madman raging. This was someone they could goad for amusement.

When Crosby began chalking on the blackboard some of the boys began tearing pieces off the blotting paper on their desks, rolling it into a ball with saliva and using their rulers to flick the soggy missiles at the ceiling just above his head.

The projectiles stuck for a few minutes, then gradually lost their grip dropping down on to the teacher's desk. One of them landed on his head.

Crosby brushed it away in disgust, then stared evilly at the boys before flying into another raging frenzy, threatening dire punishment and wildly throwing the chalk in his hand at them. Grabbing his books from the desk, he stormed out of the room.

Mr Phillips was altogether different. Down to earth and entirely sane. Under a crop of dark curly hair his eyes shone brightly like searchlights seeking out anyone who dared question his authority.

A stocky man, he brooked no misbehaviour. Whether his pupils took in the history he taught didn't overly concern him. Some kids listened others didn't. Simple. If anyone got out of line, talking, trying to read a comic below the desk, he'd launch the hard, wood backed blackboard duster at their head with pinpoint accuracy. The blow gained rapid attention. But the boys really liked him and his no nonsense approach.

Being away from home introduced an entirely new dimension to Tony's life. There was no home refuge to seek protection from difficulties. He was out on his own like the other new boarders, with no familiar friends or bonds of friendship yet formed.

The teachers were only part of his existence at Sandalwood College, the main event was surviving among his junior colleagues and in the towering presence of the senior, older pupils.

Tony thought he'd left the violence of London's east end behind. The incident when a senior boy pulled a knife on him in the train had shown otherwise. That memory was fading until he heard a conversation between two seniors in a corridor.

"Where's Dippy Roberts and Psycho Harris? Haven't seen them for a while," one asked.

"They've been expelled," the other replied.

"Why?"

"They were down in the village and some local lads told them to stay away from some girls they were dating. Threatened them."

"Dangerous."

"Yep. Pyscho and Dippy came back here, unhooked a couple of lavatory chains from the toilets and went back to the village. They smashed up the local lads with the chains putting them in hospital."

"No!"

"So now they've been expelled."

"Stupid sods threatening those two nutcases."

The boys wandered off down the corridor.

Tony hoped the college senior who'd threatened him on the train was one of those who'd been expelled. His hope was short lived.

A day later he was coming down one of the numerous back staircases connecting dormitories and rooms in the building, and starting to walk along a narrow passageway to his classroom. A door at the end of the passage opened just as he reached it. A boy a few years older than him was about to pass by, when he suddenly stopped.

"Don't I know you?" his eyes were searching for recognition.

Tony immediately realised he was the one who'd confronted him on the train. His blood ran cold.

"No," he replied, hoping his adversary would accept his answer.

A wicked smile began to emerge on the senior's face as he remembered the incident.

"You're that little bugger who dared to answer me back on the train," he stood astride to block any effort by Tony to pass.

"No-one around to see me stab you now," his aggressor swaggered.

Tony was terrified he'd pull out the flick knife. The boy began jabbing him in the chest with his finger, driving him back towards the stairway.

The jabbing became intensely irritating. Tony began imagining Billy talking to him, 'don't let some idiot bully push you around'. Swiftly he lashed out with a hard blow to

159

the boy's face. A look of shock rose as he staggered back from the impact, his hand reaching for the pain. He drew it away and saw blood from the nose bleed. Tony prepared for a counter attack.

"Don't! Don't hit me again," his enemy whimpered, moving away and taking a handkerchief from his pocket to wipe away the blood.

"Then don't piss me off again!" Tony warned, now feeling a giant in the older boy's presence.

"I won't. I won't," he promised, standing aside to let him pass.

Tony wasn't sure if it was a ploy for an attack from behind and made his way cautiously, but his adversary was too busy nursing the nose bleed to offer any more resistance.

He wasn't happy with the idea of the senior possessing a flick knife, but he couldn't report it to any teachers. That would be snitching. And anyone who snitched on others would be treated like a pariah by everyone. Life wouldn't be worth living. It was an unwritten code.

Tony managed to survive the first term at the college, absorbing a certain amount of knowledge, but needing more to learn about coping with oddballs, bad meals and avoiding being caned, especially by six foot six teacher, Mr Thompson, whose whacks on the arse literally catapulted boys across the room.

He was met by Gerry and Irene on arrival back at Paddington station for the start of the school holidays.

His mother hugged him tearfully. Gerry stood resolutely upright as usual and formally welcomed his son back with a handshake. He hoped the college was turning him into a gentleman.

"Are they a good crew there?" he asked.

"Yes dad." Tony wished his father wasn't so serious and remote. If he told Gerry what he'd really experienced there, it would be dismissed as exaggerated rubbish. Good money was being paid for a proper education and nothing would sway his dad from that belief.

Home by contrast to college was super luxury for Tony. Warmth, a soft mattress, comics, toys. Even his mother's cooking, which hadn't seemed so great, now became the best food he'd tasted in ages compared to the blandness of the Sandalwood menu.

One thing he missed in his new home were friends. He'd had no time to make any before being whisked away to North Wales. There were several other blocks of maisonettes on the new council estate, with expansive areas of grass landscaping around them. A welcome setting from the previous bomb site surrounds and he wanted to explore the new territory.

After a day of relaxing at home, he ventured out to see if he could meet others of his own age living on the estate. Descending in the lift from the top floor, he stepped out to see three boys sitting opposite on a low wall beneath the cover of the building, which was supported by rows of tall concrete pillars.

He stood wondering if he should strike up conversation with them.

"What you starin' at?" one asked, sounding less than friendly. A greasy quiff was neatly crafted on his head, just like his two companions. Tony's hair was side parted. No fancy hairstyles were permitted at the college. The trivial difference in hair immediately set him apart from them.

"I've just started living here," Tony attempted to break the style barrier between them.

"Sounds like a posh boy," another of the trio remarked.

Tony wasn't aware of it, but his time in private schooling among a better spoken class had rubbed off. The old east London accent was disappearing. And the chance of his fresh start in the new area seemed to be disappearing with it.

Other families from rundown parts of London had also been rehoused in these modern blocks of maisonettes, many bringing with them their rough street culture.

"What school do you go to?" the boys quizzed. The one in the middle of the trio slipped down from the wall, followed by his friends. They approached Tony. He struggled for a reply. He couldn't say he was going to a private school, that would really set him apart. These boys certainly weren't being privately educated. He could sense they came from the same London background as him. And anyone they judged as posh would get a hard time.

"Bury Street school," Tony made up a name hoping they'd accept it.

"Where's that?"

"It's not far away. A couple of miles."

The boys looked at each other. They'd never heard of it. They hadn't lived long in the area and gave Tony the benefit of the doubt that it existed.

The boy who appeared to be the leader of the group was taller than his companions. He wore blue jeans and a black leather jacket. Studying Tony, he took a comb from his pocket and carefully drew it through the quiff to make sure the crest remained rigidly in place.

"Where have you moved from?" he quizzed further, his mates beginning to close round Tony.

"Hardwick House. It's in Hope Street. Stepney."

"I lived near there one of the boys close to Tony's side broke in.

"Tell me the name of some shops in Cable Street," the leader with the superior quiff wanted to be sure Tony was telling the truth. He reeled off some names.

"Welcome mate," the boy declared, patting Tony on the shoulder. "But why d'ye talk in that posh way?" The boy was puzzled. It wasn't the familiar accent he and his friends spoke and knew.

"My dad tells me to talk like that."

It was true. Gerry encouraged him to speak the way of gentlemen and not like a commoner. Tony launched into his former accent to convince the boys.

"I'm Rob," the leader introduced himself. "And this is Eddie and Alfie."

"I'm Tony."

The barrier between them collapsed. He was a member of the gang.

"We're going to Richmond Park," Rob announced. "D'ye wanna come?"

Tony nodded. He heard his father mention Richmond Park, but had no idea where it was or how far. He just

163

followed his new friends as they set off down the broad grass slope descending away from the tower blocks to a road below.

After walking half-a-mile on the roadside, they came to a high wrought iron gate opening on to the park. As they entered Tony was awestruck by the fields and trees spread before him. Being whisked away to boarding school soon after moving to Roehampton, there had been no time to properly explore his new home surroundings. There was nothing remotely like this around Hardwick House.

His companions saw the look on his face.

"Ain't you been here?" asked Eddie, surprised that someone living locally didn't seem to know the place.

"No, I've been staying with my aunt for a lot of the time. She lives in Colchester," Tony half lied.

He did have an aunt who lived in that town, and he'd seen her once years ago, but had no idea where the place was located. The name just came into his head as a way of explaining why for a local person he hadn't seen the park.

Now his new friends looked puzzled again.

"My mum and dad have been ill. I had to stay with my aunt." Tony told a full lie, still terrified they would discover he was going to a posh boys school as they would see it. But to his relief, they appeared to accept his explanation.

"There's real deer in here," said Alfie. He was a wiry, thin boy whose quiff dominated his bony forehead like a giant surf wave.

"And rabbits. I've seen rabbits," Eddie added, his tubby frame and bloated round face in total contrast to his thin companion.

"They're hares, not rabbits," Rob corrected him in a surly, superior tone. "I know what rabbits and hares look like. Seen it in a book, and they're different."

Eddie disagreed, but said nothing. Rob was muscular and would give him a good kicking if he dared question his leader's authority. They walked across a field rising to a cluster of trees.

"Look, there's some deer!" Alfie pointed to the animals gathered beneath the branches, sniffing and munching at undergrowth. As they approached, the creatures looked up, growing edgy. Slowly they began to back away and then broke into a trot gaining a safe distance from the visitors.

"They won't let you get near them," Alfie declared, as if none of his friends were intelligent enough to see for themselves. The boys went back down the field to a stream running through the park.

"D'ye think there's fish in there?" asked Eddie.

"Of course there's bloody fish in there, dozy sod," Rob sneered at him. "There's always fish in streams and rivers," he announced with an air of supreme knowledge. "Look, there's one!" Rob pointed at a silver skinned fish edging slowly through the clear flowing water.

"It's a carp," said Alfie.

"No, it's a trout," Eddie disagreed.

"It's a salmon," Rob pronounced.

"You don't get salmon here." Eddie was pushing his luck disagreeing with his boss. Rob turned on him with a snarl.

"Yes, it's a salmon," Eddie corrected himself just in time.

"What do think it is Tony?" Rob tested his opinion.

Tony had no idea, and the fish was now slipping rapidly away from sight down the stream. It could have been a hump backed whale for all his knowledge of aquatic life, beyond the angel fish his father once kept in a tank at their old home.

"Definitely a salmon," he replied, not wishing to upset the delicate balance of his new friendship.

"Told you!" Rob boasted triumphantly to the other two, a smug grin rising on his face.

As they walked a little further along the bank of the stream, two young girls were approaching from the opposite direction wearing short skirts and revealing shapely legs.

Rob couldn't resist taking the lead as top guy.

"How about a kiss darlings?" he stepped towards them as they drew near. The girls began giggling. Tony thought they looked really attractive. His liking for girls was growing stronger. His younger indifferent feelings towards them was now changing to a sensation of attraction.

A well thumbed copy of Parade magazine featuring scantily dressed women, which was passed around in his dormitory at college, often led to pleasurable fantasies under the bedsheets at night.

Now Rob's would-be female conquests stopped beside him.

"You can't resist my handsome looks, can you?" he said, opening his arms for an embrace and showing off to his friends the power he had over the opposite sex.

One of the girls with blonde hair giggled again. Her darker haired companion looked at him like a piece of low life.

"We don't go out with little boys, sonny," she said. "When you grow up, we might consider you. But I doubt it."

Rob's face fell. The girls began laughing and continued on their way. The leader's companions stifled their own laughter, Alfie and Eddie in particular overjoyed at seeing their master put down by a couple of girls.

"Slags!" Rob shouted after them, desperately trying to maintain his superiority. "They were ugly anyway," he dismissed his rebuttal. That was not the opinion of his gang, but they remained silent. Tony was rapidly coming to the belief that the boy was a vacuous idiot, but he'd made some friends. It was a start.

"Let's go to the village," Rob changed the subject. All of them agreed.

Retracing their steps along the roadside they came to Roehampton village. It was largely untouched by time from the sleepy place it had been for a hundred years or more. A couple of pubs, a church, village store, newsagent and terraced houses.

But the area was under rapid change, earmarked for development to re-house thousands from the London slums. Construction workers on a plot nearby were already busy laying the foundations for a new tower block and shopping parade.

"This place is dead," Rob concluded. There wasn't a cafe, cinema, fish and chip shop, nothing he'd been familiar

167

with near his old home in south London. "Let's go to the newsagent and nick some sweets," he concluded.

Alfie and Eddie weren't keen. They didn't mind appearing tough, but they didn't really like doing anything that could land them in trouble. Tony thought it was a stupid idea, remembering his excursions into crime and the unhappiness it had brought him. He shook his head, declining.

"So you're chicken?" Rob goaded.

"Not chicken. Sweets are for babies," Tony replied.

Eddie and Alfie's jaws dropped. The newcomer was putting down their leader. Rob's face became thunderous. He stared evilly at Tony. Then the storm passed.

"You're right," he said, "just wanted to see if these two tits agreed," pointing to Eddie and Alfie. "They're still babies." He enjoyed treating them like dirt.

The balance of power was shifting. Tony began to realise that Rob was more a bag of wind than a tough guy.

"Well, since there's fuck all to do in this dump, we might as well go home," the leader concluded.

They started to make their way back along the road when not more than a hundred yards in front of them a group of five boys appeared.

"It's Dennis Taylor and his mob," Rob announced. "They think they run this place."

Alfie and Eddie looked twitchy. Rob broke into a swaggering stride. Tony wondered what trouble was brewing. Both groups grew near to each other then stopped a few yards apart.

"Your mum let you out has she?" the lead boy standing slightly ahead of his gang mouthed the insult.

Tony took him to be the boy named Dennis Taylor, wearing rolled up shirt sleeves and jeans, short cropped hair on a hard face edging for a fight.

"At least my mum ain't a slag like yours," Rob snapped back.

"No-one calls my mum a slag and gets away with it!" Dennis lashed out at Rob. His gang followed, fists flying at Tony and the boys beside him. Tony side stepped a blow and lashed out hitting his attacker's chin. The boy faltered, dazed for a second. Tony saw Eddie taking a hammering in the head and stomach. He leapt in giving the attacker a side head blow.

As his punch impacted, he felt a sharp pain in his side from an attacking kick. For a moment Tony's defence was broken and the boy he'd just hit took advantage, pummelling him in the head and splitting his lip.

From a side glance, he briefly saw Rob and Dennis rolling around on the pavement in a lashing tussle of punches. Then he saw his attacker facing him, a look of triumph rising in his eyes ready to deliver the killer blow. In the same second a move taught him by Billy flashed into his head. He grabbed his opponent by the shoulders, pulling him close and striking a swift knee blow at his balls.

The boy yelled in agony, bending forward to grasp the pain, his head bowed low enough for Tony to kick it hard and send him sprawling on the ground.

169

Eddie was taking a heavy beating from two of Dennis' gang. Tony began to move in to help when a loud shout rang out.

"Clear off you fucking sods!" The man's voice made them freeze.

"I've called the police. They're on their way."

The boys saw the man on the other side of the road. Several other adults were beginning to gather near him. The prospect of being taken in by the police rapidly brought them back to their half-dazed senses.

Rob and Dennis sprang up from the pavement, suffering the least injuries of all from just rolling around clutching each other and unable to deliver any significant blows. Quickly both gangs took off, some half limping from injury, making for home as fast as possible.

As Tony and his friends reached the safety of their own territory beside the lifts under the maisonette block, they realised Alfie wasn't with them.

"Where is he?" asked Rob.

"He ran off when the fight started," Eddie informed him, nursing a large lump rising on his forehead, his left eye disappearing into a bruised purple swelling.

"The bloody chicken!" Rob was furious. "Wait 'til I see him next."

"You did bloody good Tony," he praised the latest gang member, anger on his face turning into an admiring smile.

Tony nursed a split lip, looking at the blood from it streaked across his finger. His so called leader wasn't bearing any marks of battle, except his quiff now flopping untidily over his forehead, and his clothes dusty from rolling around on the pavement. But Tony was pleased with the praise.

"Yeah, and thanks for coming to help me out," Eddie added.

"Your a great gang member," Rob patted him on the shoulder.

It was a short lived moment of triumph.

Parting company he went into the lift taking him up to his home on the top floor. Irene took an entirely different view of the situation when she opened the door.

"What in God's name happened to you?"

"Nothing. I just fell over," Tony attempted to play it down.

"No you didn't. You've been fighting ain't you?"

Gerry appeared a few moments later as Tony stepped inside. He just stared at his son, seeing the trail of drying blood that trickled from the split lip down his chin.

"I thought we'd left all that behind," he said mournfully.

Irene took hold of Tony's head, examining the lip wound and a bruise just below his left eye.

"That's it," Gerry declared in a soft voice, masking the fury and disappointment building inside.

"Every weekday while me and your mother are out at work, you will travel to town and stay with your nan," he announced. "You obviously can't be trusted to stay at home on your own. And you will not go out with your uncle Frank if he calls round there, or any of your friends in the area."

Tony was effectively under house arrest.

"If you disobey me, I will arrange for you to remain at your college through every school holiday so that you don't come home for years."

Tony knew a few boarders, whose parents worked in faraway parts abroad, that spent the holidays staying at the college and were looked after by live-in teachers. Irene didn't think they'd be able to afford any such extra accommodation. And she wouldn't put up with an arrangement where she didn't see her son, though she realised the warning was necessary to steer Tony from trouble.

The boy's hope was that if he behaved and did as his father commanded for a while, he'd be allowed his freedom again.

"Now get your clothes off and start running the bath," Irene ordered. Tony left, head bowed. No hero in his parents' eyes.

******

THE daily journey by bus and train to his nan's became a punishing drudge for him. Confined to her flat there was little to do but read the comics Joyce provided, the American imports bought from stalls selling books and magazines at the local market.

She'd been sad when her grandson moved away, missing him and fearing he would grow distant from her in his new existence. Joyce had no reason to be fearful. Tony loved his nan dearly for her kindness and love. The comics and cakes

172

were an added bonus. But the routine of confinement became tedious.

The two days holiday over Christmas was a brighter time. Especially when Tony received a new train set. For a short while he enjoyed his father's company as they played together setting up the track in the living room and taking goes with the train. Christmas dinner of roast turkey was also a rare treat.

A few days before Tony returned to college, Frank called in at his nan's. Tony greeted his uncle with a smile and thought some money might be pressed into his hand with a magic trick.

But Frank's face was unsmiling. He nodded to his nephew distantly as if the boy was hardly there, then went into the kitchen where Joyce was putting on the kettle for tea.

Tony heard them talking in hushed tones while he sat with a comic in the living room. Five minutes later Frank came into the room.

"Can I come out with you?" the boy asked eagerly, forgetting his father's strict order to remain indoors.

"No, not today," Frank replied, still distant. He mumbled a goodbye and left.

Tony wondered what was wrong. Had he done something to offend his uncle? He'd never seen the man in a dark mood before.

What he didn't know was Parker brother, Dave, had discovered in prison that his wife Lindy and daughter Lucy were now living in Frank's new house. He was not a happy man, his wife taking up with the person he'd trusted to

173

stand-in for him and his brother, Lenny. They hadn't anticipated being given a long sentence, but incarcerated they still controlled outside finance and contacts, and had put up a big reward for anyone who eliminated Frank.

Frank had got word of it, stepping up his own security and warning his family to watch for any suspicious people or activities. His visit to Joyce that day had been to inform her that his own network had traced the three would be assassins, and that their bodies would shortly be disposed in the concrete foundation of a new office block being built in London.

He warned her the police might be calling to make enquiries about the family. Of course, Joyce was always able to play the silly old woman on the edge of senility when required. Frank could rest assured she knew nothing about her son's employment.

Tony would never know his uncle's refusal was necessary to keep him away from any high risk activity at this crucial time. He'd hoped Frank might have taken him to see Lucy at their house. She was on his mind quite a lot.

CHAPTER 7

TONY had been back at college for a couple of days after the Christmas break when he thought he recognised a familiar face in the corridor coming towards him.

He'd just come from an extraordinary lesson with ol' Drac. The ancient teacher had shuffled in as usual to take the class in his flowing dark gown, and paused beside the desk at the front to stare disapprovingly at the blackboard.

"Terrible state," he murmured, shaking his head. With that he turned and shuffled back out the room. He was right, the blackboard was in a terrible state, deeply scratched and dotted with holes, the surface appeared worn out from years of chalking and sharp missiles launched at it by previous pupils.

Everyone in class looked at each other mystified by the old teacher's behaviour. Wasting no time in his absence, they began making paper darts and flying them across the room, reading comics and challenging each other to arm wrestling matches. One boy kept watch and five minutes later warned that ol' Drac was returning. Swiftly they returned to their desks, hiding all trace of activity.

The man entered holding a paint tin in one hand, a brush in the other. Approaching the blackboard, with a shaking unsteady hand he dipped the brush into the paint and proceeded to coat the blackboard.

The boys eyes widened in amazement, the colour of the paint was orange. Not that black paint would have been suitable for resurfacing a blackboard. After a couple of minutes, Drac stopped and stood back studying the board, now streaked with orange, as if realising something was wrong. He mumbled some incoherent words to himself, turned and and left the classroom. Never to return for the rest of the lesson.

General pandemonium broke out as the boys burst into laughter and resumed paper darts, arm wrestling and taking turns at mimicking Drac shuffling on his feet and mumbling incoherently.

The amusement still raised a smile on Tony's face while making his way down the corridor after the lesson that never was. The face of the boy approaching, with dark curly hair and full red cheeks, seemed familiar to him and he was struggling to place him.

The other boy also seemed to be assessing Tony's face. They stopped, minds visibly searching.

"Spencer House," the curly haired boy said. As he spoke the penny dropped with Tony.

"Yes!"

Neither of them knew each other's names. Although similar in age, they had been in different classes at their previous school in Sloane Square. Moving in different orbits and only seeing each other in passing.

"How d'ye come to be here?" Tony asked.

"My dad's moved into the area for his work. I only started this term," the boy explained.

"Welcome to the madhouse then," Tony smiled.

"Is it that bad?" the boy seemed concerned. "My dormitory is freezing at night, and some of the teachers seem a bit odd."

"It grows on you," Tony replied sagely, already feeling an old experienced hand at the vagaries of Sandalwood College. They were interrupted by a teacher coming down the corridor.

"Stop talking. Get to your next lesson," the man's voice boomed at them.

"See you at break outside the front entrance," Tony managed to blurt as the teacher glowered considering punishment if they delayed any further.

A chill wind blew as Tony left the building at break-time wearing his dark overcoat to meet the boy whose name he still didn't know. His new companion was a few minutes late arriving.

"Sorry," he said, coming round the corner from a college side exit to the gravel forecourt at the front. "We had some nut teacher who threw the classroom bin at one of the boys, then ripped off his shoe and started beating his arse in a mad frenzy."

"Sounds like Hamilton Crosby," Tony recalled his experience of being thrashed by the nutcase.

"The bin caught the boy's face, Johnson, I think he's called, and we had to help him to the matron's surgery."

Tony shook his head in disbelief that someone with Crosby's obvious mental disorder was actually allowed to teach.

The front of the college opened on to a field leading down to a lake with a small island at the centre. Pastures beyond the college to the distant Snowdonia mountains were a welcome sight of freedom from the greyness of their

177

confinement. The boys walked across to the lake, small waves rippling in the waters.

"Hope you don't mind," Tony began, "but I don't know your name."

"That's okay, I don't know yours," his companion replied.

"Selby," said Tony.

"And mine's Harris."

It was instilled into private school boys that they addressed each other by surname. But it created a barrier to close friendship. Stiff upper lip. They decided to breach the formalities and reveal their first names.

"Mine's Clarence," his friend said sourly. "And I hate it. Don't ever call me by it. I call myself Lance."

"I promise," said Tony, and revealed his own first name.

First name terms created a bond between them strengthened by the fact they'd both been to the same school before Sandalwood College.

"Did you like it there? At Spencer House?" Lance asked as they walked by the lakeside.

"Not really," Tony recalled. "I wasn't clever enough to stay there and Mr Fitchmore hated me. He was always trying to get me in trouble."

"I thought he was alright," Lance offered a different view.

"You're not a cockney from the east end though, are you?" Tony had detected from his new friend's well rounded accent that he'd come from somewhere posh.

"We lived near the school at Knightsbridge," Lance confirmed Tony's assumption that he came from an upmarket area of London.

"My dad hated coming to live here. Well, near here. My new home's about ten miles away at Llangollen," said Lance. "His company wanted him to run a new division in North Wales, so he had to do it."

"Why is he sending you to a boarding college? Why can't you go home every day if you don't live far from here?" Tony was puzzled.

"He thinks it'll make a man of me," Lance's face looked grim. He seemed unconvinced of his father's theory.

"That's what my dad thinks too," Tony was equally unconvinced. He went on to tell Lance about some of the other strange teachers at the college and the seniors to avoid who liked picking on new boys. Their conversation was interrupted by the ringing of a hand bell echoing across the field from the college, signalling the end of break and start of the next lesson.

Tony had described Sandalwood as a madhouse to Lance, and it was only a few days later when the description was vividly demonstrated.

They'd been out for another stroll along the bank of the lake just before evening dinner, when they heard shouting and saw a crowd of boys gathering to watch something happening at a side window three storeys up on the college building. Quickly they made their way across to join the gathering.

179

"Jesus Christ! For God's sake don't!" a boy was screaming, dangling upside down outside the window, his legs tied in a fire escape harness attached to a rope.

"I won't do it again!" the boy begged for mercy, his head pointing towards a one hundred feet drop on to the paving below the building.

Tony and Lance watched in horror.

A face appeared at the window, then an arm reached out, long knife in hand preparing to slice the rope with the sharp blade.

From the distance, Tony couldn't be certain, but he thought it was the face of a senior boy he'd passed in the corridor a few times, whose wide, staring eyes instantly chilled him.

On one occasion the eyes had flicked across at him, revealing a demented mind inside that seemed to be considering a vicious attack. The senior was heavily built and out of school uniform would easily pass as an adult. That moment had passed without incident, much to Tony's relief. Even his boxing skills he feared would be crushed beneath this weirdo's onslaught.

The boy dangling upside down continued to scream for mercy, as an older pupil shouldering his way through the gathering crowd stopped beside Tony and Lance.

"That's Schizo Jackson," he told them. "Totally off his rocker."

"Can't someone stop him? One of the teachers?" asked Tony. The older boy laughed.

"They're bloody terrified of him. Terrified he'd murder them."

Schizo Jackson was now starting to slice into the rope, his victim thrashing around in a helpless frenzy. Then Schizo stopped, an evil grin rising on his face. He disappeared from the window and a few moments later the rope was hauled up on its winch. His arms reached out and he pulled the nervous wreck inside. A gasp of relief rose from the crowd thankful the boy hadn't plunged to his death.

"You're right, this place is a nuthouse," Lance had turned pale.

Tony would like to have reassured him that he'd get used to it, but he wasn't sure himself.

The drama wasn't quite over.

As the assembly began breaking up, the piercing sound of a ringing bell came from the direction of the long college drive. A police car came tearing into view, racing down the roadway. Everyone shifted round to see what new drama was unfolding.

The car pulled up sharply, tyres skidding on the front entrance gravel. Two officers leapt out and raced inside the building.

"What's happening?" a general whisper went through the onlookers.

A few minutes later the police officers emerged, dragging Schizo Jackson by the arms and struggling to contain him. A couple of teachers were trying to help, but Jackson's furious strength was proving a match for them all.

As they drew close to the car, the prisoner freed one of his arms and swung round to attack. The two teachers had already lost their tenuous hold. Swiftly an officer reached for the heavy wooden truncheon in his side holster and delivered a hard strike on Jackson's head.

The man-boy tottered for a moment, but appeared to be recovering. The policeman dealt another hard blow. This time Jackson collapsed on the ground.

In an instant he was handcuffed arms behind his back. At the same moment an ambulance was pulling up nearby, as Jackson's victim was being helped out of the building by two other teachers towards the vehicle. The boy was walking unsteadily, a nervous, shaking wreck.

An officer radioed from the police car for a secure prison van to take Jackson away. In his severely disturbed state, they were taking no risks.

"Alright! Alright! Back inside the college," a master loudly clapped his hands to disperse the onlookers.

The incident became the topic of conversation for a few days after the event in a mixture of high excitement and deep shock. The boys never learned of what happened to Schizo Jackson or his victim, the college authorities were tight lipped. But neither of them ever returned.

******

JANUARY snow began coating the surrounding fields and distant mountains delivering a freshness even to the usually gloomy grey college building. But while the weather bestowed beauty outside, the inside grew from cold to freezing.

Tony and his colleagues had barely slept the night this big freeze arrived, with wind whistling through generous gaps in the tall sash windows, which were long in need of replacement. Sheet and blanket gave little protection from the sub-zero temperature.

A couple of boys joined each other in bed, snuggling together to keep warm. The other boys in the room thought the cold was also an excuse for them to pursue another sort of closeness.

The only heating in the building came from large cast iron radiators in the classrooms. And they were shut off at night. The boys knew that the teachers had electric heaters in their private accommodation in and around the college. Even log fires in a couple of nearby cottages occupied by the most senior staff. Character building endurance was confined to the lower ranks.

"Jesus, I was freezing last night," Lance was still shivering as he met Tony from a different dormitory on their way to breakfast in the dining room.

"I had a glass of water on my bedside cabinet and there was a layer of ice on it this morning," Tony shared his experience of the night, while dipping a spoon into his warming bowl of porridge. Normally it was lumpy and tasteless. That morning none of these drawbacks stopped it from being deliciously welcome.

Little did either of the boys know that a few weeks later things would become a lot hotter, but nothing to do with the weather.

David Hollister, or Dave as he liked to be known by close acquaintances, had a lucrative enterprise on the go.

An 18 year old senior in his last year at the college, he was always looking for shady ways to make money.

Much of it involved stealing cash or watches from boys' bedside cabinets or in the sports changing room, to sell in pubs or nightclubs during the school holidays.

He'd loosened a short strip of floorboard beside his own bed, and when the coast was clear he'd raise it to store the booty below. Hollister's senior contemporaries intensely disliked their slippery eyed colleague and knew he had thieving ways. But they abided by the unwritten code of never snitching.

A mild interlude in the freezing weather had melted much of the snow to sludge, bringing to an end the snowball fights and mucking around in the crunchy downfall.

During break-time Tony and Lance had been on a short walk along a pathway at the back of the college leading to an overgrown former apple orchard. Nearing a rear entrance to the college on their return they saw Hollister standing by the door. He assessed them as two young innocents and raised a devious smile on his hollow cheek-boned face.

Tony and Lance weren't accustomed to older boys greeting them in friendship, usually ignoring the lower orders as insignificant dust. They returned wary, sheepish smiles.

"Do you want to make some money?" Dave Hollister asked.

The two boys stopped in surprise. It wasn't a question they could have anticipated.

184

"How?" asked Lance. He thought Hollister looked a bit shady and wondered if they could be entering a trap.

"It's easy. Just come along to the college art room this evening in the rest break before bedtime and I'll show you how." The older boy avoided a direct answer.

"How much money?" Tony queried.

"I reckon five shillings each for five minutes work."

Tony and Lance gazed at each other. They were suspicious of what they might be letting themselves in for. But most of the time they were penniless, save for small amounts of money occasionally sent to them in letters from their parents. Money which was always rapidly spent in the college sweet shop that opened for an hour each day.

The prospect of five shillings each for five minutes work was extremely appealing and would buy a large amount of sweets. It was an offer too good to turn down.

After the evening prep period, when pupils had to complete class work set by teachers during the day, they both made for the art room. It was situated off a back corridor that led only to a cleaning equipment storeroom at the end, so was rarely visited in the evening,

Hollister was waiting outside the art room door holding a briefcase when Tony and Lance arrived. He greeted them with another sly smile and taking a key from his trouser pocket opened the door.

"Where did you get that?" Lance wondered. Only teachers and support staff were allowed keys to locked doors.

"Ssh!" Hollister put a finger to his lips. "Quiet."

185

The boys began to have doubts about what they were getting into. But five shillings for five minutes work. They decided to continue.

Inside the art room paintings rested on easels, drawings lay on long tables and pots with paint brushes perched on shelves. Tony felt a pang of guilt as an uninvited intruder. Mr Richards, the art master, a young man with a kindly face and warm personality, was the friendliest teacher in college.

The boy was aware of his own limitations as an artist, but Mr Richards was ever encouraging, trying to bring out the best in him. This intrusion felt like a betrayal of the man's trust. But five shillings when he had nothing.

Hollister locked the door and made his way across to a small partitioned room at the back. Inside was a kiln used for firing pottery. Tony and Lance grew ever more intrigued by their mission. Hollister opened the briefcase on a workbench beside the kiln, removing a rectangular plaster cast and a strip of grey metal.

"That's lead," observed Lance. Hollister ignored him and switched on the kiln. He placed the lead in a tin tray then put it inside the kiln to melt the substance. Fifteen minutes later, wearing protective gloves, Hollister removed the tray and poured the liquid lead into the shallow circular moulds formed in the plaster cast. Now the boys were entirely mystified and asked what he was doing.

"Just wait and see," he replied curtly, placing a smooth edged plaster cast over the mould containing the lead. Suddenly they heard footsteps in the corridor outside. The boys hearts began racing as someone tried the door handle.

"It's alright," Hollister reassured them. "It's the caretaker just checking everything's locked up. He'll be gone in a minute."

Tony and Lance remained frozen until the footsteps moved away. The enterprise was not turning out to be as easy and quick as they had anticipated, but the hook of money persuaded them to persevere.

Ten minutes later, Hollister removed the top cast to reveal twenty solid lead discs. He ran a shallow pool of water in the nearby sink and tipped in the discs to rapidly cool them. After drying them, he placed ten each into small string bangs and gave them to the boys.

"Now this is your part," he said. "I want you to get a college pass for Sunday and go down to the village. There are two cigarette machines there and I want you to use the discs to get ten packets of cigarettes each from them."

"But they take half crowns for a pack," said Lance. He knew because his father sometimes bought cigarettes from street machines.

"They're the same size as half crowns," Hollister explained.

"But lead's heavy. It won't work," Lance protested.

"It will with those machines. They're rubbish. They operate on size, not weight," Hollister had done his homework. Not all cigarette machines, especially in smaller places, had yet been updated.

Tony was calculating that a half crown was two shillings and sixpence, so they'd get sixpence from each pack to total five shillings. It was nothing compared to the money he used to get doing work for uncle Frank, but since he now had nothing it was something. He knew what he'd just been asked to do was wrong, but it wasn't going to hurt anybody. Lance appeared less keen, but was prepared to go along with his friend.

Hollister gave them a slippery smile of encouragement. He would make a good profit from selling the cigarettes on to seniors who enjoyed a smoke, purchasing them from him for a few pence less than the retail price.

Pipe smoking was allowed in the senior study block, a rectangle of dwellings beside the college intended mainly for work, but used more often for listening to music on transistor radios, reading novels, sleeping and smoking cigarettes as well as pipes.

Lance and Tony arranged a school pass for the following Sunday and, after morning service in the college chapel set off on their mission to Wynngryth village a mile away, taking a back path through fields instead the usual route along the college drive and roadway outside.

Their main fear was that they might arouse suspicion feeding the cigarettes machines for a large amount of cigarette packs, apart from the fact they would look under age being seen by any locals. But the village was a sleepy place on Sundays. The sabbath was strictly upheld in this bit of Wales, which usually meant the area was largely devoid of life.

There were cigarette machines outside the closed newsagent and post office, both situated a few hundred yards apart. Taking positions, they fed the machines with the fake coins, peering nervously around occasionally to see if they were being watched. As the lead discs clunked inside the machines and they pulled open the drawers to remove the packs, Lance realised Hollister was right. The mechanisms were fooled by size. The weight didn't matter.

Nearing the accomplishment of their mission, Tony noticed an elderly man watching him from the high street corner a short distance away. The man didn't move. Just stared. It unnerved him a little. Could he be identified if anyone in authority found out? His jacket pockets were stuffed with packs of cigarettes. Shortly Lance rejoined him. The man remained, now staring at them both.

With relief they left, taking the same cross country path back to the college. For once the place felt like a refuge from potential outside danger.

They had arranged to meet Hollister at the far end of the lake beneath a cluster of trees on the bank side about half a mile from the college building. He was waiting there for them as they arrived.

"D'ye get them?" he quizzed eagerly. Tony and Lance unloaded the packs from their bulging pockets and their employer put them in a bag.

"And the money?" Tony wasn't sure if Hollister would keep his part of the bargain. He could just walk away. The boys were hardly likely to report him to the masters and implicate themselves in a crime.

Hollister's trademark sly smile rose on his lips. He wanted to keep them sweet for future missions and reached into his jacket pocket handing them a ten shilling note.

"Five each as agreed. I'll be in touch so you can make some more money." He turned and left.

Ten shillings in the boys straitened circumstances was a small fortune. They began heading back to the college across the lakeside field.

A short distance further they saw someone approaching. As the figure grew closer they realised it was Herring, a college prefect. A rank that gave supreme power not far below teacher level.

They'd had no direct encounter with him before now, but their friends had suffered at his hands, being reported to masters on trumped up reasons of misbehaviour merely because he'd taken a dislike to them. Herring carried a permanent sneer.

"What you two been doing?" he questioned aggressively, drawing close to them.

"Just been for a walk round the lake," Lance answered innocently. Herring's face registered cynical disbelief.

"I'm going to search you. Lift your arms and spread your legs," he ordered.

The boys felt demeaned by the order, but obeyed knowing if they refused they'd be reported for defying authority of a prefect searching for things they shouldn't possess. In particular, cigarettes.

And that was Herring's motive. Not to uphold college rules, but to see what he could make out of them. He enjoyed a smoke, and had many a time confiscated them from boys in the junior ranks who'd embarked early into the habit. Tree cover at the end of the lake was a favourite haunt for an illicit ciggie.

Herring harshly patted their clothes feeling for lumpy cigarette packs and caused them to flinch as he whacked

190

their crotches. Hiding packets in the groin was one of the techniques to remain undetected. But this prefect knew all the tricks.

He appeared disappointed at finding nothing as Tony and Lance resumed their dignity.

"I reckon you've been down there by the trees 'cause you're a couple of queers who've been wanking each other off." Herring vented his vile mind at not finding anything worthwhile. Tony wanted to punch the creep to pulp, but knew all hell would break loose if Herring reported him saying it was an unprovoked attack. Controlling his rising temper, he had to let it pass.

The prefect spat at the ground in front of them, sneering at them as contemptuous dirt. Then he walked off. Tony raised his fist in half a mind to go after him.

"Leave it," Lance urged. "It could have been worse if he'd caught us with the cigarettes." Tony agreed. Best to leave it be. At least they had money, and with their ill gotten gains went on to enjoy a feast of sweets from the college shop.

The call to action from Hollister never came again. A month later word went round the college that he'd been expelled along with two junior boys. It was another week before Lance and Tony learned the reason from another boy, who'd been told the story by a senior who was his older brother.

It transpired that Hollister had built a network of younger boys all eager to earn some money. They too, like Lance and Tony, had been sent on missions to get cigarettes, but from vending machines over a wider area, taking bus journeys on Sunday passes to nearby towns in Lllangollen and Wrexham. There were many more machines in these places.

As the vending machine operators discovered more and more counterfeit discs in them, they alerted the police to the possibility of major fraud growing in the area. An undercover watch was mounted and one Sunday afternoon two boys were spotted feeding the machines for cigarettes. Taken in for questioning and quaking with fear, they confessed all.

Hollister's possessions were searched where coin moulds, discs and other materials were discovered. The game was over.

For the next few weeks Tony and Lance sweated. What if Hollister snitched to the police telling who else had been involved? Would they be getting a visit from the law? They could be expelled too. Their parents would be furious. As time passed the fear diminished. Hollister it seemed, for all his faults, had at least kept the college code of silence.

******

IN the following two years, Tony and Lance generally settled into the college routine. They were never going to be academic scholars, but were good at sports. Sport, however, was not prized by the college as being important, other than for entertainment.

In school holidays, Tony still had to spend weekdays at his nan's, but was given a bit more freedom to see friends on a strict time slot. Any breach and confinement would return.

Tony hoped uncle Frank would call in during the days he spent at his grandmother's. The chance maybe to get some casual work at his clubs and more pressing, an opportunity maybe to see Lucy again. But whenever he asked Joyce if his uncle was coming round, she would avoid answering the question. It seemed she didn't want to talk about him, and he never did make an appearance. The youngster wondered what was wrong.

At the start of the autumn term, Tony now fourteen, was glad to be reunited with his friend.

Lance had enjoyed two weeks of the summer holidays with his parents at Nice in southern France and boasted a good suntan from the stay. Tony had spent a week with his parents at Bournemouth on the English south coast, listening mostly to them arguing about nothing in particular that he could make out.

Both youths had now grown accustomed to the rigours of boarding school life, but never lost the feeling of being confined in a short radius of the college. Saturday or Sunday afternoons they could catch a bus to the local towns, go to cafes and even chat-up some girls in the recreation grounds. But even that was short lived, because there was never enough time to strike up any meaningful relationship with any of them.

About halfway through the term and pining for greater freedom, Tony came up with what he thought was a brilliant plan.

"Why don't we just run away from here. Get a job and lead our own lives," he suggested to Lance while they were out strolling along a woodland path one early evening about half a mile from the college grounds.

The area was officially out of bounds without a pass, but some rules were more flexible than others, and they were enjoying the privilege of being college older boys, not having to settle in their dormitories until 9pm.

Lance took a moment to digest Tony's extraordinary idea.

"I think my parents would kill me," he concluded after giving it some thought.

"But if we plan it properly, no-one will know where we are. Then in a year or two we can let them know where we've gone. It'd be too late for them to send us back here and we'll be living our own lives by then," Tony's enthusiasm was persuasive, if not mapped out in essential detail.

Lance still needed greater convincing. They reached a stream flowing idly at the bottom of a grass embankment and were distracted for a moment seeing a large pike in the water nibbling at some algae attached to a small rock. A few moments later it slipped away.

"Where could we get a job?" Lance wasn't dismissing the plan out of hand. He bent down and picked up a stone, lobbing it into the stream.

"I'm sure my uncle Frank would find us a job at one of his nightclubs in London. Helping out with cleaning and stocking booze and fags," Tony's enthusiasm was reaching even greater heights.

"But your uncle will tell your parents. They'll tell the college, who'll tell my parents," Lance fought to maintain his thoughts in reality.

"My uncle hates my dad. He'd never tell. And if he did we could run off and find a job somewhere else."

Lance was still not entirely convinced, but the sense of being freed from the weight of lessons, always being told what to do by teachers and prefects, and the prospect of being treated like an adult were overwhelming reasons to sway him towards agreement. Though one pressing problem came to his mind.

"We've no money. How do we get to London?"

"Hitchhiking," Tony replied. He'd given the matter some thought.

During the next few weeks the youths worked out a plan. It was obvious that when they were discovered missing from the college there would be a search for them and probably the police alerted. The first step was to lay a false trail.

In their geography atlases they drew a line in red ink to the town of Chesterfield, about ninety miles east of the college, and wrote 'destination' at the top of the page. This was intended to draw anyone away from their real destination.

Hitching for lifts in college uniforms would be a giveaway. Tony and Lance were members of the college's army cadet unit which involved once a fortnight field exercises, rifle training and marching up and down the college forecourt. The cadet uniforms would be ideal. They could tell anyone giving them a lift they were engaged in

195

an initiative exercise to reach London without using any official form of transport.

The uniforms had to be put back in a storeroom at the end of the fortnightly sessions, but on the last one before their intended departure, Lance and Tony changed out of them slowly, waiting until their colleagues left. Then watchfully they smuggled them in sports bags to their dormitories, hiding the garments underneath their mattresses.

They arranged college passes for the following Sunday, with the plan to leave after lunch. That would give them time to make a good getaway before they were missed in the evening.

When the day arrived, following lunch they returned to their dormitories, usually unoccupied at this time, and placed the uniforms back in the sports bags along with a bottle of lemonade and a few packets of crisps from the college sweet shop. Refreshment to sustain them on the two hundred miles journey.

They left the college building by a side exit, and crossed the field rounding the edge of the lake to reach a style in the wood post fencing bordering the grounds. This was the crucial phase. If a snooping prefect saw them carrying bags they might be stopped and searched. Visions of Herring catching them terrified their progress across the field.

With huge relief they reached the style and climbed over. The field ahead sloped steeply down and would soon take them from the view of even the highest windows in the college. They'd travelled this terrain before and knew of a broad oak tree which they could hide behind to change into their cadet uniforms.

Discarding their college uniforms, they set off for the road half a mile away at the bottom of the field. It was a narrow country lane and not much traffic passed. For an hour they thumbed lifts from the occasional passing vehicle with no takers. Their plan looked like taking a dive from the outset.

As they began to wonder if they'd made the right call and thinking about returning to put their college uniforms back on, in a final try they thumbed an approaching dark red Ford Humber car. The vehicle slowed and stopped a short distance ahead. They ran to it. A man wound the driver window down.

"You lads looking for a lift?" he had a cheery, smiling face with neatly combed side-parted brown hair.

"Yes," the cadets answered in unison.

"Where you going?"

"To London," Tony replied.

"Oh, that's a long way. I'm only going to Shrewsbury, but you're welcome."

For Tony and Lance it was a start. They took the offer getting into the back of the car.

"On an exercise are you?" the driver asked as he drove off.

"It's an initiative test," Tony answered

"Which unit are you with?"

The uniforms made them look a few years older than their real ages. It seemed the man thought they were actually in the full time army.

His question threw them for a moment. They could hardly reveal themselves as army cadets from the college.

"The Wrexham Regiment," Lance blurted, using the name of a town near the college as the first thought that came into his head.

"Never heard of them," the man seemed puzzled.

"It's been newly formed," Tony broke in, lending backing to his friend. They hoped the driver believed them. If he was suspicious, he might turn them in. His ponderous silence was unnerving.

The cadets had noticed a woman sitting in the front passenger seat. Long auburn hair trailing over her shoulders was all they could see of her. She sat rigidly still, not saying a word as if she objected to the man beside her giving them a lift.

Further questions from the man kept them on edge, needing to feed more lies rapidly.

"Which part of Wrexham are you based?"

"In a new barracks north of the town."

"Why did you decide to join the army?"

"For action and adventure."

"Where do you live?"

"Lincoln and Norwich."

Unrelenting the queries came for another five minutes, then the man revealed he'd been in the army during the second world war joining the allied forces moving in on Berlin during the final days of Hitler's reign. Locked into memory lane, he recounted heroic moments as they fought their way towards the German city. The cadets were much relieved the questions had stopped.

After an hour or so, the car reached Shrewsbury and the man pulled up in the high street to give them instructions on where to hitch a lift next.

"Head for Birmingham and then Rugby where you can hitch a lift on that new motorway that'll take you nearly to London," he advised. "But I expect you've got a map."

As it happened Tony and Lance had forgotten to bring a map, but nodded that they did. Stepping out of the car, the silent woman turned towards them. She looked radiantly pretty.

"Good luck," she said.

The cadets smiled back, totally bemused by her sudden sociability.

Strange couple they thought, thanking the driver and leaving. But more pressing matters soon filled their minds now they realised they'd forgotten to bring a map.

The town was practically empty being a Sunday. They stopped a man passing to ask for the road to Birmingham.

"It's about half a mile away, left turn by the post office," he pointed, eyeing their uniforms as if wondering why two army personnel were asking him for directions. The youths moved on quickly fearing more awkward questions.

Finding the main road, they tramped along the grass verge thumbing lifts. This time it didn't take long before a black, Bedford flatbed carrying a large wooden crate anchored with straps pulled up. Tony opened the passenger door to be greeted by a mop of curly fair hair, wide beaming eyes and a huge smile revealing a missing front tooth.

"You lads on an exercise?" the man behind the wheel sounded enthusiastic. "Jump in. Where you going?"

"To London," said Lance, climbing on to the passenger seat and shifting along so Tony could wedge himself on as well.

"I'm going to Rugby, not far from that new M1 motorway to London." The driver pulled away.

"I'm Max. What's your names?"

The cadets introduced themselves.

"You're young recruits. Can't see your regiment badges. Which regiment you with?"

A few days before the youths had unstitched Sandalwood College Cadets badges with a pair of scissors to travel incognito. Now it was raising another question.

"Ist Wrexham Regiment," Lance was ready.

"Never heard of them."

"It's a new regiment. We're on a trainee initiative test in new uniforms that haven't been given an insignia yet," Tony came in with a bright lie.

"I wasn't much older than you two when I signed up in 1940," Max began to reminisce. Ended up fighting the Germans in North Africa. Lost some good men there."

Tony and Lance relaxed. They'd met another ex-serviceman who was only too happy to regale them with tales of wartime exploits. Apart from the occasional question of where they lived and why did they join up, Max was content to do the talking.

Every so often he amazed his passengers by being able to steer with one hand, while taking tobacco from a pouch on the dashboard with the other, placing it in a cigarette paper, rolling the tobacco inside, lick sealing it and flicking a lighter to ignite it.

After a few times, Max detected their amazement at his skill.

"They teach you a lot in the army," he winked at them.

A couple of hours later Max pulled into a large parking lot mostly filled with lorries. To the side stood a flat roofed building with Willy's Cafe emblazoned in red lettering over the entrance.

"This is our transport cafe," Max announced pulling into a space. "Care for a bite lads?"

"We haven't got much money," said Tony. "It's part of our initiative test to get to London without spending," he thought up another lie. Though it was true they didn't have much money. Just one pound.

"That's alright. You're army lads. I'll treat you," Max gave another missing front tooth smile.

There were no frills inside Willy's Cafe. Other lorry drivers sat eating enormous plates of fried food at the grubby, scored tables. The chalked menu board behind the counter offered fry-ups only of egg, bacon, sausages, with extras accompaniments of baked beans, fried bread, tomatoes, black pudding and toast. The entire place was steeped in a humid atmosphere of frying.

Behind the counter a man dished a couple of eggs and two sausages on to a plate. A well rounded woman, wearing a stained apron, ladled some beans from a pot, added fried bread and two generous slices of black pudding, then carried it to a table.

"Hello Max, how are you?" the man looked up to greet him.

"Fine Sid. I've got some army lads," the lorry driver nodded towards them standing by his side. "They're travelling to London."

Sid smiled, revealing a set of brown teeth, then raised his hand to smooth the receding layer of grey hair clinging to the last vestige of life on his head.

"What can I get you all?"

"Bacon, eggs, beans, toast and three mugs of tea," Max ordered, reaching for money in his trousers pocket.

He paid Sid and they walked across to an empty table. A radio behind the counter echoed tinny music across the cafe.

The woman in the stained apron brought their food which sat in a murky pool of grease. But Lance and Tony were starving, it looked delicious and the strong tea was wonderfully thirst quenching.

"Good ol' grub, eh?" Max smiled, seeing his army companions enjoying the meal. A little later his attention was caught by a tall, broad shouldered man entering the cafe.

"Hold on lads, that's Toddy. He does a regular drive from the Midlands to London. I'll have a word with him." Max left to meet Toddy at the counter. A minute later he returned.

"Toddy's going to Watford. That's pretty close to London. He'll give you a lift because I'm only going a few miles further."

Lance and Tony's new driver ordered his food and came over to join them. He was a young man in his thirties, bulging forearm muscles extending from his black T-shirt.

"Toddy does lots of body-building. He's the south London weightlifting champion," Max explained to the youths. Toddy smiled modestly at the flattering introduction. His crew cut hair and strong, square face belied his kindly eyes. Max went on to describe a few more of the man's competition achievements, leaving his lorry driving colleague almost writhing with embarrassment. He was not a person to boast of his successes.

"Right I've got to get on," Max took a last swig of tea then stood up. "Wonderful to meet you lads," he reached out to shake their hands in his leathery skin grip. Tony and Lance felt a pang of sadness at the parting. Max was wonderful. It was like meeting a free spirit after the rigid world of college life.

"And don't forget. If you ever find yourselves under heavy fire from the enemy, run like fuck if you want to live," Max burst into laughter, winking at them as he left.

"Great guy," said Toddy when Max had disappeared out the door. "Where do you want to get to in London?" he asked, as his fry-up arrived.

"Horseguards at Hyde Park," Lance answered. He'd heard of an army barracks based there and hoped it would sound convincing. Tony was thankful for his companion's quick thinking.

"Well you can catch a train into London from where I'll drop you off at Watford." Toddy readily accepted Lance's lie.

203

In the cab the cadets hoped their driver wouldn't probe too deeply about their so called 1st Wrexham unit. They'd realised if they could get people to talk about themselves, it warded off prying questions.

Tony remembered Max's comment of Toddy being a weightlifting champion and asked him about it.

The driver was not a boastful man and played it down saying it wasn't much. He hardly spoke at all and for a time an awkward silence fell between him and the two cadets squeezed together on the passenger seat beside. After half an hour Toddy broke the silence.

"I was a national service soldier a few years back. Posted overseas in 1956 to Cyprus where riots were breaking out between the Greek and Turkish Cypriots." Toddy was silent again for several minutes. Tony and Lance had vaguely heard there'd been fighting in Cyprus, but they had no idea what it was over or who was involved.

"It was a bloody affair. Lots of people killed on all sides and no-one's ever really won from it." Tony stared ahead at the motorway, unpleasant memories still floating around in his mind. Silence followed for several more miles.

"Do you like football?" The man's mood lightened. The cadets grabbed the lighter atmosphere.

"Tony supports Tottenham, but my club Chelsea's much better," Lance leapt in.

"They're all rubbish. Arsenal's the king," Toddy turned to them and smiled. For much of the remaining journey football was the topic as the lorry ploughed down the motorway.

It was dark when the lorry pulled up in a space beside Watford railway station.

"You can catch a train into London from here," he said.

"We're meant to hitch hike into London," said Lance. "It's part of our test. We haven't got any money." Toddy looked at them with a half smile, detecting that he wasn't being told the entire truth.

He reached across to the glove compartment and took out his wallet. "I don't know what your game is, but I admire your spirit." He handed them a five pound note.

The cadets could hardly believe their luck. Thanking him they got out of the cab. Just before they closed the door, Toddy called to them.

"If you really are with the army, I hope you never have to shoot anyone." His face fell serious again. The cadets smiled and closed the door, totally unaware of the pain the man carried for some incident in Cyprus he would never reveal or forget.

CHAPTER 8

The money Toddy had given them was more than enough to pay train connections into London. They arrived at a station not far from uncle Frank's home at just after ten o'clock.

It was dark as they emerged on to the street, and light flecks of rain scurried through the beams of the street lights.

Walking along the pavement towards uncle Frank's, the sound of piano music began to fill the air as they approached a pub. The door flew open and a man staggered out the worse for drink. His rolling eyes caught sight of the cadets.

"The army's here!" the man exclaimed. "God save the Queen," he slurred, attempting a mock salute, but his arm wavered senselessly around. The next second he spewed on the pavement. Tony and Lance stepped round into the road as the man continued to wretch.

"Jesus, where have you brought me to," Lance was starting to have doubts about their new found freedom. He'd only lived where streets were clean and houses neatly nurtured.

The litter strewn route they took, lined by gloomy dark brick terraced houses, looked like a refuge for the abandoned. The drizzle began turning to heavy rain, dampening their spirit as well as the depressing scene.

Then the setting seemed to miraculously change after a few more street turns. The houses were larger. Semis and detached properties boasting a considerable step up in wealth and the pavements virtually litter free.

Another turn and they approached uncle Frank's. Tony wrapped on the knocker. After a few moments the door opened slightly, halted by a security chain.

"Yes?" came a woman's voice, eyes peering cautiously through the gap. Tony recognised the voice as Lindy.

"It's Tony with a friend."

"Tony? No he's away at college," Lindy was dubious.

"No. It's me. I'm here."

The door closed as the security chain was slipped away allowing Lindy to open it.

"Tony! Have you joined the army?" The woman was mystified.

"No, it's a long story. We're getting wet in the rain. Can we come in?"

"Of course," she beckoned them inside. "What are you up to? Who's your friend?"

Lance nodded as Tony introduced him, then she led them into the kitchen.

"I'll make you a cup of tea. Then you can get those uniforms off to dry in the airing cupboard while I find you something to wear."

The cadets sat on chairs at the table as Lindy made the brew. Tony had noticed that she looked a lot older than when he'd last seen her. The gleam seemed to have disappeared from her eyes and there were dark shadows below them. The blue cotton dress she wore hung limply. It was as if a life force had deserted her.

As Lindy joined them at the table with the tea, Tony explained that they were runaways.

"I think you might be landing yourselves in a lot of trouble," she responded. It was not what they wanted to hear.

"We thought uncle Frank might give us jobs in one of the nightclubs. We really hate being stuck at college," Tony was hopeful of them being given a chance.

"Your uncle's out at the minute. Probably won't be back 'til the early hours."

Tony was disappointed at the news, but another hope surfaced.

"Is Lucy in?"

Lindy stared at him knowingly through lustreless eyes.

"Sorry to disappoint you, but she's away at school. Your uncle's giving her a private education."

Tony began to wonder if his great plan wasn't so great. He'd overheard a few years back uncle Frank, in a whispered conversation with his nan, scorning his dad for sending him to a private school. Now he was doing exactly the same thing for Lucy.

"You ought to go back and finish your education both of you," Lindy advised, finishing her cup of tea. "Smart people do better in this life. You've got a great opportunity to shine."

She stood up.

"Now go upstairs, get those wet clothes off and have a bath."

Tony had never seen the serious side of Lindy before. He was surprised. The boys had expected to be welcomed and receive encouragement for their bold plan. Now instead of the thrill they'd imagined of being free, it began to dawn that reality was not going to live up to the dream.

Lindy found them two of Frank's old dressing gowns in the back of a wardrobe for them to wear while their uniforms dried. They were well oversized for the youths, raising smiles all round, but temporarily did the job. Then she made them a meal of sausage, egg and chips, which considerably lifted their spirits.

When they finished eating, Lindy made up a bed in the spare room for Tony while Lance was given Lucy's bedroom to sleep in for the night.

Curiously Lance having Lucy's bedroom sent a twinge of jealousy through him. He would like to have slept in there. He wanted to feel close to the girl he'd fallen in love with, sharing at least the intimacy of her surrounds if not her presence. He wondered if she still kept the comic annuals they had looked through together.

As Lindy led them upstairs to the bedrooms, Tony saw a smiling photo of Lucy on the hall wall. Her long fair hair was cut shorter and curved in around the neckline. Her face had filled out so that she no longer looked like a little girl. To Tony she appeared even more beautiful than the last memory he held of her.

"She's growing up, ain't she?" said Lindy, observing him studying the photo. "Just like you are," she smiled. "You're a lot taller than when I last saw you. Becoming a handsome young man."

Lance stifled a laugh at her comment. Tony lowered his head in embarrassment.

Resting in bed in the spare room, the images and events of the long day flickered through Tony's mind. The different characters he and Lance had encountered. As he drifted into sleep, sounds rose from downstairs. A door opening and closing, voices, chairs scraping, clattering of crockery, all evaporating away into restful peace.

******

SUPPLIED with dry uniforms, the cadets were eating breakfast cereal in the kitchen when uncle Frank appeared at the door in a white open neck shirt and dark trousers.

"It's the army boys!" he smiled at them. "Gone AWOL eh?"

Tony was thrilled to see his uncle again. All doubts about running away from college immediately disappeared. Lindy was at the counter making a pot of tea.

"I'm told you're both looking for a job with me," he joined them at the kitchen table.

"I've told them they should go back and finish their education," Lindy came over and began pouring the tea into cups.

"I'll decide what happens!" Frank turned sharply to her. The venom in his voice shocked the cadets.

Lindy said nothing and finished pouring the tea. A light smile returned to Frank's face as he resumed talking to the youths.

"So you're ready for some real life are you?"

Tony nodded eagerly. Lance half-heartedly. He wasn't so sure about this man who he sensed was covering cunning with smiles.

Neither Lance or Tony could imagine what torment he carried. Corrupt money and power came at a price.

He'd managed to survive attempts on his life instigated by the Parker brothers' outside contacts, and as the brother's influence diminished, some of their loyal followers had joined Frank's ranks. But always there was a plot by someone who wanted to take over from him as king pin. And payoffs to bent policemen was a costly and risky business. Always a straight copper trying to infiltrate the set-up.

Life for Frank was not a happy one, continually fearing arrest, imprisonment. The price was high, but the power addictively higher.

"Well you can't work for me wearing those uniforms. The customers will think we're getting ready for another war," Frank laughed at his own remark. The cadets smiled back respectfully.

Lindy left the kitchen. She said not a word, though her disapproval filled the atmosphere. She'd lived with a criminal leader before, but she was unhappy with the prospect of two youngsters with the chance of a better life being drawn into the world of crime and corruption.

Uncle Frank took them to a clothes shop and kitted them out with jeans and T-shirts, then on to the Soho club where Tony had previously worked. Lance was totally bewildered entering a sphere he'd never before experienced.

A bar where men with eager, consuming eyes chatted to shapely young women, who seemed to encourage being touched in more than just friendly places. Scantily dressed showgirls occasionally crossing the floor, or rehearsing while the club was closed, preparing for a show.

That became a plus for the youths, at an age where their interest in the opposite sex was growing keener by the day. The downside was stacking crates and cleaning jobs, though amply compensated by the five pounds each Frank gave to them at the end of a long day. Tony had anticipated ten pounds, like the earlier times when he'd worked there, but five was still generous, and a week's wage to many in the population. However, their new found existence abruptly came to an end after just three days.

At eight in the evening, while Tony and Lance were watching television in the living room at Frank and Lindy's, the peace was suddenly disturbed by furious knocking on the front door. Lindy answered.

"Right, where are they?" Tony's father, Gerry, barged inside, his face puce with anger. "I know they're here."

Tony recognised the voice coming from the hallway. His instinct was to try and hide, but behind the sofa was hardly a good hideaway.

"What's going on?" Frank descended the stairs to see Gerry in the hall.

"I want my son and the other boy," he demanded. Frank moved in close to confront him.

"You don't force your way into my house giving your orders. You're not in the airforce now."

Gerry raised his finger.

"You hand over those boys now, or I'll call the police and tell them you're harbouring two young runaways without authority."

The mention of police coming to cause Frank trouble instantly made him draw back. He had some influence with them, but harbouring boys against the wishes of their parents was not an area he felt sure he'd be able to contain with payoffs. That was not his criminal province.

Tony had heard the confrontation and knew the game was over. He felt angry at his father spoiling the dream, him and Lance's new life, but there was nowhere else to go now. The youngsters entered the hall."You stupid fools," Gerry vented his feelings. "What were you thinking? Come on, I've got a car outside."

Gerry and Frank stared venomously at each other as the lads shuffled out.

"If you weren't Tony's father, I'd have had you sorted long before now," Frank glowered.

"And if you weren't my wife's brother, I'd have sent the police instead," Gerry snarled in return. As he left, Frank slammed the front door shut.

Lindy was standing at the end of the hall.

"I suppose you're happy now," he growled at her. She said nothing, fearing he'd give her a beating if she dared express any further opinion. But yes, she was happy. Happy the youngsters might yet have that better chance, and glad to see that the man she'd loved, before he became a tyrant, had been put down by Tony's father.

No one else she knew would have dared answer Frank back like that. Her only regret was not being able to give the boys a goodbye hug.

The drive back to Tony's home in Roehampton was largely silent as Gerry fought to contain his anger. It was tinged with relief that he knew his son and the other boy were safe.

The police had been informed of the boys disappearance from college and on a search of their belongings the teachers had come across the atlases which showed the false trail to their destination. As a result police had searched areas they were nowhere near.

Irene was going spare with worry, as were Lance's parents, all wondering if they'd come to harm. When Gerry learned what had happened, he too at first was mystified as to where they might be. Then realisation dawned. He knew Tony was fond of his uncle Frank and that he'd worked at the part-time job in his club. A sixth sense led him to the right conclusion of where both lads were hiding.

When they arrived Irene hugged her son, tears of relief streaming down her cheeks.

"I've spoken to your mother on the phone and she's been worried sick about you," Irene turned to Lance. "We're taking you and Tony to Paddington station tomorrow morning. You're mum and dad will be there, but tonight you're staying here."

Lance looked down, suitably shamed.

"You've both been very stupid," said Gerry. "And it's only because I've pleaded that you're stupid and naive boys to your headmaster on the phone, that he's agreed to take you back and not expel you."

Lance was glad of the news. He wasn't sure that working in a nightclub was the best he could do in life. Tony was disappointed. He preferred the company of his uncle, and good money away from adults who were always so serious and critical of him. But his father's will still ruled in all things.

Next morning at Paddington station Lance's parents met him. His mother tearfully hugged him then his father had a stern word about his misbehaviour before giving him a hug. Tony noted that his own father had not given him a hug or shown anything to indicate affection.

On the long train journey back, the youths hardly spoke to each other in the anti-climax to their hopeless dream of being independent in an adult world. At Wynngryth station they were met by the paranoid teacher, Hamilton Crosby, standing beside a waiting car. He'd been sent to ensure they didn't try to run off again.

As they approached, he started his nervous habit of slapping his forehead to brush back the hair continually slipping down from his side parting. The lads resisted laughing in case he began frantically beating them with a shoe. They'd tagged him as an unstable lunatic.

Back at the college they were led to the headmaster's study and paraded in front of him.

"Why did you do it?" Dr Goldacre asked in a soft voice. "You've caused a great deal of trouble." The man loomed above them, the black gown around his shoulders lending a powerful air of authority.

"I don't know, sir. Just a silly moment of madness I suppose," Lance replied.

The head glowered at Tony, waiting for his reply. He wanted to answer by saying 'because it's very boring being stuck here like I'm in prison'. But he knew if he said something that could be taken as insolent or rude, he'd be expelled. Facing the wrath of his father at such an event was a terrifying prospect.

"Because I was stupid and won't do it again," he blurted, showing the contrition expected.

"Right. Go back to your usual duties, and in the meantime the laundry staff will find temporary replacements for the uniforms you've lost. Your parents will have to pay for new ones, which I'm sure will not please them." Dr Goldacre looked at them sternly.

"In addition, all pass leave will be denied you for the remainder of the term, and any further misbehaviour, even the smallest thing, and I will have no hesitation in expelling you from my college." He pointed them to the door.

For the next few days, though frowned upon by teachers, among their own Tony and Lance were hailed as heroes and eagerly questioned about their adventures on the outside world.

The experience of what the youths had done together acted as an even stronger bond between them for a while, but as they settled back into the everyday routine it gradually started to open a divide.

Tony remained determined to escape the shackles of college life. Lance was more level headed. He'd enjoyed the escapade, but felt lost in a world he'd never before

216

experienced. He knew he wasn't ready for adult life yet. It had been drummed into him by his parents that exam qualifications were important for finding a good job.

Tony took a different view. Having a good time was his motivation, and anyway, uncle Frank had left school at fifteen to start work with no qualifications. Now he earned loads of money, probably even more than his own dad.

The moving apart was gradual. Not unfriendly, just spending more time with other friends. It was towards the end of the summer term a new alliance with another student at the college began to take shape. An alliance that would eventually lead to a major change in Tony's future.

******

THE change began unheralded while Tony was working on a pen and ink drawing of a tree during an art lesson. He noticed the art master, Mr Richards, helping an older student with some artwork.

From where he was sitting at a table, the work appeared unusual, not a conventional painting, more like something called modern art he'd seen in a magazine. The style was becoming more popular.

Tony stood up to go across and look. To him the artwork seemed to be just a mass of mixed colours and shapes.

"Do you do that if you can't paint properly?" he asked innocently.

The art master and the student looked up at him, smiling.

217

"Weston can paint very well," said Mr Richards, introducing the pupil. "He's just experimenting with shapes and colours. A new form of expression called modern art."

The older pupil was in a senior class above Tony's, and had come into the art room for extra coaching during one of his free study periods.

"I like the colours, but what's it meant to be?" He stared at the piece.

"Art doesn't have to be anything in particular. It's a freedom of expression," said Mr Richards. The explanation didn't hit home with Tony. The painting to him was a jumble, but for some inexplicable reason he liked it.

"Some of Weston's work is going to be displayed in an art exhibition near his home in Fulham during the summer holidays," the art master told him.

"Fulham! That's not far from where I live in Roehampton," Tony was amazed. Even though they were at college two hundred miles away, he and the art student had homes just miles apart.

The painter looked up again from his work, turning to Tony.

"We're both a long way from home then," he smiled.

Tony immediately took to his friendly, peaceful face and cascading brown curly hair.

"Can I come to your exhibition in the holidays?" He'd never been to an art exhibition before, and his request was driven more by connecting with a kindred spirit in the holiday who possibly shared his experience of confinement at Sandalwood College.

"Of course you can come," he said. "I don't suppose there'll be crowds waiting to see my work. You can boost the numbers by one," he smiled again. "I've got some flyers for it. I'll leave one with Mr Richards to give to you at your next art lesson."

He placed his paint brush in a jar.

"And sod to the formalities. My first name's Rudy. Rudy Weston. And you?"

Tony looked to Mr Richards expecting him to reprimand the pupil for using a swear word. None came. He introduced himself.

"Tony. Tony Selby."

"Okay Tony. If I don't see you before, I'll see you at the exhibition sometime."

Rudy took up another brush and returned to his artwork.

Tony returned to his pen and ink drawing feeling strangely happy, as if he'd embarked on a new route in life. Not art. He knew he wasn't talented at that. Just some new adventures. Rudy didn't seem to be in the same mould as anyone else he'd met. There was no logical reason for the feeling. It was just a feeling.

CHAPTER 9

TONY was glad to be at home in the summer holidays away from the restrictions of college, but disagreement with his father didn't take long to develop.

"You're going to your nan's during the week," Gerry insisted when Tony asked if he could go to Rudy's art exhibition in a few days time.

It was Saturday afternoon and his mother had just returned from shopping. Gerry sat in an armchair reading a newspaper and smoking his pipe.

"But someone I know at college is exhibiting a painting there. I said I'd go," the youngster pleaded.

"I can't trust you not to head off for your uncle."

"I'm not going there. I'm not going to see uncle Frank."

Tony turned to his mother pleading the cause. She'd just placed the shopping bag inside the door and was taking off her coat.

"Let him go if it's a friend from college," she took her son's side, entering the living room and placing her coat over the back of the sofa.

"Do you trust him not to go to your brother's?" Gerry was beginning to buckle slightly. He didn't want to appear like a tyrant to his son, but was genuinely fearful of him falling into the clutches of Frank's underworld.

"Can we trust you?" Irene gave Tony a serious gaze.

"Yes, seriously. I'm just going to my friend's exhibition. Look here's the flyer." Tony removed the leaflet from his trouser pocket, unfolding it for his parents to read. Gerry placed his newspaper to one side and studied the details, remaining silent for a few moments as he made up his mind.

"Alright, you can go. Though heaven knows why you'd want to see an exhibition of all that modern art stuff. It's not proper painting at all."

Tony couldn't care less what his father thought of it. In truth he wasn't overly taken with it himself. But that was not the point. He looked forward to seeing Rudy again. He bent forward and kissed his father on the head.

"Thanks dad."

Gerry wouldn't show it, but the affection of his son warmed his imprisoned heart.

The following Wednesday afternoon Tony entered the grand, greystone building of Fulham library in south west London, featuring tall columns each side of the black imposing doorway. A sign pointed him to a large room set aside in the building for the local art exhibition. A few visitors were studying the art works mounted on the walls as he entered.

He couldn't see Rudy and wondered if he'd been and gone. A young woman in a light yellow dress came across to him carrying a clipboard.

"Are you looking for someone?" she asked.

"Rudy Weston."

"Ah, Rudy. I think he's out the back. Hold on." The woman walked off, disappearing through a door at the far end. Tony caught sight of the painting Rudy had been working on at the college. A few colourful twirls and dyed cloth textures added since he'd last seen it, but definitely the one.

221

The woman re-appeared with Rudy beside her. He greeted Tony with an enthusiastic handshake and smile.

"Really glad you could come."

Tony was thrown for a moment. He recognised Rudy's face, but he looked entirely different out of college uniform in a bright red shirt, blue denim jacket and jeans.

Tony suddenly felt uncomfortable in his plain white shirt, blue tie, navy jacket and dark trousers with a neat crease down the front. His mother had insisted he must dress smartly for an exhibition.

"I like your painting," said Tony, not having any strong feelings for the work, but wishing to be polite.

"That's mine too," Rudy pointed to another artwork of mixed shapes and textures alongside it. He could see Tony wasn't taken by the paintings.

"There's another of mine over there," Rudy led him across the floor to a line-up of more artwork. He pointed to an oil painting depicting a seascape with a galleon in full sail on the waves. Tony's jaw dropped in awe. Rudy laughed.

"No-one believes you're a real artist if you can't paint traditional pictures," he said, seeing Tony's reaction.

"That's fantastic," Tony was still staring at the painting, deeply impressed. "It's like ones done by famous artists."

Rudy shook his head, smiling.

"But I like abstract art," said Rudy, taking Tony on a tour of the exhibition. "It's been about for twenty years in New York, but only now beginning to take off over here in Britain. It's going to be a big scene in the coming sixties."

The start of the 1960s was only a year away. Tony would be fifteen. Beyond hoping he could be an adult as soon as possible, he had no idea what Rudy was alluding to concerning the future. The changing world was as distant from him as the stars.

After showing him round, Rudy invited Tony for a cup of coffee in the small back room of the library. With mugs in hand they settled on a couple of chairs.

"Have you got much lined up for the summer holidays?" asked Rudy.

"Seeing friends and things," Tony replied. He didn't want to confess that his father was confining him to his nan's because he wasn't trusted. It would sound childish in front of someone who wasn't much older than him, but behaved in a manner more like an adult. It gave Tony a sense of higher status being treated as an equal by him.

"I'm having a party at my house on Saturday night. Why don't you come?" Rudy invited.

Tony wanted to jump at the chance, though couldn't imagine his father allowing him to go.

"I'm not sure. I'll have to check if there's something already on," he made an excuse.

"Well if you can, you're very welcome. Starts at about eight o'clock. I live in Perrymead Street, not far from here. Number 220."

Before leaving, they briefly chatted about Sandalwood College. Tony told him he hated the place.

"It's okay if you just play the game," Rudy advised. "You can get away with a lot if you do your bit. Obey the orders. Let them see you're trying. That they're in charge.

Then they'll think you're a great guy and put up with some of your antics if you don't push your luck too far."

Rudy seemed so laid back about the place. Tony listened to the advice, but was beginning to realise his own emotions got the better of him. So often reacting before considering the consequences.

"Do your mum and dad mind you having a party?" Tony was curious. He couldn't imagine his own parents allowing any of his friends into their home. Going to the pub was how they got together with people. Home was a place just for living, not fun. He'd never even thought of asking any of his friends to a party. His father would never approve.

"My parents are divorced," said Rudy. "My father works for the government abroad and my mother is usually drunk most evenings. She rents most of the rooms in our house to lodgers. The ground floor is our own private area and my bedroom is in the cellar."

Tony didn't know how to reply. Rudy's home life didn't sound good.

"Anyway, if you can come to the party, it'd be great to see you," the artist stood up. "Now I'd better get back and mix a bit with the visitors, such as they are."

Tony got up.

"I'd love to come. I'll see if I can sort something out."

"Parents eh? They can be a pain in the arse," Rudy gave a knowing look. Tony's face flushed, embarrassed that his new friend could see through him clearly.

That evening he cautiously tackled his father on the thorny subject and was met with a flat refusal.

"But I went to the exhibition and didn't run away. Why can't I go?"

"Who is this Rudy? I know nothing about him. How can I tell if he hasn't got some hare-brained scheme that will get you into trouble?" Gerry was annoyed at being interrupted while he sat reading a book in the living room.

Irene heard them through the sliding glass partition in the wall connecting with the kitchen. She stopped preparing a meal and came into the room.

"I think it's alright for him to go, as long as he's back at a proper time," she defended her son.

"I've made my decision," Gerry remained adamant.

"You can't keep him cooped up all the time. He's got to be able to do a few things on his own," Irene rounded on him. "You joined the airforce underage only a few years older than he is now. You defied your parents when they tried to stop you."

"But that was to fight a war. Not go off to a party."

"Oh, so going to a party is worse than going to fight in a war is it"?

"That was entirely different, I wanted to defend my country," angrily Gerry flung his book on the floor.

"The war's over. You keep on living it with your bloody stupid stiff upper lip. I was in the women's auxiliary. You're not the only one who fought in the war for freedom. Give the boy some."

Gerry's face was red with fury. His wife, who he considered to be of lower intellect, had confounded him. He was restricting his son for his own good, but now it began to sink in that it could be over protection. As his

225

blood pressure subsided a little he began to have a change of heart. Tony was standing silently as the verbal blows between his parents came to an end.

"Okay. You can go," Gerry relented, standing up and staring sternly at his son. "But you be back here no later than eleven thirty, or I'll get an extra lock fitted to make sure you don't leave this place for the rest of your holiday."

Tony felt ecstatic, but didn't want to show it, just in case his father thought any sign of triumph over him would lead to a change of mind.

"Thanks dad," he said softly and left for his bedroom.

"Dinner's in ten minutes," Irene called after him.

******

TONY arrived at Rudy's just after eight o'clock on Saturday night. The three-storey Victorian terraced property had a small, paved front garden with low hedges on each side.

""So you made it," his friend greeted him at the front door. "Come in, we're in the front room."

Rudy's guests were spread on chairs, a sofa and sitting cross legged on the floor. They all looked older than Tony, late teens and twenties, and casually dressed in corduroys, denims and T-shirts. Again the newcomer felt out of place in his navy jacket, pressed trousers, shirt and tie, which his mother insisted he should wear for the occasion.

As Rudy introduced him, he noticed two men and a woman chatting who wore odd clothes. Not the kind you'd see in the street.

226

One of the men had dressed in a collarless dark suit, vividly contrasting with his bright pink shirt displaying frills down the front. The other, a yellow afghan jacket and tight fit bright green trousers. The woman's white top was covered in gold glitter and silver stars. Her white skirt had broad red diagonal stripes, and was so short it barely covered her thighs.

Tony had seen skimpy dresses on the showgirls in uncle Frank's nightclub, but they'd never wear them out in public.

Rudy noticed Tony studying the group.

"They're art college students," he said, "working on new fashion designs. Those are some of their ideas and creations. A couple of big fashion houses have shown an interest. They're the sort of clothes that could go mainstream in the next few years."

Tony had the sensation he was entering a new universe, set far away from the rigid regulations of college and the never ending routine of his parents' joyless lives.

"Would you like a glass of wine?" asked Rudy.

The guests all had drinks and Tony felt he'd become more included if he joined in. Rudy poured him a glass of white.

"So you go to the same college as Rudy, do you?" one of the men asked Tony. He nodded the reply, feeling awkward in the company of complete strangers older than him.

"Well I hope you paint better than he does," chipped in a woman on the sofa, looking across at Rudy. "I just don't go with all that modern art stuff."

Rudy laughed.

"No, you're a total stick in the mud."

The woman raised two fingers at him, smiling.

Tony was struggling to strike up conversation with these people who he felt were on a different level to his world. Rudy detected his discomfort.

"This is the chat room," he told him. "They all think they're great intellectuals, not just everyday people like us." Rudy raised his voice in a wry tone making sure he was overheard.

"Oh, so speaks the great one who thinks he's better than us having his art shown in a local exhibition," another man voiced with a friendly grin. The others began laughing.

"You're just jealous," Rudy batted back. "Come on Tony, let me take you to the relaxing room."

"You'll certainly blow your mind relaxing there," someone called out as they left.

The distant background music Tony heard when he'd entered the house grew louder as Rudy led him down the hallway towards a room at the back.

"Who's that singing?" asked Tony. He'd never heard music like it before.

"Bo Diddley singing I'm A Man. He's an American blues singer. A friend of mine gets some US import records into the UK for me," Rudy explained. "Not many people have heard of him over here. Some new bands are starting to play American blues music in the clubs. Rhythm and blues they're starting to call it. Becoming very popular. Muddy Waters' songs are catching on too."

Tony was completely baffled by Rudy's explanations. The music and artists were totally alien to him. But he liked the sound coming from the room, strange though it

228

sounded, and not at all like the American crooners his mother loved to hear on the radio at home.

Inside the room three women sat on a sofa and a row of three men and a woman relaxed on the floor, legs outstretched resting their backs against the wall. The blues singer poured soulfully from a record player on a small table in the corner.

The guests nodded and smiled as Rudy introduced the newcomer. Tony had finished his glass of wine, and was starting to relax a little, the shyness beginning to fade.

"You don't exactly look thrilled to see me," Tony blurted out, regretting in the same second the words that had emerged from his mouth. They arrived without thinking.

For a moment the guests stared at this young stranger in amazement.

"Takes a lot to thrill us," one of the men on the floor called back and they all began to laugh. Tony's involuntary remark had broken the ice.

"Who's this, our surprise comedy act for the evening Rudy? What are you wearing son?" a woman on the sofa in a red satin dress grinned at Tony.

"This is my mother's special selection," Tony looked down at his clothes. "Suitable for birthdays, weddings and funerals, but best for dustbins," he blurted again. He had no idea where these remarks were coming from. They were just flowing from his mind as the alcohol worked further into his system.

His reply was a great hit. Everyone creased with laughter. They'd all suffered from what mother thought was best for them. Rudy was thrilled that his friend had suddenly melted into the scene.

"I reckon you deserve a prize," another man with dark shoulder length hair and dressed in T-shirt and jeans called to him from the floor. He held in his fingers what looked like a hand rolled cigarette. Tony had become aware of a strange smoke odour in the room, but it wasn't the same as ordinary cigarettes.

"Come and sit down with us," the man beckoned. He nudged the fair haired woman beside him to shift along making space for Tony who settled between them. "Have a drag on this," he offered the hand rolled smoke to him.

"What is it?" Tony asked. Everyone stared at him.

"Cannabis ol' son. Or a spliff, a joint, hash. Whatever you want to call it, this'll take your troubles away."

Tony wasn't sure. He had no idea what any of those names meant. But now he was glowing in his new found acceptance with the group. They were grown-ups treating him like an adult. He took a drag, inhaling. Next second he coughed violently as the smoke struck the back of his throat. The group laughed at the novice in their company.

Determined not to lose status among them he persevered, inhaling a few more times and trying to resist the irritation in his throat forcing him to cough a few more times. They clapped him for his efforts as he passed the joint back to the man beside him.

After about five minutes the room seemed to come alive, the light brighter. He felt incredibly relaxed as the blues music playing grew powerful, the emotions in the song reaching inside him. The conversation and laughs of people

230

around him more vibrant. His mind was lifting into a different plane.

Tony heard himself talking, but had the sensation it was coming from a different person.

"Feeling good?" someone asked.

"Amazing," Tony smiled.

One of the women on the sofa stood up.

"Come on Rudy, let's have some music we can dance to. This blues stuff is starting to depress me." She began swaying to an imaginary faster beat.

Rudy selected a record from a stack beside the player. The room suddenly burst alive to the sound of Elvis' Jailhouse Rock.

Soon the guests who'd been in the chat room came in to join the dancing, everyone beginning to fill the floor. One of the women took Tony's hand and pulled him up to dance with her. She looked immensely desirable to him, beautiful shapely breasts in a frilly blue blouse and a black skirt with silver embroidery in rows of waves gyrating as her hips began swaying to the song.

The woman broke into a jive dance still holding Tony's hand. He had no idea how to do it and she guided him as he clumsily tried to make the twists and spins. Laughter broke out at his inept efforts, but by now he didn't care. He'd never felt so good, so much fun in the warmth of the attractive woman's smile, who appeared not to mind that her partner was a complete numpty dancer. The atmosphere was electric. Time no longer existed.

However, in reality time relentlessly ticked on. Tony suddenly became aware of it. He had to be home by eleven thirty, or his father's anger would condemn him to hell. Glancing at his wristwatch he saw the time was just after eleven. A glass of wine and a smoke of cannabis was not quite enough to drive away the impending fury of being late home.

Tony broke away from the excitement making for the front door. Rudy saw him and followed.

"Sorry, but I've got to go or I'll miss the last bus home," Tony sounded regretful. He really wanted to stay.

"Get it in the neck will you, if you're late?" Rudy was sympathetic. Tony nodded, his veneer of adulthood slipping away as he descended again to the dictates of mum and dad.

"The crowd in there loved you," said Rudy, "they think you're a great genuine guy. I'm really pleased you could come."

"I had a great time. The best." Tony replied.

Rudy placed a hand on his shoulder.

"See you back at college then."

The thought of returning to Sandalwood brought Tony rapidly down to earth. The door closed on the music and he ran to catch the last bus home, drizzle beginning to spatter his clothes.

He arrived back home at quarter to midnight. Gerry was waiting up and looked grim as Tony entered. He thought he'd blown it. Hell would break out.

"Did you have a good time?" his father's gaze lightened. Gerry was glad to see his son had returned and not done another runner.

"Yeah. It was really good," Tony felt relieved.

"Right, I'm off to bed and you'd better too. Your mother's asleep so don't make a noise."

"I won't. Goodnight dad. Thanks for letting me go." Tony was certain he'd passed a crucial test and would now be let off the leash.

He was wrong. Next day his father ordered he should still go and stay at his nan's during the working week for the rest of the college holiday. If he did that and didn't misbehave, Gerry would consider allowing him more freedom during the next holiday. Tony was bitterly disappointed.

******

THE situation began to turn brighter for Tony at the start of the autumn term. Rudy was appointed a prefect and his friendship offered considerable protection.

The vindictive prefect, Herring, always on the lookout to catch juniors doing something wrong, or searching them to boost his cigarette supply, laid off him. Herring knew if he picked on the friend of someone bearing his own rank, the other prefects would unite to cause trouble for him. He was generally disliked by them anyway. It wouldn't take much for him to be cited as a thief for confiscating cigarettes and not reporting it to a higher authority. The unwritten code of silence could be broken for a traitor to prefect loyalty.

Tony's friendship also brought benefits. Rudy shared a room in the study block, set away from the main building, with three other seniors.

It meant Tony could sometimes join them to enjoy music from a record player in the study, as well as spend time relaxing on a sofa and chatting with them. For a while all seemed to be going well. Something had to happen to upset the run of luck.

Walking along a corridor in the main building after finishing a lesson, he saw Herring approaching him.

"You may think you're untouchable with your arty friend Rudy Weston, but there's more than one way to skin a cat," he snarled. "Your friend Lance Harris is in the headmaster's study being expelled from the college."

Tony was stunned. He hadn't seen much of Lance lately, both of them spending more time with other friends. But they still chatted occasionally. They still had a bond.

"Why?"

"He stole some money from another boy. I found it in his bedside locker with total proof it was him." Herring gave a self-satisfied grin then walked on, leaving Tony totally shell shocked.

Lance was never a thief. He'd been guilt-ridden for weeks after they'd taken cigarettes using counterfeit coins. Stealing wasn't in his bones. Herring must have done something. Of that Tony felt certain. A nasty trick to get back at him for enjoying Rudy's protection. The bastard knew it would upset him. He'd enjoyed giving him the news.

Over the next few days the whispers went around about Lance's expulsion. The only official announcement was that he'd left the college, but Herring made sure the reason was circulated.

Several weeks later Tony received a letter during the usual distribution of mail at breakfast in the dining hall. The address handwriting seemed familiar, but it was not the hand of his mother or father. He opened it. As he read the contents, his eyes grew wide in shocked disbelief. The letter was from his friend Lance.

Dear Tony,

You will know by now that I've been expelled from the college. You were my good friend, so I'm writing to tell you I did nothing wrong. I'm sure Herring got another boy, Peter Simmons, to tell him he'd had a five pound note stolen. Herring did a search of my bedside locker and found the five pound note there. Simmons said he recognised it because it had a wavy, black marker pen line in the top right hand corner.

I told the headmaster that I'd never seen the note before, but he believed Herring and said I was a wicked thief. He said I'd already been bad for running away with you from college, and there was now no second chance.

I think Herring set Simmons up for it. You know how the vile bastard can threaten people. Thought I would write to let you know. I hope you believe I'm not a thief, whatever they might be saying about me.

Your friend,
Lance

The students sitting near Tony could see the contents of the letter had deeply upset him.

"What's wrong?" one asked. "Someone died?"

Tony shook his head, folding the letter and placing it in his inside jacket pocket.

"Are you alright?" asked another.

Tony's appetite for the cereal in front of him faded. The letter tied in with what Herring had smugly said a few weeks earlier about Lance stealing money. Now he was convinced Lance had been set up. Tony felt powerless to right the wrong. He had no status in the matter and Lance's letter was no proof of innocence. 'He would say that', anyone would reply.

The shock of the letter now rose into anger as Tony sat through a history lesson. The teacher talking about the Corn Law of 1815 passed entirely over his head. Maybe someone could help to bring justice for his friend. An idea came to him that he thought was worth a reply.

******

TONY went to Rudy's study at end of lessons that day. His new friend was sitting in an armchair paging through an illustrated book of artwork by Picasso.

Two of Rudy's colleagues, Tank Thomson and Freddie Newton, were sitting at a table writing exam preparation work in their notepads.

"What's up? You're looking a bit serious," Rudy observed when Tony knocked on the door and entered.

"Have a seat," he pointed to a chair.

Tony took Lance's letter from his pocket and gave it to him. Rudy read it then looked up, a thoughtful gaze as his mind fully digested the information.

"Do you think it's true?" Rudy asked. "Not just Lance trying to put the blame elsewhere?"

"I believe him," said Tony. "We were good friends and nothing he ever did made me think he was a thief." Tony paused, remembering the cigarettes he and Lance took from the machines.

"Well, he wasn't perfect, and nor am I, but I know Lance just doesn't have a criminal personality. I don't believe he stole this money."

Rudy remained quiet, considering the situation. Tank Thomson got up, his muscular frame almost bursting out of his white shirt. His height towered over all the other college teachers, and it was obvious to see why he had the nickname Tank. Rudy handed him the letter.

"If this is true, that fucking bastard Herring needs putting down," Tank's jaw raged in his solid square head after reading it. He was not someone to mince words or emotions.

He handed the letter across to Freddie, whose appearance strongly contrasted with Tank, serious eyes carefully considering the world through gold rimmed spectacles. Freddie too expressed his disgust, but without fury.

"Herring needs to be chucked out of this college," Tank simmered, beginning to calm a little.

"And this might be the opportunity," said Rudy.

"Can I hold on to this?" he asked Tony, taking the letter back from Freddie.

Tony nodded.

"Leave it with me. I'll see what can be done."

Next day Rudy summoned the boy Peter Simmons, named in Lance's letter, to his study. Freddie was at the table revising for a physics exam in a couple of weeks. Tank was absent in a lesson.

Simmons stood neatly in jacket and trousers looking down as if expecting trouble.

"Did Herring ask you to say you'd had five pounds stolen from you?" Rudy got straight to the point. The boy shuffled his feet nervously.

"Tell me the truth and you'll be alright. I'll protect you. Lie and you will be in serious trouble," he laid out the deal. The youngster shuffled again. Freddie had stopped studying, listening intently.

Simmons began nodding, raising his head to reveal his soft, round face

"Yes," he whispered quietly.

"You're absolutely sure?" Rudy insisted.

"Yes," he whispered again.

"Okay. Thank you. Now don't mention this to Herring, otherwise I'll make life ten times worse for you than he ever could."

The boy looked troubled. Rudy hated threatening him like that, but it was essential not a word of their meeting got out.

"You can go now."

A few days later afternoon Rudy looked out the window knowing that Herring would be entering the study block enclosure. He was a creature of habit and usually nipped back in late afternoon to his own study, facing Rudy's on the opposite side, for a cigarette and an illicit glass of wine. Drinking was not allowed, but he sneaked in bottles from the local village off-licence.

Rudy walked across the centre lawn to Herring's study, knocked and entered.

Herring appeared defensive. He knew he was unpopular and on more than one occasion Rudy had told him he was an unpleasant toe-rag.

"What do you want?" he asked sharply, holding a cigarette pack in his hand.

"I know we don't see eye to eye," Rudy began in a conciliatory tone, "but I think there's something seriously wrong going on, and I know that you have an uncanny knack of catching juniors when they're up to no good."

Herring stood mystified. He did consider himself clever at knowing how to catch younger boys doing wrong things that he could use to his advantage. But Rudy taking him into his confidence seemed out of place.

"So what do you want?" he played it cautiously.

"I think there's a stash of cigarettes and alcohol that some of the juniors have been stealing from shops in the towns when they're out on Saturday afternoon passes," Rudy began to explain.

"I overheard two of them in the back corridor, talking about putting cigarettes in a hiding place covered by undergrowth near the old, disused well. You know, the well on on the far side of the old orchard."

Herring was calculating if this was some tale Rudy was making up to entice him into a trap. He looked doubtful.

"I was wondering if you want a share of what I find," said Rudy, "but that's up to you." He turned to leave.

"Why are you telling me? I know you hate me. What's in it for you?" Herring stared suspiciously.

Rudy turned back to face him.

"It's true. I haven't particularly liked you. But since my appointment as a prefect, I've come to realise that to keep order, you have to be hard on the juniors."

He paused.

"And I've also come to realise that allowing a junior like Tony Selby to come to my study was not a good idea. I knew him before I became a prefect, but now things are different. So I've banned him from entering the study block."

Herring seemed surprised at the news and began thinking Rudy was possibly starting to side with him. That perhaps he should give him a trust trail. After all, he'd be able to smell out any tricky business if Rudy was selling him a line. He considered himself pretty astute at that. And the prospect of getting some cigarettes and booze was enticing, as well as making life hell for the juniors involved.

"Who were the juniors you overheard?" he asked. Rudy wasn't prepared for the question. He had to think fast. Hesitation would blow the set-up.

240

"Who do you think they are? You should know the ones that get up to this sort of thing." He threw back the question.

A couple of names came into Herring's mind. Boys he'd confiscated cigarettes from on several occasions. Devious ones who seemed able to get hold of them in a way that mystified him. He'd threatened to report them to a higher authority, but never did because they were a good continuing supply for him.

"Johnson and Hendry," he named the boys he suspected.

"You're on the ball," Rudy praised him, while having no idea who they were in the college of three hundred pupils.

"Well, we'll take their stash, but I don't think we should report them," Herring envisaged a golden goose to protect.

"I thought you were a stickler for the rules?" Rudy frowned.

"Rules are for fools," Herring uttered, a faint smile escaping his sour face.

"I don't plan to interfere with your territory," Rudy promised. "Now are you coming with me or not?" He turned to leave again.

"Okay," Herring followed him.

They walked down the sloping stony track at the rear of the college towards the old orchard, uncultivated and overgrown for many years.

Tramping through the barely visible path almost covered in long grass and ducking under neglected apple tree branches, they approached the area of the disused well.

Now a tangle of weeds and grass covered everything around as they moved to an open area just beyond the

241

orchard. Herring protested as Rudy began crushing a path underfoot between them.

"Where's this hidden stash?"

"Not far," Rudy reassured.

The top of the old well came into view, the lower part of it obscured by the surrounding undergrowth. Rudy stopped a few yards away. A round lid of thick oak wood rested over the opening, the grain greyed by weather.

"You're not telling me that's where it's stashed?" Herring sounded suspicious.

"Oh no," Rudy replied, "that would be silly. Even a bastard like you wouldn't believe me."

In that second, Herring realised he'd been set-up. Suddenly there was rustling in the undergrowth. Tank and Freddie emerged.

"Well, if it isn't our old friend Herring," Tank boomed from his lofty height, drawing close with Freddie by his side. Freddie wasn't tall, but dressed in shirt sleeves, like the giant beside him, his wiry physique was apparent.

"What the hell's this?" Herring demanded, his voice heavy with fear.

"We just want to have a little chat about how you got Lance Harris expelled from the college," said Rudy.

"He was a thief. I caught him and he got what he deserved," Herring blustered.

"You set him up didn't you? And threatened the boy Simmons if he didn't go along with your planted five pound note plan," Rudy pressed him.

"I don't have to stay here listening to your nonsense," Herring turned to leave.

Rudy and Freddie leapt at him, grabbing an arm each and twisting them behind his back. He yelped in pain.

"Now you're going to go to the headmaster and confess what you did," Rudy ordered.

"I'm fucking not!" their victim shouted. The captors forced his arms painfully upward.

"I'll go to the head and tell him what you're doing to me," Herring threatened.

"Okay Tank, time to get rid of him," Rudy looked across to his colleague who'd been staring at the captive like dirt.

He stepped forward and gripped the edge of the well's oak wood covering. It would usually need at least two strong men to shift its enormous weight. Tank was vested with enormous strength, but even he struggled to lift it. But after a few moments, lift it he did, exerting all his force to push the covering half open across the well.

"What are you doing you maniacs?" Herring writhed, attempting to free his arms, panic surfacing in his voice.

"I think it's about a forty foot drop into the water," said Freddie.

"You're joking! You've got to be joking!" Herring now struggled more violently trying to free himself from the arm grip.

Tank approached and grabbed Herring by his jacket lapels as Rudy and Freddie released him.

"Sit down!" Tank released his lapels, forcing him to sit on the undergrowth. "Lie down."

Herring visibly shook with terror, obeying the hulk in front of him. Tank bent down and grabbed his ankles, then lifted him so he dangled helplessly upside down.

Carrying him across to the well, he hoisted his victim so that his head aimed downwards into the dark depths. Then he began lowering him.

"Jesus Christ, help me!" Herring screamed, his cry echoing round the shaft below.

"You don't have to confess to him. Just the headmaster," Rudy called.

"I will, I will," Herring shouted. "Just fucking pull me back."

"Not sure I believe you," Rudy replied.

Tank released one of Herring's ankles, causing him to swing sideways.

"God no! Please no!" he screamed, horrified he was about to be released into the watery pit. "I'll do anything you want!" He began to cry.

Tank grabbed his other ankle and pulled him upwards out of the opening, dropping him on the ground.

He got up, staring at them terrified, his face puffed red. Manic bulging eyes.

"You better change your underwear," said Rudy.

A wet patch covered the crotch of Herring's trousers.

"Then meet me outside the headmaster's office in half-an-hour. You're going to confess your lie about Lance Harris to him."

A look of reluctance rose in Herring's face.

"If you don't," Rudy warned, "next time we'll kill you."

Their victim said nothing, and began running away as fast as he could through the undergrowth.

Half-an-hour later Rudy arrived outside the headmaster's office. He waited for a few minutes wondering if Herring would turn up. He began to think his plan hadn't worked, then the prefect appeared at the end of the corridor and approached. Hate burned in his eyes as Rudy knocked on the door.

"Come," a voice answered.

Dr Goldacre sat at his desk reading through paperwork. After a few moments he looked up.

"To what do I owe this honour?" he smiled at the two prefects standing before him.

"Herring has a confession to make," Rudy cut straight to the point.

Dr Goldacre's smiled dropped.

"That sounds serious."

"It is," Rudy replied, stepping forward and handing him the letter Lance wrote to Tony. The headmaster read it then looked up at Herring with a piercing gaze.

"Is this true?"

The accused hesitated. Rudy turned his head to stare at him, conveying the dire consequences if he dared back track.

"I'm afraid so," Herring mumbled, as if a half-hearted reply would lessen the outcome.

Dr Goldacre's sunny welcome had dissolved into an approaching storm.

"Why did you do it?"

"I don't know sir. It was a stupid thing to do." Herring couldn't admit it was an act of malicious revenge.

"Do you realise you've seriously damaged a young boy's reputation?" The head was furious, his face turning puce. Herring didn't reply.

"I have no alternative but to release you from this college. I shall inform your parents, and you will leave within the next couple of days when arrangements can be made." Goldacre paused, shaking his head in disbelief. "And you are stripped of your prefect status. Now go!" he pointed to the door.

Rudy moved to leave with him.

"No wait, ."

Rudy turned back as Herring departed.

"I'm puzzled as to why this confession came about?" Goldacre quizzed.

"The student Tony Selby showed me the letter," Rudy explained. "I confronted Herring with it. He denied it to start with, but a few days later I think guilt got the better of him. He asked me to come with him to confess to you."

Rudy's mixed explanation of truth and lie seemed to satisfy the head.

"Thank you," he replied. "I think it would be best if the reason for Herring being expelled is kept under wraps as far as possible."

Rudy nodded, though he thought it would be a tall order in a place where tongues and rumours spread like wildfire.

Alone again, Dr Goldacre wrestled with his own conscience. If he wrote to Lance's parents explaining their son had been exonerated, fury would likely break out at the terrible injustice done to the boy. His job could be on the line for not properly investigating. The college governors would sack him in order to detach any possible actions against the college. Goldacre eased his conscience by deciding the youngster would probably make out okay somewhere else, and returned to reading the paperwork in front of him.

******

TONY learned of Herring's expulsion from word that rapidly spread through the college, sparking a wave of joy among seniors as well as juniors. He made his way to Rudy's study after lessons.

"What did you do?" he asked, entering to see Tank and Freddie sitting in armchairs drinking coffee and Rudy perched on the table chatting to them.

"We persuaded him to confess what he'd done," Rudy winked at his companions. They smiled. Tony could tell he wasn't going to get a straight answer at present.

"Just say we were very persuasive," said Tank.

That evening he wrote a letter to Lance saying Herring had confessed and perhaps his parents could get him back into Sandalwood.

A week later he received a reply from Lance thanking him for the information, but saying he was now at a new college that was much better. He had a fresh start and wanted to move on. He'd told his parents and they'd be writing to Goldacre asking him to put the record straight. Then the matter could drop.

Although they had drifted apart a little as friends at Sandalwood, Tony was saddened to think it likely he'd never see Lance again.

Goldacre was hugely relieved when he received a letter from the boy's parents saying that as long as he put on record that their son was innocent of the theft, they would take the matter no further. The head was happy to comply, though he wondered how Lance's parents had learned of Herring's sacking. He concluded it must have come from the boy's friend, Tony Selby. But the matter was settled and now best left alone.

CHAPTER 10

IN THE following year Tony actually felt happy at Sandalwood College with Rudy's patronage behind him. He behaved in class and at leisure, not wanting to let his friend down. Even the teachers noticed a positive change from his past uncaring attitude to knowledge.

During the holidays he spent more time with Rudy. That had been a battle at first with his father insisting he should still be in the care of his nan. But Tony totally refused.

"Do as I say or I'll throw you out in the street," Gerry raged.

"Go on then," Tony dared him.

Gerry was not going to throw his son out. It was the final veiled threat in his armoury. And Irene certainly wouldn't back him on that score. The threat hadn't worked. He relented, but warned he would definitely carry it out if there was any hint of Tony getting into trouble, or more especially, going to uncle Frank.

The relaxation stretched to Tony occasionally staying overnight at Rudy's. Music, spliffs and drink at parties. At one of them, held in the flat of the woman who'd danced with him that first time at Rudy's, she welcomed him at the door and planted a soft kiss on his cheek.

"My lovely boy," she said, sounding a little out of it on drink, maybe pot, or possibly both.

She wore a light yellow lace top and short, dark red skirt revealing enticing legs and thighs that Tony felt a strong urge to touch. The scent of her perfume seemed to be pulling him to her softness. He smiled as she stepped aside for him and Rudy to enter..

"Are you going to give me another dancing lesson?" Tony joked.

"Oh, I'm planning to give you lots of lessons," she replied with a devious wink.

They entered to the music in the living room, couples dancing, chatting, drinking. The stuffy heat by itself was intoxicating.

"I see you've made your mark with Victoria," Rudy whispered to him, before turning to greet some friends. Until that moment Tony hadn't known the woman's name. He looked around feeling lost in a crowd of strangers. Then Rudy beckoned to him. He went across to the group Rudy had joined.

"I see you've dressed down for this party," one of the men remarked. Tony wore a T-shirt and jeans, no longer feeling confined to the smart dress code his mother had previously imposed on him. Tony recognised the man as the one who'd handed him a cannabis joint at Rudy's after the art exhibition. Tony laughed, about to reply when Victoria broke in handing him a glass of red wine.

"Here's your starter for a fun night," she winked and smiled at him again.

"You're in there," grinned another man with a neatly trimmed horseshoe moustache, as Victoria disappeared between the dancers. A woman in the group laughed.

Tony felt embarrassed, but as the evening wore on, wine and the occasional drag on a spliff relaxed him, so that conversation and laughing began to flow naturally. Strangers seemed to become familiar friends.

Victoria, who had been circulating among her guests, reappeared as Tony sat chatting in a happy haze.

"You've got to come and dance with me," she grabbed Tony's hand just as Chris Montez broke into Let's Dance from the record player.

Tony had never felt so euphoric, gyrating the twist and looking into her smiling eyes. They danced on to more music until she took his hand during a pause.

"I'd like to show you something," she said, leading him through the dancers waiting for the next record to begin.

She guided him upstairs into a room. He was wondering what she wanted to show him. This was a bedroom. Beyond there being a bed, wardrobe, dresser and a teddy bear on an armchair, there appeared nothing remarkable to see. Victoria turned to him, drawing close.

"Kiss me," she invited, placing her arms around his waist.

For a second Tony looked puzzled. Totally unprepared for the amazing invitation. It didn't take long for him to accept the offer. They kissed. Victoria pressed his lips in deep passion. Tony had no experience of the powerful desire in a woman. His teeth clunked on hers.

Victoria broke away laughing.

"You're a total virgin, aren't you?"

Tony's rising penis started to deflate.

"It's alright. There's a first time for everyone," she joked, sensing his male-hood offended.

She grabbed the bottom of his T-shirt and pulled it over his head, softly stroking his chest and stomach. Then she undid his belt and zip, taking down his jeans and pants. She could see his libido was rapidly recovering. Then she stripped off her clothes and took his hand, leading him to the bed.

"Oh, my strong man," she urged him on, laying down. With her left hand she began massaging her breast and drew up her knees, slowly moving her other hand down across her stomach, opening her legs to gently stroke between the parting. "I'll teach you how a woman likes to be satisfied."

******

WHEN Tony returned to Sandalwood the next term, a sense of deep loneliness pervaded him. Rudy had left the college along with Tank and Freddie. They'd taken their exams and moved on to permanent adult life in the outside world.

Now he was a senior at the college, but at sixteen not old enough yet to be running for prefect status. And since his past attitude had been deemed a bit bolshy, the privilege was unlikely to be bestowed on him.

He enjoyed the company of friends there in his day to day life, but after the excitement of living in an adult environment with Rudy during the holidays, returning to the rigid confines of Sandalwood to be treated like a child again, began to grow unbearable. He endured it for a couple more terms, until one fateful day he had an argument with a teacher who gave him detention for not completing part of his course work.

Tony decided he would leave Sandalwood and find a job back home. But not from his own home. Gerry would explode, there'd be a dreadful scene on learning his son had decided to abandon college. Tony would seek a temporary shelter at Rudy's home. Sleep on the floor if necessary. At first he wrote a letter to his mother telling her not to worry. He had decided to leave and would be safe.

Early on Sunday afternoon and before the letter would have arrived to cause an alert, Tony dressed in casual clothes and left for the village. There he caught a bus taking him a few miles down the road, where the busy A5 route would give him a better chance of quickly hitching a lift.

His luck with getting lifts was not so great as his last escape with Lance. After a couple of car rides, the generosity of passing traffic dried up. Night began to enclose and after walking miles on roadside verges, he became exhausted, hungry and thirsty. There was a gap in the hedge running alongside the grass verge. He went through into a field and laid down in the long grass.

The comfort of a thin mattress at Sandalwood for sleeping on now seemed like a luxury. Even the unappetising food. He awoke shivering, clothes soaked by the dew. The dream of a new life seemed a million miles away. Hunger and cold sapped the spirit. A faint dawn light on the horizon silhouetted stripes of cloud, but night still held sway.

"This is hopeless," Tony said to himself, standing up. In his eagerness to escape he'd taken a few snack bars, but not bothered with a jacket. The bars had long gone. Now in two minds as to continue or give up his quest, he returned to the grass verge and began walking again to warm up. He could just make out the dark ground beneath, tripping occasionally on an uneven mound.

The road was quiet, with an hour or so to go before commuters set off on their journeys again. After ten minutes, Tony glanced back to see the lights of a vehicle approaching in the distance. Half-heartedly he began to thumb a lift, not expecting a result.

As the vehicle grew nearer he realised it was a lorry. The headlights briefly blinded him as it passed by. His heart sank. Then he heard brakes squealing a short distance ahead. The vehicle was pulling up. Tony ran to open the cab door. A young man with wavy, ginger hair stared at him under the dim interior light.

"Are you an escaped prisoner?" The driver appeared serious. For a second Tony thought he'd been discovered. He felt he was escaping from a type of prison. The man broke into a laugh.

"It's alright, I'm joking. I wouldn't have bloody stopped if I thought you were. Jump in."

Tony hauled himself on to the passenger seat.

"What's up? Running away from home?" The driver began to pull away.

Once again Tony was struck by the near accurate assessment of his situation. He began to spout a spurious story about how he'd been planning to catch a train home from a friend's house, when he discovered he'd lost his wallet. The driver interrupted mid-sentence.

"It's okay me ol' mate, I've given lifts to all sorts giving me stories why they're hitching lifts in the middle of the night. None of my business." He glanced at Tony and winked. "We're all escaping from something. I do this job 'cause I couldn't stand working all day in an office. Now where you heading?"

Tony told him.

"Well you're in bloody luck. My next delivery," he thumbed towards the back," is two hundred lavatory seats, would you believe, to a depot about five miles down the road from you."

Tony was immensely thankful at this amazing turnaround in fortune at a moment when he'd been on the brink of conceding defeat.

"So if you get caught short, I can at least supply you with a seat," the man laughed. "Now my name's Badger. It's a nickname, 'cause I do lots of night-time driving. What's yours?"

"Tony."

"Well Tony, you look a bit knackered to me. If you want to have a kip while I'm driving, feel free. I won't be offended."

Tony felt more relaxed than he'd been in a long time. The friendliness of Badger and the warmth of the cab. He took up the offer and soon fell asleep, waking only when the man pulled into a transport cafe and treated him to the most delicious fried breakfast and mug of hot tea he'd ever tasted.

Badger loved talking, probably making up for the long hours of solitary night driving thought Tony as the driver regaled him with tales of people he'd given lifts.

"I did have an escaped prisoner once," Badger went on. "I was new at this and I asked him where he'd come from. Cullingham prison, he said to me. Now give me some money or I'll fix you. He pulled a fucking knife on me," Badger turned to Tony, his face expressing the shock he'd felt at the time. "I give him a twenty note, 'that's all I've got' I told him. He took it and jumped out the cab, and disappeared in the night!"

He paused, slowing the lorry as it came to a junction.

"Don't know if they caught him. Probably. I didn't want to report it. I'm not supposed to give lifts. Company policy. It'd get me the sack."

Tony was getting to like the easy going Badger, and grew a little sad as the journey came to an end.

"There you are me ol' mate," he stopped in a road only half-a-mile from Rudy's home. "Look after yourself and don't take lifts from strangers," Badger laughed, "they never stop talking."

Tony thanked him and climbed out of the cab. The man's friendliness had lifted his spirits, but as he began to make his way along the street towards Rudy's, under a grey overcast sky threatening rain, doubt began to descend again.

Would Rudy welcome him as a fugitive from Sandalwood? Give him shelter? Or would he have discarded college life only to end up begging for forgiveness from his father? Be forced back to the ways of a child?

Badger would know what to do he thought with his devil may care attitude to life. That vestige of confidence was disappearing into the distance as his lorry joined the busy rush of mid morning traffic.

Tony knocked on Rudy's door. A few moments later a middle-aged woman with greying, untidy hair opened it. She wore a blue dressing gown and stared at him through black rimmed spectacles.

"Yes?" she shot sharply.

Tony faltered for a second at the brusque reception. He recognised her as Rudy's mother, seeing her briefly on previous visits when she always seemed to be looking daggers at him. At those times she'd usually be swaying slightly from the effects of alcohol.

"Is Rudy in?" he asked sheepishly. She turned back towards the hall bellowing 'Rudy', then shuffled away in her slippers. A few moments later Rudy appeared wearing a blue and white striped shirt and black jeans clasped by a large, brass buckle belt.

"Tony!" He stared in disbelief.

"I've left the college."

"Left?"

"I've had enough of the place. I can't stand it any more."

"Come in," Rudy placed his hand on Tony's shoulder. "Come and have a coffee. Tell me what's happened." He led him into the kitchen. Unwashed dishes and cutlery were scattered on the draining board. Rudy rinsed out a couple of cups, while Tony told him of his decision to leave.

"I feel hemmed in, imprisoned by the place," he explained.

"I know what you mean, but have you made the right decision?" Rudy made the coffee and they sat at the kitchen table.

"I don't know," Tony clasped his head. "I just can't go on there."

"Well what do you want to do?" Rudy asked sympathetically.

"I don't know that either. Get a job, live a normal life," Tony paused, looking at Rudy. "Could you put me up for a day or two while I sort something out?"

His friend could see the anguish Tony was suffering.

"You're mum and dad?"

"I've written to my mum. My dad would never understand."

Rudy thought a little longer.

"There's an un-let room on the first floor. You could stay there for now."

"Would your mum mind?" Tony feared she would object. He'd never seen her look at him in a welcoming way.

"Not while the room's unoccupied. Don't worry, I look after most of what happens round here," Rudy reassured him.

"Now by the look of it you've no other clothes or possessions with you. I'll see if I can dig out something fresh to wear. Get a bath. Bathroom first floor. Then I'll sort out some food."

258

A wave of deep relief coursed through the new lodger. For now at least he'd found a refuge. However, it wasn't long before the peace was broken.

******

THE room was small, but served the purpose with a single bed, wardrobe, table and chairs, gas oven and an electric bar heater. Tony had little money and Rudy invited him to share meals with him in the living room, where Tony had experienced his first taste of party life and spliffs.

He intended to find a job locally, maybe as a shop assistant. He didn't have any exam qualifications for better paid work.

"Do you know anyone who could help you get a job?" Rudy asked, as they sat in the living room eating a meal the following evening. Tony mentioned his uncle, how he worked in the nightclub business and the good money Frank used to pay him when he worked there occasionally.

"Why don't you go to him?"

The thought had crossed Tony's mind, but he knew his father, Gerry, hated his uncle. If he did that, God knows what trouble it would lead to. Over time, Tony had pieced together the realisation his uncle was most likely a gangster, and although he had differences with his father, he feared if both men clashed, Frank might actually murder him. He told Rudy his thoughts.

They were interrupted by loud knocking on the front door and repeated bell ringing. Rudy went to answer.

"He's here, isn't he?" a man's bellowing voice echoed down the hallway. Tony immediately recognised it as his father's. For a moment he thought of hiding, then decided the inevitable confrontation must be faced.

"Just calm down a minute," he heard Rudy say as he came along the hallway.

"I thought you'd be hiding round here," Gerry growled, seeing his son. "Now stop being so bloody stupid and come with me."

"No!" Tony stood resolute.

"Don't you disobey me! I'm your father," Gerry pushed past Rudy to make a grab at his son. Tony swiftly stepped back.

"If you don't come, I'll bloody well pick you up and carry you," Gerry lunged again, his face purple with fury.

"And if you don't calm down, I'll call the police," Rudy interrupted.

The words had a sobering effect. Gerry calmed down a little.

"What are you doing this for?" he pleaded to his son.

"College life and all that studying isn't for me. I'm trapped there. I want to live."

"What the hell do you know about life?" said Gerry contemptuously. "Nothing. And now you want to chuck away a good education. Me and your mother have worked ourselves to the bone to pay for it, and now you're throwing it away." He shook his head in disgust.

"You're breaking your mother's heart, you know."

Those words cut Tony deeply. But he couldn't be compromised by emotion. It would all end up in the same unhappy circle again. He'd contact his mother to let her know he loved and missed her.

"You're only sixteen, still a minor. I'll get a court order to make you return home," Gerry threatened.

"And I'll break it," Tony remained defiant.

"This isn't the end of it," Gerry visibly shook with anger, then turned and left.

Tony returned to the living room feeling deeply depressed. He didn't want his mother to be upset. They probably had spent a lot of money on him for a good education. But that had been their choice. He surely couldn't be blamed if he didn't want to follow the rigid path they, or more accurately, his father was determined he should take?

Rudy could see his friend was unsettled and unable to finish his meal.

"Well your dad certainly makes his feelings known," he commented. It raised a faint smile from Tony.

"I'll ask around. See if I can find some work for you," Rudy promised.

"I suppose you make money from selling your artwork," Tony surmised.

"You must be joking," laughed his friend. "It's not that easy. I've got some possible openings, but at the minute I do a part-time job at the local grocery store and work several evenings behind the bar at the George and Dragon pub in the high street. Succeeding in art is hard work."

Tony was amazed. Perhaps earning a living in the outside world was not quite as straightforward as he'd imagined.

"But right now let's relax," Rudy opened a cabinet drawer and took out a tin. "Time for a spliff."

******

OVER the next few days Tony went around the local shops asking if there were any jobs available. Some took his name and Rudy's home phone number, saying they'd call if anything came up.

Late one evening sitting on the bed in his room, thumbing through the jobs section of the local weekly paper, Rudy called in to see him after his bar shift at the pub.

"A friend of mine is opening a record shop in the Fulham Road, just a short bus ride from here. I've persuaded him to take you on as a counter assistant for a trial period," Rudy announced. "Are you interested?"

Tony sprang from the bed, hugging his friend.

"That's fantastic. Thank you so much."

"I'm glad you'll take it," Rudy smiled, "because someone's answered my mother's advert for a lodger, and you'd have to leave here in a week if there's no money coming in. She's been getting a bit ratty about you staying here for free."

"Just in time, thank you so much," Tony expressed his gratitude again.

"It isn't a lot of money my friend Sebastian Osborne is offering. Five pounds a week. But the rent's two pounds, so it leaves you a bit to live on," Rudy spelled out the terms.

262

Tony remembered the ten pounds he'd earned working just a few hours for his uncle Frank. But then he didn't have his freedom. His life dominated on all sides. It was a price worth paying. And he'd have enough money to buy food and afford the bus fare. Even to go to the cinema or a local dance night sometimes.

The following Monday he arrived at Sebastian's newly launched record shop set among a row of stores on the busy Fulham Road. It was easy to recognise with the large board 'Sebastian's Sounds' emblazoned in gold on a light blue background stretching above the shop frontage. Posters of Cliff Richard, Elvis Presley and Lonnie Donegan filled the window.

Sebastian was sorting through singles records on shelves behind the counter when Tony entered. He turned to greet the new employee, his hair styled in black and blond streaks rising stiffly at the front like a cliff edge. The young man had the largest nose Tony had ever seen, hindering his otherwise good looking face which sparkled with enthusiasm.

"Tony!" Sebastian came round the counter extending his arm to give a vigorous handshake.

"Rudy's told me all about you. Now for a start we've got something in common. I'm launching a new venture and you're on a new one too. Together we can make music," he laughed at his own joke.

"All this pop record stuff is growing in a big way, and I want you to be in with me on the wave," Sebastian's powerhouse of enthusiasm was almost overwhelming. Rudy had kept mentioning that the new decade was going to bring about amazing times in art and music. Tony's main interest in the future was earning enough money to live.

"Now we open in half-an-hour. I've circulated flyers to let people know we're here and put an ad in the local paper," Sebastian rattled on energetically. "But before we open, I'll give you a few basics on what to do."

He pointed out the racks in the centre of the shop containing album covers where customers could search for music of their choice, three booths on a sidewall for listening to samples before buying, and a board on the counter wall with the latest hit single titles chalked on it. Then he led Tony behind the counter and immediately plunged him into working life at the deep end.

The first few days just a trickle of customers came, but as word spread more started to arrive. When Saturday came, the shop was hardly able to contain the numbers entering. Sebastian was thrilled, and heartily thanked Tony for his hard work after closing the door on the day's trade. Then he handed Tony his first week's pay, contained in a sealed brown envelope.

It wasn't a lot of money, but Tony felt immensely proud in the feeling of independence it gave. At last he was a real adult earning his own living in the world. Sebastian was a hard driver, and not averse to mucking in at the counter with Tony when not immersed in the administration of the business. And he allowed his employee every other Monday off, in lieu of his Saturday work.

Tony hadn't seen much of Rudy, being so busy. His friend was often out in the evening or cloistered in his room creating artwork. Sunday was when they usually found some time together.

"I saw Sebastian the other day," said Rudy, as they met in the kitchen for a coffee. "He says you're doing really well. A hard worker."

Tony bristled with pride, he hoped his employer was happy with him and the confirmation pleased him greatly.

"And I've got some good news of my own," Rudy gleamed.

"You've sold some artwork for a huge sum," Tony made a guess, hoping it was true. Rudy laughed.

"Not yet. But I've landed a job at an art gallery in the King's Road, Chelsea. All the rich people go there. Pop stars, big name actors. I'll just be cataloguing for a start. Hosting some exhibitions. But I'm hoping I might be able to put some of my work on sale there in time."

"That's fantastic," Tony was thrilled with his good friend's chance to become a successful artist. They took their coffees and settled in the living room for a Sunday afternoon chat.

In the following months Tony saw even less of Rudy as his work at the gallery took up much of his days and evenings. Changing times also heralded a new era for Tony's fortunes. A girl about his age became a frequent visitor to the record shop.

Their acquaintance began with smiles as she listened to the latest hit singles in the music booths, occasionally buying one, and chatting to Tony about the records they liked. Her long, brunette hair and vibrant, brown eyes had an enchanting effect on him, to say nothing of the short skirts she often wore, revealing beautiful thighs and legs that he yearned to explore.

His shyness to ask her out was finally overcome one day when Sebastian was in the back room and none of the other customers were at the counter, except for the girl.

"There's a band playing down at the community centre in Putney on Saturday night," he plucked up the courage to begin, "would you like to come?" Tony waited, fearful of rejection.

"I'd love to," she smiled. Tony's heart turned somersaults.

"It's in the Wellington Road."

"I know. I live just round the corner."

"Seven o'clock be okay?"

"Fine."

Tony realised there was something important he didn't know.

"Er," he stuttered, "I'm sorry, but I don't know your name."

"Sandra."

At that moment Sandra became the most beautiful name he'd ever heard.

"I'm Tony."

"I know. Don't worry, I won't eat you. See you at seven Saturday." She smiled at him again and left.

Sebastian emerged from the back of the shop. He'd overheard the conversation.

"Don't fraternise too much with the customers. This isn't a lonely hearts club," he said, pausing. "She's a good looking girl though."

During the next few weeks they continued dating on Saturday nights, going to the cinema and dances at the community centre. Tony's clumsy attempts to follow Sandra's dance steps caused them great laughter. But on the slower numbers he'd been able to hold her close.

Shyness had blocked his overwhelming desire to kiss her, fearing she might object and stop going out with him. But finally one Saturday night, when they stepped outside the community centre for a breath of fresh air, Tony took her in his arms. They looked searchingly into each other's eyes, and softly brought their lips together. The most wonderful moment in Tony's life. He could hardly believe it. The girl he wanted so much, wanted him too.

"Would you like to come back to my room?" asked Tony, after their lips parted. I can make you a coffee. Or we could have a smoke." He'd been given some cannabis by Rudy. Tony didn't smoke the weed much, but occasionally at weekends. Sandra knew what he meant. She'd smoked joints at parties.

They crept quietly into the house and made their way upstairs. Tony had no idea if Rudy's mother might object to him inviting a female to his room, but she was probably well out of it from drink by now. However, they kept the noise down just in case she happened to be around and sober.

Tony made coffee and they sat on the bed smoking the spliff he'd rolled. After a while they kissed again and then laid down on the bed, not entirely comfortable squeezed together on a single mattress.

267

He began to stroke Sandra's breasts through her blouse. She sighed, her mouth parting in pleasure. His hand massaged her stomach, finding its gradual way down to her thighs and under her short skirt, across her tights towards her vagina. Suddenly her hand reached out to stop him going any further.

"I don't have any protection."

Tony's erection was cruelly foiled. For a second his frustration nearly broke into annoyance, but the feeling along with his passion rapidly subsided. He didn't have any protectives either. They didn't want their unplanned first embraces that evening leading to an unplanned consequence.

"It's okay Sandra. Don't worry. Everything's fine."

They sat up.

"I'm sorry," Sandra repeated. "I don't want to disappoint you."

"You're not," Tony reassured her. "I've had a fantastic time with you. It's okay. I promise," he kissed her cheek. She kissed his lips.

"Me too."

Sandra stood up, straightening her clothes.

"I'd better get home now or I'll miss the last bus, and my parents will go ballistic."

"I can't let you travel alone at this time of night. I'll come with you," Tony insisted.

"No, I'll be fine."

"No, I'm coming with you."

They caught the bus down the road for the short journey, and standing on the pavement outside, Tony saw her safely enter her semi-detached home. By now, just after midnight, the return buses had stopped operating. He began walking back just as the rain started. Within ten minutes he was soaked to the skin. But it didn't matter. Sandra had kissed him.

******

A COUPLE of evening's later another lodger at the house knocked on Tony's door. Mr Murray, a middle-aged man, lived reclusively and always seemed reluctant to engage in conversation. This visit was no different.

"There's a lady in the hall who wants to see you," he said curtly, quickly returning to his room on the floor above.

Tony thought it was Sandra and wondered why she was unexpectedly calling round. As he descended the stairs to the hall he saw the lady in question was his mother.

"Don't you love me anymore?" Irene greeted him in a reprimanding tone.

"Of course I love you mum," Tony hugged her.

"I thought you might have come home to see me," she laid into him.

"I've thought about you lots of times, but I didn't want to create another upset with dad blowing his top again."

Irene seemed to grudgingly accept the explanation. She was glad to see her son was well, but told him he looked pale and thinner, and should be eating more. They went upstairs to his room.

"It's a bit pokey in here," his mother surveyed the room disapprovingly.

"I'm fine, it suits me for now," Tony assured her.

"Why don't you come home? You're just wasting your life here. Your father says he could get you a job as a junior clerk in his law firm," Irene tried to persuade her son. "You could work your way up. Make a decent living for yourself."

The thought of being an underling in his father's office was not a persuasive idea.

"I've got a job mum, in a record shop not far from here. I told you in my letter. I'm fine I like how I'm living."

Irene eyed the room again. The aged wallpaper and skirting boards in need of redecoration. Grease on the gas stove. The wooden bed ends faded and scratched. The threadbare carpet.

"It's a dump. Come home," his mother pleaded.

"I can't live with dad. I like my independence," insisted Tony.

Irene shook her head.

"Can I make you a cup tea?"

His mother ignored the offer.

"I don't understand you. You had so much opportunity to do well for yourself," Irene began reprimanding again. "We didn't want you to be just another boy from the east end with no chances. Or a gangster like my brother, Frank, always looking over his shoulder, wondering when the early morning police will knock to stick him inside."

His mother's words confirmed the conclusion that he had reached regarding his uncle's profession. He was surprised that she readily admitted it to him.

"I won't end up like that. I don't see uncle Frank now, and I plan to make a good living for myself," Tony was growing frustrated at his mother's lack of faith in him.

"Now let me make you a drink, and let's talk about something else. My job. What I've been doing."

Irene's disappointment was visible. Her heart had been set on persuading her son to come home.

"No. I just came to see that you were alright. I'm going to get the bus back. Your father doesn't know that I've come," she turned to leave.

"I'll come to the bus stop with you, make sure you're okay," Tony didn't want her to leave like this.

"No, I'll be fine, there's no need." Irene wouldn't be defied on that front. Tony hugged her again in the hallway just before she left.

"I love you mum. I'm only sorry it's worked out this way, but I'll never lose touch with you."

Irene fought to raise a smile, then left.

This was the hardest moment in Tony's life. His mother always a tough woman, battling adversity all her life. He was her soft spot, always protective if sometimes harsh in her over zealous manner of keeping him on course in childhood. He sensed her sorrow, the bond between mother and son unbreakable. But now it stretched beyond her reach. He wiped away the trickle of tears rising in his eyes.

CHAPTER 11

IN THE following year Tony's fortunes continued to improve. His boss, Sebastian, opened a new record shop a couple of miles away in Putney. Business was booming and the venture led to Tony being promoted manager of the first shop, with an accompanying good pay rise. His boss took charge of the latest, larger premises.

The only dent in Tony's blossoming future was not being able to persuade Sandra to move in with him. His rise in wages had enabled him to rent a bigger room in the house with better decoration and fittings, as well as accommodating a double bed.

Rudy's mother it turned out was not tied by the usual convention of permitting only married couples to live together on her premises. As long as they paid rent and behaved, partners were perfectly acceptable.

For Sandra it was different, or rather for her parents.

"They'd never let me move in with you. Not unless we were married," she explained to him

"Then let's get married," Tony pleaded.

"I'm only seventeen, the same as you. We'd need our parents permission for it to be legal," Sandra pointed out.

"We could go to Gretna Green in Scotland. You can be married legally there at sixteen," Tony wouldn't give up.

"I'm still going to secretarial college, remember? I want to get a good job as a personal secretary in a big company. Earn a good living. I wouldn't want children yet."

Tony knew Sandra's ambition well. She'd often told him her plans to save money before thinking of family commitments. It made him feel a little diminished that she was staying with the education route, unlike him dropping out of the system. For the time being they enjoyed the comfort of his double bed on some Sunday afternoons, and occasionally overnight when Sandra told her parents she was staying with a girlfriend.

Another year passed in relatively settled routine, until one fateful evening when Tony sat with Rudy in the living room smoking a joint. Spending time together had become a rare event for them, both now leading largely seperate lives.

"I'm going abroad for a few months," Rudy told him. "There's a big exhibition I'm involved with in New York. And there's a top gallery that's interested in displaying some of my work. Cathy, my girlfriend, is coming with me."

Tony was thrilled for his friend. Rudy had already managed to sell some of his artwork in the London gallery where he worked. Not for fortunes, but enough to raise his bank balance.

It was also news to Tony that Rudy had a girlfriend.

"How long have you known her?"

"For about six months. She works at the gallery with me. I've been staying at her flat a lot. It's only a short walk from the gallery."

Tony had never been sure if women attracted Rudy. He'd never shown any sign of having any relationship with either sex. Just being single-mindedly intent on his art.

"She's never been here," Rudy could detect Tony's curiosity. "I'll bring her over before we go. Make sure she meets with your approval," he laughed.

"Oh, and before I forget, Victoria has invited you to a party she's holding in a couple of weeks. Remember Victoria?"

How could Tony forget her? She had stolen his virginity. But it was an act of theft that had left him a happy victim. He'd never seen her since.

"And she's moved. She's got a new place in Bow," said Rudy. "I'll give you the address if you want to go."

The name Bow suddenly took Tony back to the past. It was an area of east London not far from where he used to live as a boy. Memories sprang to mind. Little did he know Victoria's party was going to draw him back into the maelstrom of that violent past, this time with deadly consequences.

******

TONY and Sandra arrived outside Victoria's house in Bow, a magnificent three-storey, end terrace house. Tony had learned from Rudy that a few years back, Victoria had married a multi-millionaire businessman she'd met in a top West End casino.

The marriage was in haste, but the romance didn't last long. The couple had recently divorced and the settlement included the grand property in front of the two party-goers.

A man in an evening suit and bow tie answered the door. For a moment Tony thought they'd arrived at a formal occasion, immediately feeling dressed down in a brown leather jacket and jeans, Sandra wearing a yellow suede jacket over her dark red dress. Then he realised the man was a butler receiving guests.

In the broad hallway with a staircase to the side, couples chatted with drinks in hand. Their casual dress made Tony and Sandra feel comfortably in place again.

The newcomers made their way to the loud music pumping from the room at the end of the hall. The expansive setting inside heaved with guests, drinking and talking around the edges with energetic dancing in the middle. The air hung hot and stuffy, the aroma of cannabis mixing into the blue haze of cigarette smoke.

Sandra and Tony felt left out, surrounded by strangers. Rudy was busy preparing for his trip to New York and unable to come. As they made their way over to the drinks table, Tony heard a familiar voice.

"Tony! I'm so glad you could make it you handsome creature," Victoria emerged from the crowd. She wore a low cut, light blue dress with white lace edging, and swayed a little with a glass of wine in her hand.

"You look so grown-up since I last saw you. I expect you're bigger in that department as well," she nodded towards his crotch. Tony flushed with embarrassment, sensing curiosity stirring in Sandra's mind. She had no idea of the education he'd received from Victoria and he wasn't about to tell her now.

"And you have a beautiful lady by your side. You are so lucky," Victoria acknowledged Sandra, who half-heartedly smiled in return, but did not like the woman at all.

"I'm so sorry Rudy couldn't come, getting ready to go to America. He's so talented and I will miss him," Victoria was unstoppable. It was obvious to her two guests that the effect of alcohol and maybe spliffs were motivating her mind. She was more interested in talking than listening.

"Over there," she pointed, "you'll find a table with booze of every kind. Beer, wine, spirits. Go help yourselves. I've got to circulate, so I'll see you later." Within seconds she'd disappeared back into the crowd.

Tony and Sandra helped themselves to glasses of wine. A man standing by the drinks table engaged them in conversation, but he was so tanked up on alcohol he didn't make any coherent sense. A group of men and women stood at one corner smoking spliffs, and on a sofa two couples were snogging, not bothered about their hands freely exploring intimate places in full view of the room. He could see Sandra felt uncomfortable in this setting.

Tony left for a moment to go to the washroom, not sure as he walked down the hallway which was the door. He opened one.

Faces shot towards him. Couples on a sofa and squatting on the floor. Some holding hypodermic needles. One man in the process of mainlining into his arm. Tony realised they were hard drug addicts. Quickly he shut the door and found his way to the toilet.

Returning to the party room, he and Sandra prepared to leave. This wasn't their scene. Tony wanted to say goodbye to Victoria, but she was somewhere lost in the mass of people.

As they turned to go, Tony stopped in his tracks. A burst of adrenalin shot through him as he caught sight of a face. It was Lucy!

She had appeared in a gap of the crowd, chatting with two women on the far side of the room. No longer the young girl he'd seen on their last meeting years ago, but it was definitely her. He could never mistake the gentle contours of her face. Sandra saw him staring.

"What's the matter?" she asked.

"I've just seen an old friend," Tony played down the thrill of excitement coursing through him. "I just want a word."

Sandra followed him across the room.

"Lucy?" Tony neared her. She wore a short-sleeved cream top, and knee length dark red skirt. Sandra stared suspiciously.

"Tony?" Recognition dawned in Lucy's inquisitive eyes. "What are you doing here?"

"I could ask you the same," he replied.

For a moment an awkward silence fell between them. They'd been apart for so long with nothing in common since their childhood. Then the past linked them again.

"Have you still got those comic annuals, because I never got to read them all?" Tony joked.

"I've kept them specially for you," Lucy laughed.

The rest of the world disappeared for a few moments as they journeyed back to what now seemed precious times. Unspoken feelings, which back then their immaturity couldn't fully process beyond a childish sense of affection. Seeing Lucy again, Tony realised he was deeply in love with her. She still wore her fair hair long across her shoulders, but the beautiful face he remembered was now even more radiantly beautiful in blossoming womanhood.

Both suddenly realised they were the centre of curiosity. Lucy's two friends seemed eager for further information. Sandra looked definitely put out. Tony introduced his boyhood friend to her with a brief explanation of the link. Sandra shrugged her shoulders in an obvious sign of disapproval.

"Do you know Victoria?" Tony turned again to Lucy.

"No, but Sally here is a friend of hers from schooldays," she smiled at the woman beside her.

They were barely able to say another word when shouting and screaming ripped through the air from the hallway. A man in a grey suit rushed into the room followed swiftly by a line of uniformed police officers.

"Stay where you are!" the man commanded, as officers spread out to stop anyone trying to escape.

"I'm Detective Sergeant Bill Walker, and this is a drugs raid. Any one trying to leave will be arrested."

A man in the crowd tried to force his way out and two officers grabbed him.

"There are more police officers outside, so it's useless trying to get away," the DS reinforced his warning. The music stopped, replaced by yells of protest from the guests. The police started searching them, as cannabis smokers did their best to discard their roll-ups unseen.

Some of the officers were already discovering amphetamine tablets inside pockets and handbags, shepherding the guilty owners into a corner of the room.

Tony felt thankful to be clean. Sandra trembled with fear. He placed his arm around her. Two officers reached the couple standing with Lucy and her friends, ordering them to raise their arms for the search.

At that moment Tony's gaze was drawn to the detective sergeant in charge of the operation. Something about him seemed familiar. The officer was only a short distance away busily searching one of the guests. Then it struck home.

"Billy!" he called.

The detective turned and stared at him for a second, his eyes wondering how this stranger knew the usual way his friends addressed him. His eyes widened in surprise.

"Tony?"

The person the detective was searching must have thought it his lucky day. The officer stopped and approached Tony.

"What the hell you doing here? You look so grown-up. I'd hardly recognise you."

It had taken Tony a moment or so to recognise his boyhood boxing coach Billy. He'd always had a big build, but now his face was even more assertively stronger, his body broader.

"Are you clean?" asked Billy.

Tony nodded.

"Okay, follow me. I'll let you out."

"I can't go without... "Tony indicated his party. Billy shook his head. He was breaking the rules, but reluctantly conceded.

"Okay, them too. But no more."

He led them through the confusion to the front door. As they passed down the hall, Tony saw into the open doorway where the guests had been mainlining. They were handcuffed and under guard. Outside on the pavement, Billy gave a word of advice.

"I'd keep out of this place. We've had it under surveillance for some time. The woman who owns it, Victoria Ridley, has been taking the piss, using it as a drug running exchange and for prostitution."

Tony remembered that Billy's burning ambition had been to join the police force and now he seemed in his element. The man had been his great friend and protector when they were younger and he was glad to see his ambition had been fulfilled. He was also glad that Billy had yet again rescued him, along with his friends, from a difficult moment.

"I want to go home now," said Sandra, looking thoroughly dejected.

"Alright, we're going now," Tony reassured her.

"Thanks Billy," he smiled at the detective. "I'd love to meet up with you again soon. Talk about old times."

"I'm based at the local nick in Bishopsgate. You can…" he didn't finish as a uniformed officer interrupted.

"Trouble inside," he called from the front door.

"Must go. Take care," Billy disappeared into the house.

"Thanks for rescuing us," Lucy stood with her two friends, amazed at Tony's connection with the law. "You've obviously got influence in high places."

"It's a long story," said Tony. "But what about you? Where do you live? We must meet up again," he was determined not to lose contact with her either.

"Just a few miles away in Shoreditch. I'll give you my work phone number. I haven't got a phone in the flat," she opened her bag, finding a slip of paper and biro to quickly scribble the number. As she handed the slip to him, she gave his cheek a kiss. The soft touch sent a wave of arousal through him.

"Bye for now," said Lucy, as she set off with her friends for the bus stop down the road.

Sandra eyed Tony evilly, feeling completely left out. She had sensed a potential rival for her boyfriend's affection and didn't like the way she'd been ignored. Tony detected her hostility and reached out to put a reassuring arm round her. Sandra shook her shoulders to push him away.

He hated hurting her feelings. She was a true friend and lover, but he couldn't help the compulsive attraction he had for Lucy. Love was so complicated.

The couple barely said a word on the train journey back home, and when he tried to kiss Sandra goodnight at the door of her house, she pulled away and went inside without a word, slamming the door shut.

******

TONY phoned Lucy in the week and arranged to meet her at her flat in Shoreditch the following evening. It was on the first floor of a Victorian semi-detached house and only a short walk from the train station.

The rooms in the property had been converted into flats many years earlier, and the entrance hallway was badly in need of redecoration, heavily browned wallpaper, peeling ceiling paint and most of the varnished stair bannister faded to bare wood.

By contrast, Lucy's living room off the ground floor was a welcoming sight, newly repainted in light blue with prints of Mediterranean piazzas and exotic beaches brightening the walls.

"It's a bit of a dump this building," Lucy apologised, "but I've given this flat a makeover since I moved in." She wore a colourful burnt orange, long-sleeved dress.

"It's okay. I don't exactly live in Buckingham Palace," Tony empathised. He was surprised that a man of uncle Frank's wealth was allowing the daughter of his partner, Lindy, to live in anything less than luxury.

Lucy went to the kitchen to fetch a bottle of wine. They sat on the sofa to catch up on old times, brief though their encounters had been. Tony outlined the main events he'd experienced over the years, and on one of them they immediately found something else in common.

"Frank sent me to a private school miles away in Brighton," said Lucy, drawing her legs up on the sofa, the hem of her dress slipping down to her lap, revealing the enticing curves of her legs which Tony couldn't help but enjoy seeing.

"I hated the place," Lucy continued. "After a couple of years I just left. Then Frank had to send me to a local school so I could be nearer home again." She reached for her glass on the side table and took a sip of wine.

282

"Well you obviously don't live with Frank and Lindy now. Do you work nearby?"

"I do secretarial work with an insurance company in the City. It's only a short tube ride away. Not great pay, but enough to get by," Lucy lowered her legs to the floor again, ending Tony's scenic view.

"And how are Frank and Lindy?" he enquired.

Lucy's face fell, as if a dark shadow had swept across the room.

"I thought you'd ask," her voice sounded gloomy. She paused for a moment.

"If you want to know, Frank is a total bastard and treats mum like shit. I think she's on the verge of a breakdown and maybe thinking of doing herself in."

They were silent for a moment, Lucy in distant thought and Tony unsure of how to reply.

"I visit my mum from time to time, but only when he's not there. Can't stand to see him. As far as I'm concerned he doesn't exist, and Lindy would be better off if he didn't," she took another sip of wine.

"I'm sorry, I know he's your uncle. I don't mean to offend you."

"No need to apologise. I'm sorry that he's making life hell for your mum," Tony couldn't help feeling an element of guilt, if only because of the family connection. They were silent again for a moment.

"Can't she leave him? Tony ventured.

"I think the bastard would kill her if she tried. I'm sure you know what sort of business he's mixed up in."

Tony reluctantly nodded. The man he'd admired as a boy, now appeared to have become a monster. Even his mum, Irene, had said he was a gangster.

"She could come and stay where I live for a while. There's a room to let there. Might give her some time to make plans. Frank would never know where she is," Tony blurted a possible solution that he'd only half thought through himself.

"Lindy doesn't have a job. Frank won't let her work and she hasn't got a penny without him," Lucy's gloom deepened. "I've thought about bringing her here to live, but Frank knows where I am. He and his heavies would drag her back in no time."

Tony couldn't abide seeing Lucy so unhappy.

"I'll pay for her room where I live, and make sure she has food," he offered. It would be tight for him financially, but he could just manage it.

Lucy stared at Tony with a slight sign of hope in her eyes that swiftly faded.

"I couldn't stick that on you, but it's really good of you to offer."

"I mean it," Tony insisted. "Lindy's a lovely person. My uncle used to be. But he's obviously changed for the worse."

"Do you really mean it?" Lucy gazed at him earnestly. "It could bring a pile of trouble on you."

"He's my uncle. Hardly likely to kill me if he finds out."

"I wouldn't be so sure," she warned.

It was a chilling remark and Tony wasn't so sure either, but he'd made the offer and wouldn't retract. Lucy stood up and took the wine bottle from the dining table to top up Tony's glass.

"I'll have to speak to Lindy first. She might take some persuading. But I know she's desperate to get away from that tyrant and his criminal life." Lucy settled on the sofa again.

"Who's that girl you were with at the party? And who's your police friend who let us out?"

"Sandra's my girlfriend, though I think I'm in the doghouse with her at the minute. I think she's worried I know you too well and that I neglected her."

"Well I did have first call on you," Lucy joked, her mood lightening. "And the detective?"

"That was Billy. We go back a long way too," Tony recounted the tale.

"Do you have anyone else in your life?" he asked, wondering if she was already attached to someone. She smiled at him.

"No, I've had a couple of boyfriends, but nothing really serious. I suppose I've been waiting for the right person to come along," she paused, "return even."

The last remark sounded cryptic. What person? Did she mean she'd met someone who had been close to her then left? Tony felt a pang of jealousy that perhaps a lover had possessed her deep affections. He was tempted to pursue the line, but resisted prying further, fearing that her heart was set on someone else and to hear it would be unbearable. And if he told her now how much she meant to him, a rejection would be devastating.

After another hour of chatting about other events in their lives, and the world growing rosier with glasses of wine, Tony glanced at his watch.

"I'd better get going now. Work tomorrow and an early start for annual stocktaking."

"I"ll give you a ring to let you know if Lindy wants to go ahead with your plan," said Lucy as they walked to the door.

"Give me a ring anyway," Tony replied. They smiled at each other, both wondering what the other was thinking. Then he left.

On the train journey home, Tony's mind hovered in euphoria, still relishing the company of Lucy again after so many years. But the feeling was tinged with guilt, now realising that he didn't wish to spend the rest of his life with Sandra. He was very fond of her, but not in love. He sensed there would be troubled waters ahead.

******

A WEEK later and Tony hadn't received a call from Lucy. Perhaps Lindy had declined his plan. He called Sandra and arranged to take her to the cinema on Saturday night. He didn't want her to feel rejected, but now his earlier plan to marry her was no longer a bond he desired.

The chance meeting with Lucy seemed like fate was telling him to reconsider the direction of his life. That perhaps some deity had interceded.

Sitting together in the cinema, the film had little impact. Their minds were elsewhere. The magnetic force that once drew them together had reversed, acting to push them apart. Afterwards they went for a drink in a local pub. The awkward silence was broken by Sandra as they sat at a table.

"You don't have to keep going out with me."

"What?"

"I saw the way you were looking at her. I might just as well have disappeared into thin air."

"She's an old friend. Someone I haven't seen since childhood. It was a surprise meeting her," Tony protested, though he knew he was being less than genuine in his true thoughts. He didn't want to hurt Sandra's feelings by saying bluntly he was in love with Lucy. He'd have to find a gentler way if it was at all possible.

"I'm going home now," Sandra stood up without finishing her vodka and orange.

"I'll see you back," Tony got up.

"No, it's alright, I'll make my own way." Sandra picked up her handbag and made for the door.

"Please! Lucy and me are probably passing ships in the night," Tony pleaded, thinking it might be the case. Lucy had made no commitment to him. He tried to put his arm round Sandra, but she pulled away.

"I'm not going to be your patsy. Tell me you'll never see her again and mean it," she demanded. Tony couldn't bring himself to make that pledge. He remained silent.

"Thought so," Sandra stormed off. Tony became aware of the pub customers staring at him, soaking up the entertainment of a lovers' tiff.

Another week passed with no call from Lucy. Tony rang Sandra's house in an attempt to arrange a meeting again and try to explain that he had feelings for Lucy, but wanted to remain friends with her.

Sandra's mother answered the phone and frostily told him her daughter was out. Now Tony began to feel the fool. He was isolated from the woman who cared for him, and it seemed he'd been abandoned by the one he loved.

Rudy's mother had generously agreed to reserve the room to let for a short time, but she'd be pressing for rent or letting it to someone else soon. If Lindy didn't arrive in a day or two, it would no longer be available. He called Lucy's work phone the next day to check what was happening. A colleague said she wasn't in.

That evening the hall phone rang. It was Lucy.

"Is it still on? The room?"

"Yes. I thought you'd never call."

"Sorry, but it's been hard work convincing Lindy to leave. She's terrified of what might happen," Lucy explained.

"She'll be safe here. Frank won't know where she is," Tony reassured.

"We'll be there tomorrow evening. Frank will be out when we leave."

"Okay, see you then. And be careful." Tony replaced the phone receiver and went to Lindy's room to make sure it was clean and tidy for her arrival.

CHAPTER 12

THE STARK change in Lindy's appearance shocked Tony. Her once bright and happy face was now thin and drawn, hollows in her cheeks, eyes weary and defeated. She wore a floral patterned dress, but its colours did nothing to brighten the weary occupant.

"Come on in," he welcomed her to the house, kissing her cheek, and trying to avoid showing shock at her condition in case it upset her. Lucy entered carrying Lindy's small suitcase and Tony led them upstairs to the room. It had a simple layout, single bed, dresser, wardrobe, table, armchair and gas stove.

"I'm afraid it's not a palace," Tony apologised, "but I hope it's okay for now."

"You are a saint," Lindy replied, "thank you so much for helping me." Tony had never been described as a saint before and felt slightly embarrassed by the praise.

"I'll make you a cup of tea in the kitchen and let you settle down for a while. The bathroom's first left on the landing."

Lindy gave a faint smile and Lucy joined Tony as they made their way downstairs to the kitchen.

"She's terrified," said Lucy as he made the tea. "She thinks Frank will kill her if he discovers where she is."

"Well it's unlikely he'll connect it to me, and he's no idea where I live anyway."

"I've told her that, but she finds it hard to believe. Frank haunts her mind and he has some pretty nasty people working for him. Torture and murder is the way they handle punishments."

Back in Lindy's room they sat with her for a while, trying to take her mind off matters with small talk, the weather, Tony telling her about the local area and a nearby park good for a refreshing stroll.

Lindy smiled occasionally, but her mind was absorbed in the torments she'd suffered, beatings, being locked in her room and generally treated like dirt. The man who had once been kind and appeared to love her had degenerated into a tyrant as his power grew.

After a couple of hours Lucy had to leave and catch the train back home.

"Work tomorrow," she said, standing up from her perch on the end of the bed and kissing Lindy goodbye. Tony saw her to the front door.

"I'll give you a ring tomorrow to see how Lindy's getting on." Lucy looked sad.

"Don't worry, I'll make sure she's okay," Tony did his best to reassure her. He leaned forward to kiss her lips.

"Close the bloody front door, you're letting cold air in," a woman yelled.

Tony pulled back.

Rudy's mother had emerged from a door at the end of the hallway in her dressing gown and swaying slightly from drink. "It costs money to heat this house," she snarled, then returned inside.

The couple laughed at the rude interruption. A fleeting moment of light in the dark atmosphere that currently shrouded their lives. But as Lucy left, Tony felt robbed of a precious moment when he may have discovered if she felt for him. How she might have responded to his kiss.

Before going to his room, he called in on Lindy.

"I'm alright," she said, "and thank you again for helping me. I just want to get a little rest now."

Tony thought it probably a long time since she'd been able to look forward to a peaceful night of sorts. Unfortunately it was only for that night.

******

WHEN he returned home from work the following day, Tony checked to see if Lindy was okay. She looked a little better, her eyes not nervous and fearful as on the previous evening.

"I went for a walk," she told him, "had a look round some of the shops. It was good to get some fresh air," she lifted a kettle of boiling water off the gas stove and poured it into the teapot on the table. "Would you like a cup of tea?"

"No thanks, I'm about to cook my evening meal. Can I cook you something as well?" he offered.

"No, it's alright. I had a meal in the cafe round the corner. Lucy gave me some spending money." Lindy's reply cut Tony's heart. That this once strong woman should be reduced to living like this on handouts.

"I should never have married into a world of gangsters," said Lindy. Her words struck him in complete surprise. A sudden shock confession of the dejected sinner. "I've

291

brought all this on myself." Lindy held the kettle, frozen for a moment in deep thought.

"When I married Dave Parker I was very young. He seemed so exciting. I knew he was a bit of a bad lad, but I was naive, and I suppose I turned a blind eye as I realised he was getting deeper and deeper into the criminal world."

Lindy turned to place the kettle back on the gas stove, giving Tony a half smile that looked more like a grimace of guilt.

"Then as you probably know, he got sent down. Your uncle Frank and me got on well. I wanted security, especially for Lucy when she was young. Things just moved on so that we decided to live together. Once you're webbed into the gangster world it's difficult to break away."

Tony could see the painful self-reprimand she was going through. Yes, she was probably guilty of turning a blind eye, of once living comfortably off criminal activities. But if anyone was paying for it now, Lindy certainly was with her life in ruins.

"It's okay Lindy, you don't have to confess to me, I understand," Tony thought she was suffering enough. "I'm not your judge. You've always been kind to me."

This time she managed to raise a full smile.

"Thank you."

"Okay. I'll look in on you later. Right now I'm off to heat up my meat pie dinner. I lead a simple bachelor's life," he smiled in return.

He heated the meat pie downstairs in the kitchen oven, so that he wasn't far from the hall phone to wait for Lucy's call. She'd promised to call and find out how her mother was coping. Standing and eating the pie from the kitchen counter, he heard the doorbell ring. Opening the door, he had the shock of his life.

"Hello Tony, long time no see." Frank stood there in a long, dark overcoat, giving his nephew a wicked grin. His hair had greyed since Tony last saw him, but apart from a few added wrinkles, it was an unmistakably familiar face.

"You've grown since I last saw you. D'ye mind if we come in?"

A broad, heavily built man in a black leather jacket stood beside Frank. He seemed vaguely familiar to Tony. Then the second shock of the visit hit him. It was Brendan. The boy now a man, who'd been his arch enemy in childhood until they'd struck up friendship.

"Frank's right. You have grown since we last met," Brendan spoke. "Still doing boxing?" he raised his fists like a boxer, doing some pretend punches.

"What do you want?" Tony's mind reeled, knowing perfectly well what Frank wanted, doubting he could stop both of them entering and wondering how the hell he knew Lindy was here.

"I want my wife, as I'm sure you know," Frank stepped forward. Tony moved to block his way. The grin on Frank's face dropped into a threat, his eyes narrowing. "I know Lindy's here, and if you let me in to collect her without any bother we'll let it rest. You're my nephew and I don't want to hurt family."

"Who says she's here?" Tony resisted. Frank shook his head.

"If you really want to know, one of my men saw Lucy and Lindy leaving the house yesterday, when he was going there to pick something up for me. He rang me and I asked him to follow them. He got on the same train as them and saw them entering this house." Frank paused. "Good enough explanation?" He stared contemptuously at Tony.

"I've been very patient, now get out of the fucking way. I'm taking Lindy back." He pushed his nephew. Tony pushed him back.

"You're making this very difficult. I do not want to hurt someone who I've always liked," Frank shook his head again in frustration. "But Brendan doesn't mind."

In that second, Brendan aimed a blow at Tony's head. He swung sideways, but the fist glanced off the left side causing him to flinch for a moment. Brendan rushed past him. Tony swung round grabbing the back of his jacket and tugging him back. Frank's arm wrapped round Tony's neck forcing him to release his grip on Brendan.

"What's going on?" a man shouted from the landing.

"Fuck off! Frank replied, maintaining the neck grip. Now freed, Brendan turned and delivered a hard punch at Tony's face. It stunned him and blood started streaming from his nose. His lip felt split.

"I've called the police," a woman lodger yelled, joining the man on the landing. "They're on their way."

Frank released his grip. Brendan resisted delivering another blow. Neither of them wanted to meet the police in this area of London where they had no corrupting influence.

"I had such high hopes for you," Frank growled at Tony. "You could have been king pin with me. Now we are at war." Frank turned and left.

Brendan looked at Tony. "Well my boxer friend, you weren't quite quick enough to get out of that one. Your nose is running with red stuff," he laughed, and followed Frank into the night.

"What's happening?" Rudy's mother appeared in the doorway at the end of the hall, once again in dressing gown and swaying a little, but not completely out of it. "Who called the police?"

"No one. I only said that," the woman on the landing replied. "It usually works when there's trouble."

Rudy's mother looked at Tony without noticing the blood on his face.

"I don't want any trouble," she mumbled. "Anyone causing trouble will be out." She disappeared back into her room. The two lodgers present on the landing completely ignored Tony, offering no help, and returned to their rooms.

He went upstairs to the bathroom and washed off the blood. The nose bleed had stopped, but he had a swelling fat lip. Right now though he was more concerned for Lindy and Lucy's safety.

At Lindy's door he softly knocked and waited, but received no reply.

"It's me Lindy. It's okay," he called. Still no reply. Then he heard the door being unlocked, Lindy peering cautiously through a narrow gap.

"I heard his voice. He knows I'm here, He'll be back," Lindy's voice trembled in fear as she let Tony in. "He'll kill me." Then she noticed his swollen lip.

"God, what's he done to you?

"It's okay It's nothing. He's gone."

"I better leave. I don't want you hurt because of me."

"No Lindy, I'm fine. Now stay here and I'll keep you safe," Tony attempted to calm her, though realising there was a high possibility that his uncle might find a way to dispose of them both and Lucy too. He wanted to warn Lucy of what had happened, but she had no phone in her flat. She should be ringing at any moment from a street call box.

He made Lindy a cup of tea and stayed for a while to comfort her. He was amazed that Brendan had teamed up with his uncle. But thinking about it, he lived in the same area that Frank covered and his uncle would most likely expand his empire with local talent. Brendan's rough nature and streetwise personality made him an ideal candidate for Frank's criminal enterprises.

The link made him think of Billy. He was stationed in a place that probably policed that area. Perhaps he could offer some sort of protection for Lindy and Lucy.

Tony could see Lindy's hand shaking as she raised her teacup to take a drink. He glanced at his watch. It was seven thirty. Why hadn't Lucy rung yet? He began fearing for her safety. If she didn't call soon, he'd contact the police.

"Shouldn't Lucy be calling?" Lindy glanced at her watch, the same fearful thoughts began to surface in her mind. She'd just finished speaking when the hall phone started to ring. Tony rushed downstairs to answer.

"How's Lindy? Is she settling in?" Lucy asked. It was a huge relief to hear her voice and know that Frank hadn't got to her. Tony explained the unwelcome visit. She was silent for a moment.

"We'll have to get her out of there."

Tony detected her voice trembling.

"First you need to get out of your flat. Frank may be on his way even now," he warned. "Come here. At least there are people around and it won't be so easy for him to do anything if you're not alone."

Lucy fell silent again. Tony could almost feel the turmoil in her mind.

"Fuck, fuck, fuck," she exploded, the hoped for plan of salvation had been totally blown away.

"You're right. I better sling some things in a case and get over there. Might buy a bit of time to work something out. See you later. Make sure Lindy's okay." she ended the call.

Tony felt a huge weight of guilt. Through no fault of his own his idea to help had gone off the rails. He desperately needed to set it right again. He returned to Lindy to say Lucy was coming. She was deeply relieved her daughter wouldn't be left on her own.

Tony went back to the hall. He picked up one of the telephone directory books stacked on a shelf beside the phone and looked up the number of Billy's police station at Bishopsgate in the City of London.

"Detective Sergeant Walker's out at the minute," came the reply from the officer answering the phone when he rang, "should be back in half-an-hour."

"It's really important. Can you get him to give me a call?" Tony left the number and replaced the receiver, returning to keep Lindy company.

Half-an-hour later he went back to the phone. A lodger was using it and appeared to be engrossed in conversation. Tony interrupted.

"I'm expecting an important call. Will you be long?"

The man gave him a withering look. It was the same greying, middle-aged lodger, in threadbare brown sweater and corduroy trousers, who'd shouted from the landing when Frank was causing trouble. He carried on talking for another five minutes ignoring Tony. When he finished, he replaced the receiver and turned to him.

"We don't need troublemakers like you and your friends here. Find somewhere else." The man ascended the stairs looking back down in disapproval before returning to his room.

Tony was worried that Billy might have called while the phone had been engaged. He wondered if he should call the station again when it started ringing.

"Is that who I think it is?" came Billy's voice as he answered.

"It is, and I'm sorry we couldn't have talked for longer when we met the other night," Tony was pleased to hear his longtime friend's voice again.

"Picked up some people we've been after for some time. You want to stay well clear of the crowd," Billy advised. "Anyway, what's the problem?"

Tony explained for the second time that evening what had happened. Again he was met with a shocked silence.

"You're telling me that Frank Ryder is your uncle?"

"Yes."

Tony met silence again.

"Jesus! We've been after that bastard for ages. No offence, he's your uncle."

"None taken."

"And his partner is with you now?"

"She's terrified he'll kill her," Tony emphasised the gravity of the situation.

"Of all the people, I would never have guessed in a million years he's your uncle. The biggest villain on our list," Billy paused.

"You know Brendan's working for him?"

"He gave me a bloody nose."

"Were all my boxing lessons wasted on you then?" Billy laughed, but quickly became serious again.

"Stay inside. When Lucy gets there make sure none of you go outside. I'm coming over now. Where are you?" Billy took the address. "It's a bit outside my area, so it'll probably take me an hour or so."

Tony now felt a little more secure. But he couldn't settle until Lucy arrived. He dreaded Frank getting to her first. Returning to Lindy, he let her know what was happening.

"Now I've got everyone into trouble," she shook her head looking totally dejected.

"No you haven't," said Tony, "Frank needs to be sorted out. He's made your life a misery."

Lindy glanced at him with an ironic smile. "I know you mean well, but I don't think you understand what you're dealing with."

Tony knew very well he was moving into deadly territory, but maintained an air of confidence because someone had to.

An hour later Lucy arrived carrying a small case. Tony hugged her at the door, relieved to see she was safe.

"How's Lindy," she asked.

"Okay, but very frightened."

"I know the feeling," Lucy went up to her room. Tony was about to follow when there was another knock at the door.

"Who is it?" he called before opening.

"Billy. Is that you Tony?"

He opened the door.

"Has Frank been back?"

"No."

"Good. Where's Lindy?"

Tony led him upstairs and introduced him as Detective Sergeant Bill Walker.

"Just call me Billy," he said, keen to drop the formality. "Now tell me exactly why you're here and what happened this evening?"

Tony did most of the explaining. Billy looked thoughtful, digesting the information.

"You know your husband's top on our list of criminals," he said to Lindy. She nodded.

"Our problem is, he's very careful. He has a lot of people doing the dirty work for him. Petty criminals who usually take the blame if we haul them in for stealing, beating someone up or doing something they shouldn't be doing for him. And, of course, they never give up any information because they're terrified of being killed if they split on him."

He paused.

"I was wondering if you could help?" Billy directed his question at Lindy. She stared back at him in horror.

"If you think I'm going to stand up in court and spill the beans on everything I know about Frank's activities, then your living in cloud cuckoo land," Lindy answered, more in fear of retribution from her husband than defiance.

"No, I don't mean that," Billy rubbed his forehead, thinking of a way to rephrase his words.

"I mean," he paused again, "I mean you must know some people who have been to your house. Names. We've had your place under observation from time to time, sorry for the intrusion, but we can't identify who they are."

All eyes were fixed upon him, curious to know what he was driving at.

"We believe some of them are drug runners, but we think there's something even bigger going down and it's essential we stop it. I can't give you any more details about it than that for security reasons."

Lindy sat down on her bed, her face drawn with worry.

"I do know some names of Frank's visitors, but I'd definitely be signing my own death warrant if I said anything. If I went back home now, I'd get a good beating, but at least I'd probably live," she reasoned.

"What, and continue to live a life of sheer misery for the rest of your days," Billy spelled out the reality. "Is it okay if I sit down?" he pointed to a chair at the table. Lindy nodded. Lucy took the other chair by the table while Tony remained standing.

"I'll have to get the consent of my superiors, but I think I can swing a deal. If you can help me with names, then I'll make sure you'll be comfortable and secure in a safe house. Both you and your daughter," Billy glanced at Lucy. The women appeared uncertain.

If I leave now and do nothing, because nothing's all I've got, then you'll be unprotected and left totally to the lions," the detective continued laying out the bare truth. "You've dug yourselves a hole, and right now I'm the only one who can get you out of it." He waited for an answer.

"Let's go downstairs and I'll make you coffee," Tony suggested to Billy. "Give them time to think it over."

Billy stood up.

"Yep, good idea." They left the room.

"Sorry, but I can't extend the protection to you," Billy explained as Tony made the coffee in the kitchen. "It would be best if you could find somewhere else to live."

"It's okay, I'm not going to run. I don't think Frank could face my mother or my nan if he murdered me," Tony calculated.

"I wouldn't be so sure. If you notice the slightest hint of something suspicious, someone following you, ring my number. I'll let them know at the station and they'll get an officer from the local cop shop over to you," Billy took a drink of coffee. Tony thanked him for the offer of some protection.

They became less serious for a short while, reminiscing over old times, and half-an-hour later returned to Lindy's room. Lucy sat beside her on the bed. Both appeared downhearted. Billy returned to the chair by the table.

"I know it's a bloody hard decision," he sympathised, "but it'll be the best way of freeing yourselves from a life of misery in the long run. And yes, there's something in it for me too, I admit. Putting a dangerous villain behind bars, which will be good for everyone."

"How will we live? I'll have to give up my job and flat. Lindy won't have any money," Lucy questioned.

"We'll provide you with food and some money, and help you resettle somewhere else. New identities if needed," Billy outlined the prospect.

The women looked at each other, communicating their thoughts with their eyes and grim faces. After a few more moments, and knowing there was no other way to free themselves from the tyrant, they agreed.

Tony was wrestling with the possibility that he might never see Lucy again if they had to resettle anonymously elsewhere. But their safety was paramount.

"Right, well we'll move on to it now. I'll take you to a place where you can stay overnight while I arrange things. Then tomorrow we can start to talk a bit more," Billy stood up. "I'll wait downstairs while you collect your belongings."

Tony went downstairs with the detective.

"Be kind to them," he said as they waited in the hall.

"What's going on?" The lodger who'd earlier told Tony he should find somewhere else to live stood at the top of the stairs.

"There's been an outbreak of the Black Death, and I'm here from the police to tell everyone to stay locked in their rooms for at least three days," Billy replied.

The man scratched his head looking puzzled, then returned to his room. Tony smiled at his friend's remark. It was the last light moment he'd experience for some time.

Lucy and Lindy came down the stairs with their cases. As Billy opened the door for them to leave, Tony put his hand on Lucy's shoulder. She turned to him.

"I will miss you," he said, feeling his eyes welling with moisture. They leaned forward and kissed. Softly. All too briefly.

"We'd better get a move on," Billy was keen to get things in motion. Tony watched as the police officer driver who'd been waiting in the car outside put their luggage in the boot and opened the back door for them.

"Call me if you run into any trouble," said Billy as he climbed into the passenger seat. The vehicle pulled away and Tony felt himself plunged into a pit of desolate loneliness.

CHAPTER 13

OVER the next few days he kept a nervous eye open while he travelled to and from work. In the shop it was unsettling when some customers, sorting through record covers in the racks, occasionally glanced across at him standing behind the counter. Were they spying for Frank?
But nothing resulted and he began to feel confident that no-one was following him.

As well as hoping Lucy and Lindy were safe wherever they'd been taken, thoughts of Sandra came into his mind. He still felt guilty that he'd let her down, badly hurting her feelings. Although certain he didn't love Sandra, he was still very fond of her and wished they could remain on friendly terms.

He rang her home one evening in an attempt to rebuild bridges, but Sandra's mother answered again, saying her daughter was out and it would be best if he stopped trying to contact her.

The only bright spot in his life was a letter from Rudy in New York telling him he was having a great time, and that he'd managed to display some of his artwork in a major exhibition.

A few evenings later Tony sat in his room enjoying the luxury of watching a TV programme on the set he'd been saving money for some time to buy. Though reception through the small indoor aerial often gave just a fuzzy black and white image. He was interrupted by a lodger shouting up to him from the hallway.

"There's someone here from the police who says they need a word about some incident." The lodger, a young man who had recently moved in, was standing by the open front door as Tony looked down from the landing. He thought it must be Billy calling or one of his officers.

"Hello Tony," said the visitor when Tony reached the door, In that second he saw it was a heavily built man with short cropped hair and a scarred face. This wasn't a police officer. His instinct was to slam the door shut, but the man's foot blocked it. Then Tony saw a gun pointing at him.

"Your uncle Frank wants to see you," the man whispered so he wouldn't be heard by anyone inside. "Now don't do anything silly. I really don't want to shoot you. Come on out and get into the car."

Since he didn't want a bullet in him, Tony had no choice but to obey. The sodium street lights in the darkness outside reflected on the shiny surface of the limousine parked in the road. He was ushered into the back, securely hemmed between the two heavies.

"Where are you taking me?" he asked, as the man who'd threatened him with the gun climbed into the front seat beside the driver.

"To see your uncle. I've told you."

Tony felt a cold sweat breaking out. Was that true? Or were they taking him to a remote place to put a bullet in his head and bury him? The alternative of coming face to face with Frank was only marginally less terrifying.

The hour long journey continued in silence, the huge, dark suited guards on either side remained resolutely quiet and still like statues, only occasionally glancing at him as he sometimes shifted to keep the circulation in his legs flowing.

The vehicle eventually entered a main street bustling with people, traffic, and lights streaming from large department stores, before taking a side turning and entering a service road at the rear.

Tony guessed from the activity at the front that they were somewhere in the west end of London. But he couldn't place the exact location. His guards let him out and the man who'd held the gun at him led him to a back door, knocking on it. Another aggressive face in a dark suit opened it and let them in.

He was guided up a short flight of stairs and along a narrow corridor. He could hear music in the background and guessed he was in one of Frank's nightclubs. At the end of the corridor the minder ushering him knocked on another door.

"Yeah," a voice boomed from within. As the door opened Tony saw his uncle sitting at a desk, writing something in a hard cover notebook. Framed photographs of smiling showgirls in flimsy dress adorned the cream walls. Frank finished writing in the notebook and looked up.

"Thanks Ned," he said to the henchman who'd brought Tony. The man left.

Frank stared coldly at his nephew. Then a smile rose. He leaned back in the chair assuming a relaxed, friendly countenance.

"I can't understand why we have to be enemies," he said. "I loved you when you were a boy. We had a lot of fun together, and I was always generous to you."

For a moment his uncle's reminiscences touched a soft spot. It was true, Frank had been fun. They'd got on well together in his childhood. Tony could see in the years since, the stresses of running a criminal empire had aged his uncle. His taut body had also given way to the excesses of food and drink.

"I think it's you that's changed," he said.

"Life is fucking hard. Don't know if that's got through to you yet," Frank shook his head. "If you want things you've got to grab them quick, or some other bastard will. I've changed because I didn't want to end up like the downtrodden pieces of shit I grew up with," he paused, studying Tony. "You came from the same place."

Frank hoped the reminder of their lowly origins might persuade his nephew to understand his motivation. Perhaps even draw him to his side.

"But treating other people like shit doesn't make you any better," Tony could not partner with his uncle's logic. He hoped Frank might listen to reason. After all, he appeared to be offering an olive branch. Maybe he could be persuaded to treat those close to him more kindly.

"A lot of people need to be treated like shit, especially in my line of business," Frank didn't sound persuaded.

"But not Lindy."

Frank flinched at Tony's reply. His friendly approach turned sour,

308

"Don't you tell me how I should treat her. It's none of your business and you shouldn't have stuck your nose in," he leaned forward in the chair.

"Since you mention Lindy, here's the deal. Ned will take you back to your place, and I want you to tell her to come back home. Tell her all is forgiven. I don't want to make a bigger deal of this than necessary. That's why he didn't just force his way in and take her." Frank issued his ultimatum, resting back in the chair again.

"It's a bit late for that," said Tony, "she's already left with Lucy, and I've no idea where they've gone," he left out the connection to Billy in case it alerted Frank to any police operation being planned. His uncle lowered his head, considering the news, then slowly looked up, giving Tony a stony stare.

"I'm disappointed," he said. "I really had it in mind all those years back that I could make you into someone important in my business. You'd have money to live like a lord. Such a shame."

Tony began to fear the direction of Frank's thoughts.

"Being my nephew makes it very difficult for me. I'll have to think it over," Frank leaned forward again. "One last chance. Are you telling me the truth? Are they still at your place, or have they really gone?"

"They've gone, that is the truth," Tony answered with conviction. Frank rubbed his brow, then pressed a button under his desk.

"Ned will take you to a room. You'll be kept there until I decide what to do with you." Frank stood up. A few moments later his henchman Ned entered.

"Take him to the room upstairs," Frank ordered. The man nodded and waved Tony to leave. He was ushered up a narrow wooden stairway and along another corridor. Ned took out a key and unlocked a door, pushing Tony into the room. Then he slammed the door shut and locked it.

Inside were a couple of chairs tucked under a table and a brown leather armchair in a corner. Tony sensed it was an interrogation room. Interrogator facing victim at the table and the chief sitting smugly in the armchair. A brown stain on the bare floorboards chilled him as he imagined it could be dried blood. He sat in the armchair wondering what hell might be waiting for him. Surely Frank wouldn't spill the blood of his own family? His nephew who'd once been so close?

Now he wished he'd listened to his father. But Gerry was like stone. Tony had felt closer to Frank. Then his mother came to mind. Surely Frank wouldn't kill his own sister's son. Tony hadn't seen his mother for some time, despite promising he'd keep in regular contact. He'd been too possessed with himself and had neglected her. The guilt piled in. It seemed as if time was now too short to make amends for his failings before his uncle dealt the final blow.

But no. He was not going to put up with this shit. Somehow he was going to live to see justice dealt on Frank. Tony fixed the positive thought in his head with absolutely no idea how to achieve it.

******

HE was left on his own for a couple of hours. Then he heard the key turning in the lock. Brendan entered the room.

"Hello Tony? How are you keeping?"

Tony stared at him from the armchair.

"Having a wonderful time, as you can see," he met sarcasm with sarcasm.

"Glad to see you've still got a sense of humour," Brendan pulled a chair from the table and sat on it facing Tony.

"Frank's sent me to give you another chance. You see he doesn't believe you've no idea where Lindy is. He thinks she's still at your place, but doesn't want to send in the heavy mob to collect her. It'd draw too much attention," he paused, smiling with a friendly gaze of encouragement. "If you tell us where she is, you can leave and get on with your own life."

"I've told Frank that I've no idea where she's gone," Tony insisted, "that's the truth."

"Dear, oh dear," Brendan shook his head and stood up, reaching inside his suit jacket to take out a gun.

"Tell me or I'll blow your fucking brains out," he pointed the weapon at Tony's head. The terror of being shot almost forced Tony to tell him that Lindy and Lucy were in a safe house. But if Frank ever discovered where they were, it was almost certain his people would find a way to eliminate them, as well as wreck Billy's chance of destroying his uncle's empire.

Death at the end of a gun barrel stared him in the face.

"I've told you, I have no fucking idea where Lindy is. I can't tell you what I don't know. Go and search where I live. I'll give you the front door key. She's not there." Tony desperately hoped his plea would be accepted. Brendan lowered the gun.

"Okay, we're going for a trip," he walked to the door, "come on, get up."

"To my place?" Tony wondered if his offer was being taken up.

"A mystery tour," Brendan waved him out of the room with the gun, escorting him from the building to a black car in the service road at the back. A man sat in the driving seat.

"Get in," Brendan opened the back door, then climbed in beside him.

"Are we going to my place?" he repeated the question as the vehicle pulled away.

"You'll find out," came the reply. Tony began to wonder if this might be his final journey.

For the next few minutes there was silence save for the sound of the car engine revving and slowing as it edged its way through heavy traffic in the London street. Brendan broke the silence.

"You know I was totally amazed when I found out you were Frank's nephew. Small world. Seems you can't escape where you come from," he mused, replacing the gun inside his jacket as the car cleared the traffic and began moving faster.

"And dy'e know Billy Walker is a copper? A detective sergeant. You and him got on well together when we were boys," Brendan recalled.

Tony feigned surprise at the news, not wishing to let Brendan know he'd had recent contact with him.

"I knew he wanted to join the police," Tony replied non-committedly.

"That bastard is now our arch-enemy. Been trying for ages to bang us up. He hates Frank and he never liked me," Brendan looked at Tony as if aware he was holding back some vital information. Tony made no reply.

The car began to leave the city lights moving through suburbs and gradually on to a road where in the surrounding darkness only the car headlights picked out the way ahead.

"Are you going to kill me?" asked Tony.

"You're making it sound so dramatic," Brendan laughed. "I only obey orders. I'm your uncle's right hand man. He always sends me to do the dirty work he doesn't want to handle. Make sure it's done right. Oh, and sorry for giving you a wacking the other night. But that's what Frank wanted me to do," he looked at Tony again.

"You've really pissed him off. A member of his own family interfering with his private life. He's given you more chances that anyone else who's disloyal to him. And he usually tortures them first."

The car had now turned on to an uneven, bumpy road with steep grass banks on either side, highlighted in silvery grey moonlight. The area appeared isolated from any nearby homes.

313

Tony's hands felt sweaty with fear. The skin on his arms began to prickle like a heat rash allergy. The car lights illuminated high wire gates ahead. The driver pulled up and got out to release the padlock then pushed them open.

Returning to the vehicle, he drove into a large compound. In the moonlight Tony could make out the shadowy shapes of vehicles stacked in high piles on top of each other. It became obvious to him they had entered a scrap yard.

"This is the car graveyard," said Brendan, "all waiting to meet their maker and be transformed into new metal life," he laughed at his own cynical religious parody. "Do you believe in reincarnation?" he directed the question to Tony.

"Right now I'm hoping I don't have to find out," he replied, attempting to keep his nerve.

"I've got to hand it to you, you're very cool," Brendan commended him as the car pulled up again and he took out the gun. "Our enemies are usually begging for their lives by now."

Tony was not feeling cool, either mentally or physically. He wiped away the sweat rising from his forehead. He had to think of a way to escape before it was too late.

"Okay, out you get," Brendan stood by the door, waving the gun for him to exit. Tony stepped on to the dusty ground. Brendan told the driver he'd be back in about ten minutes.

With enough moonlight to see the way without a torch, he ordered Tony to start walking along the main track feeding the compound. All the time, the captive was weighing up the possibility of making a break for it. The stacked cars offered an opportunity to hide somewhere among them, but the light of the moon would give Brendan adequate vision to blast him with a bullet before he could run more than a few yards.

"We've used this place a few times," said Brendan, following a few paces behind. "Your uncle does business with the owner, exchanging a few favours for each other."

Tony wasn't interested in the crooked dealings Frank might have with whoever owned the place. He was concentrating on the possible opportunities for escape.

"Once the body is put inside one of these old cars, the crusher over on the right mangles it down to a fraction of its original size, body included," Brendan described the fate awaiting Tony. "Then off they go to a furnace for reincarnation into something else."

He laughed again at his crude reference to rebirth and the perfect solution to disposing of an enemy without trace. Tony glanced across to the shadowy outline of the crusher plant in the moonlight. A surge of terror shivered through him as the prospect of a horrifying ending drew closer, while the chance of escape moved further away.

"Turn right," Brendan ordered a little further down the track. The route took them between a row of piled cars.

"Okay stop. Turn round."

Tony obeyed, realising there was now no opportunity to escape.

"One very last chance," said Brendan, raising the gun at him. "Where's Lindy?"

"I don't know! I've no fucking idea! Are you really going to kill me? I know we started off bad when we were kids,

315

but I thought we'd become friends," Tony pleaded the link to old times in an attempt to save his life. Sweat now poured profusely from all over his body, yet he felt shivering cold.

"I only obey orders," Brendan replied.

Tony heard a click as the gun safety catch was released, the pointing barrel staring at him menacingly.

Brendan pulled the trigger, in the same second shifting his aim towards the ground beside Tony. The bullet struck a stone in the dirt and ricocheted into a spin, hitting the ground again a few feet away. He fired again, this time the missile sinking into the dust.

Tony stared at him, the silvery light sharply contrasting the contours of Brendan's face in black and grey like a charcoal drawing. His smile appeared bizarre, puzzling. The gun still in his right hand, he reached into his jacket pocket with the left.

"Here's a key to the padlock," he tossed it on the ground in front of Tony. "Wait fifteen minutes, then fuck off and find somewhere else to live quick. This small world ain't over yet." Brendan turned and walked back to the track.

Tony stood there stunned. He was still alive. For a few minutes his mind struggled to understand why he was still alive? Why Brendan had spared him? Perhaps a plea to old friendship had worked. What did he mean saying 'this small world ain't over yet'?

He stooped to pick up the key. After a few minutes in the still air he heard the sound of a car starting. The engine noise rose as the vehicle pulled away. Soon complete silence fell on the compound save for a distant owl hooting.

Tony retraced the steps back to the gate. Now the cold of the night replaced the cold of terror. He'd been taken at gunpoint wearing only a T-shirt and jeans. Reaching through the gate fence wire, he released the padlock with the key Brendan had given him. The problem remained that he had no idea of his location.

He walked back along the road that brought him to the yard, startled for a second by the dim shape of a fox suddenly scurrying across in front of him and swiftly mounting the grass bank to disappear from view.

After what he guessed was about a mile, the road reached a junction that looked more like a main route and he began walking along the grass verge. Fortunately the moon still shone brightly in the clear sky lighting the way. Cars occasionally passed and Tony started thumbing for a lift, but no-one stopped. Then ahead he saw the light inside a phone kiosk beside the road.

He checked in his pocket and found some small change to make a call. Reaching the kiosk he dialled Billy's number, which he'd made a particular point of remembering.

"Not sure if he's still here," answered the police officer taking the call, "hold on."

Tony prayed that he was still there. A minute later he heard Billy's voice.

"Yes?"

"It's me. Tony."

"What's up mate?"

Tony told him what had happened.

"You're lucky to still be alive," Billy replied, "where are you?"

Tony glanced at the location sign in the kiosk.

"Aspen Road, Billericay."

"Bloody hell! You're out in the sticks mate. Stay there and I'll send someone out for you. Whatever you do, don't go back to your place," the detective hung up.

Half-an-hour later a police car drew up beside the phone kiosk.

"Mr Selby?" an officer called from the open window. Tony nodded.

"Get in the back."

He was driven to the local police station a few miles away, feeling relieved to be returning to civilisation as the unlit roads gave way to street lights, though still well outside London and Billy's patch.

An officer made him a cup of tea as he sat in a room at the police station just off reception. No-one could tell him what was going to happen next, other than they'd had instructions for him to wait.

The hands on the wall clock ticked slowly from one in the morning to two. The only other sounds came from outside in reception, with the desk sergeant occasionally talking on the phone, and a scuffle as officers wrestled a noisy drunk into a cell beyond. Tony felt weary and began to doze, slumping back in the chair beside a table.

At half two Billy entered, startling him awake.

"You and your lot don't half cause me a lot of bother," he greeted him with a smile. Tony had never been so glad to see his ex-boxing coach.

318

"You look knackered mate," said the detective as he led Tony to his car parked outside. "I'm taking you back to my place for the night, and tomorrow we can sort out what's going to happen. Things are moving on."

The last was a cryptic remark that intrigued Tony, but at that moment exhaustion from the horror of the night overtook him. He fell asleep resting on the front passenger seat as immense relaxation coursed through him.

He awoke as the car stopped on the driveway of a semi-detached house. Low hedges on each side of the frontage.

"Welcome to Bethnal Green," said Billy opening the door to get out. Tony realised he was in an area not far from where he lived as a boy.

Inside the house, Billy took a bottle of whisky from a cabinet in the living room and poured a drink for Tony. He could see his friend was suffering from the trauma of a life or death ordeal and needed a shot of relaxant. As he began to unwind a little, Tony noticed the framed photograph of a smiling, auburn haired woman on a shelf between a couple of ballerina ornaments.

"That's my wife, Ellie," said Billy, seeing his curiosity. "She's in the police force too. The uniformed side. She's on a training course at the minute and won't be back 'til the weekend."

It was news to Tony that his friend was now married. He rested in an armchair, enjoying another glass of whisky, as Billy settled with a drink on the settee extracting more information from him about the compound where he'd nearly met his maker. He didn't want to distress Tony further, but was keen to learn as much as possible.

319

The drink now began to relax Tony to the degree that nothing much seemed to matter for the moment. Billy saw it was time to let go of the questioning.

"You can sleep in the spare room upstairs," he said, "we use it for friends staying sometimes. The bathroom's next door to it," the detective got up.

"Anyway, right now you need to get some rest and so do I. I've got to be at work early tomorrow, but we'll talk when I get back," he took Tony's empty glass.

"Sorry to keep you up so late," Tony apologised, glancing at his watch to see it was nearly four in the morning.

"That's alright, in this job I'm used to it."

"I really appreciate your help."

"That's alright too. I was often helping you out when we were boys, so I'm used to that too," Billy smiled. "Now I want you to rest tomorrow, take it easy for a while."

"I'll have to ring in sick for work," said Tony as they made their way upstairs. He was concerned about the record shop.

"There's a phone in the hall. Now get some bloody rest. Tomorrow I'll send someone round to get some clothes and things from your lodgings. Stay inside the house while I work things out."

They parted as Billy headed for his room at the end of the landing and Tony to settle in the spare room. Images of guns being pointed at him and imaginary sounds of machines crushing cars haunted him as he lay in bed. After a while exhaustion and whisky granted him merciful sleep.

IN the morning Tony rang work to say he'd be off for a couple of days with flu. Billy had gone, but left a note on the hall table saying 'help yourself to food in the kitchen'.

He wasn't hungry, but ate a bowl of cornflakes. He began to feel entirely lost in the empty house and wanted to go home. To do something instead of just hanging around. Flipping through the pages of magazines on the living room coffee table passed a bit of time. Then he tried to get into the story of a book or two on the bookcase shelves. But his mind kept wandering to all the recent events, in particular Lucy and Lindy. Were they safe and well? What was Billy working on? Something he'd said about 'things moving on'. What things?

Billy returned in the late afternoon bringing a travel bag with some of Tony's belongings. He'd also bought some tinned steak and kidney pies to heat for dinner later.

After changing into fresh clothes, Tony joined the detective in the kitchen for coffee.

"Are Lucy and Lindy okay?" he asked the question uppermost in his mind.

"They're fine," Billy answered, leaning back on the kitchen counter with his coffee in hand, "though obviously they don't like being corralled for their own safety."

He paused, taking a drink from the cup. "And no, don't ask me where they're being kept," he said, anticipating the next question.

Tony readily accepted the fact.

"Oh, by the way I nearly forgot, the officer I sent round to collect your things said some woman was calling for you at the same time he was there. Sandra I think he said her name was. D'ye know her?"

"Someone I knew," Tony replied sadly. He was surprised by the news, believing she'd decided to cut all links with him.

"Love stuff?" Billy enquired.

Tony nodded.

"Is she involved in any of this business?" the detective looked concerned.

"No. She knows nothing about it."

"Good, we don't want any more complications. And don't contact her, not yet," he insisted.

Tony wanted to ring Sandra wondering, if like him, she desired to rebuild bridges too, remaining at least as friends. On the other hand she may have gone round to throw something heavy at him. Whichever, he understood it was wise for now to follow Billy's orders.

They ate their steak and kidney pies and settled with coffee in the living room for a while. For Billy it was only a short rest.

"Right, I'm going back to the police station and won't be back until the morning. Got a few things to sort out," he announced.

"Don't you ever get any proper sleep?" asked Tony.

"Not much. There's a bunk bed in one of the storeroom's at the station where I can get a few hours rest sometimes," he grinned, leaving Tony to wonder whether it was true or a wind-up.

"More importantly," he continued, "tomorrow I want you to meet someone."

"Meet who?"

"You'll see tomorrow," Billy got up from the armchair. "As I've said, things are moving on."

The repeat of this cryptic remark annoyed Tony, but he knew it would be pointless to press for an answer. Billy was obviously unprepared to give any more information at this moment.

"You can watch the TV if you like. And help yourself to a drink. Sorry to coop you up like this, but it's very important you stay out of sight right now." Billy left. The front door closed and on hearing the key turning in the lock, Tony feel like a prisoner.

In his isolation he had the urge to ring Sandra to find out why she had called in at his lodgings, but resisted the temptation. He also felt guilty about not contacting his mother for ages. Though even if he wanted to go against Billy's wish, his parents didn't have a home telephone.

Next morning he found a note on the hall table.

'Didn't want to wake you. I nipped back early this morning. One of my men will pick you up at ten o'clock and take you to meet me. Left a spare key so you can lock up when you leave. Billy.'

Once again his friend was being mysterious, leaving him entirely out of the loop. It was nearly nine o'clock. He'd slept more peacefully and for longer than expected. At ten precisely, a black Vauxhall Victor pulled up on the driveway.

As he watched from the kitchen window, he saw a man getting out wearing a dark red pullover and blue jeans. He'd been expecting to see a police car, and wondered if this was a visitor not connected to the police. Surely Frank hadn't found out where he was hiding? The doorbell rang and Tony was in two minds whether to answer or not. The whole business had unsettled his nerves. But he couldn't be cowed. He opened the door.

"Tony?" the man greeted him. He had short dark hair and a moustache, which made him look older than his mid-twenties. "DS Walker sent me. I'm Detective Constable Tom Radcliffe. Call me Tom," the officer held up his identity card putting Tony at ease.

In the car, the detective lifted the radio microphone from its holder on the dashboard.

"We're on our way."

"Okay," a tinny voice burst back, which Tony just about recognised as Billy, at the same time realising he was in an undercover police car.

Twenty minutes later the car pulled off the main road into a cafe car park. The sign 'Jack's' was emblazoned in red above the entrance to a white, flat roofed building.

"DS Walker's inside. I'll leave you to it," said Tom.

Inside the cafe Tony had the surreal sensation he was entering what seemed like an episode in a crime thriller. The secretive nature of the business. He saw Billy sitting at a table in the far corner away from other customers and beckoning him over. Someone was in the seat beside him. As he approached, he could hardly believe what he was seeing. It was Brendan. In a state of shock, he made his way to them, wondering if he'd lost his mind.

"You look as though you've seen a ghost," Brendan smiled. "Come and sit down," he indicated the seat opposite.

"Sorry to surprise you," Billy apologised," but this whole thing needs to be kept under wraps, so we have to meet like this."

"Don't tell me, Brendan's really a detective," said Tony, surmising the next revelation as he sat down.

"You must be bloody joking," Brendan laughed. "I'd rather be dead."

"Shush, keep it down," Billy raised his finger to his lips fearing they'd be overheard. "This is all very secret and only a few of my own men know about it."

"Yes, because a lot of other coppers are a load of corrupt bastards," added Brendan.

Billy ignored the remark, but knew there were bad apples in the force. A waitress came to the table.

"Two more coffees please love. And Tony?" he asked.

"The same."

The waitress left and the detective continued.

"You're wondering why Brendan's here," he stated the obvious. "Well he wants to see your uncle Frank brought down as much as you."

The news came as yet another shock to Tony.

"He's fucking the whole operation up," Brendan broke in." I need to take over the business. Push him out of the way."

"Yes Brendan, you've told me that many times, now just button it," Billy demanded.

"Thing is Tony, your uncle has got himself into some deeply serious waters," the detective lowered his voice. "Something that could endanger national safety. This is outside of his grubby business in sleazy nightclubs and drug dealings."

Tony's head was beginning to spin with each new revelation unfolding.

"Lindy has supplied us with some names of people she's overheard visiting Frank's house. They match with people who the government agency MI5 are particularly interested in."

Now Tony thought this really was moving into a fantasy tale, but he knew Billy was no fantasist.

"Frank is planning a meeting with a gun runner called Alan Baxter. In Northern Ireland at the minute there's a growing underground build-up of a para-military force calling themselves the Irish Republican Army. They want to take the Northern part of the island back from British rule. It's believed in government circles they are intending to launch attacks."

"Attacks on who?"

"Anyone I guess who wants to stop them. The government is worried about security in Northern Ireland and over here on the UK mainland." Billy had only a limited briefing of what was happening on that front. The Irish Republicans hadn't been a serious problem for the British government for nearly half a century, and most people in the UK had no idea what they were about now.

"But that's not the point of what we have in mind," Billy didn't want to complicate matters. "Frank is getting himself involved with this gun runner Baxter. Investing money to help him purchase ex-military weapons from corrupt arms suppliers, and selling them on to countries where there's political unrest."

"Frank's a fucking idiot. Doesn't know what he's getting himself mixed up in," Brendan interrupted again.

"Three coffees," the waitress arrived, placing the cups from a tray on the table. Billy waited until she was a good distance away.

"Frank knows that Baxter is planning to sell weapons to a para-military force building up in Northern Ireland who want it to remain under British government rule. They call themselves the Ulster Volunteer Force. They oppose the Irish republicans. If both sides start getting arms, mayhem could break out over there, and maybe even spread to our towns and cities over here."

Tony had no idea anything like this was going on. His mind worked hard to grasp the nature of this undercover secrecy.

"But all that aside, it presents us with the perfect opportunity to dismantle Frank from his criminal empire," Billy explained.

Tony couldn't make the connection to see how that was possible, and he was also finding it difficult to understand why Brendan would go along with a plan to unseat Frank. After all, he was his uncle's right hand man.

"What's in it for you?" he asked Brendan, who returned a smile, shaking his head.

"You know when we were kids, I thought you were a walkover. Then Billy showed you how to hit back. You got good at it, but the thing that's always held you back is being so nice. Believing in justice, being fair."

He looked down for a moment before firmly fixing his gaze. "What's in it for me is getting rid of Frank and taking over the business. I should think it's fairly bloody obvious why I'm here."

Tony looked at Billy. The person who'd wanted to rigidly uphold law and order. Had he changed? Joined the low life? Billy could read Tony's thoughts from his bewildered face.

"Takes a thief to catch a thief," he said. "Brendan helps me with information and so I give him a steer now and then. That's how the world works."

Together they made him feel like the most stupid innocent who'd ever walked the earth.

"Right, that's enough for now. I just wanted to give you some background," said Billy. "I know you'd like to see your uncle pay for the hell he's put Lindy and Lucy through, and I wanted you to know Brendan's on board with us. Both of you will play a key part in my plan. That's if you want to?" he gave Tony a penetrating look.

"Yes," he replied. "I'm not that fucking innocent."

The detective set off with Tony back to the house while Brendan returned to his home territory.

"What surprises me is that you want Brendan and me on board. Surely you must have people in the force who could help you with this?" asked Tony as Billy drove back.

"I should think that's obvious. I can trust both of you not to say anything to Frank. You both have vested interests in toppling him," Billy explained. "And I'm suspicious that there are some police officers feeding Frank with information, so I want it to be a tight operation. Brendan is also involving two of his own trusted people who want to see Frank brought down."

"You mean you're trusting three villains to help?" Tony was amazed. Billy paused for a moment, concentrating on entering a road junction before continuing.

"If this all goes wrong, the government will deny any involvement. It will look like gang warfare and nothing connected to politics. And I'll just be a copper working in the line of duty chasing criminals."

"And me?"

"An innocent bystander," said Billy.

Tony had agreed to help, but now began to wonder what he was really getting himself into.

"And if you ever breathe a word about the Irish stuff I've told you," Billy warned, "you'll find government agents sticking you in a dark cell and you'll blow my chances of going any further. It's all top secret stuff."

"Give me some credit. You've made me feel a naive fool as it is," Tony snarled. "And I'm fed up with all this secrecy. Tell me what the hell you've got planned."

"Sorry," Billy apologised, "I'll tell you what I've got in mind when we get back."

CHAPTER 14

WHEN they returned Billy made some coffee and they settled in the living room. He got straight to the point.

"Have you ever used a gun?"

"Christ no! And I'm not going to shoot my own uncle," Tony was adamant.

"I'm not asking you to shoot him, I just want him off the scene. It's for self-defence if you need it," Billy reassured him.

"Don't worry, I'll show you how to use one," Billy stood up and walked across to a cabinet, opening a drawer and taking out a photograph.

"Baxter the gun runner is going to have a meeting with Frank at his country house in Essex," he continued.

"Frank's got a country house? It was yet another revelation for Tony.

"He's done well on crime," Billy showed him the photograph. It was an aerial shot showing a large house set in countryside with a long drive and several outbuildings. Tony could hardly believe his uncle had done so well to afford a place that must have cost a fortune.

"Anyway, Frank and Alan Baxter plan to discuss importing illegal weapons into London's docklands for onward shipment to the para-military UVF group who want to defend British rule in Northern Ireland. But Frank doesn't know Baxter is also planning to divert some of these arms to their enemies the IRA."

Tony took a drink of his coffee, absorbing the information.

"Some people in Baxter's network over here are unhappy with his double dealings and see a pile of shit coming down on them if these para-militaries discover his duplicity. They don't want trouble from them. They're terrified they'd be hunted down and assassinated by them in revenge." Billy took back the photo from Tony and replaced it in the drawer.

"The plan is for Brendan and me to kill Baxter while he's with Frank. Then Baxter's network will cease all arms shipments to these para-militaries. End their involvement."

Tony was stunned that Billy would be prepared to commit murder. His friend noticed it.

"Better that than weapons going on to cause even greater killing and likely involving innocents," he justified.

"But how will that get Frank?"

"Frank doesn't realise it, but Baxter got him to sign some documents showing that he agreed to supplying arms to both sides. MI5 has copies, and when Baxter is dead, they'll be passed on to both para-militaries. Frank will be looking over his shoulder constantly, because even his band of ruthless killers would be no match for these diehards seeking revenge. His best option will be to disappear, probably abroad."

"So how do I fit in?" asked Tony, fascinated by the web of intrigue he was entering.

"We don't want to take out Baxter at Frank's country house, because he has security guards who could complicate things. Baxter is going to take him for a trip to his own place at Brussels in Belgium. They'll go by car to a small airfield five miles away, where they plan to fly in

331

Baxter's private plane," Billy returned to sit in his armchair. "That will be their weakest point with only a driver and two security guards." He looked at Tony. "Follow?"

Tony nodded.

"We will drive to a small countryside road in a wooded area about a quarter mile from the aerodrome and park up. Brendan and one of his people will be in another car blocking the narrow road leading to the airfield, pretending it's broken down. Putting on balaclavas, they'll shoot Baxter and his security guards, and lock Frank in the boot for the local law to find him with documents implicating his part in illegal gun running."

"Yes, but what will I do?" Tony was still puzzled.

"I want you to stay with the car in the wood. That's the one we're planning to make our getaway in. When we've parked up, I'll be leaving you with it and joining Brendan to make sure he does a good job. You'll have the gun just in case any of Baxter's men escape and find you and the car. You'll have protection, but I doubt they'll get that far."

Now the danger he was facing really hit home with Tony. They were all a band of ruthless killers, even his good friend Billy.

"But the local police will investigate it," he saw a flaw in the plan.

"Gangsters killing each other as I said. It'll make no more news than that. And authority in high places will control the depth of investigation, which won't go far."

The detective saw the doubt, even disapproval in Tony's expression.

"It's the lesser of evils," Billy assured him. He stood up. "Anyway, that's for a couple of days' time. Right now I reckon we should get something to eat and then spend a couple of hours relaxing in front of the TV. I've got a bit of time off. That is, unless someone calls me into the station."

Tony joined him in the kitchen where Billy got out the pan for a bacon sandwich fry-up.

"Tomorrow I'll show you a map of the area we'll be going to," he explained, over the sizzling of frying bacon. "And give you some practise on how to use a gun."

The coming showdown was not Tony's only worry. Because Billy didn't want him to contact the outside world for now, he was unable to ring work. If he stayed away much longer he'd be facing the sack. But then with the coming event, he might not be around to worry about it. The thought was hardly a consolation.

******

ON the morning of the operation Billy went through the plan of action one more time with Tony. Then after checking their guns were loaded, set off in the car.

The detective had obtained special permission from a government Home Office department to allow his friend into the police firearms practise gallery, and he was now confident Tony could handle the weapon.

He was also certain the getaway car they were travelling in would be parked far enough away from the shootings not to come under fire. But he wanted the 'just in case' insurance of his man being armed.

333

Tony wore the gun under his brown leather jacket in a shoulder holster.

"Are you sure you're okay? Nervous?" Billy asked.

"A bit," Tony replied, playing down the anxiety he really felt.

"Natural. Everyone gets keyed up on an operation involving firearms. You just have to hold your nerve. Be watchful and remain positive."

The car moved away from the built-up areas of the city on its north-west journey out of London into the county of Essex, leafy narrow lanes gradually replacing the urban sprawl. As they neared their destination, Billy took a turn on to a single track road with woodland on either side. A little further he steered the vehicle on to the flat vergeside covered in yellow autumn leaves and stopped.

"Right. This is where I leave you for now," he announced. "I'm planning to be back here soon with Brendan and his man," Billy climbed out of the car. "As I say, guard it with your life," he closed the door and disappeared into the wood.

After a few minutes Tony felt isolated just sitting in the vehicle. He stepped out. The air was still and birds shrilled in the trees. No other cars passed. This was truly a remote spot. Another five minutes passed and he wondered how the operation was progressing.

Another couple of minutes passed and he heard the drone of an aeroplane growing louder, soon catching sight of the light aircraft flickering through the thinning tree leaves as it made a landing descent not far away. Was it Baxter's plane arriving at the airfield?

The lack of any other sound except for birdsong began to make the setting seem eerie. Were Billy and the others okay? Should he see if they needed help? The quiet didn't last long. Several gunshots echoing through the woods shattered the stillness.

Had Billy been shot? He felt no concern for Brendan. The world would probably be a better place without him. But he couldn't just leave Billy if he'd been hurt. Now feeling useless standing there, he removed the gun from his shoulder holster and set off into the woods following the direction of the firing he'd heard.

As he edged cautiously around the trees, shouting broke out. He moved quickly towards the commotion and through an opening in the tree trunks ahead saw a car with the bonnet open. Raising the gun, Tony approached the vehicle, stepping out on to the narrow road. At first he could see no-one.

Then his eyes caught sight of three bodies spread on the ground near the vehicle. Two men in dark suits, guns in hand, their shirts heavily stained with blood from gunshot wounds to chest and stomach. Another overweight man had blood seeping from the blown away side of his head and spattered across the shoulder of his overcoat. Tony had to force himself not to throw up from seeing the horrifying spectacle.

Another gunshot rang out from down the road. Tony sped off in its direction. He rounded a bend and caught sight of a hooded figure raising a gun at him. Tony froze. The figure lowered the weapon.

"I nearly fucking shot you! What are you doing here?" The balaclava covered Billy's head.

"I came to help," Tony shouted back, greatly relieved at not stopping a bullet.

"I said not to leave the car. Frank's escaped, if he finds it he could hotwire start it and get away," Billy was furious.

Another hooded figure appeared on the road, calling to the detective.

"Frank's headed across the field and Brendan's after him. Come on."

"Coming," Billy replied.

"You're planning to kill Frank, not lock him in the car boot," Tony suddenly realised.

"Get real Tony. What the fuck d'ye think we really planned? This ain't a gentleman's game. Get back to the car."

"No, I'm coming with you." Now Tony was furious at being double crossed and once again treated like a stupid innocent. Ridiculously perhaps, he felt he could play a part in saving his uncle's life. Imprisonment for him yes. But killing, no. Frank was after all his mother's brother.

Billy wasn't waiting to argue. He set off. Tony followed.

The detective veered off the road into the wood following his hooded partner. Soon they reached the edge where it opened on to a field. Another hooded figure a few hundred feet ahead was running up a grassy incline towards a farmhouse at the top.

Tony reached the field as Billy and the other man had already covered a good distance up the slope. The farmhouse appeared to be their target.

As he neared, he saw the three men laying flat in the long grass just below the top of the incline, keeping themselves out of view from the farmhouse. Tony laid down beside them.

"What you doing here?" a voice from the balaclava next to him whispered. It was Brendan.

"Seeing Billy going back on his word not to kill my uncle," Tony replied.

Brendan laughed, gun poised in hand pointing up the slope.

"I'll go round the back of the farmhouse this way," Billy whispered from the left side of the group, indicating the direction with his firearm. "Brendan go right and Ely cover from the front," Billy named the other man whose identity Tony hadn't known.

"You stay here," Billy ordered Tony. "I don't want your death on my hands."

Tony had other ideas, mainly to try and persuade them not to kill his uncle, though presently the odds seemed against him. He made no reply to the order.

Ducking low, Billy crept along the side of the incline to reach a line of trees bordering the farmyard forecourt on the left. To the right, Brendan headed for the cover of a barn. Ely crawled further up the slope enough to see across the forecourt and farmhouse frontage by just raising his head. Tony followed suit.

For a while all was quiet, broken only by the sound of a cow mooing in a distant meadow. Then the hum of a light aircraft as it came into view low in the sky on a landing approach to the aerodrome.

Tony grew edgy wondering what was happening at the farmhouse. He wouldn't be able to save Frank's life just laying on the grass. He had to do something and decided to take Billy's route towards the cover of the trees.

As he began to crawl he heard Ely quietly calling to him.

"You go any further and I'll shoot you."

Tony stopped, sensing a gun pointing at him with no idle threat.

Gunshots suddenly exploded from the direction of the farmhouse. Ely sprang up and raced across the forecourt towards the building to take cover behind a blue Vauxhall Velox car parked near the front. Tony was torn between following him or sticking to his plan for approaching from the cover of the trees like Billy. He chose the trees. The front approach would make him too much of an open target.

Reaching the tree cover he cautiously moved from trunk to trunk to gain a side of the farmhouse. He could see a door and a second floor window above it. The door was half open. The gunfire had ceased. Foreboding silence ruled.

A few moments later two gunshots came from inside the building. Tony broke cover from the trees and raced across the stony ground to the side door. Bolts top and bottom were sticking out. It had been smashed open.

He raised the gun and stealthily stepped inside to a lobby. Wellington boots coated in dried mud stood beneath dark blue overalls hanging on hooks above. A brown leather riding saddle rested on a table to the side. The menacing silence dominated again.

Another door leading further inside was also half open, the keyhole lock shattered by gunfire. Keeping his own firearm raised, Tony moved warily into a short corridor opening on the right to a utility room. A twin-tub washer churned blissfully unaware of the tension mounting around it.

Turning to continue along the corridor, a crouching figure leapt at him from the room. Next second he felt an arm tightening round his neck, his gun hand gripped by the wrist and painfully twisted forcing him to drop the weapon.

"Jesus, I nearly bloody killed you again," Billy whispered furiously in his ear, releasing the grip and removing his balaclava. "Pick up your gun. Now you're here, you might as well be useful." The detective could see Tony was not going to be excluded from the hunt.

"We think Frank is upstairs. Brendan's covering from the other side. Keep back for now, and for God's sake obey my orders. Your life depends on it." Billy made his way along the corridor, which opened on to the hallway and a flight of stairs.

Tony held back and shortly saw Brendan appearing from a doorway across the hall. He too had discarded the balaclava. Billy gestured his partner to follow him upstairs. As he placed his foot on the first step a voice shouted at him.

"Stay back!"

Frank appeared on the landing his left hand twisting a woman's arm behind her back, a gun in the other pointed at her head. Her young face was drawn in terror, the shoulder of her blue dress torn in the struggle when she'd tried to escape from the intruder who'd found her hiding in her bedroom.

"Throw your guns down," Frank ordered. Billy and Brendan hesitated. Frank pressed the gun barrel hard into the side of the woman's head causing her to wince in fear. His opponents dropped their weapons.

"Now move towards the front door, open it and get outside. Try anything and the woman's dead."

Billy and Brendan obeyed, keeping an eye on any opportunity to outwit their target. But presently he held the ace card.

With his back pressed tightly against the corridor wall to try and keep out of sight, Tony saw Frank arriving at the bottom of the stairway with the hostage. Confrontation while the woman was his prisoner would prove too risky. Tony's mind reeled for a plan. Ely was taking cover behind the car parked at the front. He decided to join him. Together one of them might be able to distract Frank while the other moved in on him. Tony had begun to realise the chance of pleading for his uncle's life was becoming an impossibility.

Leaving the farmhouse, he retraced the cover of the trees and ducked back below the grass slope incline. Looking up he saw Billy and Brendan outside the farmhouse, but no sign of Frank coming out yet. Swiftly he ran across the forecourt to join Ely in the cover of the parked car. It was almost his last moment yet again. Ely swung round, gun aimed at the unexpected visitor, trigger micro seconds from being activated.

"You fucking idiot. What are you doing here?" Ely greeted him, balaclava still covering his head.

"I thought we could work something out together," Tony crouched beside him.

"Just stay down," Ely grunted.

Frank came out of the house with his hostage and ordered Billy and Brendan to move back a good distance as he began moving towards the parked car. It was obvious he was planning to use the Vauxhall car to escape, using his captive as insurance for safe passage.

Tony decided his uncle's vulnerable moment would be when he'd have to release his hostage to bundle her into the vehicle. In that moment she'd briefly be free from his grasp. He whispered the thought to Ely, but the man didn't want to know. As Frank drew within ten feet of the car, Ely suddenly sprang up.

"Shoot her and your dead!" he shouted pointing the gun.

"I don't think so," Frank replied, blasting him with a bullet. Ely jerked as the missile seared through the balaclava and sunk inside his forehead, catapulting him lifeless on his back. Tony nearly shit himself seeing the body beside him and realising any moment he could be the next.

He desperately struggled to hold his nerve and fought to stop his hands shaking. Nestling tightly from Frank's view to the side of the vehicle, he now had only seconds to act.

Frank forced the woman to the rear of the car, releasing her and pushing the gun barrel into the small of her back. He reached with his other hand for the keys in his jacket pocket that he'd taken from her. Unlocking the boot, he prodded the terrified woman with the gun to make her climb inside. She resisted briefly until Frank punched her hard between the shoulder blades causing her to cry in pain and obey.

Hidden crouching at the side, Tony couldn't see what was taking place, but could hear Frank's orders. At the slamming shut of the car boot, he knew he had to swiftly act.

Frank walked to the driver door, pointing his gun at Billy and Brendan warning them to stay back as they tried to move in closer. Tony worked his way round to the rear of the vehicle. He heard Frank opening the door and sprang out, raising the firearm at his uncle's back.

"Drop the gun," he commanded. Frank froze. The voice seemed familiar, but not in context. It couldn't be?

"I don't want to shoot you uncle Frank, but I will if you don't drop the gun," Tony offered the ultimatum. Frank could hardly believe it, his own nephew threatening him. Slowly he turned his head.

"Don't move any further," Tony ordered. Frank ignored the command sensing his nephew faltering. He turned to face him.

Just twenty feet away, Billy and Brendan were identically thinking of rushing in. But they'd be sitting targets and doubted Tony would pull the trigger on his uncle.

"I never thought I'd live to see the day when the little boy closest to my heart would turn traitor on me," Frank stared at Tony, shaking his head in disappointment. "It's no surprise toe-rags like Brendan wanting me out of the way. But you?"

The kind uncle who used to do magic tricks for him, give him money, treat him like the father he'd wished for flashed through Tony's mind. He couldn't shoot that man.

"I had such plans for you," Frank smiled, raising his gun.

"Go on then, shoot me. Your own flesh and blood," Tony dared him, lowering his weapon. Frank grabbed the opportunity and pressed the trigger.

A loud shot rang out.

Frank staggered forward as the bullet from his gun struck the ground beside Tony. Frank shuddered. A look of surprise on his face. His legs tottered slightly, his hand gripping the gun wavered. Then he pointed directly at his nephew again.

Tony had no choice. He fired his gun, the bullet tearing into Frank's chest sending him careering backwards. Another gun blast sent Frank staggering forward again, swaying then falling face first dead on the stony forecourt. Blood oozed through his jacket from two gaping wounds in his back. Tony was momentarily mystified by their appearance. Then he saw a man in a muddy overall approaching from the side of the farm building, shotgun raised and pointing at him. He'd obviously blasted Frank from behind.

"Don't shoot!" Billy cried out. "We're on your side."

The man continued pointing the shotgun at Tony, who stood in a daze. He'd lowered his own weapon not caring if the man shot him. He was sick of the violence he'd been born into and could never seem to escape. Now he'd killed his own uncle. His nan's son. His mother's brother. He threw the gun away. Right now death would be welcome.

And that poor bloody woman in the car boot. She'd done nothing wrong. Ignoring the approaching armed man, he stooped to get the car keys from his dead uncle's hand.

"I'll do it," he heard Billy, who took the set and went to the boot.

"What the bloody hell's going on?" the man with the shotgun demanded. "Who did this to my daughter?" he saw her as Billy helped the young woman out.

Brendan placed an arm across Tony's shoulders.

"You did bloody well mate. For a second I thought you were a gonna."

Tony shook him off. The last thing he wanted was praise from another violent criminal and now probably Frank's successor.

The young woman shook uncontrollably as she stood freed from her prison.

"Daddy, daddy," she clutched her father. The man placed his left arm around her, still clutching the shotgun with the right while uncertain of his present company.

"It's okay Karen your safe," he comforted her.

Billy picked up the gun Tony had discarded and approached him.

"Go back to the car with Brendan and he'll drive you back to my place. I've got some sorting out to do here and I'll see you later."

Tony hated the prospect of spending another moment in the presence of Brendan, but not as much as staying in this scene of carnage. Taking a last look at his uncle's blood soaked body he set off with Brendan back to the car in the wood.

On the drive back he was revolted by the cheerful mood Brendan appeared to be enjoying.

"That's solved a lot of problems," he said with relish.

Tony kept silent, the events still revolving in his mind.

"You came through really well," the driver by his side continued, completely unaware of his passenger's depression. "I could find you some well paid work if you want to join me. You'd earn ten times what you get now."

Tony had taken enough.

"I know he was an evil bastard, but I've just shot my own uncle. So give it a rest."

A mystified smile rose on Brendan's sinewy face.

"Your upset. It'll pass," he dismissed the harrowing events that had happened as if they were nothing. Tony ignored the remark, realising a psychopath was incapable of understanding anyone else's emotions.

Back at Billy's house he closed the front door as Brendan drove away, and settled for a spell of brief peace and solitude away from the outside world. He poured himself a glass of whisky from the cabinet and let the liquid warm him, releasing a glow of relaxation through his body.

Tony was slumped on the living room sofa when hours later Billy returned.

"Jesus, what a day," he entered the room looking pale and exhausted. "Turned out to be a right bloody mess." He flopped into the armchair. "My superiors will roast me tomorrow." He looked across at Tony.

345

"You did a bloody good job mate in the circumstances. For a second I thought you'd bottle it, but you held out."

Tony stared back unimpressed.

"Yeah, I know he was your uncle. Must have been really hard, but don't feel too bad. That bloke with the shotgun blew half his insides out. Frank would never have lived anyway."

"Oh, I feel much better now," Tony replied sarcastically. They fell silent for a moment.

"What have you been doing at the farmhouse?" he asked.

"I had to call in a government team looking at the build-up of paramilitaries in Ireland. Frank and Ely will officially be disappeared from the face of the Earth. Nothing at that farm or near it will ever have happened."

"What about the man and his daughter. Surely they'll tell someone?" Tony couldn't see how the incident would be kept secret. Then a terrible thought struck him. "You haven't killed them?"

Billy smiled.

"No. We haven't killed them. A good sum of silence money is going their way. But on the condition they never breathe a word to anyone what happened." Billy paused. "Or some of the money will go to their funeral costs."

Tony began to hate even more the dark underworld Billy had entered.

"I don't really want to say it," Billy stared grimly at Tony, "but I wouldn't be able to protect you either, if you ever said a word about what happened."

Tony knew exactly what he meant. The thought had already occurred to him.

"D'ye fancy something to eat?" Billy changed the mood and stood up. Food was the last thing on Tony's mind.

"No, I'm going to bed and try to get some sleep, though God knows how."

"Cheer up ol' friend. You can go home tomorrow. The coast is clear now," Billy gave him the welcome news, which did cheer him.

"Lucy and Lindy? Can they go back home."

"Not sure. Can't say yet," Billy was unwilling to give more information. "Well I'm bloody starving. Got to get some food. I'll see you in the morning," he left for the kitchen. Tony sat a little longer wondering if he'd ever see Lucy again, then made his way upstairs to bed.

He had a restless night without much sleep, and was in the kitchen early next morning drinking a cup of tea when the detective came down.

"There's some tea in the pot," he told Billy, who was reaching for a couple of chocolate snack bars in a cupboard.

"No, it's okay, I'll grab a coffee at the police station. Can't be late for a debrief meeting about yesterday's fiasco. Probably put back my chances of making inspector for a while." He turned to Tony as he placed the chocolate bars in his jacket pocket.

"I know right now you're thinking I'm a shit. But I'm sure you'll understand in time that the rules sometimes have to be broken. I wish it was different."

347

Tony was beginning to come to the same conclusion but even if he'd wanted to reply, his friend was already heading out of the room.

"When you leave," Billy called back, "post the key through the letterbox. Look after yourself and I'll be in touch." Seconds later the front door closed. Tony finished his tea and packed his belongings, then left for the train station a short distance down the road.

******

WHEN he arrived at his lodgings, Rudy's mother greeted him in the hallway clothed in the usual dressing gown she wore at home. The cord from the electric iron she held trailed to the floor as she stared at him sourly through wrinkled eyes.

"You're behind with the rent."

"Yes, sorry. I had to go away for a few days. I'll bring it down to you in a minute," Tony apologised.

She glared at him doubtfully. So many tenants over the years had made such promises, then sneaked away never to return.

Snatching the trailing cord in her other hand, she walked off down the hallway, mumbling under her breath as she returned to her room.

After freshening up and a change of clothes, Tony went downstairs to the hall phone to ring his boss at work. Billy wasn't the only one expecting a hostile reception from a superior. He'd been away for more than the couple of days he'd said he would be.

"I thought you'd left the country," Sebastian, the record shop owner greeted him.

"I'm sorry. I've been really ill. I just couldn't call in," Tony knew it sounded a lame lie.

"What did you have, Bubonic Plague, Yellow Fever?" Sebastian registered his disbelief.

"I won't let you down again," Tony could hardly tell him the truth of his absence. Even if he could, it would sound more ridiculous than a phony sickness story.

"I know you won't," his boss replied, "I've got someone else in. I had to close the shop for two days. You're fired. I'll send a cheque for what you're owed in the post." The phone went dead.

Tony returned to his room. It was no more than he'd expected and he didn't feel any loss. It was time for a change. He'd never rise to anything higher working for Sebastian in a small record shop. For a few hours he rested, then went out and bought a local paper to search through the jobs column. The irony struck him that he'd be looking for work just to exist, while a violent criminal like Brendan would be rolling in money.

A few days later he decided it was time to visit his mother. She'd be giving him a dressing down for not being in touch for some time. He could live with that, but seeing his dad would not be pleasant. Even harder would be carrying the knowledge he'd shot her brother and could never say a word about the incident, if he wanted to continue living.

At the flat, Irene poked her head out the door giving him a curious gaze.

349

"Oh it's you. Been so long I hardly recognised you," her sarcasm flowed. Inside he said sorry for not keeping in touch and began to think he'd spent a lot of time now apologising.

"I'll put the kettle on. Your dad's upstairs," Irene went into the kitchen. Tony settled in the living room. Cowboys were embroiled in a shoot-out on the TV in the corner. Irene loved her television, 'it's a bit of company' she'd often remark.

She brought the tea on a tray into the living room and placed it on a small table, settling with Tony on the sofa.

"Still working at the record shop?" she asked.

"Tony nodded as his mother poured tea from the pot into a cup and handed it to him. He didn't want to say he'd been sacked. That would lead to more questions as to why and what would he do next. Stuff he just didn't want to talk about right now.

Irene chatted about her aches and pains, some clothes she'd bought and didn't like, gossip about someone in the flats having an affair, and how the toilet upstairs wasn't flushing properly. Her son dutifully listened while his mind drifted into wondering if he'd ever see Lucy again.

"Your nan's very worried," Irene's words suddenly wrenched him from his thoughts. "She says your uncle Frank seems to have disappeared. Some people called round at her flat asking if he'd been there. They said no-one knows where he's gone."

It was the subject Tony dreaded. He knew exactly what had happened to his uncle. He'd helped to kill him. But he couldn't say a word. The memory of firing a bullet into

Frank's chest vividly returned. His dead body covered in blood.

"Has he been in touch with you?" asked Irene. Tony hesitated.

"No, I don't know where he is." The answer was true. He had no idea where Frank's body had been disposed. He hated lying to his mother and wanted to leave the flat, but the moment was interrupted by his father entering the room, dressed smartly in a tweed jacket and neatly pressed beige trousers.

"Hello son," he greeted him stiffly.

"Hello dad," Tony felt an icy barrier between them.

"Still working at the record shop?"

Once again Tony felt compelled to lie. He knew his father disapproved of him ever working in what he considered a lowly occupation, and was now likely to start lecturing him on how he should have remained at college to get qualifications leading to a better life.

On that, Tony was coming round to the same conclusion. He'd been considering signing up for an adult education course. But he couldn't bear to admit it to his father and have him gloating on the fact he was right all along.

"Well I've got to go out now. I'm meeting with some friends at the British Legion club for a member's fiftieth birthday celebration," Gerry made his excuse to leave.

"You mean you're off for a boozy piss-up," Irene realistically described the event, lifting the teapot to pour Tony another cup. Gerry eyed her savagely. She eyed him back defiantly. Tony anticipated a furious row. Nothing had changed between them.

351

"Cow!" Gerry spat at her, then left, slamming the front door behind.

"Glad he's gone out, gives me some peace," Irene began to pour Tony's tea.

"No, it's alright mum. I've had enough," he didn't only mean tea.

"You going now?" Irene looked surprised. "You haven't been here five minutes. I hardly see you."

Tony felt guilty that his mother would be upset if he left at that moment. He conceded another cup of tea, and stayed for another half-an-hour of listening to her ailments and local gossip.

He left feeling alienated from the world, everyone busily rotating in their own concerns while he currently approached the road to nowhere. Lucy in an unknown universe with Lindy. Sandra the woman who had cared for him now existing far from his reach. He'd managed to fuck up everything.

******

SANDRA wasn't quite so far away as he'd imagined. A few evenings later a lodger called at his room to say someone was at the front door asking to see him.

Tony was puzzled. He wasn't expecting any visitors and was unsure if it was friend or foe. Cautiously he descended the stairs feeling a cold draught coming in from the open doorway. Then he saw Sandra standing just outside with a young man beside her.

352

"Hello Tony," she greeted him. "We were passing so I thought I'd call in to see you." She wore a black three-quarter length overcoat against the night air. The man beside her in a fawn duffle coat, which seemed a size too large for his thin frame. He looked at Tony nervously, as if knowing Sandra had once been his partner and that seeing them together might spark jealously.

"Great to see you again," Tony welcomed her. "I tried to contact you by phone a few times, but your mum said you were out."

"Did she?" Sandra shook her head. "She never told me."

"Come in for a minute, I'll make you a coffee."

"No, it's okay," Sandra declined. "Just wanted to see how you are, and say no hard feelings."

"I'm sorry if ..." Tony began.

"No, it's alright," Sandra stopped him. "That's the way it is sometimes. "Kevin and me are off to the cinema down the road," she turned her head indicating the boyfriend beside her. "Maybe see you again sometime."

As she walked away Tony wondered if the visit was to demonstrate that she could carry on with life perfectly well without him. Or was it intended to make him jealous and draw him back? He closed the door feeling certain they'd never meet again. Lucy was the woman he wanted. The one never far from his thoughts. And right now he was certain he'd never see her again either.

******

TWO weeks later Tony returned from an interview for a sales assistant in a department store a few miles away at Wandsworth. He was convinced he wouldn't get the job. It would be less money than he'd been earning and his lack of enthusiasm for the position probably showed.

The trauma he'd been through at the shooting had entirely changed his outlook on life. It could all end so abruptly. His own was going nowhere and he felt certain he could do so much better.

Entering the hallway back at his lodgings he saw two suitcases resting against the wall. The living room door opened.

"Tony," Rudy came out to greet him, dressed in black leather jacket and trousers. "We're just back from New York. It's been a fantastic time."

A woman appeared in the doorway.

"This is Cathy," Rudy introduced her. The woman smiled approaching him, her blue silk dress covered with round silver sequins. Vivid red streaks highlighted the blonde, shoulder length hair and her hazel eyes sparkled in greeting as she bent forward to kiss Tony on the cheek.

"Rudy's told me so much about you," she said. "Your days at college. How both of you stuck that place is beyond me."

It was beyond Tony too, but he didn't press the point.

"We got married in New York," Rudy announced excitedly, "and we've got plans to open an art gallery of our own in London."

Tony congratulated them. It lifted his spirits to see two happy people after the depressing days he'd been through.

"We're going to throw a party soon and you've got to come along," Rudy's enthusiasm brightened the atmosphere. "But right now we're a bit jet lagged. Not long back from the airport." He bent down to lift the suitcases. "Time to get some rest. We'll see you later. You can tell me what you've been up to."

Cathy smiled at Tony then followed Rudy upstairs. The couple's happiness disappeared with them as he stood alone again in the hallway.

A few days later to Tony's surprise he received a letter offering him a job at the department store. The owner was opening a new record section and felt his experience of sales in the growing popular music business would be invaluable. It wasn't the position Tony had applied for, though better he thought than an assistant in the furnishings department the company had advertised in the local paper. This wasn't a step change in life, but a stop gap to at least earn a living for now.

The hurdle he faced in finding work further afield was not having a car. Over the next few months he took driving lessons and was fortunate to pass the test first time. Not having much money, he was able to scrape just enough to buy an older two-tone blue and white Ford Sedan. It spluttered a lot on starting and juddered sometimes on the road, but offered him a new freedom to travel.

Rudy threw his party later than originally planned, spending much of the time at Cathy's flat in fashionable Chelsea a few miles away, near where they intended to open their art gallery.

"It's costing us a fortune to set up," Rudy explained to friends over the noisy music and chatter at the party. "But I've got some up and coming artists who are keen to put their work on display there. If we can crack this, fingers crossed, we can launch some amazing art on to the scene and make a lot of money into the bargain."

Tony was surprised to hear his friend talking about making lots of money. He'd always thought Rudy interested in art for its own sake, not just for money. He knew America was a country highly driven by commercial enterprise and thought the ethos must have rubbed off on Rudy while he'd been there.

The atmosphere in the room held a heavy concoction of cigarette and cannabis smoke. Alcohol flowed freely. Bob Dylan, Elvis, The Beatles, Buddy Holly sang their emotional hearts out. Everyone appeared to have a partner. Friends all around them. Someone tried to sell him some LSD on a sugar cube. But it wasn't drugs or alcohol that could lift his depression.

Tony wondered how happy any of these people would be if they'd shot their uncle in the chest. Helped to kill a member of their own family. The guilt continually weighed him down. Feeling alone without a partner, he decided to go for a walk in the cool night air.

Edging his way through the party-goers, he made his way towards the front door. As he left the room, he was met by a balding, middle-aged lodger, half-undressed with braces stretched over his white string vest.

"Bloody noisy sods," the man glanced disapprovingly towards the party room. "Glad I didn't have to look for you through that lot. There's a phone call for you."

Tony went to the phone in the hall wondering who it could be. He wasn't expecting a call. He heard a voice, but couldn't make it out with the party noise dominating. The phone cable was just long enough for him to open the front door and listen outside.

"It's me, Lucy," the voice came again.

"Lucy?" Tony was stunned.

"Yes, how many times? What's all that music?"

"Just a party."

"Having a good time?"

"No I'm not. Where are you? I've missed you so much."

For a moment Lucy said nothing.

"Will you come and meet me?" she asked, breaking the silence.

"Of course I will. Where are you?"

"I'll be at the White Bear cafe. It's next to Harlow train station."

"I'll get there. Might be an hour or so," Tony promised. He climbed into his car praying the temperamental engine would start. A cough and splutter and it blasted into life.

His depression evaporated as he pulled away. The sound of Lucy's voice and the prospect of being re-united expelled his demons. Lucy was only forty miles away on the north east outskirts of London, but to get there involved the clutter of busy Saturday night traffic.

He arrived at the White Bear cafe nearly two hours later to see light streaming through the steam covered window

357

blocking the cold outside. Pushing open the front door, he looked around. Two men in railway uniforms sat at a table eating their meals. Another in dirty, torn clothes was mumbling to himself, clasping a cup of tea.

"What do you want mate?" the cafe owner with an unwelcoming gaze called to him from behind the counter. Tony ignored him as he caught sight of Lucy sitting in the corner a mug on the table. She wore a light yellow jacket and now had a bob hairstyle, the sides curling across her cheeks.

"I thought you weren't coming," she said as Tony sat down opposite at the table.

"The traffic was terrible," he explained, distressed to see how pale she looked.

"You've got a car? I thought you'd be coming by train."

"It's an old heap, but it gets me around. Just," he smiled. She smiled back. It lifted him to see a spark of light in her sad face.

"Remember the comic annuals?" she asked.

"I'll never forget them."

"D'ye want something to eat or drink mate," the cafe owner shouted from the counter. "This ain't a social club."

"Two coffees," Tony shouted back.

"What's happening?" he turned back to Lucy, "are you still meant to be in hiding?" Tony lowered his voice.

"Billy thinks I'm safe now, but said it might be best if I stayed out of sight for a couple more weeks," Lucy replied. "He says there's been a lot of blood letting. People loyal to Frank unhappy with Brendan taking over. But most of them have been disappeared."

358

"So did Billy tell you everything that happened?" asked Tony, curious to know how much she'd been told.

"Only that Frank had been killed in a gangland confrontation, and that Brendan had been involved."

Tony wanted to unburden his mind and tell her the complete story. But he'd sworn secrecy to Billy, and since his life could be at risk if he ever divulged the information, he didn't want to put Lucy unwittingly in the same position. It was enough she knew the outcome.

"How did Lindy take it?" he asked.

"She felt relieved. But sad that it had to come to this."

"Right, two mugs of coffee," the cafe owner in a dirty blue apron interrupted, slamming the drinks down on the table. "We don't normally do table service here," he stared aggressively at Tony. "But sir can pay me on the way out if he so wishes." The man returned to the counter.

"The thing is, I can't stand being cooped up any more. I want to get back to a normal life," Lucy sounded drained.

"And Lindy?"

"She's a lot happier away from it all. She's waiting for Billy to arrange a new identity for her. Start a new life. I don't know what I'll do if she does. I might never see her again." The spark of light that had briefly risen in Lucy's eyes faded. Tony reached out for her hand resting on the table.

"Where is she? Where have you been staying?"

"A house about a mile from here. The police safe house."

"Do you want to go back there?"

"No, I never want to see the bloody place again. I've been living like a prisoner. Food supplied, but never able to go out without fearing for my safety. I can't stand it any more."

"But your mother, Lindy, if you don't go back?" Tony could see Lucy was being torn apart.

"She said I have to get on with my life. Don't let it be ruined," her eyes were filled with tears.

"What do you want to do?" Tony pleaded.

"Just be normal again."

"Come on, I'll take you back to my place," he knew Lucy wanted to get far away from the confinement of the safe house. They stood up. Tony took hold of the untouched coffee mugs and slammed them down on the counter.

"Your coffee looks like dirty dishwater. I don't pay for rubbish," he said to the owner standing by the till preparing to take money for the drinks. The man looked startled, weighing up if he should insist on payment or forget it. As the couple left he chose to forget it.

******

THEY didn't speak for a while at the start of the car journey back. Tony broke the silence with a thought puzzling him.

"What I can't understand is how Billy could web himself up with Brendan? When I knew Billy back in our boy days, he hated criminals, bullies, people who used violence to get their own way."

Lucy said nothing for a moment considering Tony's dilemma.

360

"I think he has to work with the devil to know what's happening in hell," she replied.

Tony had never thought of it like that. He was impressed by her understanding. They fell silent again for a while.

"Billy said you were there when Frank was killed," Lucy wasn't sure if Tony knew she'd been told.

"It isn't a moment I want to remember, or a moment I can forget," he glanced across at her. "Can we talk about it later?"

After travelling several miles, the car developed engine trouble and Tony spent some time tracing and fixing an electrical fault. The couple didn't arrive back at his lodgings until the early hours of the morning.

The party music no longer echoed loudly round the house, replaced by quieter romantic songs. Most of the guests had left. A couple stood in the hallway locked in a loving embrace and oblivious to their entry.

"Come on," Tony led Lucy up the stairs to his room.

"As you know, it's not a palace here, but the best I can offer you for now," he took off his leather jacket and lobbed it on to the bed.

"It's a palace to me after that confinement," Lucy reflected.

"Would you like a coffee? Something to eat?" he asked. Lucy shook her head.

"I expect you're really tired. You can have my bed and I'll sleep on the armchair."

"I am tired," said Lucy, "but I've been stuck in that safe house for ages, and right now I'd like to go for a short walk. Just feel free again."

361

"Okay. I'll come with you."

They stepped into the street, the quiet of the early hours noticeable by the absence of people and cars that continually passed in the daytime.

After a while they came to a bridge across the River Thames, and halfway along stopped to watch the rippling water flowing beneath. Then Tony turned to Lucy and took her in his arms.

"I love you," he said, "I've loved you since we first met."

"Have you? I've never been sure," Lucy looked uncertain.

"Ever since you shared your comic annuals with me," he smiled. Lucy laughed.

They kissed as the light of a new daybreak began surfacing on the horizon.

I hope you enjoyed *A Fracture In Daybreak*. If you also enjoy supernatural stories I've written many, which are listed on the following pages.

As a taster, here's the first part of my popular ghost story novel.

DEADLY ISLAND RETREAT

CHAPTER 1

THERE are times in life when you wish you could turn back the clock. Reset the moment when you agreed to do something that seemed a good idea at the time, only later to find it was a big mistake.

That's how the episode began after an old friend, Lawrence Keating, rang me one day.

"Alex, how are you keeping? I've bought an island off the west coast of Scotland. Come and spend a few days with me."

Lawrence was the only person I knew who would have enough money to buy an island. We'd met five years earlier at a business college. The fact that we were both aged 22 and shared the same birth date in May had instantly connected us.

He was the flyaway student, brilliant in sales and marketing strategies to the extent his knowledge often exceeded the tutors. But he was modest with it. Friendly, the life and soul of the party. No-one could be envious or annoyed with him.

"You've bought an island? That's amazing." I was impressed, though not surprised Lawrence could do something like that.

"It's not exactly a sun-baked paradise island, but fantastically atmospheric," he said. "There's an old mansion there that needs a lot of renovation, but I've got plans in hand for it. Come and meet me."

As it happened I was between jobs. That is, having recently lost my job as manager of an office equipment store which had gone into liquidation. I wasn't a brilliant student like Lawrence, but the difference in ability didn't stop us from enjoying each other's company at the college.

"Where should I meet you and when?" I asked.

"Why now. No time like the present. I've got a motor launch moored at an old fishing harbour at Tullochrie on the north west coast of Scotland. The island's about five miles offshore there. It's called Fennamore. You might have heard of it."

I hadn't, but then I wasn't an expert on Scottish islands.

"It's a long drive from London. It'll have to be tomorrow," I told him. "I've a few things to sort out."

"All right. Tomorrow. There's a pub by the harbour called the The Ship Inn. I'll meet you there."

"It'll be about two o'clock," I said.

"Okay, but don't be late. See you then." Lawrence hung up.

That was him all over. Driving people to agree to something before they'd hardly had a chance to take it in. That was the secret of his success.

Fortunately his invite had come at the right time. Being between jobs I had a bit of time to spare. There were a couple of interviews lined up, but not for another week. And I hadn't seen Lawrence in over a year. It would be good to meet up again.

My girlfriend, Rosie, was away on a training course from work and wouldn't be back for a few days. She was in sales for a cosmetics company and forging ahead with a great career. By coincidence, her course was only sixty miles away from the coastal town in Scotland where I'd agreed to meet Lawrence.

It was an eight-hour-drive from my London flat in Fulham and I arrived at Tullochrie just before two o'clock. Lawrence was standing outside The Ship Inn, wearing black chinos and a light blue shirt patterned with yachts and motor boats. The seafaring theme had obviously grabbed him.

His fair hair, blue eyes and square jawline gave him an assertive look that immediately instilled confidence. You could see how this would literally give him a head start in convincing business partners and customers that he was their man.

"Alex, you wonderful person. It's fantastic to see you again," he greeted me with a hug. "Isn't this an amazing place."

I looked around, taking in the colourful boats bobbing gently on the harbour water, seagulls gliding in the breeze, and the rippling sea beyond stretching to the horizon. Grey stone cottages bordered the harbour front and sides, with narrow lanes at each end leading into the small town behind.

"Inspirational isn't it?" Lawrence placed his arm around my shoulders. "So great to see you again."

He was always over the top with everything. But that was his magnetic charm.

"Making loads of money?" he asked.

"Not exactly at this minute," I answered honestly.

"Never mind," he smiled. "I can give you a steer to some amazing investments. Make you rich overnight."

"Great," I replied. "But right now I feel really knackered after a long drive. Can we get something to eat?"

"Sorry, sorry. I'll buy you lunch. Come on."

We entered the pub and after boosting my system with steak pie and chips downed with a beer I felt renewed.

As we made our way along the harbour to where Lawrence's 30-foot, blue and white motor launch Pioneer was berthed, he recited all the technical details about the boat. He'd already filled my head with many of its features over lunch. His enthusiasm was unstoppable.

If only I'd know what was to come, I'd have turned back at that moment and driven home to London. As it was, my horrific future was already unfolding.

Outside the harbour the sea was choppy and the launch bounced furiously over the waves. I wasn't the best seafarer and my stomach began to protest.

Lawrence was in his element.

"Yippee," he yelled, and accelerated causing the craft to whack into the waves even harder.

"Soon be there," he called to me from the wheel, as I sat on the deck enduring the violent impact and feeling like death.

"There's Fennamore island!" he shouted excitedly a short while later. I glanced ahead. The outline of the island was partly covered in a blue-grey mist, giving it a mysterious, almost threatening appearance, as if a warning to stay away.

"I own that," Lawrence announced loudly, bristling with pride as he began turning the launch towards a small inlet. The opening led to a curved pebbly bay with a projecting stone jetty to the side. The bay waters were calmer and with the boat no longer furiously bouncing I began to feel better. Lawrence steered the craft alongside the jetty.

"There's the house," he pointed to a large greystone mansion, which it would be difficult to miss given its size. The steeply pitched slate roof was pitted with extensive patches of moss. A ledge spanned the building just below the roof line with gargoyles perched on each side of the facing corners, fanged teeth and vicious claws projecting into the skyline.

The building loomed at the top of a steep slope overlooking the bay. I felt uncomfortable in its towering presence. The tall, leaded-light front windows seemed to peer curiously like a collection of eyes assessing the new arrival to their island domain.

Lawrence had no such qualms.

"Come on, let's get inside," he called tying the boat ropes to capstans on the jetty. I grabbed my overnight bag and followed.

We walked up the steep gravel track dividing a wide grass slope rising to the house. The view on each side as we neared the top opened across fields and a distant spread of pine trees to the right shrouded in mist.

Crunching yet more gravel underfoot across the broad forecourt at the top, we reached a short flight of steps taking us to the stately oak door entrance.

"Isn't it amazing," Lawrence continued to enthuse.

"Yes," I agreed, "but you've definitely got your work cut out."

As we grew closer to the building I could see much of the stonework was eroding with age and neglect, cracks in places and the wood frames on many of the windows rotting.

"I've got great plans for this place," Lawrence's spirit was undeterred. "Just needs money and a lot of TLC. The last owner Lord Ernest Loftbury died broke. The place had been falling apart for years. That's how I got the island and house for a knock down price. No-one could see its potential like me."

The oak front door began to open. An elderly man in a white, open neck shirt and grey trousers appeared. There was no sign of welcome on his grizzled face, merely an unemotional stare.

"This is Andrew McKellan, my butler, caretaker and general maintenance man," Lawrence introduced him. "And this is our guest, Alex Preston, a good friend of mine

369

from college days," he announced, slapping me on the shoulder.

The man just nodded acknowledgement of my presence and held out his hand to take my travel bag.

"Andrew will drop that in your room and his wife, Laura, will bring us some coffee and cakes in the sitting room." Lawrence beckoned me inside as his employee left with my bag.

The entrance hall was huge. A vast candelabra hung above the setting, attached to a chain stretching two-storeys up to the roof. Dark wood panelling filled the expanse, with a wide stairway to the right sweeping up to balconies overlooking the hall on the first and second floors.

It was a grand setting, but now tarnished with age. Many of the glass beads in the candelabra were missing and the remainder coated in dust. The panelling and several doors off the hallway looked faded and scuffed.

Within moments of us entering an elderly, grey-haired woman emerged from a side passage at the back of the hall. She was wearing a green apron scattered with patches of flour and held a ladle in her left hand.

"This is Laura, Andrew's wife," my host made the next introduction to me. The woman wasn't as impassive in her greeting as her spouse, raising the semblance of a smile in her craggy, aged face, but was far from overwhelmed by my arrival.

"Laura is an amazing cook," Lawrence placed his arm around her shoulders, which made the woman look distinctly uncomfortable. I gained the impression husband and wife bore some sort of resentment towards us.

She ducked from under Lawrence's embrace and returned down the passageway.

"Where did you find them?" I whispered to him. They didn't look like people he would choose to suit his outgoing personality.

"They're old family retainers. I'll tell you about it later," he whispered back, then walked across to one of the doors off the hall.

"Come in here," he opened it. "This is the former sitting room."

More dark panelling surrounded the large room with a bay window at the far end. It was empty apart from a brown leather sofa and a couple of armchairs.

The broad fireplace was ornately fashioned with a carved wood mantelpiece surround. Above it hung the portrait of a middle-aged man with a bushy, dark moustache and neat side parted hair. He stared down at us austerely, an air of superiority in his gaze. Lawrence saw me studying the oil painting.

"That's the late Lord Ernest Loftbury. A gentleman of the English aristocracy and the last in a long bloodline to own the island."

An uneasy feeling that the lord in the portrait was somehow not gone from the place came over me. His image seemed so alive. Penetrating, calculating eyes.

"This will make a great conference room," Lawrence surveyed the setting, his enthusiasm unbounded.

"Conference room?" I was puzzled.

"Yes, I plan to turn the place into a getaway for businesses. Where executives can find relaxation as well as getting down to the nitty gritty of sales expansion strategies. An island retreat."

"It's not exactly a sunny isle," I pointed out.

"That's the point." Lawrence walked across to the bay window overlooking the side of the property. "It's for mental and physical toning. There's another large ground floor room that I'll convert into a gym and sauna. And another for a swimming pool. This place is enormous. Twenty upstairs bedrooms alone."

His imagination was soaring. I had to admire his get up and go.

"And, of course, loads of room on the island for a boot camp, outward bound, golfing, tennis and sailing from the bay. The potential's enormous." He paused. "But there's a lot to clear up and renovate first."

I joined him at the bay window. The large lawn outside and flower beds were overgrown with weeds.

"But it can all be done."

At that moment Laura entered the room with a tray of coffee and cakes, placing it on a small table in front of the sofa.

"Let's have a quick bite and drink, then I'll take you for a tour round the island in the launch before it gets dark."

As we settled down on the sofa for the snack, I felt distinctly uncomfortable with Lord Loftbury staring at us from the portrait.

Discover what horrors are waiting in the haunted island mansion:

DEADLY ISLAND RETREAT
by Geoffrey Sleight
Available on Amazon

MORE BOOKS BY THE AUTHOR

THE GHOSTS OF HARCOURT GRANGE
Strange apparitions in a haunted country house

THE LOST VILLAGE HAUNTING
Ghosts return from an old Victorian coastal village

EMILY'S EVIL GHOST
Horrific past murders come vividly to life

DARK SECRETS COTTAGE
Shocking family secrets unearthed in a haunted cottage.

THE RESTLESS GRAVE
A ghost returns to seek vengeance for his death

THE SOUL SCREAMS MURDER
A family faces horror in a haunted house.

THE BEATRICE CURSE
Burned at the stake, a witch returns to seek horrific vengeance.

The sequel BEATRICE CURSE II.

A GHOST TO WATCH OVER ME
A ghostly encounter exposes deadly revelations.

VENGEANCE ALWAYS DELIVERS
When a stranger calls – revenge strikes in a gift of riches.

THE ANARCHY SCROLL
Perilous fantasy adventure in a mysterious lost land.

All available on Amazon

For more information or if you have any questions
please email me:
geoffsleight@gmail.com

Or visit my Amazon Author page:
viewAuthor.at/GeoffreySleight

X (Twitter): @resteasily

Your views and comments are welcome and
appreciated.

Printed in Great Britain
by Amazon